Deborah Challinor has a PhD in history and is the author of eleven bestselling novels. *The Silk Thief* is the third in a series of four books set in 1830s Sydney, inspired by her ancestors — one of whom was a member of the First Fleet and another who was transported on the Floating Brothel. Deborah lives in New South Wales with her husband.

www.deborahchallinor.com

By Deborah Challinor

FICTION

*Behind the Sun*
*Girl of Shadows*
*The Silk Thief*
*A Tattooed Heart* (forthcoming)

*Tamar*
*White Feathers*
*Blue Smoke*

*Kitty*
*Amber*
*Band of Gold*

*Union Belle*

*Fire*

*Isle of Tears*

NON-FICTION

*Grey Ghosts*
*Who'll Stop the Rain?*

# Deborah
# CHALLINOR
## The Silk Thief

**HarperCollins***Publishers*

**HarperCollins**_Publishers_

First published in Australia in 2014
by HarperCollins_Publishers_ Australia Pty Limited
ABN 36 009 913 517
harpercollins.com.au

Copyright © Deborah Challinor 2014

The right of Deborah Challinor to be identified as the author of this work has been asserted by her under the _Copyright Amendment (Moral Rights) Act 2000_.

This work is copyright. Apart from any use as permitted under the _Copyright Act 1968_, no part may be reproduced, copied, scanned, stored in a retrieval system, recorded, or transmitted, in any form or by any means, without the prior written permission of the publisher.

**HarperCollins**_Publishers_
Level 13, 201 Elizabeth Street, Sydney NSW 2000, Australia
Unit D1, 63 Apollo Drive, Rosedale, Auckland 0632, New Zealand
A 53, Sector 57, Noida, UP, India
77–85 Fulham Palace Road, London W6 8JB, United Kingdom
2 Bloor Street East, 20th floor, Toronto, Ontario M4W 1A8, Canada
195 Broadway, New York NY 10007, USA

National Library of Australia Cataloguing-in-Publication entry:

Challinor, Deborah, author.
 The silk thief / Deborah Challinor.
 ISBN: 978 0 7322 9677 3 (paperback)
 ISBN: 978 1 7430 9905 6 (ebook)
 Female friendship—Fiction.
 Women convicts—Australia—Fiction.
 New South Wales—History—1788–1851—Fiction.
A823.3

Cover design by HarperCollins Design Studio
Cover images: Woman © David et Myrtille / Arcangel Images; The entrance of Port Jackson and part of the town of Sydney, New South Wales [picture] / drawn by Major Taylor, 48 Regt., engraved by Robert Havell, 1769–1832, National Library of Australia, nla.pic-an5575513; background image by shutterstock.com
Map on page vi uses detail from _Map of the town of Sydney 1836_, Dixson Library, State Library of NSW — Ca 88/7; adapted by Laurie Whiddon, Map Illustrations
Typeset in 10.5/16pt Sabon by Kirby Jones
Printed and bound in Australia by Griffin Press
The papers used by HarperCollins in the manufacture of this book are a natural, recyclable product made from wood grown in sustainable plantation forests. The fibre source and manufacturing processes meet recognised international environmental standards, and carry certification.

*This one is for my beautiful great-nephew,
Oscar Jack Anderson, born on 16 January 2014*

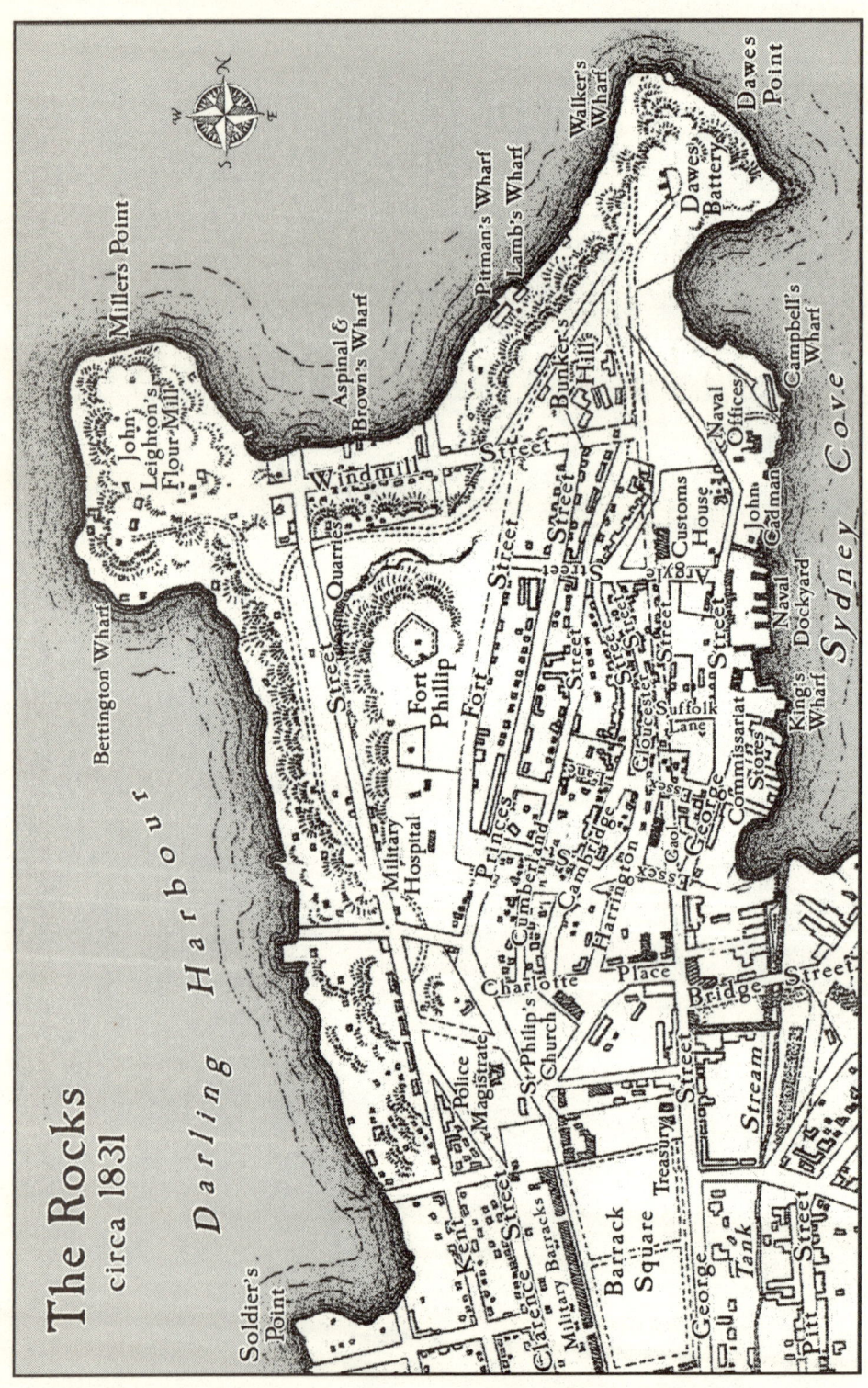

Part One

# When the Melancholy Fit Shall Fall

# Chapter One

*Early Monday morning, 11 July 1831, Sydney Town*

Harrie Clarke hadn't slept at all well. She'd tossed and turned, worry nipping at her like a hungry rat, her dreams getting as twisted as her sheets; and when Angus the cat had come in he'd selfishly spread himself across half the mattress. And now someone was tapping on her window. Except that was impossible — her room was high up in the attic.

Grateful for the rag rug on the cold floorboards, she crossed to the window and peered down past the shingled slope of the roof. Dawn was still several hours away and there was hardly any moon — she couldn't see a thing. During the day her eyrie at the top of the Barretts' two-storey house afforded her a view of the roofs, privies and dank yards of those who lived below on Harrington Street (and, unfortunately, of the gallows within the walls of Sydney Gaol), of the streets of the town to the south and west, and of Sydney Cove and the governor's enormous private gardens to the east. Now, however, in the velvet darkness, her ears and nose were more use to her than her eyes. She heard the susurration of small waves on the cove's shore, the strident call of a night bird and the tuneless singing of a drunk somewhere down near George Street. As always, the nearby cesspits tainted the air even up here, undercut by yesterday's rendered tallow from the soap and candle works in the next street, mixed with wood smoke from hearth fires and the pleasant briny tang of the sea.

But as her eyes adjusted to the night's shifting shadows, she made out the barest outline of a lone figure standing below in the backyard, its pale face turned up towards her. A raised arm drew back and something small and hard bounced off her window, making Harrie flinch. A pebble?

Her visitor was a boy, and she guessed from the way he held himself it was Walter Cobley. But what had gone wrong, to make him rouse her so early on a Monday morning? Had something happened to Friday in the night? No: Walter knew nothing about her gruesome midnight errand.

Harrie lit the bedside lamp, keeping the flame low. Angus, awake now, gave a soft meow as she slid her feet into slippers. The air was chilly but she didn't bother with a robe. She made her way downstairs, treading gently on the creaky risers so she wouldn't wake anyone, and let herself out through the back door.

He was waiting for her, his lanky form detaching from the yard wall as though he were made of smoke.

She whispered, 'Is that you, Walter?'

'I need help, Harrie.' His voice cracked and he cleared his throat, the sound close to a sob. 'I've done something bad.'

She lifted the lamp, and almost dropped it. Walter's shirt, jacket, face and hands were splattered with some dark substance.

'Walter! Is that blood? Are you hurt?' She took a step towards him, but his scruffy little dog, Clifford, crouching protectively in front of him, growled menacingly.

'Shut up, Cliffie. It's not mine. It's Amos Furniss's.' Walter swallowed audibly and stared down at his hands — held before him palms up, fingers spread — as though they belonged to someone else. 'I killed him, Harrie.'

Her heart stopped, then lurched into a wild, thumping rhythm. 'Amos Furniss? You've killed Amos Furniss?'

Walter nodded.

'But ... where?'

'In the old burial ground.'

Harrie went dizzy as the enormity of what he'd done overwhelmed her. She was confused, too — Friday had gone to the cemetery, not Walter. She had the most hideous thought. 'Is Friday all right?'

'I suppose. I dunno.' Walter wiped a trembling hand over his face, smearing tacky blood across his cheek.

'What do you mean?' Desperate to hear about Friday, she wanted to grab his shoulders and shake a useful answer out of him, but he was clearly suffering from shock and she knew it wouldn't do any good. 'What happened, Walter? Tell me.'

Walter squatted so suddenly Harrie thought for a second he'd collapsed. But he was only crouching to pat Clifford, his blood-sticky hands running along the dog's hairy back, drawing in comfort stroke by stroke.

'I followed her to the burial ground.'

'Friday? Or Clifford?' she asked. Clifford was actually a bitch despite her masculine name, and Harrie wanted to be very clear about who was who in Walter's story.

'Friday. And I seen Furniss so I hid while she gave him the money. Then when she'd gone I followed him to the Bathurst Street gate and I stabbed him. To death.' He raised his head, his teeth bared in something not even close to a smile. 'And I'm bloody glad I did, Harrie. He deserved it.'

She nodded: she knew why Walter had killed Furniss. The shock of his news had for some reason heightened her sensory perception — she could taste the cold in the air and feel the darkness on her skin, and she fancied she could actually hear the bones in her neck grating together. She shivered.

'And I thought I'd feel ... I dunno, happy or something,' Walter said. 'But I don't. I feel funny. I feel sick.'

As if to demonstrate this, he retched and, narrowly missing Clifford, heaved up a little puddle of watery vomit.

Harrie patted his back as he spat out a long string of saliva, and this time Clifford didn't growl at her proximity. This close, Walter smelt like a freshly slaughtered cow and she felt her own gorge rise. 'Where's Furniss now?'

'Still at the burial ground.'

Harrie waited until he'd spat some more and wiped his mouth on his sleeve. Then she said, 'Walter, listen to me. Did anyone see you leave? Or on George Street near the burial ground gates? Is that the way you came here?'

He shook his head. 'I come back along York Street.'

'But did anyone see you?'

He shrugged and settled his hand gently on Clifford's head. She licked his mucky fingers. 'Maybe,' he said. Then he nodded miserably and started to cry.

Harrie dressed hastily, not caring that her shift was on backwards, and wrapped her shawl around her shoulders. She glanced at the rocking chair under the eaves, but it was disappointingly empty. She felt sick, and a leaden, almost painful, sense of doom had settled in her belly.

She'd despised Amos Furniss herself, but now there'd be another dead soul to creep around in her mind and torment her. Liz Parker and Gabriel Keegan, then Jared Gellar and now Furniss. And poor, darling Rachel, of course, though unlike the others she'd been a tremendous comfort since she passed. So many folk whose paths she and Sarah and Friday had crossed had died. Is it us? she wondered. Are we somehow responsible for all those deaths? Am I?

She crept back downstairs. Walter was still there, hunched against the wall in a crouch, head resting on his arms, Clifford at his feet. The dawn was still a good hour or so away. Harrie knew she'd have time to get to Friday's, then Leo's, then back again before the Barretts awoke.

'Come on.' She offered Walter a hand up. 'Let's get you home. Leo'll know what to do.'

Walter extended his own hand; in the light of Harrie's lamp they both eyed the blood staining his skin and the rims of his fingernails. He withdrew it, and pushed himself off the cobbles.

'Quickly, love, have a wash.' Harrie indicated the bucket beside the rainwater overflow barrel, and wondered why he hadn't done so already. The shock, probably.

'I lost me hat,' he said forlornly.

'Never mind, we'll get you another,' Harrie said, as though she were talking to a five-year-old.

Walter splashed his face with cold water and scrubbed at his hands while Clifford helped herself to a noisy drink from the bucket.

'Why did you come here?' Harrie asked as they hurried along Gloucester Street towards the turn into Suffolk Lane. Worried that someone out early would see the state of Walter's clothes, she'd given him her spare shawl to wrap around his shoulders. 'Why didn't you go straight home?'

'Oh.' Walter stopped, dug around inside his jacket and brought out a pouch. 'This is for you.'

Harrie didn't have to look inside to know what it contained. Her heart sank yet again. 'The money?'

He nodded.

'How did you know to follow Friday last night? How did you know who she was meeting?'

'I were listening when you and her were talking about it at Leo's,' Walter confessed. 'When she were getting her new tattoo?'

Oh God. Harrie felt as though her insides were turning to water. After all these months, was their secret finally out? What had she and Friday said that day? She really couldn't remember. She was having trouble remembering all sorts of things lately. Nervously, she asked, 'What, exactly, did you hear?'

'Friday said something about Bella and two hundred quid. And that the money were to be delivered to Furniss at the old George Street burial ground last night. At midnight. And something about a lady called Janie and some babies missing out? You said you haven't got much money to give. So I got it back for you.'

He didn't appear particularly pleased with himself — unsurprisingly he still looked like a boy shocked silly after stabbing a man to death — but Harrie knew him well enough to understand that he needed acknowledgment for retrieving the money, whatever other awful thing he'd done. So she said, 'I'm grateful for that, Walter. We all are. Thank you.' Though there would be hell to pay when the blackmail money remained undelivered and Bella discovered that Furniss was dead. She would immediately assume that Friday, Sarah or herself had killed him. Bella already knew, after all, that they were capable of murder. God, why hadn't Walter thought of that? But he was only a boy.

'Walter, when Friday and I were talking, did we say why we were being blackmailed?'

He shook his head.

Harrie allowed herself a sigh of relief, and slipped the pouch into her skirt pocket. 'Did you tell Leo what you heard?'

'Hell no. He would've clipped me ears for listening at the door.'

'Oh, love, he's going to do more than clip your ears. Do you not realise how much trouble you're in?'

'He'll tan me hide, won't he?'

'Probably.' Instead of following Suffolk Lane down to George Street, Harrie turned into Harrington.

'Where are we going?'

Harrie patted Walter's arm reassuringly. 'To make sure Friday got home all right and to tell her what's happened. Then we'll get you back to Leo's.'

It only took them a couple of minutes to arrive at the Siren's Arms, the hotel owned by Friday's boss, Elizabeth Hislop. A lamp burnt outside the pub's front door, but the windows on the upstairs accommodation floor were all dark. Harrie and Walter followed the carriageway around to the stable yard at the back, and stood staring up.

'Which one's Friday's?' Walter asked in a loud whisper.

Harrie wasn't sure; it was hard to tell from outside on a dark night. 'I think it's that one,' she said, pointing. 'Throw something. See if we can wake her.'

Walter tossed a small stone towards the mullioned window. It hit the glass with a clack and bounced off.

Nothing happened. He threw another one. And another. Finally the window opened and a tousled head appeared. 'Who the hell's throwing bloody stones?'

'Friday!' Harrie called up as loudly as she dared. 'It's me. Let us in!'

'Harrie?'

'It's me and Walter. We have to talk.'

The window banged shut. 'Don't worry,' Harrie assured Walter, 'she'll let us in.' And then she realised that Walter wouldn't understand why it was so important she tell Friday what had happened, and that when he did understand, he'd feel even worse than he did already. But that couldn't be helped. Not now.

Clifford growled, then a voice behind them said, 'Oi!'

Harrie almost jumped out of her boots and Walter started so wildly he fell to one knee.

'What d'you think you're doing?' It was Jack Wilton, Elizabeth Hislop's coachman and factotum, and he was hefting a wood splitter in one brawny hand.

'Jack, it's me, Harrie Clarke. And Walter, from Leo Dundas's.'

Jack took a step forwards on stockinged feet and squinted. 'Christ, it is, too. What are you doing out here in the middle of the night?' He glanced at Walter. 'And why's he wearing a woman's shawl?'

The back door of the pub opened and Friday Woolfe appeared, a robe thrown over her nightdress, her wild hair unbound and falling almost to her waist. She carried a lamp, its flame illuminating her bare feet. 'Harrie? What's wrong? What's happened?'

'Are you all right?' Harrie demanded.

'Me? I'm fine. Why?'

Harrie glanced at Jack. 'We need to talk. It's important.'

Friday understood immediately. 'Thanks, Jack.'

'Sorry we woke you,' Harrie added.

Jack shrugged, yawned, said, 'I'll get back to me pit then, shall I?' and trudged off to his room above the stables.

'Come upstairs,' Friday said.

Harrie, Walter and Clifford followed her. She locked the door to her room and dug around in her dressing table drawer for a small bottle of gin. 'What's going on, Harrie? What's Walter doing here? And why's he wearing your shawl?'

As Walter sat on the chair before the dressing table, Harrie sank onto Friday's bed, relieved beyond words to be sharing the awful predicament caused by what he'd done. 'Walter overheard us at Leo's the other day and last night he followed you.'

'You sneaky bugger,' Friday said. 'You must have kept your head down. I didn't see you.'

'Weren't meant to,' Walter mumbled.

'He waited until you gave Furniss the money,' Harrie went on, 'then he killed him.'

Friday choked on a mouthful of gin, shooting it out of her nose like a whale's blow and coughing until her face turned puce.

Harrie talked on over her racket. 'And then he took the money back.' She removed the pouch from her pocket and dropped it on the bed. 'He thought he was doing the right thing, but now Bella's going to think we killed Furniss. So she'll either kill us in revenge, or she'll tell the police what we did and we'll hang.' Her voice rose and she was powerless to stop it. 'It's over, Friday. We're going to die and we'll all go to hell for our sins.'

Friday gave one last cough and wiped her mouth on her sleeve. 'Calm down, love. Here, have a drink.'

'I don't want one,' Harrie said, her mind darting back to the dreadful episode with the wine in Hyde Park last year.

'Just drink it, will you?' Friday thrust the bottle at her. 'Call it medicinal.'

As Harrie took a tiny, hesitant sip, Friday turned to Walter, whose pale, narrow face had gone even whiter, and said, 'Really? You actually killed him?'

Walter nodded miserably. 'But I didn't think … I'm sorry. I just wanted to make Furniss pay, and get the money back. For Harrie. For all of you.' He swallowed anxiously. 'Why will you hang?'

'Best you don't know. Where's Furniss now?'

'In the burial ground, where I left him.'

'Christ. Does Leo know?' Friday asked Harrie.

'Not yet. We're on our way.'

'Do you want me to come with you? I'll never get back to sleep now.'

'Oh, would you?' Harrie felt teary with gratitude. She really wasn't looking forward to Leo's reaction when he discovered what Walter had done.

'Nearly morning anyway.' Friday slipped out of her robe and drew her nightdress up to her waist, revealing long white legs and a very shapely bare bottom.

'Friday!' Harrie inclined her head towards Walter.

'Oh. Right. Look away, love,' Friday said.

But Walter, utterly exhausted, had nodded off, his chin on his chest, a dangling hand resting on Clifford's head.

Friday tut-tutted. 'Look at him. Twelve years old and a murderer already. What a bloody tragedy. It's all Furniss's bloody fault. The only real crime is poor Walter had to top the bastard himself. Someone should have shoved him off his twig ages ago.' She pulled her nightdress off over her head and unselfconsciously stooped to rummage through a pile of clothes on the floor. 'Where the hell are my boots?' she exclaimed, loud enough to startle Walter awake again. He gawped at her nude form for a moment, then quickly looked down at his hands.

'Hurry up and put something on,' Harrie urged. 'Was that them at the bottom of the stairs?' She'd noticed an abandoned pair as they'd come up.

Friday sniffed the armpits of yesterday's shift, made a face and put it on anyway. 'Could be. I was in a bit of a state when I got in last night. Had a couple of drinks.' She stepped into her skirt then struggled into the fitted bodice, swearing under her breath as she did up the fiddly little buttons down the front.

Harrie snapped, 'For God's sake, will you hurry up!'

'Christ, I'm not giving you gin again,' Friday muttered.

A sharp knock came at the door — everyone froze.

'Friday? What's going on in there?'

'Shite,' Friday hissed. 'It's Mrs H.'

'Friday! Let me in!'

Elizabeth Hislop's master key rattled violently in the door and it opened, revealing her enveloped in a shapeless woollen robe, with a frilled nightcap atop her grey hair, which during the day was concealed by a luxuriant auburn wig. The candle she carried cast shadows across her face, making enormous cavities of her nostrils, accentuating the bags beneath her eyes and turning her plucked brows into evil flaring wings. Walter let out a squeak of fear. Clifford growled.

'Morning, Mrs H,' Friday said.

'Barely. Harrie, what are you doing here?' Elizabeth demanded. 'And who's this?'

Walter lifted his feet onto the seat of his chair, laid his head on his knees and curled himself into a ball.

'We're just leaving, Mrs Hislop.' Harrie prayed she hadn't noticed the blood on Walter's jacket.

But Elizabeth had. She marched over to him, her candle's flame flickering madly, and levered up his unwilling head. 'You're that boy of Leo Dundas's, aren't you?' Clifford aimed a snarling nip at Elizabeth's ankle, but she kicked out with a velvet slipper and sent her flying.

Wretchedly, Walter nodded.

'And does he know you're here, in the boudoir of one of my girls, covered in blood?'

'No, he doesn't,' Friday said. 'We're just about to take him home.'

Elizabeth's eyes narrowed and her mouth puckered like a cat's bum as she waited for an explanation. When none came, she let out a great, worried sigh. 'I hope you're not in trouble. Any of you.'

'Nothing we can't sort out,' Friday lied as she pulled on her jacket. 'Back soon.'

Dawn still hadn't arrived but the darkness had diluted somewhat in expectation, and there were a few more folk abroad. They walked the short distance from Harrington Street down to George, turning into the narrow alleyway alongside the Sailors' Grave Hotel. A faint light glimmered across the uneven cobbles from the window of one of the two downstairs rooms in Leo's tattoo shop.

'Is he normally up this early?' Friday asked.

Walter shook his head. 'He's going to kill me.'

'No, he isn't,' Harrie soothed.

The door was on the latch; they pushed it open, went through the darkened room where Leo did his tattooing, and found him next door, sitting at the table drinking tea in a fug of tobacco smoke.

'Where the hell have you been?' he barked, his normally sun-weathered face almost as pale as his silver-grey hair and short beard. 'I've been out looking for you everywhere. And what's that all over you? Good God, don't tell me it's blood!'

'I ... I've ...' Walter stammered.

'Would you like me to tell him?' Friday offered.

'Tell me what?' Leo demanded.

Walter scooped up Clifford and held her as though burping a baby. She licked his face, leaving a shiny trail on his cheek. 'I followed Amos Furniss to the burial ground tonight. Last night. And I killed him. I had a knife and I killed him.'

Leo sat in stunned silence for a long moment, then shot to his feet and slapped Walter hard across the face. Clifford whipped her head around and bit Leo's hand. Leo grabbed her by the scruff of the neck, tore her from Walter's arms and tossed her yelping and growling across the room onto the cot beneath the window, then clutched Walter to him in a tight embrace. Walter, his face pressed against Leo's wiry chest, burst into tears.

'You stupid bloody boy,' Leo muttered as he rocked Walter. Blood from his hand soaked into the back of Walter's filthy jacket.

Friday searched for something to staunch the flow, snatched up a grubby tea towel from the table and tapped him on the shoulder. 'You're bleeding everywhere.'

Leo let go of Walter, wrapped the tea towel around his hand, resumed his seat and gestured to Walter to sit opposite. Friday wondered vaguely if Leo would get rabies from bad-tempered Clifford.

'Where's Furniss now?' Leo asked.

Walter sniffed loudly and wiped his nose on his sleeve. 'Everyone wants to know that.'

Leo shot an alarmed glance at Harrie and Friday. 'Everyone? Who the hell else knows?'

'Just us,' Friday said. She didn't think Mrs H counted, as she didn't actually know what had happened. She raised her eyebrows at Harrie for confirmation.

Harrie bit her lip. Her face was nearly as bloodless as Leo's. 'He thinks he might have been seen, on the way back from the burial ground. Don't you?'

'Maybe,' Walter said. 'On York Street, after I come out. It were really dark, but.'

'Did you speak to anyone?' Leo asked.

'No. I kept me head down.' Walter hesitated, then added reluctantly, aware he was admitting to an error of judgment that could only make the situation worse, 'And I made really sure Cliffie were quiet.'

'You had the dog with you,' Leo said flatly. 'Christ. So when Furniss's body gets found they'll call for witnesses, who'll come forwards saying they saw a boy near the burial ground with a hairy little dog. You never go anywhere without that bloody animal, lad. Everyone knows you. Why didn't you think?'

'There's hundreds of dogs in this town,' Friday said. 'And surely dozens of boys with dogs.'

Leo shook his head. 'Not that look like her.'

That was true. They all stared at Clifford, who turned around on the cot and presented her arse.

Leo sighed: a small one, but it was filled with tremendous sadness and regret. 'You can't stay here now, lad. You'll have to go back to England. Preferably on the next ship out of port.'

Walter looked desperate, and as though he were only now realising the true consequences of his actions. 'I can't. I've no money. I can't afford the passage.'

'I can,' Leo said.

'But I want to stay here, with you.'

'You can't. Not now.'

'But —'

'No!' Leo was adamant. 'If you stay, you'll hang. I'm not having that on my conscience. I'll go down to the docks this morning.' He stared for a long moment at the bloodstained tea towel around his hand, then made a fist with his other hand and slammed it on the table. No one said anything. At last he unwound the towel and poked at the ragged, weeping punctures in the flesh below his thumb and muttered, 'Bloody dog.' Then he sighed again and said, 'I know why you killed him, and I don't blame you, but how did you know where he'd be? Last night?'

Walter's eyes flicked to Friday and Harrie, then quickly away. He knew he'd already caused them enough trouble. 'I followed him.'

Leo shook his head. 'Walter, lad, I can always tell when you're not telling me the truth. Pass me that brandy on the shelf, will you, Harrie? And a bit of clean rag from the cupboard?' Harrie did as asked. While Leo poured the alcohol — perfectly good drinking brandy, Friday noted — over the wound on his hand, he said amiably, 'Now, I'll ask again. How did you know where to find him?'

'I did follow him,' Walter said. 'I waited outside where he lives, in the bushes, and I followed him.'

Leo made a sceptical face. 'How did you know he'd be abroad?'

'Didn't. I were going to wait there every night till he were.'

'But ... why now?'

Walter shrugged. 'Dunno. It were time.'

Leo fixed him with a pointed stare. 'Is that the truth, lad?'

'I swear.'

Friday and Harrie hardly dared to breathe. Leo still didn't look convinced but at last he nodded, and took a swig of the brandy.

'Bit early in the day, I admit, but desperate times,' he said, offering the bottle to Friday, who knocked back several enormous gulps. Returning the brandy to the shelf, he added pointedly to Harrie, 'You don't drink,' and to Walter, 'and you're too young.'

There was nothing in the *Sydney Herald* later that morning about a (fresh) body discovered in the old burial ground, but by midday everyone on the Rocks, and no doubt across all of Sydney Town, had heard that a murder had occurred. Perhaps it would be officially reported in Tuesday's edition of the *Sydney Gazette*.

Yawning her way around the fruit and vegetable hall in George Street market, Harrie overheard a woman telling someone that she had it on very good account that the corpse had been hacked to pieces with nothing less than an axe or a hatchet, and Friday, ducking into the Fortune of War for a quick morning gin on the way to warn Sarah, heard that the victim's entrails had been drawn out to a distance of ten feet in all directions around the ruined body. Friday made suitable noises of disgusted fascination, but doubted Walter had bothered to hang around to mutilate Furniss to that extent, though he might have harboured the rage to do it. She'd seen it herself, in his eyes.

The bell over the door chimed as she entered Sarah and Adam Green's jewellery shop just after nine o'clock. Sarah was at a cabinet, rearranging a display of cufflinks and tiepins.

'How did it go last night?' she asked without preamble.

'Is Adam in?'

Sarah tensed. 'No. Why?'

'We need to talk.'

'What's wrong?' Sarah closed and locked the cabinet door. 'What's happened?'

'Furniss is dead.'

'Oh God, Friday, you didn't.'

'Not me, Walter.'

'Walter!'

Friday nodded. 'He followed me to the burial ground, and after I'd handed the dosh over he stabbed Furniss to death. And took the money back.'

Sarah subsided onto the stool behind the counter. 'Shit. That means —'

'Bella'll be roaring.'

'Christ,' Sarah said. 'What do we do? She'll think we killed him. She'll have our guts for garters.'

'Maybe, but how much do you think she really cared about Furniss?'

'Not at all, I'd say. Who would?'

'Exactly,' Friday agreed. 'She'll be more interested in getting her money.'

'Our money,' Sarah grumbled.

'And she won't get it, will she, if she's had our throats cut or we're swinging from the gallows.'

'So you think we're safe?'

'No, but we may have a bit more grace than we think.'

Sarah snorted. 'I can't imagine using the words "Bella" and "grace" in the same sentence.'

'This is all a big bloody game to her, remember,' Friday said.

'Is it? Really? How do you know?'

'If she really hated us, she'd've dobbed us in by now, wouldn't she? Just to see us hang. If you were her, wouldn't you?'

'Probably.' Sarah nodded. 'Yes, I would've. So why's she buggering about blackmailing us?'

'I'm sure the money's coming in handy, but I can't help feeling she's playing with us.'

'Why can't we just tell her it was Walter?'

Friday stared at her. 'God, Sarah, that's a bit mean, even for you. She'd kill him. You wouldn't really do that, would you?'

Sarah took just a tiny bit too long to answer. 'No. He's a good lad, Walter.'

'Though, actually, we could tell her,' Friday said after a moment's thought. 'He'll be gone soon and then it won't matter. But do you think she'd believe us? A twelve-year-old boy murdering a brawny, handy cove like Furniss?'

'Except Walter did kill him, didn't he? Why will he be gone soon?'

'He thinks he might have been seen leaving the burial ground,' Friday said. 'And he had bloody Clifford with him. Everyone knows Clifford. Leo's trying to get him on the next ship back to England.'

'Well, if Walter was seen, and he's accused of killing Furniss, won't we be in the clear as far as Bella's concerned?'

'Only if she believes he did it: but what if she doesn't? He won't be here to go to trial and be proven guilty.'

'God.' Sarah rubbed her hands over her face. 'Who's got the dosh now?'

'I have. I'll get Matthew to put it back in the bank.'

'Will we pay it again?'

'Bugger that. I've already handed it over once. It's not my fault if it came back.'

'Bella won't see it like that, though, will she?'

'So I should run up to Cumberland Street and shove it under her door?'

'Don't be stupid,' Sarah snapped.

'Well, what, then?'

'I don't know. Wait and see, I suppose.'

Monday was Friday's normal day off, so she went home for a sleep, then in the afternoon returned to Leo's to find out if he'd been able to secure a passage for Walter back to England.

Leo was putting the finishing touches to a sailor's tattoo — a ship in full sail with *Homeward Bound* scripted beneath it — so she went through to the other room, hung the kettle over the fire, put her feet up and lit her pipe. There was no sign of Walter or Clifford.

Leo appeared half an hour later, wiping his ink-stained hands on a cloth, smelling of fish oil and raw alcohol.

'Is there any tea in that pot?'

Friday nodded and poured him a cup. 'Where's Walter?'

'With a friend. Can't stay there, though. And he's not safe here. Folk know this is where he lives.'

'Do you really think he'll be fingered? There was bugger-all moon last night.'

Leo shrugged and pulled out a chair. 'Can't be too careful. This is the lad's life we're talking about.'

'Did you get down to the wharves this morning?' Friday asked.

'I did, and I can't get him passage before Thursday, not even with a hefty bribe. So I need somewhere to hide him till then. Any ideas?'

'Well, that's easy. My room at the Siren. He can sleep on the floor. Or Sarah might put him up at her house. She's got a couple of spare rooms.'

'No, lass. If you or Sarah are caught concealing him, you'll be charged with aiding and abetting a murderer. You'll swing beside him. Use your head.'

Friday hadn't thought of that, and made a face.

Leo laughed. 'You've swanned around pleasing yourself for so long you've forgotten you're a bonded convict, haven't you?'

'I have not.'

'You have. All it'll take is one foot out of line and you'll be back in the Factory as quick as you please.'

'I'm sick of folk telling me that,' Friday grumbled.

'But both feet out of line — and harbouring a murderer would definitely be considered both feet — and you'll be for the gallows.'

Friday was also getting a bit sick of Leo. 'You think of somewhere to hide him, then. You're the one reckons you know this town inside out.'

'Just the arse end of it, lass.' Leo frowned and tapped on the table with a teaspoon. 'Trouble is, I don't want any of my friends caught hiding him. And anyone who isn't a friend would sell him up the river for the reward.'

'There's a reward? Already? Bloody Furniss won't even be properly cold yet.'

'Oh, he'll be cold, all right. I heard he was stiff as a board when they found him. And gnawed to shreds by rats.'

'Still, it's a bit early to be offering a reward, isn't it?'

Leo shrugged. 'You see my point, though? About where to hide him?'

'Well, I'm fond of Walter,' Friday said, 'but I certainly don't want to hang just for giving him a blanket and a bowl of porridge.'

'And I don't want him caught at all, and this'll be the first place the police will look.'

'If someone actually does finger him.'

'Better to be safe than to mourn him,' Leo said.

'What time does the ship sail?'

'On Thursday? On the late tide. Just after dark.'

'So, that's three nights and three days away,' Friday said thoughtfully.

'It is. Why?'

'Can you have Walter in the yard behind the Siren tonight? Better make it just after dark. Bring his travelling things, and food and drink for three days. But don't bring the dog.'

Friday had an idea.

# Chapter Two

Sarah stood against the high wooden fence in the stable yard behind the Siren's Arms, merging with the shadows, almost invisible. She was good at that. The air was cool again tonight and steam rose off a pile of manure, freshly deposited on the cobbles. Jimmy Johnson, the stable boy, had emerged from the tack room and walked right past her to take the horse, sweating and blowing and skittering sideways, as its rider had dismounted, and hadn't even seen her. She felt smug. She'd not been out skulking in dark corners for months and was pleased to note she hadn't lost her knack for melting into the background.

She did wish Leo and Walter would hurry up, though. Her feet were getting cold. She raised her face to the sky, now the deep, dark blue of a very fine Burmese sapphire, and watched as a river of bats streamed overhead, heading north.

At last Leo arrived, Walter trailing after him, his collar up and his cap pulled low over his brow. Sarah stepped out of the shadows.

'Sarah.' Leo touched the brim of his hat.

'Leo. She's not here yet.'

'She said near dark.'

Sarah nodded. 'Don't worry, she won't be far away. Got everything you need?' she asked Walter.

He turned slightly, revealing the sea bag slung over his shoulder.

The gate between the stable yard and the alley leading to Elizabeth Hislop's brothel on Argyle Street rattled and creaked open. Friday appeared and beckoned. They stepped into the narrow lane and followed her — the white gauze of her flimsy robe almost glowing in the gloom — to the gate at the other end, where she signalled a stop with a raised hand.

'I've drawn the drapes across the back windows, but someone could come out to the bog at any time, so we have to hurry. Plus, I'm bloody freezing.'

'This might be easier if you told us what you're planning to do,' Leo said.

'There's a cellar under the house. No one ever goes down there. You get in from the outside but the door's always locked. That's why we need Sarah.'

Leo frowned. 'Is it habitable?'

'Dunno, haven't looked. But it must be fairly dry. Mrs H stores furniture in there. Anyway, got a better idea?'

'No.'

'Well, there you go. Sarah, you ready?'

'Always.'

'The door's just to the right of the steps. It's easy to see.'

Friday unlocked the gate and let Sarah through. She crossed the cobbled yard behind the house, passing the whiffy privy and the clothesline, and headed straight for the cellar. On her left, wooden stairs ascended to the brothel's back entrance; in front of her, two steps led down to a low door set into the house's sandstone wall. The door had two hefty locks built into it. From her burglary satchel she selected an assortment of tools, and in less than five minutes had both locks cracked, though they were stiff from disuse. She turned and waved at Friday.

Quickly the other three joined her. Friday cautiously pushed the door: it creaked open onto more wooden steps — steep and extremely rickety — and a dense blackness that smelt dryly of dirt and of something vaguely organic, like mushrooms.

Friday dug in the pocket of her robe for matches, lit her lamp and handed it to Sarah, who said, 'Why do I have to go first?'

'I don't like small spaces.'

Sarah had forgotten that. She took the lamp in one hand, gathered her skirts with the other, and carefully descended the stairs, each riser protesting beneath her weight, such as it was.

The cellar had been excavated into the hill on which the house sat, Argyle Street rising with the slope, the raw rock surfaces pointed for stability but nothing more. The remainder of the cellar walls — those not underground — were made from roughly mortared sandstone rubble. When they reached the bottom of the stairs, Leo, who was close to six feet tall, could stand comfortably.

The space wasn't, in fact, small: it appeared to extend to the four corners of the house above and did, as Elizabeth had informed Friday on an earlier occasion, contain a fair bit of furniture. Many pieces were draped with sheeting, giving them a neglected, even ghostly, appearance, but others stood naked, their surfaces dulled by accumulated grime and a dry sort of mould. Visible were three or four nightstands with doors missing, a listing dining table against which were propped several headboards, three battered bureaux, a chaise with exploding stuffing, a cheval looking-glass frame minus the actual glass, a couple of battered travelling trunks piled against a wall, half a dozen wooden chairs in various states of disrepair, two coat stands with broken arms, and a dented and tarnished brass fender.

'Doesn't she throw anything out?' Leo asked.

'Shush.' Friday pointed urgently at the floor above. 'Someone'll hear us.

'What's this?' Sarah said, kicking a long, rolled-up tube on the ground. 'Carpets?'

An absolutely *gargantuan* spider shot out the end of it, scuttling straight for her skirts. She let out a strangled squeak and leapt back at least five feet.

'God, that's a big one,' Friday remarked. 'Hope you're not scared of spiders, Walter.'

Walter stepped forwards and stamped on it.

Leo said, 'Lucky Clifford's not here. She'd eat that. Oh, sorry, lad.'

Shrugging, Walter stared down at his boots.

'You don't need me any more, do you?' Sarah asked. 'I'll wait in the alley.'

'Hang on,' Friday said. 'What do we do about the locks?'

'Nothing. The door'll look locked when you close it. As long as no one tries it, we'll be fine.'

'But if they do?' Friday persisted.

'I'll say I broke in,' Walter said.

Leo patted his shoulder. 'Good lad. But it won't come to that.'

Friday said to Sarah, 'Well, in that case, you might as well go home. Thanks for your help.'

'Thank you,' Walter echoed.

'My pleasure,' Sarah said. 'I'll come and see you off on Thursday, shall I? Is that all right?' she asked Leo. 'Which wharf?'

'King's. You can, if you don't make a fuss.'

'As if,' Sarah said. She never made fusses. She scooted up the steps and disappeared outside.

'Right,' Leo said to Walter, 'you've enough food and drink to last till Thursday, and half a dozen candles. Do *not* go out, do you hear me? And get some sleep. You'll need it.'

'Why?' Friday asked.

'He's working his passage on the ship.'

Friday pecked Walter on the cheek. 'I can't visit you down here in case someone sees me, but I'll come and see you off, too, eh? And I know Harrie'll want to as well.'

'It'll be a proper little party, won't it?' Leo's voice caught slightly. He pulled Walter into a rough hug. 'Get some rest, son. I'll be back on Thursday evening.'

'I will,' Walter said.

After closing the cellar door firmly behind Leo and Friday, he took a candle from his jacket pocket, lit it and dripped wax onto the dining table, and stuck the candle in it. Then he carefully slid his sea bag off his shoulder, set it on the old chaise, and loosened the ties.

'Come on, out you come,' he said.

Clifford exited the sea bag head first, sneezed and shook herself violently. Her left ear was inside out. Walter folded it the right way.

'Now, what were you wanting for supper? Sausage, cheese or a nice bit of pork pie?'

On Tuesday morning the *Sydney Gazette* reported in rather lurid detail — *macabre circumstances, abandoned graveyard, frenzied stabbing, blood-drenched clothing, blind, staring eyes* — the discovery of Furniss's body, together with a statement from two witnesses who had come forward to report seeing a boy and a dog in the vicinity of the old burial ground. There had been no accompanying illustration of the allegedly encountered boy (or dog), so clearly the witnesses had not got a good look, but still, the sighting was a worry. Also, an anonymous benefactor was offering a reward of fifteen pounds to anyone able to provide reliable and accurate information leading to the apprehension of the murderer or murderers.

Friday convinced Elizabeth Hislop to give her Thursday night off, but only in exchange for a full explanation of what Harrie and Walter had been doing in her room in the small hours of Monday morning.

Elizabeth was appalled — not at Friday's description of Furniss's grisly demise, but at the abuse he'd meted out to Walter on the *Isla* two years earlier, which had ultimately driven the boy to claim such a bloody revenge.

'Serves the bugger right,' she said. 'The author of his own fate. Still, that poor lad. To think what he must have endured.'

'I know,' Friday agreed. 'I don't blame him for sticking the bastard.'

'He'll hang if he's caught.'

'He won't be. He's sailing this Thursday for England. Which is why I'd like the time off, to say goodbye.'

Elizabeth checked the roster. 'I'll swap you with Hazel. She won't mind.'

'Thank you,' Friday said gratefully, and somewhat guiltily, given that Mrs H was unwittingly hiding Walter in her cellar.

On Thursday she knocked off work just on dark, skilfully inducing her cully to finish his session fifteen minutes early and wondering whether Leo had collected Walter yet. She'd better get a move on herself if she wasn't to miss him before he boarded. She changed into her street clothes and made her way down Argyle Street, turned right onto George and headed south until she came to King's Wharf adjacent to the Commissariat Stores. The ship — Friday didn't know what sort it was: she only knew about sailors, not what they sailed on — swarmed with crew as supplies were loaded on and packed away, and the wharf itself was crowded with lumpers scurrying about hefting last-minute crates and barrels and boxes. The light had vanished from the sky now, revealing a cheese-coloured crescent of moon, and great flares burnt along the wharf, illuminating sweating faces and turning ordinary men into ghouls.

She found Sarah and Harrie lurking at the base of the towering Stores buildings.

'Where're Leo and Walter?' she asked.

'We saw Leo a few minutes ago,' Harrie said. 'He's got Walter out of sight somewhere, in case the police are watching the wharf.' She glanced around nervously, peering into the shadows. 'What if they *are* watching? What if they're hiding, waiting to grab him? Though I can't see anyone, can you?'

'You're not supposed to,' Sarah said. 'That's the point.'

Friday calmly surveyed the Stores, the darkened street and the shoreline. 'I can't see anyone, either. Surely they couldn't keep an eye on *all* the wharves? There aren't enough of them, for a start.'

'Probably not, but Leo's right. It's better to be safe,' Sarah said.

They observed in silence as a pair of watermen rowed out into the cove, trailing a warping rope attached to the ship about to set sail. Then came a splash as the ship's great anchor was heaved over the side of the rowboat.

'Where *is* he?' Harrie fretted. 'It'll leave without him.'

Friday pointed. 'There they are.'

Leo ambled towards the wharf in no apparent hurry, Walter beside him, his sea bag over his shoulder. Leo gave a casual wave.

'Isn't this a bit obvious?' Sarah asked as she, Harrie and Friday caught up with them.

'We're all right,' Leo said. 'I've had a look around. There's no one here.' He caught sight of the ship's captain and raised his hat.

Several loud crashes echoed as the hatch covers on deck were closed, half a dozen lumpers trotted down the gangway, and the bosun blew his whistle to call all hands to the capstan.

'They're preparing to warp out, lad. Time to go.' Leo wrapped Walter in a tight hug, his chin resting on the boy's head. When he pulled back, his eyes glistened. 'Take care of yourself, do you hear me?'

Walter nodded and said thickly, 'I will.'

Leo dug in his pocket and handed him several gold coins. 'For when you get home, to start you off. *Don't* show anyone aboard. Bloody sailors. Can't trust 'em.'

Walter burst into tears. So did Harrie.

One after the other, Harrie, Sarah and Friday hugged him. Friday and Sarah each gave him a five-pound note — Walter had never had so much money in his *life* — and Harrie presented him with two beautifully made white linen shirts.

He seemed unable to control his tears. 'I don't want to go,' he sobbed. 'I want to stay here with you.'

'It's too late for that,' Leo said gently. 'Go on, off you go.'

Walter wiped his nose on his sleeve, drew in a huge breath, and trudged off along the wharf. At the top of the ship's gangway, he paused for a moment to wave, then stepped onto the deck and was gone.

'Well, that's that,' Leo said, dabbing at his eyes with his cuff.

But it wasn't. Walter reappeared a moment later accompanied by the captain, who, gripping his ear, marched him back down the gangway. At the bottom, Walter bent down to tip Clifford out of his sea bag, then was escorted smartly back up to the deck.

Clifford, barking her head off, raced up after him on her short little legs, but was set upon by a burly seaman wielding a boat hook. When she dodged past that he kicked her, sending her flying to crash onto the unforgiving boards of the wharf. The bosun's whistle blew, the gangway was raised, and the ship began to move slowly away. In a fit of complete dog hysterics, Clifford raced alongside, barking and yapping and yelping, until she ran out of wharf.

'Oh, stop her!' Harrie cried. 'She'll jump in.'

Clifford sat down, raised her scruffy head, and let out the most piteous howl as the ship's stern drew past her.

'Oh, Leo, please, why don't you take her home?' Harrie pleaded.

'Because I value my fingers. She doesn't like me. She's a one-boy dog.'

'Friday? What about you?'

'I hate dogs. And Mrs H'd kill me. You take her if you feel that sorry for her.'

'Oh, I *can't*,' Harrie said. 'I wouldn't be allowed. She'd be a danger to the children. Sarah, *you* take her. Please?'

'Me? I don't want a dog. And especially not that one.'

'She'll be all right,' Leo said. 'She was feral before she latched onto Walter. She'll survive.'

'She's *still* bloody feral,' Friday muttered. 'I'm going to the pub. It's too cold out here.'

Saying goodbye to Walter had been more unsettling than Friday had expected. She'd been fond of him, but she hadn't expected to feel quite so teary at his departure. Also, when she'd hugged him he'd said something very odd in her ear.

He'd whispered, 'There's a dead body in that cellar.'

Sarah hurried up George Street, her shawl pulled tightly around her shoulders against the night air's winter bite, increasingly convinced with every step she took she was being followed. Three times she turned, and though there were indeed folk walking a short distance behind her, she knew instinctively they weren't responsible for her discomfort. Finally, the feeling became so overpowering she ducked off the footway and down the side of a building just past the Hunter Street intersection, and waited.

A minute later, a small, scruffy head peeked cautiously round the corner.

Sarah sighed. She picked up a pebble and threw it. 'Go on, bugger off!'

Clifford flinched, but didn't run away.

Sarah threw another stone. It bounced off the top of Clifford's head. She whimpered, but still she didn't run.

Sarah immediately felt guilty. She glanced over her shoulder. She could go home that way, behind the houses and shops, following the course of the foul-smelling Tank Stream, but she suspected the damned animal would only follow her. Why her, anyway? Surely she could tell Harrie was a much softer touch?

She sighed again, stepped back out onto the footway and, ignoring the dog, continued along George Street. At the intersection with King she risked a look back, and swore: Clifford was still trotting along behind her, though — *oh, for God's sake* — now she was limping.

Sarah went around to the rear of her house and entered the yard through the back gate, shutting it quickly, though not quickly enough to prevent Clifford from scooting through on three legs and limping with startling speed up to the porch, where she collapsed on the mat.

Following her, Sarah said, 'You can't swindle a swindler, dog. I know what you're doing. Now bugger off.'

Clifford let out the most pathetic whine and rolled onto her back, revealing a front paw that appeared to be quite deeply cut. Then she sat up and held out the wounded limb.

'You hurt that on purpose, didn't you?'

Very slowly, aware her hand could be bitten at any moment, Sarah crouched and allowed Clifford to rest the bleeding paw in her palm. The long, straggly hairs around the dog's toes were matted with blood, which quickly pooled in Sarah's hand. She dug in her pocket for a handkerchief, tied it around the paw, stood and stared down at the animal.

Clifford gazed up at her, head on one side, brown button eyes brimming with mute appeal.

'Oh, for Christ's sake.' Sarah picked her up and opened the back door.

Adam was in the parlour, reading *The Last of the Mohicans* in front of the fire, stretched out on the sofa with a tumbler of brandy at his elbow. His crow-black hair lay unbound over his collar, rolled shirtsleeves revealing strong, pale forearms.

'Did you have a nice evening?' he asked without taking his eyes from his book. As far as he knew, Sarah had been visiting Harrie.

'Yes, I did. Very nice.'

Clifford sneezed. Adam put aside the adventures of Hawkeye and his Mohican friends, sat up so his slippered feet were on the floor and eyed the dog in Sarah's arms. 'Is this evidence of George Barrett's latest racket? I hope you didn't pay for it.'

His comments were playful, but his face and tone of voice carried an undertone of wariness. Sarah was suddenly alert. 'Of course not.'

Adam took a sip of his brandy. 'You weren't at Harrie's tonight, were you?'

Sarah settled Clifford on the floor in front of the fire, to give herself a moment to think. 'What makes you say that?'

'I followed you down to King's Wharf. I saw you meet Friday and Harrie there.'

'You followed me!' Sarah exclaimed. That made sense. The little hairs on the back of her neck had been prickling all night. 'That wasn't very nice, Adam.'

'It wasn't very nice of you to lie to me.'

For a second Sarah considered insisting that she'd told him she was meeting Harrie, not going to Harrie's house, but decided she didn't want to. Deceiving him in the first place had made her uncomfortable enough. 'I had to.'

'You never have to lie, Sarah. Not to me. Not any more.'

I bloody do, she thought.

'What were you doing down there?'

'Did you not wait to find out?' she asked, and immediately berated herself for being sarcastic. Adam had been home from the penitentiary at Port Macquarie less than a month, and already she'd forgotten the desperate vows she'd made to God never to be rude, unpleasant or unkind to him — or anyone — ever again, if only he was returned to her. But, of course, she didn't believe in God.

'I saw you were safe,' he said. 'I decided I could wait until you got in.'

Sarah dithered, furiously trying to concoct a suitable story.

'I'm prepared to sit here all night until you tell me,' he added. 'And after that, you can explain to me why there's a smelly little dog asleep in our parlour.'

Clifford *was* asleep. Cheeky tyke.'

Sarah sat on the sofa. 'Leo Dundas's boy got himself into a bit of trouble the other night.'

'The lad who was ship's boy on your transport? William, isn't it?'

'Walter.' Adam had only met him once.

'Nothing serious, I hope.'

'It was, actually. The cove found murdered in the old burial ground on Monday morning? Amos Furniss? That was Walter's handiwork.'

'But he's just a boy.' Adam was stunned.

'He was even more of a boy when Furniss was getting stuck into him on the *Isla*.'

'Really? My God. And that's why he killed him? In revenge?'

'Yes, and bloody well warranted it was, too, in my opinion. But he and Clifford were seen leaving the burial ground.'

'Who's Clifford?'

Sarah pointed at the hearthrug. 'Her. Walter left for England tonight. He tried to sneak her onto the ship, but she was chucked off. I don't know why she chose me to follow home. I don't even like dogs.'

'Why is she called Clifford? That's a man's name.'

'Don't ask me.'

Adam stared at Clifford for a moment. 'But what were Walter and Furniss doing in the burial ground in the first place? And why did you and Friday and Harrie have to see Walter off? Why couldn't Leo Dundas do it?'

'We didn't *have* to, we wanted to. We were fond of him. And Leo *was* there. You must have just missed him.'

Adam's eyes narrowed and he slowly shook his head. 'No, this just doesn't feel right to me. You're talking about helping a murderer flee the colony. That was an awful risk for girls in your position to take.'

'What position?'

'For God's sake, Sarah, you're convicts. Imagine if you'd been caught! So come on, tell me. Why?'

'Why what?'

'Sarah! Don't treat me as though I'm an idiot. Did you owe the boy something? Was that it?'

Sarah swallowed. Sometimes she wished her beautiful, talented, passionate husband wasn't quite so clever.

'Well?' Adam demanded. 'Did you?'

'No! We didn't. Stop interrogating me.'

'So what was it, then?'

She was overwhelmed then with a desire to tell him everything, about Keegan, Bella and the blackmail — the lot. It would be such a relief. He'd know what to do. He could talk to his charmingly crooked friend, Bernard Cole, who'd lived in Sydney for ages and knew certain useful people who did all manner of work if the price was right, and perhaps even come up with a plan that would get rid of Bella forever.

She began, 'Friday was in the burial ground on Sunday night —'

His face blanching suddenly in the firelight, Adam exclaimed, 'My God, are you saying *Friday* murdered Furniss? Sarah!'

'No, I'm *not*. Christ, Adam. It was Walter. Walter killed him.'

Sarah watched him blow out a shaky sigh of relief and slump back on the sofa, and her heart thumped with sick dread. She'd come so close. If he was that horrified by the idea of Friday committing murder, what would he think if *she* confessed to it?

Adam took another, rather large, sip of his brandy. 'So what was Friday doing there?'

Sarah tried to change the subject. 'Do you *really* think she's capable of murdering someone?'

'Oh, probably not.' Adam waved away the suggestion. 'It's just that she's big and strong and her temper, well … sometimes she gets that look in her eye. Mind you, so do you.' He didn't laugh. 'You haven't answered my question.'

'About?'

Adam's eyes narrowed again, his face hardened, and Sarah knew she'd pushed him too far this time. 'Friday in the burial ground. Was it something to do with the blackmail?'

Sarah got such a terrible shock it felt like a physical blow, and she thought for several moments that she might faint. She heard herself say, 'What blackmail?'

'Look, I know Furniss worked for Bella Shand. I asked around because it's obvious you and Friday and Harrie loathe her, and I've always suspected there's more to all that than what you've told me. Bella Shand *is* blackmailing you, isn't she?'

Sarah stared at him, fear making her skin tingle unpleasantly, and said as calmly as possible, 'What makes you think that?'

She felt sick and, though she was only feet from the fire, the sweat in her armpits was cold and clammy. She dreaded to hear his answer but she had to know how much of their secret he'd worked out.

'You've always needed a lot of money,' he said, 'but you never seem to spend it on yourself.'

'It's for Janie and the babies at the Factory. I've told you that.'

'But not all of it, surely. And I know Friday contributes to this fund of yours, and Harrie, when she can. I overheard you talking one day — and no, I *wasn't* deliberately eavesdropping.'

Sarah stayed silent, too frightened to speak in case he asked the next — obvious — question.

'So this is what I think might have happened,' Adam said. 'I think Friday was in the burial ground on Sunday night, meeting Furniss to hand over money. Either the boy Walter was there officially with Friday, or he followed her for some reason. After the transaction was made, Walter killed Furniss.' Adam frowned. 'So what happened to the money?'

'Keep going, Mr Know It All,' Sarah snapped. She was angry, and frightened, because the scenario he'd conjured was so accurate.

'Because it was your business in which Walter became embroiled,' Adam went on, 'the three of you felt you needed to arrange for him to leave the colony. Am I right so far?'

Sarah sighed. She'd sighed a lot tonight. 'Not quite. Yes, Walter did follow Friday. We had no idea he planned to kill Furniss. It was Leo who organised his passage on the ship, not us. We saw him off because we *are* fond of him. I got to know him quite well when you were away, through Harrie working for Leo. I don't blame Walter for what he did. The filthy cove deserved it.'

'Did Friday see him kill Furniss?'

'No, he waited until she'd gone.'

'And my question about the money? I take it you *are* being blackmailed?'

Sarah nodded. 'Yes, we are.' She closed her eyes for a second. God, it *was* a relief to finally tell Adam. About that, at least. She literally felt as though some grindingly heavy weight had been lifted from her shoulders, if only by a fraction. 'Walter took the money back off Furniss.'

On the rug Clifford let out a loud, whistly snore.

Adam said, 'So now Bella's right-hand man is dead, she's owed a blackmail payment, and she's bound to think —'

'We killed him.'

'Why didn't you tell me any of this, Sarah?'

'Because it's no one else's business.'

'Not even mine?' Adam's gaze was level, but he looked disappointed.

Sarah hesitated, then said, 'No.'

'So no one else knows about the blackmail?'

'No.' Though Sarah had wondered what Friday might have said to Elizabeth Hislop.

Adam sat quietly for a moment, his eyes downcast.

Oh God, here it comes, Sarah thought, panicking.

'Sarah, why is she blackmailing you?'

'I can only assume she's taken against us,' she said, deliberately misinterpreting the question.

'That's not what I mean, and you know it.'

She paused, thinking furiously, then said, 'During the voyage out, on the *Isla*, one of the convict women, a really nasty piece of work by the name of Liz Parker, was murdered. Friday hated Liz's guts and Liz hated Friday's. Liz was found suffocated in her bunk in the middle of a terrific storm when everything on board was utterly chaotic. It was never proved who killed her but the finger was unofficially pointed at Friday.'

'Did she do it?'

'No, she was above deck at the time watching what everyone thought was the *Flying Dutchman*. The captain didn't bother to pursue the matter. Liz was a troublemaker and I think he was glad to be rid of her. Everyone else was. But after we arrived Bella demanded money in exchange for her not informing the governor that Friday had murdered Liz.'

'But can she prove it? She can't, can she?'

'After Liz Parker died, two of her crew, Becky Hoddle and Louisa Coutts, went to work for Bella. Apparently they'll swear they saw Friday murder Liz.'

'But why would Governor Darling listen to Bella Shand? She's just a convict.'

'No, she isn't. Be sensible, Adam. She's Clarence Shand's wife, and Clarence Shand is a wealthy and influential man. We can't risk not meeting her demands. We could go to the gallows.'

'But not all of you, surely?'

Christ, she'd nearly made a mistake. 'Bella's said she'll tell the governor Harrie and I concealed the fact we knew Friday committed the murder. I told you, she's really taken against us.'

Adam rubbed his chin while he pondered her predicament.

Sarah hardly dared to breathe, hoping he would believe her. Aspects of her story were true, but she'd concocted the tale from several different episodes. Horrible Liz Parker had indeed been murdered on the *Isla*, but it was likely Bella Jackson, as she'd been before she'd married Clarence Shand, had done that herself, throttling Parker to death with her bare hands. Friday, however, was in fact guilty of murder. So were she and Harrie. They'd kicked Gabriel Keegan to death in revenge for him assaulting their beloved friend Rachel Winter, who'd died giving birth to his child, Charlotte. Bella had discovered what they'd done, and had been blackmailing them ever since.

'I can see why you're so worried,' he said at last. 'I can. But I really doubt the governor'd pay much attention to a bonded convict. And she is still a bonded convict, you know, even if she is married to Clarence Shand. And I doubt the evidence of her cronies would carry much weight, either.'

'Don't forget she has the money now to *pay* the right people to listen to her, if she really wants them to.'

Adam made a face. 'Yes, I suppose she does.' He knew as well as anyone else in Sydney Town that the way to get anything done, legal or illegal, was to hand over money. 'Why does she dislike you so much? Do you know?'

Sarah shook her head. The less she said now about the strange relationship she, Friday and Harrie had with Bella Shand, the better.

'Well, Christ, you can't keep paying her forever,' Adam said.

'No, we can't. We thought we'd done a deal with her when we told her it was Jared Gellar who'd stolen her Maori heads. She agreed then to stop blackmailing us. But then she double-crossed us and sent another demand, which is what Friday was doing in the old burial ground on Sunday night — giving the money to Furniss.'

'How much money?'

'Two hundred pounds.'

Adam's dark eyebrows shot up. 'Bloody hell, Sarah!'

'I know.'

'How much has she demanded to date?'

'Three hundred and fifty.'

'And you've paid it?'

Sarah nodded.

'Good God. That's a bloody fortune! No wonder you've been desperate for money. And the three of you have raised all that yourselves?'

'Friday puts in a lot,' Sarah said. 'She's sitting on a gold mine, remember.'

'That's absolute highway robbery. That's …' Adam tailed off, unable to think of another appropriate description. 'With any luck someone will kill her,' he said suddenly. 'That would solve your problem, wouldn't it?'

Sarah opened her mouth to tell him they'd already considered that, and that she'd imagined him masterminding such a solution only minutes earlier, then thought better of it.

Adam stood, crouched beside Clifford still wheezing and whistling in front of the fire, and, before Sarah could warn him, extended his hand. Clifford whipped her head around and snapped at his fingers.

Launching himself backwards and sitting down hard on the sofa, Adam said, 'Christ! Did you see that? Vicious little bugger.'

You cunning article, Sarah thought — that performance on the back porch had better not have just been a ploy to get inside the house. Warily, she approached Clifford and held out her hand, palm down, fingers protectively curled. Clifford licked Sarah's knuckles, then ducked her head so Sarah's hand was positioned above her bony skull, clearly hoping for a scratch. Sarah laughed out loud.

'It can't stay here,' Adam said. 'Bad-tempered little devil.'

'I know. I don't want a dog.'

'It's probably got rabies. And definitely fleas.'

'I know. Are there any of those sausages left from supper?'

\* \* \*

Friday did go to the pub, but only stayed for a few drinks before she headed for home. She couldn't get Walter's last whispered words out of her mind. When she got back to the Siren's Arms, she grabbed a couple of candles from her room, then hurried along the alleyway to the brothel. A gentleman was dithering in the backyard taking gulps from a hip flask, which, exasperatingly, meant she had to loiter in the shadows until he finally made up his mind and went in, then she shot across to the cellar and tried the door. It was unlocked — which it would be, as neither Leo nor Walter had had keys to lock it after they'd left — so she lit a candle and descended into the musty, dry darkness.

Walter had left evidence of his stay — meat bones picked clean (the rats had no doubt made short work of anything else remotely edible), ale bottles coated with stalactites of candle wax, and a very faint whiff of shit. Being a fairly tidy boy, he'd probably buried any mess he'd made, Friday thought, or at least done his best to cover it, as there wasn't much dirt down here: the floor had been beaten solid. She chipped the old wax from the ale bottles and wedged in fresh candles to afford herself more light, and stood with her hands on her hips, wondering where to start.

Walter had apparently found it easily enough, though, so surely she wouldn't have to look too hard. There just weren't that many places you could hide a corpse down here. Buried under the floor, maybe? Unlikely, if you couldn't even bury a turd. She took a candle and toured the cellar, peering closely at the ground for signs that the earth had recently been disturbed, lifting dustsheets and moving furniture she thought Walter might have managed to shift, but found nothing except the product of his bowels. Then she looked *inside* furniture — a clothes press tilted against a wall, every drawer in the scruffy old bureaux (as if you could stuff a corpse in a drawer), a sideboard, and something else with a lot of cupboards in it she didn't know what to call. And then she spotted them — two good-sized travelling trunks, one on top of the other against the far wall. What an idiot. Why hadn't she noticed them straight away?

Both were covered with hard, scuffed leather, and studded with countless brass rivets, but when she rapped on them they each made a hollow knocking sound, as though lined inside with something very solid. She gave the top trunk a hearty shove — it barely moved. The lid was at eye height and the lock, she saw by the light of her candle, had been forced. Someone — Walter, no doubt — had spent some time cutting through the tough old leather, then digging at the wooden frame beneath, around the escutcheon plate, and had levered the plate away, leaving the inner workings of the lock exposed. Friday set the heels of her palms against the rim of the lid and pushed upwards — it rose, nothing holding it down but gravity.

But she wasn't tall enough to see inside. Her belly fluttering with apprehension — what would she find? — she fetched a doorless nightstand, tipped it on its side and climbed onto it. Holding the candle high, she screwed up her face, closed one eye, squinted down into the murky shadows of the trunk and saw … nothing. It was empty.

'Shite.'

She'd been right, though; the trunks *were* lined — with some sort of beaten metal. Well, this one definitely was.

She jumped off the nightstand and examined the lock on the bottom trunk. That, too, had been forced. But why had Walter done that? Surely he couldn't have moved the top trunk by himself? Bent almost double, holding the candle barely a foot above the ground, she shuffled around until she spied what she was looking for — gouge marks in the hard dirt. What the hell could he have used? And then it came to her — the shelves in the clothes press.

Grunting, she shoved the top trunk back a few inches to make a little ledge against which to lean two of the shelves, wedged their ends firmly into the compacted dirt, then, grunting *and* swearing now, moved to the other end of the trunk and shunted it back again so it stuck out over the makeshift ramp. Straddling the shelves and digging her fingers into the trunk's riveted seams, annoyingly breaking a fingernail in the process, she strained mightily and hauled it towards her. Everything was fine — it really was — up until the moment the bloody thing tipped over, took off and got the better of her, hitting her in the chest and knocking her flat on her back. *Christ*, it was heavy. How the hell anyone actually travelled anywhere with it packed, she didn't know. Praying that no one in the house overhead had heard the almighty thump, she struggled to her feet and took a couple of deep breaths to steady her nerves. She'd be black and blue tomorrow.

She eyed the bottom trunk. Now that she *could* open it, she wasn't at all sure she wanted to. Had Walter hesitated? Had he crouched here, on his knees with the cellar's shadows rearing over him, wondering what he might find if he lifted the lid? What had made him curious anyway? Had he ... smelt something? Cautiously, Friday leant forwards, put her nose near the ruined lock, and took a very hesitant sniff. Nothing. Or perhaps just a hint of something reminiscent of very old boots, or coats or curtains.

Oh God, maybe he hadn't smelt anything at all — maybe he'd *heard* something. A scratching or a tapping? Or something — *someone* — pleading to be let out?

She was beginning to wish she'd waited until daylight to do this.

'Oh, you gutless bloody wonder,' she said out loud.

Before she could change her mind, she yanked up the lid of the trunk, raised her candle and peered in.

Walter had been right; there was a body. Friday knew who it was, of course. Or rather, who it had been. She'd had her suspicions for ages.

It — he — lay curled on his side, facing her, as the trunk wasn't long enough to accommodate him laid out on his back: he must have been moderately tall when alive. He was still fully clothed, though the fabric of the once off-white trousers was almost universally stained a scabrous brown, as was the linen shirt still neatly in place beneath the crusted, dark waistcoat and heavy coat. Around the neck was wrapped a red neckerchief, also stained. The feet were hidden in solid black boots. The whole ensemble, however, had collapsed, as there was nothing inside it now to give it form but a cage of bones.

The rust-coloured skull still retained remnants of the flesh that once covered it, mummified shreds that curled up like fingernail parings, and long, dried tendons stretched from jaw to neck beneath the neckerchief. The eyes had gone, of course, but the yellowed teeth remained, including two gold incisors in the upper jaw. Some of the hair — cut short, iron-grey — remained on the skull, but most of it was scattered around the bottom of the trunk, and over the neckerchief, so perhaps he'd worn a beard. Also gleaming near the head were two small gold hoop earrings.

His peaked cap had been placed near his belly. His arms had been arranged in front of his chest: several finger bones had become detached from the right hand, but the other was complete, held together by dried tendons, with a gold band hanging loosely from the ring finger. There was very little smell, and obviously the rats hadn't been able to get at him. If they had, there'd be nothing left at all but bones, a few buttons and the gold.

Friday thought, God, mister, you must have *really* ruffled her feathers.

## Chapter Three

Harrie gazed unseeingly at a bin piled with broad beans, the fat pods a bright and poisonous green, trying to get her bearings, trying to focus, trying to work out what on earth she was doing there. The costermonger's rough voice barked in her ear and she started, the noise of the crowded fruit and vegetable market rushing back into her head to drown out the ringing silence that pulsed there with every thump of her heart.

'Pardon?' she said, flexing her tingling hands. Her chest burnt and she could barely breathe.

'Them beans. Do you want any more or not?'

She glanced into her basket. She'd already bought some. She shook her head and managed to croak, 'No, thank you.'

The costermonger rolled his eyes and turned his attention to someone else. Harrie hurried away, her head down, mortified that she'd had one of her 'turns' in such a public place. If this kept happening, soon she would be scared to leave the house at all. It was too noisy here in the market sheds and there were so many people. She'd give anything to be at home in her attic bedroom, safe in bed with her head under the blankets.

Tears stung her eyes. She'd been doing so well, she really had, especially while Sarah had needed her when Adam was away. But now ... she was feeling as poorly as she ever had. She was having trouble sleeping again, though sometimes during the day she could barely keep her eyes open; the voices in her head were back; and her stomach roiled with dread, gnawing away at her like rats trying to eat their way out of her belly. She was full of rats now, the most vicious and hungry being Gabriel Keegan. He never stopped chewing at her.

Still clammy and sweaty and wondering if she was going to be sick, she stood near one of the shed's exits to get away from the smell of not entirely fresh produce, and fanned her face with the piece of paper on which she'd written her shopping list. Three months ago she could easily have kept a list of everything she needed in her head, but not now. It wasn't necessarily that she forgot; it was more that she became confused. Twice lately she'd come out and bought what she'd already purchased just the day before. She dared not tell anyone. She was terrified her master, George Barrett, would send her back to the Factory, though she knew Nora, his wife, would defend her staunchly. She would hate to leave the Barretts. George and Nora's children — Abigail, Hannah, Sam and baby Lewis — were dear little things, and she would miss them dreadfully. Not to mention that if she was returned to the Factory, she'd be an additional drain on Friday and Sarah, who'd have to support her as well as Janie and the girls.

For now, she just had to get home with the shopping. She closed her eyes and drew deep breaths in through her nose, filling lungs that felt constricted by iron bands, then slowly let the air out through her mouth. She did that ten times, and finally her heartbeat began to slow. After a minute, she opened her eyes and looked at her shopping list. Carrots and a cabbage, that was all she had yet to buy.

She made her way back into the shed. As she did, a knot of four scruffy-looking boys, dodging and weaving around other shoppers, appeared out of the crowd and deliberately kept pace with her. They were perhaps nine or ten years old, all barefoot and wearing their caps pulled down low. Two were smoking pipes, the cheeky sods. Her throat tightened again and panic rose like vomit in her chest. She veered hard right and hurried down a wider aisle. The boys wheeled with her, like gannets above a school of fish, and closed in. Harrie wanted to scream out for help: could no one else see what was about to happen? As they approached, she plucked her purse from her basket and tucked it inside her bodice. Suddenly she was briefly surrounded, the stink of tobacco smoke and sour, unwashed bodies flooding her nostrils, and then they were gone.

She checked that she still had her purse, and the silver and black enamel locket containing Rachel's hair was safely around her neck. Relief melted through her. Nothing had gone from her basket either, though something had been added: instead of one note, now there were two. Dumbly, she stared at the new addition — a single folded and sealed sheet — then picked it up, her heart thumping wildly. Her name was written on one side — no surname, just *Harrie*.

She opened it with trembling hands, cracking the seal and sprinkling shards of red wax over the broad beans in her basket. It said:

*To Friday Wolfe, Sarah Morgan, Harrie Clark,*
　*I know you killed Furniss. That is now two murders.*
　*You now owe me £400.*
　*Be at the Kent Street entrance to the old burial ground at ten o'clock this Friday night with the money, or I will immediately inform the police and you will all HANG.*
　*B*

Harrie only stopped herself from fainting by biting her cheek so hard that her mouth filled with blood.

Sarah peered down into the trunk. 'How long do you reckon it's been here?'

'About five years,' Friday said.

Elizabeth Hislop's cellar looked somewhat different during daylight hours. Needles of bright, white sunlight pierced the gloom at random angles, admitted by cracks in the rough mortar dashed across the sandstone rubble walls, themselves riddled with tiny gaps. Motes of dust floated in the still air, momentarily illuminated as they passed through splinters of light, and rats, spiders and cockroaches — at night only audible but unfortunately during the day all too visible — scuttled about their business.

'Then why hasn't it all rotted away?' Sarah said. 'Why isn't it just bones? It's still got bits of dried skin and stuff stuck to it.'

Friday shrugged. 'Maybe because it's dry down here? Or because the trunk's lined with tin? I don't know. Just be grateful he doesn't stink.'

'Not tin, lead.'

'That'll be why the bloody things are so heavy.'

'And you're sure it's Mrs H's husband?'

'Who else could it be? Look at the earrings and the teeth: the cove was obviously a sailor. Mrs H's man was a sea captain. She told me herself she'd had enough of him beating the shit out of her when he was drunk. And ...' Friday leant into the trunk and tilted the skull to reveal a ragged hole in the centre of a web of cracks '... she does own a pistol. And this is her cellar.'

'So he hasn't been at sea forever and a day like she says,' Sarah remarked. 'He's been mouldering away down here?'

'Looks like it.'

'What are you going to do about it?'

'You're going to help me put this trunk back where it was, because it's too bloody awkward for me to lift by myself, then we'll lock the cellar door behind us with your special keys, then we're going to forget about it.'

'Why?'

'Because I don't care. Do you?'

'It's none of my business.'

'Good.' Friday closed the lid on the bottom trunk. 'Come on, help me lift the end of this other trunk onto these bits of wood. If you hold it so it doesn't fall off, I'll push it up.'

'What about the locks? Anyone looking properly will see they've been forced.'

'Can you fix them?'

'I pick locks, I don't repair them.'

'Too bad, then. We'll just have to hope Mrs H never comes down here.'

Sarah's eyebrows went up. '"We"? I wasn't the one poking my nose into someone else's business.'

Friday suddenly raised her hand; they both froze. Above them, two sets of feet crossed the floor and someone called Friday's name.

'Mrs H,' Friday whispered.

Nothing happened for several seconds, Elizabeth called out again, then the footsteps moved towards the rear of the house. The back door opened.

'Friday, are you out here?' Mrs H called.

Sarah and Friday dared not even breathe. Friday prayed she'd closed the cellar door properly.

Then Mrs H's muffled voice said, 'I'm sorry, Harrie. She's not rostered on this morning. Are you sure Jack said she was over here?'

Harrie? Friday and Sarah stared at each other. What was Harrie doing here?

Harrie said something inaudible.

Mrs H said, 'Well, if she was, perhaps she's gone back to her room. Is it urgent? I'll come over with you, if you like.'

She and Harrie descended the back steps. Their footsteps receded across the cobbled backyard and the bolt on the gate rattled as they passed through into the alleyway.

'Quick, help me get this bloody thing back where it belongs,' Friday urged.

After a bit of shoving and swearing, both trunks were finally back in their original places. Friday swept her boot over the gouge marks in the dirt floor where the shelves had been — a waste of time, really, given the tell-tale state of the locks on the trunks — shoved the shelves back inside the clothes press, and crept up the steps to the cellar door. She paused.

'Sarah?'

'What?'

'How the hell did Walter move that top trunk back all by himself?'

'I don't know,' Sarah said, 'and right now I don't care. Has Mrs H gone?'

Friday opened the cellar door a crack. 'Can't see or hear them. Got the keys ready?'

'Yes. You go down the alleyway after them, I'll lock up.'

'No, I'll wait for you,' Friday said.

'Why? So we can both get caught?'

'I *said* I'll wait.'

'Christ. Hurry up, then,' Sarah snapped. 'Open the door.'

They slipped out. Friday stood with her back to Sarah, her gaze darting between the gate, the house's back door, and also the privy, in case someone unexpectedly materialised from its whiffy depths.

'Done,' Sarah said. 'Let's go.'

They caught up with Mrs H and Harrie at the bottom of the staircase inside the Siren's Arms. Harrie looked awful. Her face, even her lips, had leached of colour and she was breathing far too fast and sweating visibly, though it was hardly a warm day.

'Harrie? What's wrong?' Friday asked. 'What's happened?'

'Where have you been?' Elizabeth demanded. 'We've been looking everywhere for you. Hello, Sarah.'

'Harrie, what's the matter?' Sarah echoed.

'She's had some sort of dreadful shock,' Elizabeth said unnecessarily. 'She arrived at the house about a quarter of an hour ago, Friday, asking for you. I've offered tea, and brandy, but she only wants to see you.'

Friday was struck by a horrible, if irrational, thought. 'Can you not talk, Harrie?'

'Of course I can talk,' Harrie said, despite the fact her voice was wobbly.

Friday nearly wilted with relief, though that didn't last long.

Harrie thrust a folded piece of paper towards her. 'I got this. At the market, this morning.'

'Oh, shit,' Sarah muttered.

'It's another blackmail demand, isn't it?' Elizabeth asked.

Sarah gasped, then fixed Friday with a venomous glare. 'For God's sake. You bloody fool. You and your big mouth! Why don't we just put an advertisement in the newspaper?'

'Well, do you expect us to believe you haven't told Adam?' Friday fired back, her face flaming. Bloody Mrs H; she'd told her that in confidence.

'I can't keep it a secret from my husband, can I?'

'He does know? Since when?' Friday demanded, immediately leaping for the higher moral ground. 'And who the hell has *he* told, eh? We swore we'd never tell anyone.'

'That's rich, coming from you. Anyway, Adam'll keep his mouth shut.'

'Don't mind me,' Elizabeth said. 'Or Harrie. Look at the colour of the poor thing.'

'Stop it!' Harrie cried, her hands over her ears. 'Just stop it!'

'I'm sorry, Mrs H,' Sarah said. 'This is our business. Could we have some privacy?'

It was a cheeky request given that they were standing in the middle of Elizabeth's pub, but she gave a single nod and said, 'I'll be in my office if you need me,' then turned and walked off, only the sharp rap of her boot heels on the floorboards betraying her tension.

'Not here,' Friday said. 'Upstairs.'

They retreated to Friday's room. She locked the door, produced a bottle of gin and sat on the bed to read the note. 'Jesus Christ. Four hundred!'

Startled, Sarah stared at her. 'What?'

'She wants four hundred quid this time. And she actually says she'll go to the police if we don't pay it. And we'll hang.' Friday handed the note to Sarah, slumped in the chair in front of the dressing table.

Grim-faced, Sarah read it. 'Who gave this to you?'

Beside Friday, Harrie took a deep, hitching breath. 'Some boys, at the market. They crowded around me and I thought they were going to take my purse, but they didn't. They left that in my basket.'

'Did you know any of them?'

Harrie shook her head.

Friday said, 'Bella probably paid the little buggers.'

'But how did she know I'd be at the market?' Harrie asked. She swallowed: her throat made an audible noise.

'You do the shopping every day, don't you?' Friday asked.

'Nearly. Has she been spying on me? She has, hasn't she?'

'I doubt it. She knows you're in service. That's what housegirls do.' Friday did wonder, though. She wouldn't put it past Bella to be keeping an eye on them.

'But how did they know who to give the note to?' Harrie went on. 'How did they know that I'm Harrie Clarke?'

'Well, I suppose she told them what you look like.'

'But how does she know?' Harrie's voice went up an octave. 'How does she know what I look like?'

Sarah and Friday shared a deeply shocked glance. Very gently, Sarah said, 'We were on the *Isla* with her, remember? And in the Factory. She knows who you are, Harrie.'

Harrie stared at her in confusion, a red flush creeping up her face.

'Love, are you all right?' Friday asked.

'I ... Yes, I just ... I forgot.'

To cover the awkward moment, and because she didn't want to think about what it might mean, Friday rose, noisily opened her window, sat down again and took a massive swig from her flask.

'We can't pay. We don't have four hundred pounds. Do we? How much is in the Charlotte fund?' Sarah asked.

'About sixty-five,' Friday said, stifling a burp. 'That and the two hundred Walter took off Furniss doesn't add up to four hundred. We'd still be a hundred and thirty-five short — and it would leave us with absolutely nothing for Janie and the girls. And Janie's due a payment for Pearl soon. We just can't do it.'

A moment of silence ensued. It stretched on and on until Friday couldn't bear it.

'Fuck it. We'll have to borrow it.'

'Borrow it?' Sarah was incredulous. 'A hundred and thirty-five quid? That'll certainly improve matters. Christ, Friday.'

Friday took another defiant mouthful of gin, and wiped the back of her hand across her mouth. 'Then tell us your clever idea, Mrs Smartarse.'

'Well, going to a bloody moneylender won't help, will it?'

'No! Not a moneylender. We can't!' Harrie exclaimed. Her mother, Ada, had once got herself into terrible trouble after borrowing five pounds from a shylock.

Friday frowned. 'Who said anything about a moneylender?'

'You did,' Sarah said.

'I did not.'

'Who the hell else would lend us that kind of money?'

'Mrs H. She's already offered.'

Sarah drew in a long, nostril-flaring breath and let it out again, visibly struggling to calm herself. 'What exactly have you told her? You promised you wouldn't tell anyone, Friday. You swore.'

'I had to tell her. She guessed. Anyway, you made the same promise.'

'She guessed?' Sarah was appalled. First Elizabeth Hislop, and now Adam. 'What did you say to her?'

'She doesn't know it's Bella. She just knows I'm being blackmailed. I haven't told her anything else. But she did offer to help with money. How much have you told Adam?'

Now it was Sarah's turn to go red. 'He'd guessed as well, sort of, except he's got as far as working out it's Bella.'

'Bugger.' Friday raised her bottle again, drank, and let out another loud burp. 'When did you realise?'

'He confronted me when I got home the other night. He'd followed me down to King's Wharf.'

'God, Sarah, did you actually tell him you were seeing Walter off? That was a bit stupid.'

'Hardly. I'd said I was going out to visit Harrie.'

'Not very trusting, is he?' Friday said.

Sarah ignored her. 'He'd pieced things together around what happened in the old burial ground, because of Furniss, and he was nearly right. He'd already worked out that Bella's blackmailing us, though not why, thank Christ.'

Harrie, who had lain down with her head on Friday's pillow, groaned at the reminder of their crime. Friday patted her hip comfortingly.

She asked, 'So why *does* he think she's blackmailing us?'

'I told him she hates us, and that if we don't keep paying up she's threatened to tell the governor that you murdered Liz Parker on the *Isla* —'

'Oh, thanks very much.'

'I told him you didn't. I also told him Bella's threatened to shop Harrie and me to the governor for lying on your behalf.'

'And he believed you?'

'I think so. But I can tell you, I didn't enjoy lying to him,' Sarah said bitterly. 'And he's really shocked at the amount of money she's been demanding.'

'I bloody well am, too!' Friday said. She sighed. 'So is that everyone who knows? Just Adam and Mrs H?'

'And Walter,' Sarah added. 'But he's out of the picture now.'

Friday gave Harrie's flank a gentle push. 'Harrie, have you told anyone?'

Harrie sat up and looked at her hands, resting in her lap. 'No.'

'Not even Mrs Barrett or Leo? Not even in confidence?'

'No.'

'What about James?' Sarah asked.

'James?' Harrie blinked. 'Why would I tell James?'

'He's been to see you a few times lately, hasn't he?'

'Yes, but I wouldn't tell him that.' Harrie let out a high-pitched and rather hard-edged laugh. 'We're getting along quite well, at last.'

She stood and moved to the window. In the yard below, the stable boy, Jimmy, was shovelling up horseshit. There were no doubt flies all over it, even in winter. Rowie bloody Harris was a fly, buzzing endlessly around James, being indispensible as his live-in housegirl. Not that James was horse dung, of course, though, honestly, he must be just as thick, Harrie thought, if he couldn't see how much Rowie's presence was a thorn in her side. And her heart. There was something about that girl she really didn't like.

Oh, she knew James wasn't sleeping with her — James just wasn't that sort of man — but the very idea of it still drove her wild with jealousy. Well, she thought she knew it, in the bright light of day, but at night, when she was lying in bed and couldn't sleep and her room was at its darkest and so was her mind, the nasty, insistent voices in her head would whisper to her, do you really know James that well? Are you sure he isn't sharing Rowie's bed night after night? She would imagine their naked, writhing bodies, the sweat from their passion dampening the sheets, and snap! she'd be caught in the trap and round and round her tortured thoughts would go; Rowie was so much prettier than her, so much more self-assured and confident, and, of course, thoroughly at ease with manipulating men. And now she'd taken Harrie's place — her potential place, at least — in the home of the man for whom Harrie felt so much. Whom she loved. Those were the nights she barely slept at all.

'Harrie?' Sarah said. 'Are you still with us?'

Turning away from the window, Harrie said, 'Why *would* I tell him? Why would I tell him I'm being blackmailed because I kicked someone to death?'

'Well, you know, you haven't been yourself lately,' Friday said. 'Er, again.'

Harrie realised then that Sarah and Friday must have noticed the change in her. Her heart sank. She hadn't been fooling anyone. 'No,' she mumbled. 'I haven't said anything to a soul.'

'Will I talk to Mrs H, then?' Friday asked.

'A hundred and thirty-five quid,' Sarah said, shaking her head. 'How will we ever repay her?'

Friday flapped her hand dismissively. 'Easy. It's not that much. We'll make it a proper business arrangement. She can withhold it directly from my wages.'

'That's not a business arrangement,' Sarah said. 'That's you getting your pay docked.'

'She won't take it all. She's far too soft-hearted. I'll have plenty left over.' Friday didn't care, as long as she had enough in her pocket to get drunk whenever she felt like it. 'And you can pay your usual contribution to me, Sarah, to pay me back, instead of into the Charlotte fund. That'll work, won't it?'

'No, it won't. We need my money going into the bank. We can't not support Janie and the girls.'

'Shit. That's true.' Friday hadn't thought of that.

'I can give what I make from my flash straight to you,' Harrie said, referring to the money she earned drawing tattoo designs for Leo Dundas. 'Except for what I send home.'

What Harrie made from her flash wouldn't make much of a dent in a one hundred and thirty-five pound debt, but Friday and Sarah were far too sensitive to Harrie's feelings to say so.

Instead, Sarah, who had the best head for figures and whose job it was to balance the Charlotte fund, said, 'No, that should go into the bank as well, otherwise we're going to get very confused. We should make repayments to Friday from the account.'

'So am I talking to Mrs H or not?' Friday asked.

Sarah said, 'Let me think about it for a couple of days.'

'Well, you'd better hurry up. We've only got four more days before we have to bloody well pay the bitch.'

Leonard Dundas finished washing his breakfast dishes, dried them and put them away on the shelf. Then he stoked the fire, opened the window in the small room that was his kitchen-cum-parlour, and tossed out the dirty water from the washing basin. He wondered how Walter was getting on, and he wondered, too, where Clifford was. He was fairly confident that one of the girls would have taken her home — he just wasn't sure who'd been brave enough.

It was so quiet without Walter. He missed him desperately, and Clifford, regardless of her nasty temper. Perhaps he'd get himself a cat. Cats were more independent than dogs. Far more self-serving and arrogant as well, that was true, but more able to look after themselves. There'd always been at least one cat on every ship he'd sailed in all the years he'd been at sea, taken aboard as both ratter and mascot. Yes, that's what he needed — a cat.

He sat on the cot under the open window and tamped tobacco into his pipe. No, he didn't need a cat, and he knew it, though he still might get one. He needed human company. He was lonely. It was time to visit Serafina Fortune, and not just for a glimpse into his future. He'd lost track of the number of times he'd asked her to move in with him, but she wouldn't. She said she liked her independence. She was just like a bloody cat herself, Serafina was. Sleek, moody, mysterious and more than a little bit arrogant. He told her that if she looked into her own future, she'd see in it a perfectly nice existence for the two of them, even if she was twenty-five years younger than he was, but she refused. She swore she'd never poke around in her own future, but sometimes he suspected she already had, and that's why she wouldn't share her life with him.

He'd never married, though he'd loved several women and slept with many more. When he was younger and a sailor, he'd believed it unfair to marry then leave a wife ashore by herself for such long periods, but now, when he slid into the cold and empty bed in his little room upstairs, he wondered if he might have made a mistake. He'd fathered several children that he knew of. He had a daughter in Japan, where he'd lived for some time, and a son in England, long grown now, whom he'd not seen for more than fifteen years, and a son born in Sydney to a woman with whom he'd had a short fling while he'd been in port, before he'd settled in New South Wales. He'd offered to make provision for that child on a subsequent visit, but the mother had declined. The boy had gone to sea at a very young age and Leo rarely saw him, though he'd heard he was quite the young gamecock, and he did occasionally run into the boy's mother, with whom he remained on friendly terms. In Leo's opinion, finding Walter huddled among a stack of barrels behind a pub in Harrington Street, his arms wrapped around that scruffy little dog, had been a blessing — a last opportunity to raise a child properly.

Then Walter had killed that devil Furniss, and Leo had known that the only thing he could do for the lad was put him on a ship back to England, even though it had almost broken his heart. He was sorry about what had happened — to the very marrow in his bones — and regretted it immensely. He should have killed Furniss himself. Walter would have been robbed of the satisfaction, but no twelve-year-old boy was equipped to shoulder that sort of moral burden. He would pay for it one way or another as he grew up.

There was one thing he could still do for the lad, though. He went to the mantel above the fireplace and took down a wooden box, opened it and withdrew a folded sheet of paper, which he'd found tucked into his jacket pocket after Walter's ship had sailed. Walter must have scribbled it out at Serafina's — she'd hidden him that first day after the murder. It was untidily sealed with three fat blobs of her distinctive pale rose sealing wax — one over the long join and one at the fold at each end — which was a bit excessive. Three blobs were also quite rude, implying that the bearer of the letter could not be trusted not to peep inside and read the contents. Leo, however, knew that Walter had trusted him implicitly, therefore that much wax must mean the lad was trying, in a clumsy way, to protect him.

Accompanying the note had been another, this one not sealed. It said:

*Deer leo*
  *Plees giv this lettar to Bella shand on Cumbarlind street.*
*It wil save Harry and fryday and Sara. I wil not forget yu.*
  *Walter*

Leo wouldn't forget Walter, either. Every time he read the note, especially the last sentence, his eyes teared up. He'd deliver the sealed letter this morning. But Bella Shand? What the hell did the girls think they were doing getting involved with that nasty piece of work?

Leo stood several feet back from the gates, eyeing the dogs with distaste and more than a touch of fear. Muscles bunched with hostile tension, they stood with their snouts pushed though the wrought iron pickets, strings of spit hanging from their jaws, growling like hellhounds. He wondered if there was another way in. Surely visitors didn't have to run the gauntlet past these beasts every time they called? Or, given the rumours he'd heard about some of the unpleasant characters Bella did business with, perhaps that was the point? Still, he wasn't standing out here shouting himself hoarse until someone came to let him in.

He crunched across the gravel at the back of the house, which actually faced the street, past tidy garden beds and a statue of a naked cherub wielding a trumpet, until he came to a small door in the far end of the building, fortunately on this side of the fence. He knocked and waited. Eventually a shifty-eyed woman opened it.

'Yes?'

'Mrs Shand, please.'

'Who's asking?'

'My name is Leonard Dundas.'

'What's your business?'

Leo made a well-educated guess concerning the subject of Walter's letter. 'Amos Furniss.'

The woman stared at him sourly for a moment. Then she said, 'Hold on,' and shut the door in his face.

Leo had a horrible few minutes of wondering if she was letting the dogs out so they could race around the house and surprise him.

She opened the door again. 'Come in.'

He followed her down a hallway, then past a staircase and into a light-filled reception room. French doors led to a verandah with a stunning view of Sydney Cove, though this morning the doors were closed against the briskly cool winter weather.

Bella Shand sat at an expansive writing desk against the wall opposite the French doors. Leo, who had never met her, had expected her to be old and ill-favoured, perhaps even grotesque — physical traits that would be commensurate with her reputation — but she wasn't. She was quite attractive in a sharp, hawkish sort of way, though extremely thin. She was possibly in her thirties, though her thick face paint made it difficult to judge her true age. Her coal-black, heavily ringletted hair gleamed (surely such shine and abundance signified a wig?) and she was certainly beautifully dressed, even Leo could see that. He could also see why Clarence chose to marry her: privately, Clarence might prefer men, but she would make a good foil.

Inherently, however, there was something deeply unpleasant about her. She seemed ... reptilian. Also, a very fierce intelligence burnt behind her eyes. Leo decided he would do very well not to cross her, and prayed he wasn't about to do just that.

'Mr Dundas,' she said. She didn't smile.

She had an unusual voice, too. Low, but very rich and full. Alluring and quite mesmerising.

'Mrs Shand.' Leo offered his hand.

She rose to meet him. 'Amos Furniss,' she said without preamble.

'Aye. I've been asked to deliver to you a letter. I gather it concerns him. Or rather, his death.' Leo retrieved Walter's note from his jacket pocket, hoping like hell it did. He would look an absolute fool if it didn't.

Bella took the letter, returned to her chair, broke the seals and read it quickly. 'Who wrote this?' she demanded. 'A half-trained monkey? Who's this Walter Cobley?'

'Writing isn't his strong suit.'

'Is this true, what he's said?' Bella held up the letter.

'I don't know. I haven't read it.'

Bella looked as though she didn't believe him, but said, 'He says *he* killed Furniss, not Friday Woolfe and her crew. Who is he? Why would he kill Amos Furniss?'

Shocked, Leo thought, *Friday? Why does she think Friday murdered Furniss?* But, keeping his face neutral, he said, 'Walter was a victim of Furniss's thoroughly unpleasant habits. He had the great misfortune of sailing with Furniss on the *Isla*.'

'That *child*?' Bella looked vaguely startled. 'The ship's *boy*?'

'Aye.'

'But how do you know him?'

'He jumped ship. I took him in. He's been lodging with me ever since.'

'Where is he now?'

'Long gone.'

'Back to England?'

'Let's just say he's gone,' Leo said. 'I care for the lad.'

Bella drummed her manicured fingernails on the polished surface of her desk, then said, 'Well, I have to say, Furniss reaped what he sowed.' She glanced at Leo. 'But we all do, don't we? I'd like you to take Friday Woolfe a message, if you will.'

'How do you know we're even acquainted?'

Bella stared at him unblinkingly. 'I know a lot of things, Mr Dundas. Will you take her a message or not?'

Leo briefly considered agreeing, providing Bella told him why she thought Friday had killed Furniss, but suspected he'd have more luck getting the answer from Friday herself. Bella Shand would probably lie. She clearly didn't like Friday — he'd heard it in her voice when she'd said Friday's name.

'I will,' he said, 'but I won't be involved in any transaction that might cause Miss Woolfe or her friends harm.'

Bella shrugged nonchalantly. 'Of course not.'

Lighting a taper, she slotted a nib into a silver holder and wrote a short note, blotted the ink, then folded it. From a flat wooden box she selected a stick of jade-green wax, and held one end over the taper's flame, turning it around and around so each side warmed evenly. Finally the wax melted sufficiently and, not bothering with a wafer, she placed a blob across the join and pressed down with a seal.

Then she started all over again.

Oh, for God's sake, Leo thought, get on with it.

In the end she sealed the letter four times.

'You're even ruder than Walter,' Leo said.

Bella's eyes narrowed unpleasantly. 'I beg your pardon?'

'You can assume I won't look. I have more integrity than that.'

And he *wouldn't* look. He'd find out some other way.

Elizabeth opened the front door. 'Good afternoon. May I help you?'

'Aye, I'd like to see Friday Woolfe, if you please.' The man smiled.

He was probably her age, tall, had fair hair greying to silver tied back in a neat cue, a moustache and a short beard, gold earrings and a gold tooth. Obviously a sailor. The tars loved Friday.

'I'm afraid she's fully occupied for the next few days. If you'll give me a moment, I'll check the appointment book. She might have something on Saturday.'

Apparently amused, the man shook his head. 'You've got the wrong end of the stick. I'm not a customer. I just need to talk to her.'

'I'm sorry, I don't believe I caught your name.'

'I haven't said it. It's Leo Dundas.'

'Oh, you're the tattooist!' Elizabeth offered her hand. 'You know, I can't *tell* you what your tattoos have done for my bank balance. The gentlemen love them. Friday's my most popular girl.'

'Aye, well, I don't think that's the reason she has herself tattooed.'

'No, but still, every cloud.'

'You're not keen on the art of tattoo?'

'I wasn't. I must admit I did think they were, well, cheap. But lately I've come to appreciate them.'

'Now that you've seen the contribution they make to your coffers?'

'Something like that, yes,' Elizabeth confessed. 'Friday can probably see you for fifteen minutes, if you don't mind waiting.'

Leo didn't. Elizabeth gave him the choice of sitting in her office, or in the salon with a waiting customer and three of her girls. Leo, never averse to the sight of an attractive young lady, chose the salon.

'Afternoon,' Leo said to the cove already settled on the sofa, his top hat balanced on his knee.

'Good afternoon.'

'Proper weather for staying indoors,' Leo remarked as he sank into an armchair by the robustly banked fire.

'It is that.'

A blonde girl with lovely brown eyes and a temptingly full bosom gave him a welcoming smile. 'Good day, sir. I'm Connie. Do you have a specific appointment or would you like to choose?'

'Yes!' a gorgeously plump lass with shining brown hair said enthusiastically. 'You can have Connie, or me — I'm Hazel — or you can have Loulou.'

Loulou, Leo presumed, was the petite, raven-haired beauty on the end of the sofa fluttering her eyelashes at him.

'Actually,' he said apologetically, 'I'm here to see Friday.'

There was a delicate but deliberate snort of derision from Loulou. He fixed her with a stony-faced gaze: she stared right back, not bothering with the fluttery eyelashes now. He looked at his watch and wondered if the other cove was waiting for Friday as well.

When she pranced in minutes later, she stopped short and said, 'What are you doing here?'

The man on the sofa stood.

So did Leo. 'We need to talk. In private.'

Connie and Hazel tittered, highly entertained.

'Just one minute!' the other man exclaimed. 'I have an appointment!'

Friday walked slowly across the floor towards him, her hips swinging and the semi-transparent fabric of her robe sliding away from her long, long legs. Leo was amused to watch her wrap muscled but lithe arms he himself had expertly tattooed around the cove's neck and whisper in his ear. He reddened immediately, but nodded and returned to his seat, his hat over his lap.

Friday beckoned: Leo followed her out of the salon. As they passed the open door to Elizabeth Hislop's office, Elizabeth called out, 'Any more than fifteen minutes, and you charge him!'

Leo couldn't tell whether she was joking or not.

'I take it the little dark one, Loulou, doesn't like you,' Leo said as they climbed the stairs.

Flicking him a sour look, Friday said, 'She hates my guts, and I hate hers. Bloody light-fingered, too. Did Harrie tell you someone tried to break into the safe here last year? It was her, I'm sure of it. *And* she's spying on me.'

'Really? Why?' Leo asked, but Friday had clamped her mouth shut.

On the first floor she ushered Leo into a small, smartly furnished bedchamber, and closed the door.

'What's happened?' she asked immediately.

Leo remained standing. 'I've just been to see Bella Shand.'

Friday had been on the alert minutes earlier; now every nerve in her body was jangling. 'Why? You don't even know her.'

'Young Walter left a letter, to be delivered after he sailed.'

'Did you open it?' Friday demanded. Bloody hell, what had Walter said about them? What did Leo know?

'I did not. It wasn't addressed to me.'

'Did Bella tell you what it said?'

'He admitted to killing Furniss.'

'Christ, really? What did Bella say?'

'She wanted to know who Walter is, if what he'd written was true, and where he is now.'

'What did you tell her?'

'I said it was true. She said she remembered Walter from the *Isla*. But as to his whereabouts, all I said was he'd left Sydney.'

'She must know he's on a ship for England.'

'I'm sure, but what can she do about it now? Friday, you do know why Walter wrote that letter, don't you?' Leo asked. 'He did it to protect you, so she wouldn't come after you and Harrie and Sarah.'

'I know, but …' Friday stopped, realising that Leo was staring at her, arms crossed, eyebrows raised.

'What I don't understand is why *would* she have come after you?'

Friday said nothing, feeling her face begin to burn. She sat on the bed.

'Unless,' Leo went on, 'perhaps she thought you, or maybe Harrie or Sarah, killed Furniss.'

'Shut up,' Friday said.

Leo ignored her. 'But for her to think that, she must have known that at least one of you was in that burial ground with Furniss when he died. So, was it you, Friday?'

'It's none of your business.'

'What were you doing there?'

'Really, Leo, I can't tell you.'

Leo took Bella's note from his jacket pocket. 'You can if you want this.'

'Is that from her? To me?'

'Yes, but you're not getting it till you tell me exactly what's going on.'

Friday put her face in her hands. God. Their secret was starting to seep out like whey from a cheese press. Forced now to say something, she admitted that they were making regular blackmail payments to Bella, then repeated the story Sarah had given Adam and said it was to stop her from telling Governor Darling that she, Friday, had murdered Liz Parker aboard the *Isla*.

'And did you?' Leo asked.

'What a rude question,' Friday said, much more at ease now she'd steered the conversation away from the dangerous truth.

Leo waggled Bella's letter.

'No, I did not, though I felt like it. She was a right bitch, Liz.'

'Then who did?'

'Bella did it herself.'

Leo handed Friday the letter and leant on the windowsill, looking down on the traffic passing on Argyle Street, to give her some privacy.

She broke the seals and read what Bella had written, not knowing what to think at all, it was that unexpected. 'Thank Christ for that,' she said eventually.

Leo asked, 'Good news?'

There was no point to hiding this part of it from him any longer. 'She sent Harrie a note yesterday. Well, some scruffy little guttersnipes dropped it in her basket at the markets. She was demanding four hundred quid — *double* what she'd told us to give Furniss last Sunday.'

'The night he died?'

Friday nodded.

'And did you deliver the money?'

'I tried but Walter took it back off Furniss's body.'

'Did you see what happened?'

'No, I'd gone by then. To the pub.'

Leo rubbed at his beard. 'Four hundred. That's steep. Can you pay?'

'Don't have to.' Friday waved Bella's letter. 'She says here she accepts we didn't top Furniss. She probably knew what the bastard was doing to poor little Walter all those months on the ship. She only wants the original amount. But she wants it this Friday night.'

'And that was two hundred?' Leo whistled. 'It's still a fortune. How will you pay it?' Then he realised they already had paid it once. 'How the hell did you get hold of that sort of money?'

'We save it. I make a lot here, and Adam pays Sarah a good wage, and Harrie, well, Harrie pays what she can. She puts in everything you pay her for the flash, you know, except for a bit she sends home every month. Anyway, she doesn't have to pay much. Me and Sarah owe her.'

'What for?'

'She kept us all together for the first eighteen months after we met. We wouldn't have managed if it hadn't been for Harrie.'

'And now she's falling apart.'

'You've noticed.'

'Aye, I have. It's a worry.'

Friday tucked the letter into the top of her corset and stood.

'Would you have paid four hundred?' Leo asked, moving towards the door.

'If we'd had to.'

'Christ, lass, how would you have raised that sort of money in a hurry?'

'We already had the two hundred, and a bit more. We'd have had to borrow the rest.'

Leo opened the door. 'I could have helped there. I've a bit put away.'

'You mightn't have got it back for a while,' Friday said as she crossed the landing, her robe floating behind her and her riotous copper hair fanning out across her back. 'There's other things we need to pay for, as well.'

'Such as?' Leo eyed her shapely calves.

Friday stopped and turned towards him. 'A mate in the Factory. Janie's raising our friend Rachel's child, Charlotte, together with her own little girl, Rosie. They depend on us. And we won't be letting them down, no matter what.' She hesitated, then said, 'You asked before why Lou would spy on me. Because she's working for Bella, that's why. I'm bloody well sure of *that*, too.'

# Chapter Four

The wall on Kent Street surrounding the old Sydney burial ground was six feet high, but did little to contain the stench seeping from the sour clay behind it. Not even the sharp chill of the winter night could stifle the smell.

'Bloody hell,' Sarah said, adjusting the woollen scarf over her mouth and nose. The place always stank, especially during summer, but during daylight hours you could rush past, holding your breath, without the risk of turning an ankle on the rough street surface. Only those with absolutely no sense of smell — or who had nefarious intent, as it was rumoured to be a meeting place for rogues, footpads and other lowlifes — deliberately loitered in the burial ground's vicinity.

'It's worse inside,' Friday remarked. She raised her lantern. 'Are you all right?' she asked Harrie.

Harrie nodded, her nose hovering an inch above a posy of lavender and daphne. She wasn't all right, though. She felt sick with nerves. What if Bella herself turned up to collect the money? She was terrified of coming face to face with her. And why here again? Furniss had been killed here, so surely the police would be on the alert, but Sarah said it was smart of Bella — folk would be giving the burial ground a wide berth, wary of being attacked themselves by a murderer not yet apprehended.

Harrie wished Leo was hiding in the shadows, watching out for them, but he wasn't. This was their business, not his. She'd felt ashamed when Friday had told her and Sarah that Leo also knew about Bella's blackmail now — Lord, Sarah had been angry! — because she'd never wanted to lie to Leo, about anything, but Friday had fed him the version of the story involving Liz Parker, so at least he didn't know what a horribly wicked person she was. He'd hate her, if he did. True, he hadn't hated Walter for what he'd done, but Walter was a child and he'd been very badly mistreated. She was a grown woman of almost twenty and had no excuse for her sins. No excuse at all.

She was glad she'd come tonight, even though she had the jitters and her knees were wobbly and she badly wanted to sit down but there was nothing to sit on. She was even a little bit proud of herself. When Sarah had told Friday she would come with her to the burial ground, Harrie had been dismayed because she'd known she'd have to volunteer, too. But she'd realised that if she could summon the guts to do that, then perhaps she wasn't as useless and as powerless as she felt. And the more she thought about it, the more the idea became a small victory, for her anyway, even if they were handing over their hard-earned money to a nasty, blackmailing bitch. So here she was, vaguely triumphant, dizzy and wanting to be sick.

Stamping her feet against the cold, Friday said, 'She might send Brainless Becky and Lumpy Louisa.'

'Would she trust them?' Sarah asked.

'She trusted Furniss.'

'She knew she could hunt him down, you mean.'

'Then she can definitely hunt down Becky and Louisa. Pair of lardarsed hedgewhores.'

The gate in the wall opened with a discordant creak; Harrie, Sarah and Friday all jumped. A woman stepped through. She wore a shawl draped over her head and across her nose and face, revealing only her eyes. Obviously not Bella, however — this woman was too short and more rounded in the body.

'Money,' she said in a muffled voice, extending her hand.

The movement of her clothing sent out a waft of tuberose, powerful enough to compete with the stink seeping from the burial ground, and Friday was struck by a terrible suspicion. She'd know that cheap scent anywhere. She lifted her lantern.

'It's you! It bloody is!'

The woman's eyes widened in alarm, and as she took a rapid step sideways her shawl slid back from her forehead an inch or so, revealing dark, gleaming hair.

Friday exploded. 'Lou, you fucking bitch! I bloody knew it was you!'

Lou whipped out a knife, its blade glinting in the lantern light, and demanded, 'Give me the money!'

Sarah withdrew the pouch containing the two hundred pounds from an inside pocket of her cloak. As she stepped forwards, Lou made a jerky lunge towards her, slashing wildly. Horrified, Harrie could see that Sarah was about to walk directly into the upward arc of the swinging knife, and shoved her out of the way.

Lou missed Sarah altogether and as her momentum carried her past, Friday tore her shawl off her head with one hand, and punched her in the jaw with the other.

But it wasn't Lou.

It was Rowie Harris.

Stunned, Friday gaped at her.

'Stop staring, you gulpy cow,' Rowie spat. She rubbed her jaw, then snatched the pouch out of Sarah's unresisting hand and backed away. 'What did you expect? You think you're so special, don't you, with your precious little crew no one else can join? But you're not. None of you. You're no better than the rest of us. Convict slags, the lot of you!'

She ran off down the street, then skidded to a halt and called out, 'And you, Harrie holier-than-bloody-thou Clarke, I've been having the loveliest time fucking your James Downey. He'll never want you now.'

As Dr James Downey tied his black silk cravat in a simple Gordian knot — there'd be no ridiculous, neck-contorting sartorial arrangements such as 'the Mathematical' or 'the Mailcoach' for him — he realised what was missing; no tantalising smell of cooking eggs and toasting bread. And now that he thought about it, he hadn't heard the usual sounds of Rowie banging pots around this morning either. Uncharacteristically, she'd taken Friday evening, Saturday and Sunday off, to visit a friend, she'd said, but had assured him she'd be back late last night, in time to see him off to work this morning. Perhaps she'd slept in, which would be unheard of.

He opened his bedroom door and peered out: the parlour was as empty as it had been when he'd retired last night. And the fire was cold. How inconvenient. He had to be at the surgery in half an hour.

It occurred to him then that Rowie might be ill. He'd reluctantly agreed to take her on — in fact had been coerced into it by his partner, Dr Lawrence Chandler — due to menstrual complaints preventing her from working as a prostitute for Elizabeth Hislop. Perhaps she was suffering a severe relapse and was unable to drag herself out of bed.

He went outside — the only way to reach Rowie's accommodation adjoining the house — and knocked on her door. There was no answer. He waited a moment, knocked again, then cautiously entered. He hadn't been inside Rowie's room since she'd moved in, but he was fairly confident it didn't normally look like this. There was nothing on any of the surfaces, the clothes rail across one corner was bare, and the bureau drawers sagged open, empty. She appeared to have gone, taking all her things with her.

Why? He'd thought she'd seemed happy here. He closed the door and returned to the house to make himself some breakfast. After an unsatisfactory meal of rubbery fried eggs and burnt toast, he left his dishes, cutlery and the greasy cast-iron frying pan in a basin of cold water to soak, and shrugged into his coat. He was puzzled. Should he look for Rowie? But where would he start? Perhaps she'd met a man and run off with him. If that was the case, good luck to her. There had never been anything intimate between them, but now that he'd become accustomed to someone cooking his meals, attending to his domestic chores and generally cleaning up after him — an arrangement he'd resisted for some time due to his fear of gossip — he'd decided he quite liked it. Surely it wouldn't be that hard to find another housegirl. A wife, of course, would be infinitely preferable, but there was only one woman he was interested in marrying, and Harrie was turning into rather a long-term project. But that was all right. He was prepared to wait for her.

He settled his hat on his head, picked up his bag and stepped outside into the cool morning air, locking the door behind him. Damn, he'd have to find someone to tend the garden now, too. Rowie had looked after that as well. Strolling down the gravel path, to his delight he suddenly noticed Harrie standing on the street, the brim of her bonnet framing her pretty little face and a woollen shawl tucked around her trim figure. Actually, she was looking a little too trim these days, in his opinion.

'Harrie! What are you doing out this early?'

By way of an answer she raised her bare hand and slapped him hard across his face.

'Ow!' His hand flew to his stinging cheek. 'What was that for?'

'You know,' she said bitterly. 'How could you?'

'How could I what?'

But it was too late: Harrie was off down the street, her skirts flashing and her bonnet slipping, only the ribbons saving it from flying off.

'Harrie? Harrie!' Part of him desperately wanted to go after her, to stop her and find out what was wrong, but then the stuffy, strait-laced and proper side of him — the ex-navy captain and genteel doctor with a public practice — told him much more forcefully that upstanding gentlemen did not chase women down the street.

So he watched helplessly as Harrie ran away from him.

Harrie didn't know how long she'd been wandering around. She'd come out early on the pretence of buying bread for the Barretts' breakfast, but her intention had definitely been to confront James before he left for the surgery. She'd agonised since Friday night about the foul gob of poison Rowie had spat out at the burial ground, and while her common sense — and Friday and Sarah — had told her the revelation had been nothing more than a barb of pure nastiness, her heart had believed Rowie. And it still did. The voices in her head had been right after all. She had confronted James, but she'd barely said to him anything she'd wanted to say. The depth of his betrayal had rendered her virtually speechless. She felt even worse now, and she hadn't achieved anything.

She had so wanted him to be different. She'd so wanted him to be decent. She'd thought he was.

And she'd been wrong.

But this is what happened when you did the sort of things she'd done. This is what happened when you sinned. You paid.

The streets were busy now. It must be nearly mid-morning. Nora Barrett would be very angry with her when she got back, and quite rightly so. She'd not been there to make breakfast, Samuel and Hannah had been due for baths this morning, and Abigail had wanted help with casting on the first row of a scarf she was knitting. She'd let them down. Blinking back tears, she crossed the street and headed north towards home.

Outside the bakery near the corner of George and Jamison streets, the one that sold the moist pound cake and the good, crisp ginger biscuits, she came across a small boy sitting on the edge of the footway, his bare feet in the muddy gutter. Seeing his tear-stained little face and snotty upper lip, and already feeling distraught and terribly on edge, Harrie couldn't help weeping herself.

She crouched beside him. 'Where's your ma?'

The boy looked at her and cried even harder. So did Harrie. She retrieved her handkerchief, blew her nose, folded it over to find a clean bit and wiped his top lip, and tried again.

'Is she in the bakery?'

He shook his head, his dark curls bouncing.

'Are you lost?'

Scratching at the ground with a short piece of stick, he nodded.

'Have you got a name, sweetie?'

'Davey.'

Poor wee thing, Harrie thought, grateful to have someone to think about other than herself. He could only be about four and his dirty little feet were quite blue with cold.

'Where do you live, Davey?'

He shrugged, the shoulders of his grubby, patched, too-big jacket rising and collapsing.

'On the Rocks?'

He nodded.

'What street, do you know?'

'I'm hungry.'

Harrie stood and offered him her hand. He scrambled up and went with her into the bakery, where she bought him two eccles cakes, which he scoffed in a minute flat. She hoped to God he wasn't living on the streets.

Outside she asked, 'Do you live in a house, Davey? With a ma and a father and brothers and sisters?'

Apparently much happier now he'd eaten, he said, 'Got a mam and that.'

'But you can't remember where you live?'

A woman exiting the bakery said, 'That's Davey Doyle. Lives at the poor end of Cumberland. Always running off. His grandma'll tan his hide.'

Harrie felt very slightly taken advantage of, but never mind. 'Come on, let's get you home, shall we?'

Davey held her hand all the way to the Charlotte Place end of Cumberland Street, where he pointed out a small, rubble-stone cottage with a low shingle roof, two windows at the front — with shutters, not glass — and a single chimney.

'Is that your house?' Harrie asked.

Before Davey could answer, the door flew open and a stocky woman marched out and grabbed him by the ear.

'And where the hell have you been?' she demanded.

Davey squawked and stood on his tiptoes to relieve the pressure.

Harrie winced. 'I found him down on George Street.'

The woman proceeded to whack Davey's arse, changing her grip from his ear to his forearm, yanking it up and propelling him around in a circle with the force of her blows. 'He does this every couple of months, you know. Fair scares the shite out of me, so it does.'

'Are you, er, Mrs Doyle?' Harrie asked.

'I am.'

Harrie watched her as she finished thumping Davey. She was well rounded, somewhere in her late forties, and not unattractive despite the lines life had etched on her face and the grey threads woven through her dark hair.

Letting Davey's arm drop, and rather confusingly giving him a quick, rough cuddle and a loud kiss on his grubby cheek, she said, 'Thank you for bringing him back, lass. Don't matter how much I paddle his arse, he still does it. He'll be the death of me, so he will. Worries me sick. It's Biddy, by the way. Biddy Doyle. Davey, say thank you to the nice colleen.'

Rubbing the seat of his pants, Davey mumbled, 'Thank you.'

Biddy turned towards the cottage door, now crowded with four youngsters aged between about fifteen and ten, all staring curiously out, and ordered, 'Maureen, take him inside and give him a good wash. Them feet are filthy! And put some tea on, there's a good lass.' To Harrie, she said, 'What's your name, dear?'

'Harrie. Harrie Clarke.'

'Would you be wanting a nice cup of tea? Sure you would. You look cold.'

Startled, Harrie swallowed, then nodded. 'Yes, please.' There was an element of kindness about Mrs Doyle that appealed to her, despite the smacking she'd dealt out to Davey. She reminded Harrie of her own mother, before Ada had become so very ill. And she was already going to be in trouble with Nora: arriving home a further half-hour late wasn't going to make things any worse.

Inside the cottage there was little space; it was a single room partitioned by a curtain, behind which Harrie glimpsed an iron bedstead. A hearth at the other end was cluttered with cooking implements, alongside shelves containing plates, bowls and mugs. An appetising smell wafted from a pot simmering over the fire. A large wooden crucifix hung on the wall and a double mattress made up with a woollen blanket on the oilcloth-covered floor took up one corner. An oblong table with mismatched chairs occupied the centre of the room, scattered with pieces of unfinished sewing. There clearly wasn't a lot of money coming in, but the house was clean, and the children warmly dressed. Apart from Davey and his bare feet.

'Have a seat, take the weight off,' Mrs Doyle said, gesturing at the table. 'Just move those bits and pieces out of the way.' She sat down herself, with a barely disguised groan. 'Sew yourself, do you?'

'Some. I'm assigned to a family with four children. I look after them and tend to the household chores. I'm a sempstress and a broderer by trade. My mistress is a sempstress, too, so I help her a lot.' Briefly, Harrie considered mentioning her part-time job drawing flash for Leo, but decided against it.

'Oh, I'm not that clever with a needle,' Mrs Doyle said. 'Thanks, love,' she added as Maureen set down two cups and saucers and a teapot.

'I'll go out and get the water for Davey's feet,' the girl said.

'Good lass. I just do drawers and shifts and the like and sell them into the draper's,' Mrs Doyle went on. 'And kiddie's clothes. I hawk those on a stall at George Street market on Tuesdays, Thursdays and Saturdays, though I'm thinking of moving down the Haymarket.' She gave Harrie a sideways look. 'And I know you're thinking I must be a convict, but I'm not. Immigrated here years ago.'

'I am. I stole some silk from a shop,' Harrie confessed. 'And Mr Doyle? What does he do?'

Biddy Doyle let out a laugh. 'Not much you can do from a coffin. He passed years ago.'

Harrie kept her eyes on her teacup, desperate to prevent her gaze from sliding towards the children.

'Go on, ask,' Mrs Doyle prompted, clearly amused. 'All my children are grown now and gone. Two of the boys are at sea, though one's home on shore leave as we speak, my youngest. The three eldest were Frank Doyle's kids. I had them in Ireland but then Frank was transported, so I followed him two years later. When I arrived, I found Frank had married himself a new wife. Good old Frank.'

How awful, Harrie thought. 'Did you bring your children with you?'

'Oh, yes. They were all quite little. I had four more by another man, and my youngest had a different father again.' Mrs Doyle beamed. 'Eight children, I've not lost one and I've raised them all on my own, so I have. It seems years ago now.' She seemed faintly surprised. 'Well, that's because it was, I suppose.'

'So these children ...?'

'Maureen, Rosalyn and Terry are my second eldest daughter's kids, she's away to a big house in Liverpool, working as a housegirl, and Cathleen and Davey are my middle daughter's. She's in the gaol. Always was a tearaway.' Mrs Doyle sighed. 'Not a husband between them. I've more or less brought these up as my own. Still, that's what grandmothers are for, isn't it?'

Harrie wanted to say that she'd done very well for herself, but it didn't really look as though she had. Mortifyingly, Biddy Doyle seemed to read her mind.

'Don't let the house fool you, dear, draughty shitehole that it is. We've quite a stash put away, haven't we, lovies?' The children nodded energetically. 'Soon, I'll have enough saved to buy at least two houses, so we'll live in one and let the other, and I'll be a Rocks landlady. Married yourself, are you? How's your tea? Still hot?'

'Yes. I mean, no, I'm not. And yes, it is, thank you.'

'I'm surprised, a pretty girl like you. That lovely hair, though you could do with a good feed, if you don't mind me saying. How long's your lag?'

'I've just over five years to serve.'

'From seven?'

Harrie nodded. The door opened and shut: Harrie assumed it was Maureen with the water so she didn't turn, and started when a male voice said, 'Mam, you didn't tell me we were having visitors.'

She did turn in her seat, then, to see one of the most beautiful young men she'd ever encountered. He was tall, long-legged and wide in the shoulder, but Harrie barely noticed any of that, she was that entranced by his face and extraordinarily dark eyes rimmed with thick black lashes. Dark stubble dusted his chin and upper lip, and heavy brunet curls fell untidily to his collar. Most men would look like a girl with an effeminate hairstyle like that, she thought, but not this one. Definitely not this one. But he couldn't be any older than her. Even younger, perhaps. He flashed a smile full of white teeth and she felt it in the pit of her belly.

'Where have you been?' Mrs Doyle demanded. 'And where's our ham bones? My son, Mick,' she added to Harrie. 'Went out yesterday to do the shopping. Being helpful.'

Mick shrugged. 'Sorry, Mam, I was waylaid, so I was.'

'Waylaid at the pub.' Mrs Doyle snorted. 'Where did you sleep last night?'

Mick was saved from answering by Davey scampering around the table and tugging on his distinctly crumpled trouser leg. 'What did you bring me?'

Scooping him up, Mick plucked a shilling from his ear. Davey shrieked in amazement. 'Hang on, I haven't finished yet,' Mick said, burrowing a hand into Davey's jacket pocket and finding a large twist of aniseed balls.

Harrie smiled, charmed. She could see that his mother was, too. And no doubt always had been.

Mick put Davey down and patted his backside. 'Go on, be a good lad and share them with the others.'

'Go gentle on that bum,' Mrs Doyle warned. 'He's just had a walloping for running off again. Miss Clarke here was, kind enough to bring him back.'

'That was nice of you,' Mick said, treating Harrie to another devastating smile. 'Thank you.'

Feeling unaccountably flustered, Harrie stood. 'My pleasure. I should be going. Thank you for the tea, Mrs Doyle. Very nice to have met you, er, Mr Doyle.'

Mick laughed. 'It's Mick.'

Harrie nodded and collected her bonnet and basket. As she moved towards the door, Mick stepped in front of her and opened it, revealing a cross-looking Maureen with a bucket of water in each hand. The communal pump must be miles away, Harrie thought. They stood aside to let her in. As Mick followed her out, Harrie heard Mrs Doyle call to him, but he shut the door on her.

He settled a hand on her arm, sending a jolt of heat through the fabric of her jacket all the way up to her shoulder. 'Come out with me, for a drink. Thursday night at the St Patrick's Inn. Do you know it?'

She stared at him, shocked at his audacity. 'I couldn't!'

He grinned and she got that melty feeling in her belly again.

'Why not?'

Her face was flaming. 'I don't ... I just can't.'

'Sure you can.' He touched her cheek with the backs of his fingers and she felt her skin ignite.

She couldn't. It was out of the question. Wasn't it?

The St Patrick's Inn was packed, the din was raucous — shouts, roars of laughter and the thump of tankards on wooden tables — and a pungent blanket of pipe smoke hung five feet above the floor. Clutching her reticule, Harrie hovered just inside the door, sure that any minute now everyone would turn and stare at her. Not accustomed to going into hotels, she'd worried herself sick that she'd be the only female present, but far from it; she could count at least a dozen already.

She had no idea how to conduct herself in this sort of situation. She should have brought Friday — she knew what you were supposed to do in a pub. But Friday would only have told her what she'd already realised; that Mick Doyle wasn't the right man for her. A wave of panic swept through her and for a moment she couldn't get enough air into her lungs. No matter how much Mick thrilled and fascinated her, this was wrong and she didn't belong here. But just as she turned to go Mick appeared, looking even more breathtaking than he had at his mother's house, and took her elbow. All her doubts deserted her.

'My love, you came! I knew you would.' He bent and kissed her neck, his lips soft and warm. She suppressed a shudder of delight. 'Come and have a drink, meet my mates.'

His mates? Harrie felt a sharp stab of disappointment; she'd imagined it would just be the two of them. But she allowed Mick to guide her through the mass of bodies to a table, at which sat possibly the strangest assortment of men she'd ever seen, and that was saying something in Sydney Town.

'Listen up, you lot,' Mick said. 'This is the beautiful and charming Miss Clarke.' He then proceeded to introduce his friends one by one without giving her time to respond, which she couldn't do anyway as the noise was so great and she was completely unable to think of what to say beyond 'hello'.

Rian Farrell, a dashing, rather stern-looking young man with fair hair tied in a cue, was apparently captain of the schooner on which Mick sailed.

'But that's not why Mam calls him Captain,' Mick said. 'It's because he went to the Royal School in Armagh and knows the right knife to use.' Then he gave a hoot of laughter, which alarmed and completely mystified Harrie.

Captain Farrell nodded and bid her a polite 'Good evening'.

Beside him sat a slightly older man Mick introduced simply as Pierre. Pierre was small and wiry, wore his hair in a plait, had a face like a little monkey except for a thin moustache and tapered Vandyke beard, and sported three gold teeth. He greeted her with, 'Bonsoir, Mademoiselle.'

'Bayou Acadian,' Mick explained.

Harrie had no idea what that meant, either.

'And this is Running Hawk, our first mate.'

Running Hawk inclined his head in greeting. He also wore his hair in plaits, a very long, oiled black pair that fell against his chest, and was dressed in trousers and the sort of soft, loose shirt Harrie thought might be more suitable for bed. His skin was olive, but nowhere near as dark as that of the absolute behemoth of a man sitting next to him taking up the space of two ordinary folk. His complexion was as black as midnight, causing his teeth to shine a luminous white when he smiled, stood, bowed slightly and extended an enormous hand. Very cautiously, Harrie shook it.

'Good evening, Miss Clarke,' the huge man said in excellent English. 'I am delighted to meet you.'

'Gideon's from Africa,' Mick said. 'And this is Te Kanene.'

Te Kanene was Maori, from a tribe called Ngati Kahungunu on the east coast of New Zealand, and not pleased to see her, Harrie suspected, given his disapproving look. He had protruding eyes, a hooked nose, and a beautiful tattoo over his entire face. You'd better watch out, she shocked herself by thinking, Bella'll be after you. Even though he was very young — they all were, in fact — his bearing and arrogance were that of a man much older. Harrie didn't like him at all.

And neither did she like the Englishman, John Sharkey, the last to be introduced. Barely glancing up from his tankard of ale, he was missing several teeth, had a scar that ran from his temple to his jaw and wore his red-brown hair raggedly short, a thick gold hoop in each ear and a sullen expression.

Harrie thought they looked a pack of absolute pirates.

'Fancy a drink, my love?' Mick asked.

'I'm sorry, I don't drink,' Harrie said.

Mick was aghast. 'Ah, you do so. Everyone drinks!'

Harrie shook her head. 'Really, I don't.'

Mick slid his arm around her waist. 'My love, come on. Just a small one? What do you fancy?'

Not wanting to make a fuss by continuing to refuse, she gave in and asked for a glass of wine. It had rendered her extremely drunk last time, but at least she knew what it tasted like. And she could nurse one glass all evening.

'Wine!' Mick laughed. 'You'll be lucky to find that here.'

But off he went to see what he could do. Harrie sat on the bench next to Pierre, whom she thought seemed the least threatening of Mick's mates.

'You have known Mick long, Mademoiselle Clarke?' he asked in a heavy French accent.

'No, not really.'

'Then run for your life while you still can,' the one named Sharkey said, and roared with laughter.

Harrie ignored him. 'Excuse me, but where exactly is Acadia? I'm not sure I've heard of it.'

'Ah, well, that is because she is not really a place, not any more. She is …' Pierre gripped his chin with his thumb and forefinger and stared at the ceiling, apparently searching for inspiration. Abruptly, he tapped his head. 'In these days, she is something we carry in here. The bayou — now she is a real place. You have heard of Louisiana?'

'Oh, in America?'

'Oui! What an educated mademoiselle you must be!'

Mick returned and insinuated himself between her and Pierre. Harrie looked at the drink her gave her, a tumbler filled with amber liquid.

'Is this wine?'

Mick shook his head. 'Brandy. A good drop, though.'

Harrie sniffed it, and took a tentative sip. The liquid burnt her tongue and throat, but within seconds she felt a pleasant, calming warmth spread through her chest. She took a bigger drink — a gulp, in fact, hoping the alcohol would steady her nerves.

Twenty minutes later she noticed her glass was empty. Mick, who was being absolutely charming and very, very attentive to her, got her another one. When he returned with it, he slid his arm comfortably around her waist, gently but sensuously kneading the flesh over her hip. Everything he said was so funny, and she laughed at his witty comments until her eyes streamed. James wasn't funny, she reflected between giggles. James was always so very serious. And James would never dare show his affection for her in public like this. But that was because James didn't have any affection for her — he'd squandered it all on that slag Rowie Harris. Suddenly, Harrie's excellent mood evaporated.

'My love,' Mick said, tapping her bottom lip with his finger. 'Where's that beautiful smile gone?'

'I drank it,' Harrie said, and held out her tumbler.

By the time she'd had four more glasses of brandy, everything was getting very disjointed. Someone said, 'That's enough, Mick.' It might have been the one they called the captain but she wasn't sure. The mean one, with the scar, kept leering at her and laughing. She really didn't like him. And when Mick was getting her another drink Pierre offered to escort her home, but she didn't want to go home, she was having a good time.

She was bursting for a wee, though. There must be a privy somewhere. She swivelled sideways on the bench and raised a leg to climb over it, stood, lifted the other leg, got tangled in her skirts and had a horrible, profoundly disconcerting moment as the floor hurtled up to meet her.

Mick and Pierre picked her up. Someone else cackled with laughter.

'Fresh air,' Harrie said as she swatted at her skirts.

'It's out the back,' the one with the long plaits said. 'Go with her, Mick.'

'No!' Harrie pushed him away.

And then she was outside in the cold. She staggered round and round past piles of barrels and crates, the pressure on her bladder worsening by the second, but couldn't find anything that looked like a privy, so she lifted her skirts and squatted by a wall, almost weeping with relief. And after that she couldn't find her way back into the pub. Finally, she followed an alleyway and found herself out on Gloucester Street near the St Patrick's front door. A part of her knew she should just keep walking and go home, which was only just up the street, but she'd left her reticule and bonnet inside. And Mick was still there — Mick, who made her feel attractive and special and wanted. So she went back in, the noise and heat and smoke hitting her like a slap in the face.

There was another tumbler of brandy on the table, waiting for her.

And then it was just her and Mick outside and she could barely stand up. He was kissing her and his mouth was soft and lovely but a bit beery and he smelt of fresh sweat. He said he loved her. His hands on her skin were so very warm, a cat was yowling somewhere, and her skirts were in the way and there was a quick, sharp pain. And then she was being sick, and sprawled on the stairs at home, and Nora Barrett was in her nightdress telling her to get up to her room right now.

And then, while she was on her knees over the po being sick a second time, Rachel came, sitting in her favourite spot in the chair beneath the eaves, rocking slowly, her luminous eyes filled with empathy and love. And everything was all right.

While Harrie had been getting drunk at the St Patrick's Inn with Mick Doyle, James Downey was having dinner at the Australian Hotel with Matthew Cutler. Having become friends on the *Isla* during the voyage out from England in 1829, they'd been meeting there more or less every fortnight since. They rarely saw each other beyond the confines of the Australian, though Sarah and Adam Green's wedding had been one such occasion. At thirty-two James was barely five years older than Matthew, but, in Matthew's opinion, he behaved as though the difference were closer to twenty years, insisting he was too busy with his work as a doctor to attend most social events or entertainments. Not that Matthew made regular appearances on Sydney's social circuit himself: he was only a junior in the office of the Colonial Architect and as such not likely to be invited to the town's smarter soirees. Lately, though, he'd been out and about more, squiring Sally Minto.

'Not popped the question yet?' James enquired bluntly as he pushed his plate away.

'Sally? No, not yet.' Matthew stifled a sigh. James asked the same thing almost every time they had dinner together and it was beginning to get on his nerves. He always knew what would come next.

'What's stopping you?'

'The time's not been right.' Sally Minto was a nice girl — sweet and attractive and fun (usually) — but for Matthew, the time to ask her could only ever be when there was not a shred of doubt left in his mind about Harrie Clarke's availability.

'You said that in May. And last month.'

Matthew dabbed at his mouth with a napkin. 'No, I didn't.'

'Yes, you did.'

'You've been irritable all night, James. What's wrong?'

James poured himself a third glass of red wine, which was out of character. Matthew frowned.

'Several things, actually, if you must know. My servant has disappeared, God only knows where, and moments after I made that somewhat inconvenient and irritating discovery, Harrie arrived at my house accusing me of something of which I have no knowledge, because she wouldn't actually tell me what my crime is supposed to be. Then she slapped my face and hared off down the street!'

'Really?' Matthew didn't think that sounded like Harrie at all. She was normally such a gentle sort of girl.

'Yes, really.'

'Well, did you hare off after her?'

'No, I did not.'

'Why the hell not?' Matthew asked.

James stared at him as though he were mad. 'Because … well, I'm a doctor. It's not the sort of thing one should be seen doing, is it, running down the street after a girl?'

'Have you been around to the Barretts' to see her since?'

'No. She struck me, Matthew.'

'She might have thought she had good reason.' And Matthew knew exactly how to find out what it was — he'd ask Friday the next time she gave him money to be put into the girls' bank account, which he'd opened under his name. They couldn't open one because women weren't allowed them.

'What good reason?' James asked. 'What have I done?'

'Well, you'd know if you'd bothered to run after her, wouldn't you?' Matthew pushed his own plate aside. 'And why didn't you tell me all this when we sat down?'

'I don't know. It's not the done thing, is it, pouring out one's woes before the soup course has even been served?'

'Do you know, James, you're one of the most stubborn people I've ever met. Go and sort it out. And I don't know why I'm saying this. I should be delighted Harrie's slapped your face. Go on, go and talk to her.'

James's expression was grim. 'No. Not this time. I've decided I do have limits. And anyway, Matthew, I'm not sure it's any of your business.'

# Chapter Five

*August 1831, Sydney Town*

A little over three weeks later Harrie lay in bed. The sky through her attic window had turned faintly pink and the first of the morning's birds had begun their sweet, and not so sweet, calls, sending Angus the cat's ears into fits of twitching. These days, the sound filled her with a deep, grinding dread. It was almost six o'clock: the Barretts would be awake soon and she should be getting their breakfast on the table. She told herself she must get up, but just couldn't, as though her arms and legs were completely disconnected from the rest of her. She lay rigid, a tear trickling from her left eye down her temple and into her hair.

Angus yawned, stretched, jumped off the bed and scratched at the door. He'd wee on the rug again if she didn't let him out.

Harrie closed her eyes. On the count of five, she'd make a massive effort, roll over and sit up.

One. Two. Three. Four. Five.

Oh God.

One. Two. Three. Four. Five! And at last she was up. She sat with her legs hanging over the side of the bed, staring at her bare feet. They looked thin and white, like strange little sea creatures. Like someone else's feet.

Angus scratched again.

She stood, grasped the nightstand as a wave of dizziness washed over her, then opened the door. His sleek tail flicked across her bare ankle as he trotted out onto the landing.

And then the sick feeling welled up, followed by a mouthful of spit and a sharp pressure under her diaphragm. She tucked her hair behind her ears and reached under the bed for the po, just in time to catch the rush of vomit. She rinsed out her mouth with water, spat into the po and emptied it all out the window onto the roof. Bird breakfast.

She peered into her looking glass. She didn't look any different, except for the shadows under her eyes. She was, though. Normally very regular, this month her courses were a week late. She was expecting.

But she'd known that even before she'd missed. She'd been nine years old when her mother had fallen with her stepbrother Robbie — and even older when her stepsisters Sophie and Anna had arrived — so she was more than familiar with the signs of pregnancy. Her mother had been sick very early too — almost from the day she'd caught.

And though she couldn't remember everything that had happened that night at the St Patrick's Inn and on the way home, she was pretty sure she knew what she'd let Mick Doyle do to her. She'd been sore down there and had bled a little the next morning, and, well, she could remember what he'd felt like. She thought she could remember something else, too.

He'd never called her by her given name. He'd never called her Harrie.

James did. James had been calling her Harrie for a long time.

But perhaps she'd just forgotten what Mick had called her. She'd been very drunk. Again. How she'd behaved disgusted her, but she expected no better of herself, not any more. And now she would pay the same price as all the other girls who did what she'd done.

A gentle knock came. 'Harrie? Are you up?'

Harrie opened the door to see Nora Barrett holding Lewis. In his sleeping gown and cap — as was Nora — he was wriggling and waving his arms and looked grumpy and dribbly, his face red, the result of teething.

'I won't be a minute. I'm just getting dressed,' Harrie said.

Nora wrinkled her nose. 'Have you been ill?'

Harrie nodded. 'I must have eaten something yesterday.'

'Do you need another hour in bed? I'm up now, I can get the breakfast.'

'No, really, I'm all right. Thank you. Did you want something?'

Harrie felt profoundly guilty. Although Nora had given her an earwigging the morning after she'd come home drunk, she'd not told Mr Barrett and hadn't mentioned it since, which Harrie thought was extremely decent of her, given that it was the second time she'd arrived home drunk and covered in sick. And now here she was, demonstrating her gratitude by getting pregnant to a man she barely knew, like a common tart.

'I can't find the laudanum,' Nora said. 'I need it for Lewis's gums.'

'I put it in the blue and white willow jar on the mantel. I found Hannah helping herself the other day.'

Lewis started to grizzle and Nora joggled him. 'Harrie?'

'Yes?'

'There's nothing you want to tell me, is there?'

For a second Harrie was very tempted to confess her awful predicament, but embarrassment and shame overwhelmed her and she shook her head.

'Hello, dear.' Biddy Doyle wiped her hands on her apron and called over her shoulder, 'Put the kettle on, Maureen, there's a good lass!'

'Not on my account, thank you, Mrs Doyle,' Harrie said. 'I can't stop. I was just wondering whether Mick was home.'

'Mick? Sorry, love, he's gone back to sea.'

'Has he? When, exactly?' In an odd way Harrie felt relieved: at least that explained why he hadn't made any effort to see her since the night at the pub. On the other hand it meant she couldn't expect any help from him. But what sort of help had she thought she might get?

Mrs Doyle made a face while she worked it out. 'Eleven days ago? Or was it twelve?'

Which had still given him well over a week in which to visit her. And he hadn't. And he'd said he loved her.

'How long will he be away, do you know?' Harrie asked.

'Oh, I never know that,' Mrs Doyle said. 'Sometimes it's three months, once it was nearly a year. It depends on the captain's cargo.'

Something had been bothering Harrie. 'Mrs Doyle, how old is Mick?'

'Seventeen. Why?'

Harrie winced. Two years younger than her. But he'd looked so much ... more of a man. She shook her head and turned to go, but Mrs Doyle put out a hand and stopped her.

'Are you well, dear?'

'Pardon?'

'Are you feeling well?'

She knows, Harrie thought. 'Yes, thank you.'

'If you need help, you come back,' Mrs Doyle said. 'I mean that. You're welcome here any time.'

Friday lay face down on a padded bench, her cheek resting on her folded arms and her skirt pulled up past her bare knees. Leo was working on the bat tattoo Harrie had designed and then drawn onto her calf at the start of July, before Walter had killed Furniss and everything had come so close to disaster. Had that only been seven weeks ago? It felt more like a year.

Leo had completed the bat's outline then, and now he was tattooing the complex and colourful patterns that filled the outstretched wings. His needles hurt, especially where they stabbed into the fresh scar tissue where Furniss's dog had torn into her, but she relaxed into the pain, embracing it, letting her mind drift free of everything that was worrying her.

'I thought I might start Harrie on the needles,' Leo said, breaking into her pleasant state of detachment.

'Is she ready? She's not, er, I don't think she's that well.' Friday didn't want to say outright that she and Sarah thought that once again poor Harrie's mind was coming unstuck.

Leo dipped the brush he held in his left hand into a tiny pot of pigment. 'No, I don't think she is, either. That's why I thought I'd start her, to give her a distraction.' He touched the needles to the ink-saturated brush, and bent over Friday's leg again. 'She was good there for a while, during that business with Jared Gellar. I thought she was coming right.'

'She was. She did come right.' Friday thought about Harrie's ongoing belief that she could see and talk to poor dead Rachel. 'Well, sort of.'

'So what's set her off again?'

'I don't know.'

Leo applied an extra hard jab of the needles.

'Ow!'

'You must do. You and Sarah know her better than anyone.'

Friday considered for a moment; she most certainly couldn't tell him about Harrie's guilt over Gabriel Keegan. 'Well, there's the blackmail. Also, when we handed over the last lot of money, a girl was at the burial ground to collect it. I thought it was Lou, from Mrs H's. I told you about her?'

Leo nodded.

'But it wasn't her. It turned out to be someone called Rowie Harris, who was James Downey's housegirl.'

'The doctor cove who's been after Harrie?'

'Mmm.'

'So this Rowie's been working for Bella Shand?'

'Yes, the bitch. And I bet feeding Bella everything James knew about us.' As well as everything I'd told her about how much money we've got, Friday thought guiltily.

'And that upset Harrie?'

'It gave us all the shits. We had no idea. She even worked for Mrs H for a while. She was supposed to be my friend.'

'So how did she end up working for James Downey?'

'Oh, long bloody story, and I don't even know now if it was true.' Though when Friday thought back, Rowie's physical problems probably were real. How could she have faked something like that? 'She was always on the rag and couldn't work. Mrs H fired her but found her a job with James.'

'And *that* upset Harrie?'

'Shut up, will you? I'm trying to tell a story here. I think Rowie might be a bit mad.'

'Like Harrie's going mad?' Leo interrupted again.

Friday was silent. No one had said that out loud before, not in such a matter-of-fact way, except for Harrie herself, and it sounded shocking. Brutal. 'I don't know. Yes, I suppose. It's different with Harrie, though. Harrie's ours.'

Leo said, 'I'm sure it is different when it's someone you love. Why do you think Rowie's mad?'

'She said some bizarre things.'

Leo snorted. 'Then we're all mad.'

'She told Harrie she's been shagging James.'

'She probably has. He's a bachelor, isn't he?'

'You don't know James, Leo. He's one of the few men I know decent enough not to fuck the servants.'

'Thanks very much.'

'And he thinks the sun rises and sets on Harrie. No one else'd ever be good enough. He wants to marry her.'

'But she believed this Rowie?'

'Yes, she did. And she's been all over the place mood-wise ever since. She was flat as a pancake for a couple of days afterwards no matter what me and Sarah did to try and cheer her up, then she was so chirpy and bright we thought she'd been on the jar, except she doesn't drink, and then she was miserable again, but even worse. Frightened, even. And that's the way she's stayed.'

'She was in yesterday with some new flash,' Leo said. 'They're good, very good, but, well, *disturbing* I suppose is the best word to describe them. I'll show you when we're finished.'

'No, show me now.'

Leo sighed, wiped away the blood oozing from the flesh he'd just tattooed, rose and opened the cabinet where he kept his papers. On top sat a leather folder, which he gave to Friday. Propping herself on her elbows she opened it and thumbed through the drawings inside. The theme was skulls and bones: skulls wearing crowns of cypress, with Harrie's trademark bats flitting from empty eye sockets or gaping jaws, and crossed bones wreathed in lobelia or surrounded by other beautifully rendered flowers.

'Christ,' she said, slightly taken aback. 'I know cypress represents death and despair, but what are these other ones supposed to mean?'

'Wormwood is bitter sorrow and I think marigold is cruelty and jealousy.'

'And the love-lies-bleeding?'

'Hopelessness.'

'God, she's really gone to town, hasn't she?'

'But with such tremendous skill. These will have real appeal.'

'Really? Flowers? To rough-as-guts tars?'

'Sailors take their tattoos seriously, lass, you know that, and these are art. No one else'll be doing the Jolly Roger like this.'

Friday reached down and poked an itchy bit on her new tattoo. 'How do you know about what all these flowers mean, anyway?'

'You'd be surprised, what I hear sitting on this stool. Folk talk about anything and everything. That's why I think Harrie should start on the needles. It'll take her out of herself, give her something to think about other than whatever that cove Downey has or hasn't done.'

'You don't like James, do you?'

'I've never met him.'

'You don't, though, do you?'

Leo sat down again and picked up his brush and needles. 'No. I don't.'

'Why not?'

'If he fancies Harrie as much as you say he does, why doesn't he just marry her? What's stopping him?'

'Silly bloody Harrie is.'

'Is she? Why?'

'Have you got all day?'

'Give us the abridged version.'

Friday tried to think of the best way of describing to Leo, without letting any cats out of bags, everything that had contributed to Harrie's loss of faith in herself, and couldn't, except for saying, 'She thinks she's not worthy of him. Though naturally she doesn't want anyone else to have him, because she loves him.'

'Not worthy? Just because she's a convict?'

'No, it's more than that. And now there's this business with Rowie.' Friday looked back at Leo, her eyes hard. 'The next time I see that two-faced bloody cow I'm going to give her such a dewskitch.'

'Keep still, will you?' Leo said as he tapped rapidly at Friday's skin with his needles. 'So, what are we going to do about it?'

'Rowie Harris?'

'No, bugger her. I mean Harrie. She can't keep going the way she is.'

'Well, if you want her to spend more time here, learning how to tattoo, you'll have to do some sort of deal with Nora Barrett. She is Harrie's boss, don't forget.'

'George Barrett, more like. He's the coney-catcher in that family. It's him who'll be demanding compensation. Nora won't see a penny.'

'Who signed Harrie's papers?'

'George. I already pay him a retainer for Harrie's services.'

'On top of what you pay her for her drawings?'

Leo nodded, forgetting that Friday couldn't see him.

'Leo?'

'That's right.'

'You think a lot of her, don't you?'

'I do,' Leo replied.

'She doesn't spend any of that money on herself, you know.'

'I know. You told me. She's got a warm and generous heart, Harrie,' Leo said. 'Just a very messed-up head.'

The last time Friday, Harrie and Sarah had visited the Parramatta Female Factory together, at the end of February just after Sarah and Adam's wedding, they'd had a very unpleasant argument on the way. Then, as now, Elizabeth Hislop had kindly lent Friday her landau, and Jack Wilton to drive it. It had been summer then and they'd all sweltered in the heat, especially poor Jack, perched outside on the driver's seat. It was much cooler this time, and the girls were grateful Mrs H had left a pair of woollen rugs folded on the seats. So was Clifford, curled up on the edge of the one Sarah had spread over her legs.

Usually at least one of them went out to see Janie and the babies every few weeks, but with the Furniss business and everything, their regular pattern of visiting had been disrupted. Feeling guilty because no one had been for ages, they'd included extra treats in the swag they had today.

An hour into the journey, Friday waved her hand in front of her face. 'God, Sarah. Was that you?'

'Hardly!' Sarah replied. 'It'll be her.'

Friday glared at Clifford. 'What have you been feeding her?'

'It's not what I feed her. She eats anything. Even carrion.'

'Christ.' Friday raised the shade on the window, letting in cold but blessedly fresh air. 'I don't know why you had to bring her, anyway.'

'Adam won't look after her by himself. He says she gangs up on him.'

'How can one dog gang up on someone?'

'I don't know.'

'Could you draw the shade again, please?' Harrie asked. 'I'm cold.'

An hour later Sarah asked Harrie if she was feeling all right. 'Is it Clifford? Do I need to put her outside with Jack?'

'No, it's not her.'

'You look very pale.'

'It's the carriage,' Harrie said. 'It's rocking a lot.'

Shortly after that she lunged wildly for the door, thrust it open and vomited. Friday grabbed the back of her skirt so she wouldn't tumble out onto the road while Sarah hastily knocked on the wall to alert Jack. The carriage stopped and they heard him jump down, then swear as he almost stepped in a puddle of spew.

'She's sea-sick,' Friday explained as she helped Harrie out of the landau.

Inspecting the door for traces of vomit, Jack said, 'We're not at bloody sea.'

'Funny, you weren't sick last time.' Sarah climbed down after them. 'What's happened to your cast-iron stomach?' Clifford bounced out of the carriage behind her and trotted off, head down, happily following the long trail of sick.

Wiping her mouth on her handkerchief, Harrie shook her head. 'I must have eaten something. Do we have anything to drink? My mouth tastes awful.'

'There's Janie's stout,' Friday suggested.

'That's for her breastfeeding,' Sarah said.

'We've a dozen bottles. One less won't go amiss.'

'I don't drink stout,' Harrie said. 'It's alcoholic. You know I don't drink.'

'It's that or gin,' Friday said.

Harrie made a face. 'The stout, then.'

'You're not going to do it again, are you?' Jack asked. 'Mrs H'll have me balls if you spew in her carriage.'

'I don't think so. Perhaps I should eat something, just in case.'

Friday climbed back into the landau and rummaged around in various bags until she found a bottle of stout and a fresh bap. She pulled the cork out of the bottle with her teeth and handed the bottle down to Harrie.

She took a few cautious sips — the stout was very strong but was better than the taste of sick — and swished it around in her mouth then spat it out. She upended the bottle to tip out the rest but Friday snatched it off her.

'Oi! That's perfectly good beer! Swap you for this.'

Harrie exchanged the stout for the bap and they all got back into the carriage.

Jack held the door. 'All set? Are we off again?'

'No,' Sarah said. 'Where's Clifford?'

Friday laughed. 'Quick, let's go.'

'Don't be so mean,' Sarah said.

'You actually like her!' Friday was amazed.

'I do, sort of.'

'She's all we've got left of Walter,' Harrie reminded her.

'I suppose that's true.' Friday leant past Jack out the carriage door, put two fingers to her mouth and gave an ear-piercing whistle.

Seconds later Clifford appeared from the bushes at the side of the road, twigs stuck in her hair, bounded up the carriage step and collapsed on the seat, panting.

'Remember,' Jack said to Harrie, 'if you're going to heave again, for Christ's sake, bang on the wall.'

Harrie knew she wouldn't be sick a third time today — there was very little left inside her to throw up. As the carriage started off again, she nibbled the edge of the bap, trying not to catch the eye of either Sarah or Friday.

Friday took a swig of stout, then grinned. 'If you weren't so prim and proper, I'd be wondering if you were knapped.'

'Oh, don't be so stupid,' Sarah said. 'She's obviously eaten something that hasn't agreed with her.'

Harrie kept her eyes on her bap.

The rest of the journey out to Parramatta passed uneventfully. Jack dropped them off outside the Factory's high wooden gates, then drove into town to the nearest pub to refresh the horses and himself.

Friday banged on the wicket until the porter grumpily let them in.

'Got any contraband?' he demanded, eyeing the baskets and clinking bags hanging off them.

'No,' Friday replied.

'Prove it.'

Sarah handed the man a folded one-pound note.

'You can't bring that in,' he said, nodding down at Clifford. Clifford bared her teeth and growled. 'No beasts allowed.'

Sarah gave him another half-sovereign. The porter pocketed the money and went back to his little sentry box, whistling. They trudged across the beaten, hard-packed ground to the second set of gates in the inner wall, this pair smaller but just as firmly closed.

Friday shouted, 'Glad, it's us! Are you there?'

A rattle, then, 'Hold on!' A door in the gate swung open, revealing a middle-aged woman in the Factory Sunday uniform, her greying hair tied back under a non-regulation, bright red headscarf. 'Mornin', girls. Haven't seen yous for a while. Been busy?'

'We have and we feel like right shites,' Friday replied as she stepped through.

'Morning, Gladys,' Sarah said.

'Hello, Gladys,' Harrie echoed.

Gladys spotted Clifford and stepped smartly backwards, clamping her skirts around her skinny calves. Then she let out an amused cackle. 'Bloody hell, I thought it were a giant rat for a minute! Whose is it?'

'She's mine,' Sarah said.

'Hope you didn't pay for it,' Gladys said.

'I inherited her.'

Friday handed Gladys her usual block of tobacco for turning a blind eye to their contraband.

'Thanks, love. You're looking a bit peaky,' Gladys said to Harrie. 'Poorly, are yis?'

'Not really. My stomach's feeling a little delicate.'

'Well, you'd better not come in here, then. Everyone's got the shits.'

'Everyone?' Sarah said, alarmed.

Gladys sniffed her tobacco appreciatively. 'Well, nearly. I'll tell Janie yous are here. The visitin' room's empty.'

As Gladys scuffed off across the yard in too-big clogs, avoiding puddles left by recent rain, Friday warned, 'Hang on, there's Mrs Gordon and Dick the Bitch.'

They squeezed themselves and their bags of forbidden swag into Gladys's cupboard-sized gatehouse as Ann Gordon, matron of Parramatta Female Factory, and her unpleasant assistant, Mrs Letitia Dick, crossed the yard and disappeared into Mrs Gordon's quarters.

'You're on my foot,' Sarah said to Friday.

'Sorry.'

'Have they gone?' Harrie asked, her nose pressed into Friday's sweaty armpit. She was feeling queasy again.

'Yep. Let's go.'

The visitors' room was as bare and unappealing as it had ever been. They sat down to wait. Janie Braine arrived a few minutes later, a toddler parked on each child-bearing hip. Friday pulled out a chair for her but even before she'd eased herself onto it, Harrie had grabbed Charlotte off her and was cuddling the little girl, kissing her grubby face and smoothing her silver-blonde hair. She was walking and talking now and beginning to look noticeably like Rachel, except for the mahogany-brown eyes she'd inherited from Gabriel Keegan. Rachel's had been a startling cornflower blue.

'Hawwie!' she said, which apparently was how you pronounced 'Harrie' when you were eighteen months old.

'What a clever little girl you are!' Harrie exclaimed. 'And so pretty!'

'And me!' announced Rosie, now just over two years old.

'Yes, sweetie, you're gorgeous, too,' Harrie agreed, leaning over to tweak Rosie's plump cheek.

Rosie wasn't pretty, but she was extremely sweet and she was cheerful.

'Say hello to your aunties,' Janie said, passing Rosie around for kisses.

'Have they been well?' Friday asked. 'Glad said everyone's had the shits.'

'Lots have. The bloody flux, the doctor reckons. We been all right. I had a bit of a loose guts a week or so ago, but I come right. There's some been pretty sick, but, and we've had a few deaths.'

'Is Sharpe still the doctor here?' Sarah asked.

Janie nodded.

'Quack,' Friday said.

Janie asked, 'Whose dog is that outside?'

'Mine,' Sarah replied. 'Why?'

'Bad-tempered little bugger. Had a go at Pearl as we come in. Growled its bloody head off.'

Sarah went to the room's single window. From it, she could see Janie's minder Pearl standing in the yard smoking her pipe, but she couldn't see Clifford. 'Where is she? The dog, I mean?'

'Lying just outside the door.'

'She can be quite protective,' Sarah said.

'I thought it were bloody rabid. Rosie wanted to pat it and I daren't let her.'

Friday began to empty the bags and baskets onto the table. 'We've brought you loads of nice things. I'm sorry we haven't been for ages, Janie. There's just been so much to do with, well, with this business with Adam and everything.'

Friday, Harrie and Sarah had decided from the outset not to tell Janie they were being blackmailed by Bella Shand. There was nothing to be gained; she would only feel guilty about them having to finance that as well supporting her and the babies, including Pearl's fee as Janie's minder. Theft was rife in the Factory and Janie, in possession of the food, alcohol, tobacco and other tempting comforts they smuggled in to her, was a prime target. Janie was a tough girl and perfectly able to look after herself, but not while also caring for two small children. They'd also decided not to mention today that the Charlotte fund was running low. What Janie wasn't aware of, she couldn't worry about.

Janie waved her off. 'Don't worry about it. We been fine.'

'I didn't know if you needed more clouts but I made you some,' Harrie said.

'Rosie's out of them now, but Charlotte's still not quite got the hang of the pot,' Janie said. 'Not at night time, anyway.'

'And I hemmed you a few cloths for, you know, your courses,' Harrie added. 'For when you start again.'

'That's kind of you. Thanks, love. I have had a show or two. That reminds me, next time can you be a sweetie and bring me a new shift? Just something plain. I've only got the one and it's knackered. I've mended it till there's more patches than anything else and that bugger Tuckwell in the store won't give me a new one.'

Harrie nodded, thinking she'd make Janie two. With extra lace.

'And we got you some stout, for your milk,' Sarah said. 'Or have you finished with all that now?'

'No, Charlotte's feeding fairly regular and Rosie still has the odd nurse. It's better than the shite they get fed here.'

'God, girl,' Friday said, 'your tits'll be round your knees. Harrie, are you going to share that baby, or hog her all day?'

Harrie passed Charlotte across to Friday.

Janie laughed. 'They were round me knees after I had me second one, never mind nursing these two.'

'And I've made the girls some more little gowns, and a bonnet each,' Harrie said, unfolding the clothing from her basket. 'They grow so fast at this age.'

'Oh, them're lovely! Thanks, Harrie.'

Then out came the pots of preserved food, and dried fruit, biscuits, smoked sausage, cheese, sweets, soap, various ointments, a bottle of laudanum, trinkets for bartering, three blocks of tobacco, matches, and three bottles of gin for Janie. Also placed on the table was a cloth purse containing money to pay Pearl, and for bribes so Janie could keep her contraband.

Her eyes lit up. 'Oooh, lovely! Look at all that food! You're spoiling us.'

'Well, if you're healthy you're less likely to get sick,' Sarah said, distracting Rosie, whose little fingers were pulling at one of her earrings.

'How's Adam?' Janie asked. 'Settled down again all right?'

'More or less. He was very thin when he came home and he's had a bit of trouble putting the weight back on, but the doctor gave him some powders the other day, so that might help.'

'What sort of powders?'

'An anti-infestation emetic. Said he might have some sort of creatures living in his intestines.'

'That's romantic,' Friday said.

'Yes, it is,' Sarah agreed. 'He's been in and out of the privy since he started taking them.'

'What about his mood?' Janie asked. 'No hard feelings about being set up by that Gellar cove?'

'Well, yes, plenty of those. But with Gellar dead there's not much he can do about it.'

Janie nodded; she knew all about that, Harrie having written and told her. 'So will yous be getting back into the burglary business?'

'Not for now. We think it's probably sensible to stay on the straight and narrow for a while. Even though Gellar confessed to framing Adam and his conviction was quashed, shite sticks, doesn't it? Best to lie low.'

'It must be nice to have him back,' Janie said.

'It is, it's lovely.'

Janie raised her eyebrows at Harrie. 'And what about your Dr Downey? How's it going with him?'

'It isn't,' Harrie said flatly.

Janie's homely face fell. 'What? You said in your last letter everything was coming right! Now what's the matter?'

'The matter,' Friday said, 'is that Rowie bloody Harris told Harrie she's been hopping into James's bed.'

Janie gasped. 'No! The bitch! What a Little Miss Roundheels! How did you find out?'

'Harrie and Rowie got in a fight on the street,' Friday said, which was the truth, after a fashion.

'Did you face up to him about it?' Janie asked. 'What did he say?'

'He didn't deny it,' Harrie replied, though she hadn't exactly asked the question of him outright.

'The dirty lustyguts! Typical, but,' Janie said. 'Will you fight for him?'

'No!' Harrie's eyes filled with tears. She took Charlotte back off Friday and settled her on her knee, cuddling her as though to ward off her unhappiness. 'She can have him. I don't care.'

'You bloody do so,' Janie said. 'Look at you. You're all pale and puffy and your eyes look funny. You look sick as a dog. I were wondering what were wrong.'

'She whipped the cat on the way here,' Friday said.

'You spewed? You poor thing. Did you eat something bad?'

Harrie shrugged and even more tightly cuddled Charlotte, who wriggled and whined and held her arms out for Janie. 'Tittie, Ma.'

Janie took her and, in one practised movement, uncovered a breast and popped Charlotte onto it. 'Is this Rowie still at the doctor's house?' she asked Friday. 'You could go round and give her a bloody good dewskitch and tell her to pack her bags. That'd see her off.'

Friday and Sarah exchanged a glance. Surely she wouldn't be, not now she knew they were aware she was working for Bella. She'd be worried they'd tell James. Or was she gambling on the likelihood they wouldn't want him to know they were being blackmailed?

'Is she?' Friday asked Harrie.

'I don't know,' Harrie said, and she didn't. She'd been too frightened and angry and dismayed to find out. If Rowie was still there, surely that must mean James *was* sleeping with her? She hadn't accused him outright when she'd seen him, but he had to have known why she'd been so upset. He'd pretended he hadn't, but he'd certainly looked guilty. To her, anyway.

Janie said, 'Well, bloody well go round and find out! Ah-ah, don't bite.' She tapped Charlotte sharply on the head, making her blink and screw up her face.

'No,' Harrie said. 'I told you, I don't care.'

'So you're just giving up, just 'cos he's been humping some tart?' Janie demanded. 'When you didn't want him? When you've been making him wait and wait and wait? He's a man, Harrie. They all have needs, you know, even boring ones like your doctor.'

Harrie's hands crept up to cover her ears.

Sarah reached out and pulled one away. 'Don't do that. Pretending you can't hear isn't going to get you anywhere.'

Harrie lashed out and hit her, striking her full across the side of the head. Sarah's head snapped sideways.

A terrible, ringing silence filled the little room. Rosie started to cry.

'Bloody hell, Harrie,' Friday said, 'what's got into you? Are you all right, Sarah?'

Sarah nodded, though her face had gone as white as mistletoe berries.

Harrie slowly crumpled until her head and arms were on the table and her shoulders started to shake with great, almost silent sobs.

Appalled, her eyes wide with shock, Janie took Charlotte off her breast and covered herself. Glancing at Friday and Sarah, she mouthed, 'What's wrong with her?'

Friday moved around the table and bent over Harrie, her hands on her heaving shoulders. Unfortunately Harrie chose that moment to rear up, and smacked Friday in the face with the back of her head.

'Shit!' Friday clapped her hands over her nose, her eyes watering fiercely.

Sarah barked out a laugh.

'It's not funny,' Friday said, dabbing at the blood now trickling from her battered nose. 'Christ!'

Harrie turned to peer up at her. 'Oh God. I'm sorry.' She faced Sarah. 'I'm so sorry. I didn't mean to do that.'

Again Sarah nodded, the single, terse movement of her head conveying forgiveness, tolerance and acceptance of Harrie's fraught condition.

'Christ, girl, you are in a state, aren't you?' Janie said.

Harrie nodded miserably.

'But why?' Friday asked nasally, sitting down again, a handkerchief clamped over her nose. 'James *has* been a shit.' She hesitated. 'Well, Rowie said he's been a shit. But so what? It's like Janie says. You can't expect him to be as pure as new bloody snow. You didn't expect that, did you? No one's that gulpy, not even you. It's something else, isn't it?'

Shame at her predicament — her foolishness — flooded Harrie. Her face burnt at just the thought of telling them. She shook her head. 'It's just … everything. And I'd rather not talk about it any more, if you don't mind.'

When it was time to leave, Friday looked out for brain-addled Matilda Bain in the yard; as had become her habit she had a gift for her. But the wizened old woman was nowhere to be seen.

'No Matilda today,' she remarked.

Janie looked upset. 'I meant to tell you before, but then there was the business with Harrie.'

'Tell me what?'

'When I said a few folk had died from the flux? Poor old Matilda were one of them.'

'Oh,' Friday said, her face falling. 'Bugger.'

'She were old, but,' Janie said. 'And sick and weak. It's mostly the old ones and the babies what's going.'

'Still,' Friday said.

'I know.'

'Did you hear that?' Friday said to Harrie and Sarah. 'Old Matilda's died.'

Sarah wasn't too bothered, Matilda had been a mad old bat, but Harrie was sad. Dysentery was an awful way to die. And Matilda had been the only other person she knew who could see Rachel.

### *Late August 1831, Liverpool, England*

Malcolm Leary leant over the ship's rail, hoicked and spat a gob into the swift and filthy tidal waters of the Mersey River. He was a sailor by trade, but on this voyage he'd be sitting on his arse watching some other poor gulpies do all the work — unless, that was, he got so bored he couldn't stand it and pitched in, though that certainly wouldn't be happening unless there was money on offer. Or, at the very least, rum.

He was glad to be under way. Once he made up his mind to do something he liked to get on with it, no mucking about. The ship was a barque, a little on the small side, but she was sound and he could feel from the way she rode the river's undulations she would be fairly fleet. According to the first mate, she carried a half-cargo of quality printed and glazed cottons from several Lancashire manufactories, plus about sixty emigrants shoe-horned onto the steerage deck, their worldly possessions piled into the remainder of the hold.

Malcolm squinted into the wind at the diminishing view of Salthouse Dock, from which the ship had set sail, riding on the coat tails of the outgoing tide. He loved Liverpool: the noise and filth and industry of the city, the sleepless docks lining the Mersey for miles and miles, and the river itself, swarming with ships and boats, rising and falling twice a day, breathing in and out like England's heartbeat. In an hour or so they'd be into the Irish Sea, then heading south towards the belligerent North Atlantic. He'd sailed the North Atlantic dozens of times himself, mostly on American and Canadian crossings, but also en route to Australia, though the latter not for some years. This would be his first antipodean voyage since before his older brother, Jonah, was transported in 1825.

At the thought of his brother — of his brothers — Malcolm spat again, and wiped his mouth with the back of his hand. Jonah could be a reasonable cove, at least some of the time, but the other, the hell-cursed Bennett — Malcolm could barely even think his name without cringing. Thank Christ their father had died without ever knowing what he'd spawned. He'd been a cruel and manipulative old bastard, but no father deserved such a son.

Malcolm had chosen to take his chances at sea while his mother and father groomed his two brothers to one day take over the family's network of criminal enterprises, which extended across Liverpool and beyond. It wasn't the villainous nature of the family business he'd objected to — it had been the tyranny of his parents. His mother, Ansilla, came from a long line of powerful and successful crooks, and in marrying professional criminal Bartholomew Leary, she'd chosen a mate as greedy as she was. After their wedding she'd retained a tight grip on both the purse strings and the business, a grip that hadn't loosened even after Bart's death. While alive Bart had resented this, and worried that Ansilla, whom he believed favoured Malcolm's four sisters over Malcolm, Jonah and Bennett, would leave the girls with a greater share of the family's considerable fortune. In truth, Malcolm knew, she loved all her children; it was just that his sisters, irritatingly, were far more capable than the boys in the family, especially where money was concerned.

What Bart had done to safeguard the boys' financial future had been extraordinary, and while on his deathbed in 1824, he'd revealed his stratagem to Malcolm and Jonah. Bennett had been gone from the family home for almost two years by then, Bart under the impression he'd simply run off to London on a whim, because no one had had the guts to tell him the truth, which had been that Bennett had been discovered in a profoundly compromising situation. Bart explained to his two remaining sons that in 1820 he'd stolen a large amount of gold bullion from a bank, then hidden it very carefully. Immediately after the robbery he'd commissioned the tattoos, which of course Malcolm and Jonah already knew about, as they each had one on their backs, and so did Bennett. Malcolm remembered getting his all too clearly. At the time he'd been a twenty-six-year-old sailor and already inked, but this one had really hurt because it had taken so bloody long. And he'd deeply resented it as yet another example of his father's bullying. By the time he, Jonah and Bennett had all been tattooed, they'd realised they each carried a different section of the same map. But a map of what? Infuriatingly, however, at the time their father would only say that one day they would thank him.

As Bart lay coughing up blood and wheezing out his last breaths, he'd at last told Malcolm and Jonah that their tattooed maps revealed the hiding place of the stolen bullion, but that all three maps had to be consulted together. This was to stop one or another brother taking all the gold for himself. It was to be shared among the three of them, and not with their sisters, and certainly not with Ansilla, who knew nothing about the arrangement. None of the females in the family did.

Like hell they'd share it with bloody Bennett, Malcolm had thought at the time, though he hadn't said it, wanting to spare his fatally ailing father. He'd caught Jonah's eye and known he was thinking the same thing.

As soon as Bart was dead, he and Jonah had examined each other's tattooed maps in minute detail, but their father had been right — having only two sections of the three wasn't enough, and Malcolm and Jonah hadn't the faintest idea where Bennett, with his third section, might be. Soon after, Jonah had been caught by the watch robbing a warehouse, and transported the following year.

Malcolm had retired from the sea in 1829, after episodes of dizziness and shortness of breath had sent him to a physician in the city of New York. This worthy had advised he was suffering from an imbalance of humours resulting in water on the heart and so, with no other trade, and having spent most of his earnings on grog, gambling and women, Malcolm had no option but to return to Liverpool and work for his mother, who was managing the family business extremely efficiently by herself. She was in perpetual mourning, however, for Jonah transported to New South Wales, and for Bennett, who for some twisted and unfathomable reason she continued to love, though not so much for her late husband, Malcolm noted. In fact, not at all.

She welcomed him home and gave him a job collecting debts: he was comfortable terrorising folk, and indeed had killed several men in brawls. He realised after a while, however, that his sisters were being paid far more for overseeing the crews that operated the city-wide rackets, and running the brothels, which brought in the bulk of the family's wealth. When he'd complained, the deflating response he'd received from Ansilla — that he was actually getting paid what he was worth — had set him on this course for Australia, to find Jonah. His brother's seven-year sentence would be over shortly and Malcolm planned to bring him back to Liverpool.

And it wasn't just Jonah he intended to track down. A few months earlier, in a pub off Dock Road, he'd been holding forth about his search for his brothers (but not why he intended to find them — he wasn't that stupid) and some cove had suggested that Bennett might also have been transported. Swattled at the time, Malcolm had dismissed the idea, but when he'd sobered up he'd decided it had merit. Bennett was as flash as the rest of the family, and God knew he had some disgusting perversions that were bound to get him thrown in gaol sooner or later. Why wouldn't he end up on a transport to New South Wales? And the more he'd thought about it, the more convinced of the possibility he'd become. It would explain a lot — the family had heard nothing at all from Bennett since he'd left all those years earlier. Within a week, he was one hundred per cent sure Bennett had been transported.

Malcolm assumed he'd be able to locate Jonah through the proper convict authorities. Bennett, too, though he thought it highly likely he'd find his younger brother chained to the wall in the darkest, most rat-infested recesses of some dank New South Wales gaol. And if Bennett couldn't, or wouldn't, come back to England, then that was all right with Malcolm — they didn't need all of him, just the skin off his back. He knew Jonah wouldn't be averse to a bit of violence; Jonah loathed Bennett as much as he did himself.

He'd booked a cabin with money borrowed from one of his sisters, telling her he was off to America to find his fortune. She'd laughed at him, but lent it to him anyway — at eighteen per cent interest. They were all the same, the women in his family. He'd dared not ask his mother for a loan: she would have wanted to know what it was for, and he'd never been able to lie to her face. Not when it really mattered. He thought she might miss him, though, while he was away. She really did love her children, no matter what else you said about her. It's just that she showed it in such backhanded ways.

# Chapter Six

*Mid-September 1831, Sydney Town*

Nora Barrett hoisted baby Lewis higher onto her hip and knocked on the front door of Elizabeth Hislop's Argyle Street establishment. She didn't particularly approve of prostitution, but accepted it as inevitable, given human nature. The nature of men, that was. She didn't entirely approve of Harrie's friend Friday, either, partly because she drank far too much, but mostly because of her job. Surely the girl could learn to use a needle and thread to sew a couple of pieces of fabric together or something, rather than earn her money opening her legs for all and sundry? On the other hand, Friday was extremely attractive and Harrie said she made huge amounts doing what she did, so in a way Nora didn't blame her. And she was, Nora had to admit, often kind and unfailingly loyal, if a bit rough around the edges, and Harrie adored her. Harrie adored Sarah Green as well, whom, no matter how hard she tried, Nora found very difficult to get to know. They were as thick as thieves, the three of them.

So why, then, were Friday and Sarah being so damned blind?

Nora heard heels clacking across floorboards inside, and the door was opened by a short, round woman in her fifties wearing an expensive wig and a beautifully made dress of very fine indigo worsted with black braid accents.

This must be the famous madam herself, Nora thought. For a moment she wished she'd worn one of her own better dresses, then chastised herself for her vanity; she was here about Harrie, not to show off. She wondered who had made the woman's gown.

'Good afternoon,' she said. 'I'd like to speak to Friday Woolfe, please. Is she at work today?'

'May I enquire who's calling?'

Cautious, Nora thought, and quite rightly so. I could be anyone. I could be the police in disguise with a rented baby. She stifled a tiny smile and hoisted Lewis again. 'My name is Nora Barrett. Friday is a friend of Harrie Clarke's, and I'm Harrie's mistress. It's Harrie I'd like to discuss with Friday.'

The woman in the doorway relaxed slightly. 'I'm afraid Friday isn't here today. I'm Friday's mistress, Elizabeth Hislop. Very nice to meet you, Mrs Barrett. I've met Harrie. Lovely girl.'

'She is.'

'Would you like to come through?' Elizabeth asked. 'I can take you around to the hotel. Friday may be in her room there.'

Nora hesitated.

'Unless you'd rather walk around to the Harrington Street entrance?'

Telling herself not to be so silly, Nora said, 'Thank you, I'm obliged.'

Nora followed Elizabeth through the house, along the alleyway to the Siren's Arms and up the hotel stairs to Friday's room.

'It's her regular day off so she may have gone out,' Elizabeth warned as she knocked.

But Friday was in. 'Hello, Mrs Barrett,' she said as she opened the door. 'What are you doing here?'

'I've come to talk to you about Harrie.'

Friday was instantly on the alert. 'Why? Is she all right? Sorry, come in.'

Nora said to Elizabeth, 'Thank you for your help, Mrs Hislop.'

'My pleasure, Mrs Barrett.' Elizabeth lingered a moment, then retreated down the hall.

Friday closed the door. 'What's happened? Is Harrie all right?'

Eyeing the open bottle of gin on Friday's nightstand, Nora put Lewis on the floor, where he immediately started crawling around, hampering himself by kneeling on his gown. Without waiting for an invitation Nora sat in the chair at Friday's dressing table.

'No, she isn't all right,' she said. 'And I really thought you and Sarah would have noticed by now. You are supposed to be her best friends.'

Friday sat on the bed, slightly taken aback by Nora's sharp-tongued opening salvo. 'Well, she isn't happy, we know that. Did she tell you about the business with James and his housegirl?'

Nora shook her head.

'We heard, well, Harrie heard that James has been sleeping with her. I know that upset her badly.'

'When was this?' Nora stood to rescue Lewis, who'd hauled himself to his feet and was tottering along clinging to a chest of drawers.

'About two months ago.' Friday poured herself a drink. 'Would you like some gin?'

'No, thank you. So, July? Late July?'

Friday thought about it. 'Something like that.'

'That would fit.' Nora plonked Lewis in the middle of the floor again. 'Did you know that a week after that, she went out and got drunk?'

'What? Harrie? She did not.'

'She did so. I don't know where she went or who she was with, but she came home in a complete state, drunk as you like and sprawling all over the stairs. Thank God she got up to bed without waking George. And she was as sick as a dog the next morning.'

'She never said a word.' Friday shook her head in amazement. 'Mind you, after that last time with Matthew, maybe she was embarrassed. That's twice now. I'd like to know who she went out with.'

'Yes, so would I. Because she's had her head in the po just about every morning since.'

Friday stared at her. 'What do you mean?'

'I mean, you silly girl, that I think she might be expecting.'

'Expecting? As in …?'

'Yes.'

'Harrie?'

'Yes.'

'But Harrie's a virgin!'

'If she is, she's a virgin whose bubs are suddenly getting bigger, who vomits every morning, who hasn't used her rags for the last two months, and who seems desperately unhappy. Really, Friday, how could you and Sarah not notice?'

Harrie, caught for a baby? Shocked to her core, Friday blurted, 'But we don't live with her! How could we have noticed?' But they had noticed, hadn't they? They just hadn't recognised what they were seeing.

'Oh, for God's sake, Friday, you're a woman of the world, and Sarah's not stupid, either. Surely you must know something about being with child?'

'But … whose is it?' Friday said, utterly mystified. 'Who's the father?'

'I don't know, do I?'

'Have you asked her?'

'No, I bloody well haven't. It's none of my business.'

'Well, it sort of is. You're her mistress,' Friday said.

'And you're her damned best friends,' Nora shot back so sharply that Lewis got a fright and started to cry. She picked him up and patted his back. 'You have to talk to her, Friday. Make her understand what she has to do.'

Friday took a colossal gulp of gin and said, 'What does she have to do?' Though she knew, of course, and it wasn't very nice.

'What do you think? What would you do if you were unmarried, a bonded convict, and expecting?'

Friday knew what she'd done when she'd found herself pregnant, and in retrospect she often wished she'd made a different choice. It would have saved a lot of heartache and guilt. 'I'd get rid of it.'

'Yes, and so should Harrie.' Nora put Lewis down again.

Oh God, Friday thought. Harrie loved babies.

'She'll lose her position with us if she wants to keep it,' Nora went on. 'George just wouldn't tolerate it. He'd send her straight back to the Factory.'

Friday said, 'She'd have to go back anyway, to have it. And then she'd be stuck there for the next four years until the kid could go into the orphanage. God, what a nightmare.' Of course, if James was the father — and, let's face it, who else could it be? — surely he'd ask Harrie to marry him. But what if she kept on being silly and turned him down? She definitely couldn't keep the baby then.

Nora sighed. 'I have to be honest, Friday. I really don't want to lose her, but I'm not going to be the one to tell her to get rid of it. That's not … that's not my decision to make. Though I do think it's the most sensible thing to do.'

'So you think me and Sarah should tell her? What a shit job. Thanks a lot, Mrs B.'

'Well, do you think she can make a decision like that herself? With the way she is at the moment?'

Lewis had crawled over to Friday and was now pulling himself up by her skirts. She took his hands and helped him to balance. 'What do you mean?'

'She's not right, is she? You said so yourself. She's been talking to herself in her room again at night. I've heard her. Well, it's either to herself or she thinks she's seeing that poor soul Rachel's ghost again.'

'Bloody hell,' Friday muttered.

'And I've been having to get her out of bed in the mornings, and I've never had to do that in the past. She's usually up before the birds. Oh, when I knock she pretends she's just got back under the blankets to get warm, but I know. She isn't dressed, her hair isn't brushed, she hasn't cleaned her teeth.'

'How do you know she's being sick?'

'Her room in the mornings nearly always stinks of vomit. I've been making a point of checking. And it doesn't matter how much lavender she puts in there, I can still smell it.'

Friday let go of Lewis's hands. He collapsed on his backside, screwed up his face to cry then changed his mind, suddenly distracted by her toes.

Letting out an enormous sigh, she said, 'God almighty. Well, if she is caught, I wonder if she even knows. She's not very —'

'Of course she bloody well knows!' Nora snapped. 'She might not have slept with thousands of men like some girls have —'

'Probably not actual thousands.'

'— but she has younger sisters and a brother. She'll have been old enough to have helped out when her mother was expecting. Of course she knows.'

'So why hasn't she told us?'

'I don't know, but you need to do something about it before it's too late.'

Friday frowned. 'If she's only, what, seven or eight weeks along, she won't quicken for another eight. There's plenty of time before we might have problems finding someone to do it.'

'For God's sake, I'm not thinking about the fact that it's against the law, I'm thinking about Harrie! The longer the damn thing's in there, the harder it'll be to winkle it out.'

Friday was quite shocked. That was a harsh thing for a woman with four children of her own to say.

'Don't look at me like that,' Nora went on. She pointed at Lewis, happily unravelling a piece of wool from the carpet. 'Much as I love him now, he certainly wouldn't be here if things had worked out the way I wanted them to. He was my seventh pregnancy. I never planned a fourth child and I certainly won't be having any more. I've got a business to run.'

'Do you know someone who can do it?' Friday asked.

'No one reliable. Obviously. I thought you might, with your line of work.'

'Never been caught.' Not here, anyway, Friday thought.

Nora stood and scooped up Lewis, the piece of wool trailing from his hand. 'Will you and Sarah come round to my house tonight and talk to Harrie? George'll be at the pub, just for a change, and I'll make sure the children are in bed. The sooner this is sorted out the better.'

Friday opened the door. 'Any particular time?'

'About half past seven? Will that suit you? Can Sarah get away, do you think?'

'Sarah can do what she likes these days.'

Harrie opened the door, surprised to see Friday and Sarah standing on the steps. But she'd known something was up; Nora had sent Abigail next door to visit her friend, and Sam and Hannah to bed half an hour early. Sam had trotted off fairly happily but Hannah had thrown one of her tantrums at the injustice of it, her howls and cries spearing right through Harrie's head.

'Come in,' she said, knowing they'd tell her why they were here soon enough. In her heart, which felt like it had suddenly grown too big for her chest, she thought she probably knew anyway.

Upstairs, Friday and Sarah sat on the sofa. Nora appeared, busied herself stoking the fire, then pulled out a chair at the dining table. Harrie perched on the edge of an armchair. Everyone looked at her, making her feel self-conscious.

'How are you feeling?' Friday asked, giving Angus the cat — rubbing himself against her legs and shedding all over her skirt — a gentle kick.

Exhausted, Harrie thought. Terrified. 'All right.'

'Still feeling sick?'

Now Harrie definitely knew why they were here. She closed her eyes.

Sarah's voice: 'Harrie, are you expecting?'

Harrie opened her eyes. 'Yes, I think so.' The words were coming out of her mouth, but the voice didn't sound like hers. It sounded like some other stupid girl's. But it was said now and she couldn't take it back. What a relief.

'For God's sake, why didn't you say something?' Sarah asked.

Harrie couldn't be bothered explaining. They would only tell her she was a fool for feeling so embarrassed. She shook her head.

'Are you sure you are?' Friday asked.

'I've missed twice, and I've been sick.'

'And you actually, you know, did the deed?'

'Christ, Friday,' Sarah said. 'She's not that naive.' She looked at Harrie. 'Are you?'

'I must have,' Harrie whispered. 'I was drunk. I'm not sure what I did.'

'Well, have you asked him?' Friday demanded.

'I can't. He's gone back to sea.'

Friday's mouth fell open. 'What? James has?'

'No, it wasn't James!'

A red flush of anger surged up Friday's face. 'Are you saying some dirty bloody cove you didn't even know took advantage of you?'

Harrie said, 'No, I did know him. Or I thought I did.'

Friday had moved to the edge of the sofa, apparently poised to go racing off down the street after the culprit. 'Who? Who was he?'

'His name's Mick Doyle. He's … a sailor.' Harrie dared not tell them he was only seventeen.

'And he picked you up?' Friday persisted.

'No. I met him at his mother's house the Monday after …' Harrie glanced at Nora, who knew nothing about Bella Shand's blackmail.

'Just after I heard about James and Rowie Harris. He invited me to the St Patrick's Inn. I went, and I drank too much, and I think I must have let him have his way, but I can't really remember.'

'What were you doing at his mother's house?' Nora asked. 'Who is she?'

'Biddy Doyle. Her grandson had wandered off. He's only four. I found him and took him home.'

Nora had heard the name; if she was remembering correctly, Biddy Doyle was a sempstress who made women's undergarments of quite good quality.

Friday said, 'And he's back at sea now?'

'Who?' Harrie was getting confused.

'Bloody Mick Doyle!'

'Yes.'

'Does he know about …?' Sarah waved vaguely at Harrie's middle.

'No, he doesn't.'

'Would he marry you? Would you want to marry him?'

'No and no!' Harrie felt her temper disintegrate. 'What would be the point? He can't even remember my name! I made a terrible mistake and now I have to fix it.'

Friday asked carefully, 'What do you mean by "fix it"?'

Harrie thought this would have been quite obvious. 'I have to get rid of it. I can't have it. I can't keep it.' She frowned as Nora, Friday and Sarah glanced at one another, nonplussed. 'What?'

'We thought you wouldn't want to do that,' Sarah said.

'That day I was sick on the way out to Parramatta? That was feverfew leaf tea, double strength. It didn't work. I can remember my mother telling me never to use slippery elm bark because it's so dangerous, so it was either feverfew or pennyroyal. Perhaps I should have gone with the pennyroyal.'

Sarah shot a sharp look at Friday — the emergency packet of slippery elm in her drawer had been purchased on her recommendation.

'I thought you wanted babies,' Friday said. 'You're desperate to look after Charlotte.'

'Friday, shut up,' Sarah hissed.

'But it just doesn't seem like Harrie.'

'Would *you* want to keep a child you'd got during a drunken night with someone you barely knew?' Harrie demanded. 'It would forever remind me of what I'd done. And even worse, why I did it.'

'I kept mine,' Friday said. 'Didn't have a clue who her father was.'

'Do you have a child?' Nora asked, startled.

'I did. She died.'

'Oh. I'm sorry.'

'Why did you do it, Harrie?' Sarah asked.

'Why do you think?'

'James?'

Harrie nodded, because that more or less summed it up.

'And you say you only met this man once?' Sarah said. 'And you went to the pub with him and let him …' She tailed off. 'I'm not a prude —'

'Yes, you are,' Friday said.

Sarah looked vaguely apologetic. 'I just never imagined you doing that.'

Harrie kept her gaze on her hands, resting in her lap. 'I know. But he was beautiful. And he paid attention to me.'

The sadness of her statement silenced everyone.

Then Nora said brusquely, 'So, what would you like to do?'

Harrie sagged against the back of her chair and closed her eyes momentarily as at least some of the tension drained from her neck and shoulders. She'd been so worried Nora would send her back to the Factory should she find out.

'I need to find someone who can help me get rid of … it.' She'd almost said 'the baby', but it wasn't a baby, it was a mistake. 'Someone who'll do it properly. But I don't know of anyone.'

'I do, but I wouldn't recommend her,' Nora said.

'Mrs H will know.' Friday smirked. 'I'll ask her. She'll get a hell of a fright. She'll think it's me.'

'No, I think I might speak to Mrs Hislop myself,' Nora said suddenly. 'As your mistress, Harrie. I mean, you are my responsibility. Do you mind?'

'No. I don't mind,' Harrie said gratefully. She'd been dreading the prospect of creeping down alleyways and knocking on doors.

'You do realise Mr Barrett can't know about this?' Nora said.

Harrie looked at her in horror. 'Oh, no, I wasn't going to tell him.'

'I should think not. This is women's business.'

As soon as she got home that night, Friday barged into Elizabeth's office.

'Come in,' Elizabeth said dryly as Friday sat down.

'Harrie's caught for a baby,' she said in a rush.

'Your friend, Harrie?' Elizabeth was aghast. 'The one who wouldn't say shoo to a goose?'

Friday nodded.

'Fancy that. Her doctor?'

'No. She got mashed and some randy Irish tar got his leg over.'

'Good God. She let him? A *paddy*?'

'Doubt it. He would have forced her. She can't remember.'

'Well, why didn't someone stop it? Where were you?'

'Bloody not there, obviously,' Friday snapped, swallowing a huge lump of guilt.

'And where's the bugger now?'

'I don't know. Halfway to China, probably.'

Elizabeth sat back in her chair. 'Is that why her mistress was here earlier? Nora Barrett?'

Friday nodded. 'She wanted me and Sarah to go round tonight and talk to her. Nora thought she might be in trouble, but Harrie wasn't saying.'

'And?'

'And we did, and she admitted it.'

'I suppose she wants to keep it?' Elizabeth rolled her eyes. 'Silly girl.'

'No, actually, she doesn't. Well, she says she doesn't.'

'That's very wise. She'd be ruined.'

'What? Her reputation?' Friday snorted. 'She's already ruined. She's a convict girl, remember?'

'No, her life. She'd never drag herself out of the muck with a child to raise, not on her own.'

'It's not completely unheard of.'

'No, but it's very bloody hard work.' Elizabeth reached for a piece of paper. 'I can give you the name of the woman I use for the brothel. No, in fact I'll contact her myself, if you like. Won't be cheap, though. It isn't, for a reliable and safe service.'

'Well, that's what I've come to tell you. Nora Barrett wants to talk to you herself. She knows you'll know who to go to, and I think she feels responsible for Harrie. She really is quite fond of her and she doesn't want to lose her. So expect a visit.'

'Oh, good. I'll look forward to her looking down her nose at me.'

The next day Nora walked to the southern end of Cumberland Street until she came to what she thought was probably the right house, according to the directions the draper on Gloucester Street had given her, and knocked on the door. It was certainly a very humble home, but she tried not to be judgmental about these sorts of things. Too often.

A small, snot-nosed boy answered the door.

'Hello, love. Is your grandma home?'

'Gran!' the boy bellowed before running off, his bare feet slapping the oilcloth floor.

A tired-looking woman appeared from the gloomy interior, her hair pushed under a house cap and a shawl tucked into the waistband of her apron. 'Afternoon, missus. What can I do for you?'

'Good afternoon. I'm Mrs Nora Barrett. Am I right in assuming you're Mrs Biddy Doyle?'

'You are.'

'Good. Well, I'm Harrie Clarke's mistress. I believe Harrie knows your son — Mick, is it?'

Biddy Doyle hesitated, then said — very cautiously, in Nora's opinion — 'Yes. Why?'

'Is he at home at the moment?'

'No, he's at sea.' The little boy reappeared, half concealing himself in his grandmother's skirts. Mrs Doyle shooed him gently away, telling him to go and play with his sister. 'What's he done?' she asked.

'Harrie's expecting.'

Mrs Doyle sighed heavily. 'I thought she might be. She had that look about the eyes. She's a lovely colleen, too, so she is. I'll skin that little shite the next time I see him.'

Nora was moderately surprised: she'd expected, if not denial, then at least a censorious finger pointed in Harrie's direction. But if Biddy Doyle had known her son was such a gamecock, why hadn't she warned Harrie?

She said so to Mrs Doyle.

'I did try, but the door was literally shut in my face. And anyway the lass was swept off her feet. They all are, more's the pity. And now look what's come of it.'

'Yes, now look.'

Mrs Doyle crossed her beefy arms. 'What do you want from me?'

'I want you to pay for the abortion, as your Mick obviously isn't here to clean up his own mess. I can't see why Harrie should have to bear the burden of that expense herself.'

'That's fair,' Mrs Doyle said without hesitation. 'Who will you take her to? You have to be careful, you know. There's some right butchers in this town.'

'I don't know yet.'
'Why don't you give me a day? I'll do some asking around.'
'Thank you. But discreetly, please.'
'Of course.'
'I'll call again tomorrow afternoon.'

As soon as Nora Barrett had gone — there was a woman with airs, eyeing the house as though she wouldn't keep chickens in it — Biddy shrugged into her coat, told Maureen to watch the little ones and marched off down the street. She turned right into steep and pot-holed Essex Street, stomping along so angrily she slipped and nearly went on her arse, then left at the gaol corner onto George. A few minutes later, puffing quite badly now, she came to the Sailors' Grave Hotel, ducked into the alleyway down one side and rapped on the door of Leo Dundas's tattoo shop.

'It's open!' came a familiar voice.

'You busy?' Biddy barked as she sailed in.

'Nice to see you, too, Biddy,' Leo said. 'It's been a while.'

Biddy could see he was alone. Looming over him as he sorted through a pile of old illustrations, she said, 'Do you know what that bloody son of yours has done now?'

'That son of ours, you mean.'

'He's only gone and got a nice young colleen in trouble!'

'But he's only seventeen,' Leo said.

'Oh, you fool! How old were you when you fathered your first child?'

Leo couldn't really respond to that. 'Well, what do you want me to do about it? It's a bit late for a father and son talk, don't you think?'

'You've never had any talks with him.'

'You never wanted me to.'

'That's true,' Biddy agreed reasonably.

'Where is he?'

'At sea, and I don't know when he'll be back.'

'So what do you want?'

'The girl's mistress has asked me to pay to get it seen to. I think you should, Leo. He's your son and you've got more spare money than I have.'

'How much will it cost?'

'God knows. Depends on the abortionist.' Biddy knew Leo was aware she had mouths to feed at home and was saving hard for their future. He wouldn't begrudge her this. She added, 'I'll pay out of my savings, and you can give me the money back.'

'Sounds fair,' Leo said.

'Good. Thank you. It won't stop me feeling any better disposed towards the little bugger the next time I see him, but at least it'll get that high and mighty Nora Barrett off my doorstep.'

Leo frowned. 'Nora Barrett? What's she got to do with it?'

'She's Harrie's mistress. Harrie's the girl who's expecting.'

Biddy watched as Leo's face drained of colour. 'Harrie Clarke? Mick's got Harrie Clarke in trouble?'

Biddy nodded.

Leo snatched up a bottle of the shark oil he used to mix his pigments and hurled it at the wall.

Nora called at Biddy's house the following day. Biddy said, on opening the door to her, 'Afternoon, Mrs Barrett. I've the names of one or two women who come recommended, but I'd like to meet them first. You can't be too careful.'

'Why should you be the one to meet them?' Nora asked, skewered with both suspicion and jealousy.

'He's my son. I feel responsible. And I'm paying.'

'I believe it should be a joint decision. She's assigned to me.'

Biddy shrugged, knowing she had the upper hand because she held the purse strings.

Nora had been doing a bit of organising herself. 'I went to see Elizabeth Hislop this morning, the madam in Argyle Street?'

'I've heard of her,' Biddy said.

'Mrs Hislop, as you'd expect, has contacts.'

'I've no doubt she does, but why should she be bothered? She doesn't even know Harrie.'

'She does.' Nora saw the look on Biddy's face, bristled, and said, 'And before you go getting any unfounded ideas about Harrie's character, she has nothing to do with the brothel. Harrie's very good friend Friday Woolfe works for Mrs Hislop.' Nora didn't think Friday would mind being outed as a prostitute to Biddy Doyle, and if she did, too bad. 'Mrs Hislop is happy to help, as a favour to Friday. And to Harrie.'

'Help doing what?'

'I thought we could all sit down together, look at who's available and decide who we think would be best. As you say, you can't be too careful.'

'No, you can't,' Biddy agreed. 'My eldest boy's sister-in-law died last year after she paid some slattern to get rid of a baby. Four kiddies under six left behind. Tragic, it was. Just tragic. When should we meet?'

'Now, if you can manage.' Elizabeth Hislop had said any time that afternoon would suit her.

'I'll get my coat.'

Together they walked down to Harrington Street, and told the rather good-looking young man behind the bar at the Siren's Arms they had an appointment with Mrs Hislop.

When Elizabeth appeared, Nora definitely wished she'd dressed up this time. Today Elizabeth was wearing an even smarter gown of dark green taffeta with fashionably puffed sleeves and trimmed with the most exquisite black guipure lace. Nora suspected she'd done it on purpose. Still, at least she didn't appear anywhere as down at heel as Biddy Doyle, in her skirt of drab and that coat that had to be a man's. That was the trouble with the Irish — they never seemed to care how they looked. Or behaved.

'Mrs Hislop,' Nora said, 'this is Mrs Biddy Doyle.'

'Good afternoon, Mrs Doyle. Nice to meet you,' Elizabeth said, offering a soft, well-manicured hand.

'Good afternoon to you, Mrs Hislop.' Biddy took Elizabeth's hand in her own, rough and reddened as it was by chopping wood and laundering for five.

Elizabeth said, 'Please, come through to the private reception room. I've arranged tea and light refreshments.'

She ushered them into a small, cosy salon furnished with a sofa and two armchairs arranged around a fireplace, and invited them to sit. Nora left her hat on, though Biddy removed her bonnet and set it beside her on the sofa. A girl with a tea trolley appeared, poured everyone a cup, then retreated.

'Do try the cakes, or perhaps a scone,' Elizabeth said. 'They're very good.'

Nora considered a gingerbread heart — they did look delicious and she could actually smell the ginger — but waited to see what Biddy would do. She wasn't going to take anything if Biddy didn't. She glanced up and saw the other woman watching her, a tiny smile on her face.

Oh, to hell with her. Nora took two gingerbread hearts.

Biddy helped herself to a scone.

Elizabeth approached the trolley, piled a scone, two jam tarts and two gingerbread hearts on a plate, and resumed her seat. 'Shall we get down to business?'

Biddy waved a hand in front of her face while she swallowed a mouthful of scone. Nora didn't know why people did that. George did it all the time. It only drew attention to the fact that he'd put too much food in his mouth.

When she could speak, Biddy said, 'Mrs Hislop, pardon me for being blunt, but I'm not sure I understand why you're involved.'

You do so, Nora thought, I've already told you. Eyeing Elizabeth, Nora observed her polite smile becoming just the tiniest bit forced.

'As a favour to Friday Woolfe,' Elizabeth said. 'And of course to Harrie herself. She's a good girl and it would be a tragedy to allow a single foolish mistake to ruin her entire life. Don't you agree?'

'That I do.'

'Good. And I presume you're here because your son's responsible for this very unfortunate state of affairs.' Elizabeth popped half a jam tart into her mouth.

'That's right, the little shite,' Biddy said with no hint of embarrassment whatsoever. 'And I'm paying for it. Being someone that's lived on the Rocks for many years, I have a lot of friends and acquaintances, so I do. I've been told of several women who might provide the service we're looking for.'

'I, too, know of someone,' Nora said. 'But I don't believe she'd be suitable in this case,' she finished lamely.

Elizabeth said, 'I have a very good relationship with a woman who has taken care of my girls with most satisfactory results. A Mrs Turner. I recommend her highly.'

'Ann Turner?' Biddy sounded disappointed. 'She's on my list.'

'Don't scowl, Mrs Doyle,' Elizabeth said. 'It's not a competition. Who were you going to suggest, Mrs Barrett?'

'Oh, well, a Mrs Parks, from over on Phillip Street. But I really wouldn't recommend her. Not for Harrie.'

'Wouldn't you?' Elizabeth asked. 'Why not? How can you be so sure she isn't suitable?'

She knows damned well how I know, Nora thought, the old cow. 'I've heard that her methods aren't always reliable.'

'We don't want that, then, do we?' Elizabeth said. 'And you, Mrs Doyle? You implied you had more than one suggestion?

'Yes, Mrs Turner, and the other name given to me was a Mrs Leggett.'

Nora said, 'Is she related to Hattie Leggett the midwife, I wonder?'

'She is Hattie Leggett the midwife.'

'Oh, yes, I've heard of her,' Elizabeth said. 'Though I didn't realise she lent her hand to all aspects of the business. So, we have Mrs Parks, whose methods don't always work, Mrs Leggett, whom none of us knows, and Mrs Turner, whom I can personally recommend. I don't think there can much argument, do you?'

'How much does Mrs Turner charge?' Biddy asked.

'Five pounds.'

Biddy's brows shot up. 'My Christ, that's steep.'

Nora shrugged. She wasn't paying for it. 'It's cheaper than raising a child.'

'There is that,' Biddy agreed.

'What's Mrs Leggett's fee, do you know?' Elizabeth asked.

Biddy said, 'Three pounds.'

'I fully understand why the lower figure may be more attractive to you, Mrs Doyle,' Elizabeth said, 'but I'd prefer the higher amount were paid for what surely must be a better service. Please allow me to make up the difference.' To Nora's alarm, she added, 'Unless, Mrs Barrett, you'd prefer to make a contribution? Harrie is your assignee after all, and you clearly have a motherly interest in her welfare.'

Christ, Nora thought, she didn't have two spare pounds. She'd have to take it out of the money she kept so carefully hidden from George.

Biddy licked butter off her fingers. 'Don't worry yourselves, either of you. I can pay a fiver quite comfortably, so I can.'

Elizabeth and Nora stared at her.

After a moment, Elizabeth, sounding slightly put out, said, 'Oh, well, good. Are we agreed on Mrs Turner, then?'

Relieved, Nora nodded.

'Lovely,' Biddy said.

'Harrie will need help afterwards,' Elizabeth warned. 'Mrs Barrett, you may or may not know that the results of the procedure usually aren't immediate. They may take a day or so to come on. When they do, she'll be in pain.'

'I'll confine her to bed. I'll think of something to tell George. My husband,' Nora explained.

'Very good. I'll make the arrangements with Mrs Turner immediately. I don't see any point to waiting. Who should go with Harrie? I think I will,' Elizabeth said, at exactly the same time as Nora and Biddy also said, 'I will.'

Sensibly, Biddy said, 'We can't all go. Why don't we ask her?'

Harrie chose Friday and Sarah to accompany her when she went to see Mrs Turner first thing in the morning a few days later.

Ann Turner lived at the Bent Street end of O'Connell Street, in a cottage on a long, narrow lot that extended from O'Connell to High Street. Her home was tidy with a green-painted door and drapes at the windows. A gravel path flanked by clumps of early hyacinths led to a small front verandah, though the yard was more dirt than grass. It looked nice to Harrie, the sort of house she would like to live in herself. She wondered if Mrs Turner had children, and if she did, whether she'd ever considered killing them before they'd been born.

When Friday knocked on the door, it opened so quickly Harrie suspected the woman must have been watching through the window.

'Harriet Clarke?' she said to Friday.

'Not me, her,' Friday said. 'Are you Mrs Turner?'

The woman nodded. She was in her thirties perhaps, pleasant-faced and neatly dressed.

'Not all of you, just Harriet.'

'I can't do it without my friends,' Harrie said.

'Then I can't help you, dear.' Mrs Turner closed the door.

Friday knocked again, and kept on knocking until it opened a second time.

'I'm sorry,' Mrs Turner said. 'Was I not clear?'

Digging in her reticule, Friday produced a five-pound note and flapped it. 'On top of your fee. Am *I* being clear enough?'

Mrs Turner looked at the money, made a hesitant face, then took it. 'You can come in, all of you, and you two,' she said, nodding at Friday and Sarah, 'can attend her, but please keep out of the way and let me get on with my work. I can't afford to be distracted.'

Sarah and Friday crowded in before she could change her mind.

Inside, the house echoed its tidy outside appearance. A kettle hissed over a fire — probably not the cooking hearth, it was too small — and a rug-covered sofa, an armchair, a dining table and a small writing desk filled the space. In one corner stood a walking spinning wheel, the kind you stood up to use. Harrie hadn't seen one of those since she'd left England.

'Now, Harriet, are you absolutely sure this is what you want?' Mrs Turner asked. 'Once I start there'll be no turning back.'

'Yes, I am. I'm sure,' Harrie said, though it sounded to her ears as though someone else were saying the words. There was a ringing noise filling her entire head, and she was dizzy and felt sick and needed to lie down.

'Mrs Hislop said you've already tried feverfew tea?'

Harrie nodded. 'All it did was make me vomit.'

Several doors led off the main room, and it was towards one of these that Mrs Turner pointed. 'Go through, dear, take off your boots and stockings, and lie on the bed. If you're feeling unsettled, help yourself to the laudanum. It's included in the fee. I'll just wait for the water to boil.'

Harrie *was* feeling unsettled. She was terrified, and now she couldn't make her legs move.

'Come on,' Sarah said gently, and took her hand.

The room was small, and furnished with a single cast-iron bed minus its footboard, a chest of drawers topped with a lace runner and a pungent-smelling pot pourri, and several wooden chairs arranged against the wall. Above one chair hung a sampler on which was embroidered; *For God so loved the world that He gave His one and only son/that whoever believes in Him shall not perish but have eternal life. John 3:16.* A large oilcloth had been spread across the bottom half of the bed, over the end and onto the wooden floor. A sheer gauze curtain covered the window and a lamp burnt brightly on a small table, which also held a pair of folded towels and a tray covered with a linen cloth. Beside it stood a small brown bottle.

Harrie took a long sip from it, grimacing as the bittersweet laudanum slid down her throat. How many other girls and women had been in this room? It must've been hundreds, because she could hear the lonely, unformed voices of their unwanted and discarded babies, whispering to her like the rustle of the branches of an ancient tree in a restless wind.

'Go easy, love,' Friday said. 'You'll knock yourself out.'

Good, Harrie thought. She sat on the bed and untied the laces on her right boot with hands that wouldn't stop shaking. She just wanted this to be over so she could go home and pretend none of it had ever happened.

'Here,' Sarah said. She crouched and eased off Harrie's other boot, then helped her to lie down. The oilcloth on the mattress made an unpleasant rasping noise. She rolled Harrie's stockings down and off, then smoothed her skirts over her legs again. 'All right?'

Harrie nodded, though she wasn't.

'Where the hell's that woman?' Friday grumbled.

'Right behind you,' Mrs Turner said as she carried in a bowl of hot water, an apron draped over her arm. She set the bowl on the table, tied the apron around her neck and waist, and rolled up the sleeves of her dress. While she dipped her hands into the hot water, she said, 'Girls, you do understand, don't you, that what I do here is against the law?'

'Well, yes,' Friday said.

'I wasn't happy about all of you being here, but you are, so the less said about it the better. If I go to gaol, or worse, God help me, there'll be even fewer clean and competent hands available to do this. And then what will happen to girls like Harriet? Now, dear, did you have a tot of the laudanum?'

Harrie nodded.

'And how far along do you think you are? Mrs Hislop did mention it, but, well, you're the one who knows exactly, aren't you?'

'Eight weeks,' Harrie said.

'Good. Nice and early. I'll just have a feel, to make sure.' Harrie grimaced with embarrassment as Mrs Turner pulled up her skirt and pressed at her lower belly with stiff fingers, poking quite hard just above her pubic hair. 'Yes, that feels about right. Shall we start, then?'

'Will it hurt?' Harrie asked. She couldn't see how it wouldn't.

'I won't lie, dear. Yes, it will, but it won't take long. I've done this many dozens of times.'

'Successfully?' Sarah asked, rather sharply.

Mrs Turner hesitated for the briefest of seconds. 'Usually.' She dried her hands on a towel and picked up another. 'Now, I need you to move down so your bottom's right at the end of the bed. And I want this towel underneath you. That's right, tuck your skirts well out of the way.'

Harrie wriggled down as requested.

'Raise your knees, please, and set your feet on the oilcloth.' Mrs Turner selected a long sewing stiletto of bone from the tray and knelt on the floor at the foot of the bed. 'My goodness, that's a nasty-looking boil on your backside. How long have you had that?'

'I don't know,' Harrie mumbled. 'A week?' A boil on her arse was the least of her worries. She stared up at the ceiling; there was a crack in the rough plaster and she was sure something with nasty, glinting eyes was peering though it at her.

'I can give you a receipt for a good plaster to put on that. Should help to clear it up. You'll have to lance it first, though. Remind me before you go. Right, I'm starting now.'

Harrie jerked and cried out sharply.

Mrs Turner sat back on her heels. 'Hmm. There doesn't seem to be much room in there. I barely even got my fingers in. Harriet, dear, how many, er —'

'One,' Friday said. 'She did it once, and she caught.'

'Oh dear, you poor thing. Let's see.' Mrs Turner pushed herself to her feet, her knees cracking like snapping twigs, took a slim glass tube from the tray and smeared a balm over the end of it.

Sarah looked at Friday, appalled. Friday gave a tiny shake of her head, warning her to keep quiet and not to frighten Harrie.

Harrie turned her head towards the chairs against the wall. Rachel was there, her hands folded in her lap, sitting quietly.

'Help me,' Harrie pleaded.

'It's all right,' Rachel said. 'I'm here.'

Mrs Turner knelt again. She inserted the tube, peered into it, said, 'That's better,' then carefully introduced the stiletto.

A knife drove up into Harrie's belly and a shriek burst out of her. She slapped her hands over her mouth and squeezed her eyes shut, but the noise kept coming out in a long moan, like a cow in mortal terror. Then someone's hands were on her head, soothing and cool, but the pain got worse and worse, searing deeply into her innards until she knew she couldn't bear it. She heard Rachel telling her to hold on, and then Sarah's voice, then came a small release of pressure in her abdomen, and at last the pain began to ease.

'That should do it,' Mrs Turner said as she got to her feet, the stiletto in her hand slick with blood.

Harrie opened her eyes. Rachel had gone.

'How are you feeling, dear?' Mrs Turner asked. 'A bit uncomfortable? That's to be expected. Did you bring anything with you for the blood?'

Friday and Sarah helped Harrie to sit up. She glanced down between her legs and saw that the towel beneath her backside was stained an alarmingly dark red.

'I think … in my reticule.' She could barely gather her wits, she was that shocked.

Friday dug around and found a cloth, and a cord to go around the waist to hold it up. 'One isn't going to last long, is it? We'd better get you home.'

Mrs Turner dipped a washcloth into the bowl of warm water and passed it to Harrie. 'Here, dear, clean yourself up.'

'What happens now?' Sarah asked as she gathered up Harrie's boots and stockings. 'Is that it? Is it done?'

'Yes, it's done, but the foetus won't be expelled straight away. That could take up to a day or more.'

Sarah eased the bloody towel from under Harrie, dropped it on the floor and crouched to help her put on her stockings and boots. 'What if it doesn't come out? Will that mean it's still alive?'

Harrie felt her gorge rise and she retched, making a noise like Angus when he had a fur ball. Her eyes watered viciously, and she started to cry properly.

Mrs Turner turned her back and busied herself rinsing her instruments in the water bowl. 'No, it won't be alive. I do know what I'm doing, you know. It's more likely to mean an obstruction of some sort, preventing the foetus from coming away. But if that does occur, you can't come back here. There'll be nothing more I can do.'

Again Friday and Sarah looked at each other.

If that did happen, Harrie would most certainly die.

# Part Two
# Let Her Rave

# Chapter Seven

As arranged, Jack took Harrie home in Elizabeth Hislop's carriage. Nora put her straight to bed, telling George when he appeared for his dinner she'd been taken ill.

And she was ill, bleeding heavily and suffering severe cramps. By late afternoon she worsened and, convinced she was dying, wanted Friday and Sarah, but Friday was on duty at the brothel until ten that evening and Sarah was also busy at work. At six o'clock Nora sent Abigail to fetch her: she arrived as soon as the shop closed, leaving Adam to organise his own supper.

She flinched as she entered Harrie's little attic room — Nora was changing the bed linen and the chamber smelt faintly like an abattoir. The sheets dumped on the floor were stained with a shocking amount of blood, and Harrie's face and lips were absolutely white. She was wearing a shift pulled up around her waist, and a wad of cloths was folded between her legs.

'My God, Mrs Barrett, how long has she been like this?'

'A couple of hours.' Nora pushed her fair hair off her face with the back of her wrist. 'The flow was steady earlier, but I think the baby's coming away. I'll never get the stains out of this linen.'

Sarah took Harrie's hand. It was cold and limp, like a dead fish. 'How are you feeling, love?'

'Rachel? Is that you?' Harrie's eyes were glazed and a sheen of sweat gleamed on her brow.

'It's Sarah, sweetie. Are you in pain?'

Harrie groaned.

'Do we need a doctor?' Sarah asked Nora.

'What for? What's a doctor going to do?' Gazing down at Harrie, she bit her lip. 'I don't know. Maybe.'

'I was thinking of James Downey,' Sarah said.

'James Downey? Her suitor? Don't be stupid, girl. Do you think he'll still want her after treating her for a botched abortion?'

Sarah's heart lurched. '*Is* it botched?'

'God. I just don't know. Shall we wait another hour? I've given her plenty of laudanum. She's full of it.'

Harrie let out another low moan and rolled onto her side. Sarah wondered if she *had* another hour.

'Help me get another sheet under her, will you?' Nora asked. 'I've just put a couple of clean cloths on her.'

The door opened and Hannah stuck her head around it.

'Hannah, get out!' Nora snapped.

Catching sight of the bloody sheets on the floor, Hannah's eyes were huge. 'Da says he's hungry and where's his bloody supper.'

'Oh, for God's sake.' Nora straightened, her hand pressed into the middle of her back. 'Tell him to get it himself. I'm busy.'

'Is Harrie dying?' Hannah asked, and burst into tears.

Nora hurried over and gave her a quick cuddle. 'Of course she isn't.'

'But she's got a really bad bleeding!' Hannah wailed.

'Yes, I know, but she'll be all right, don't worry. I know, why don't you and Abigail get your father his supper? You're such big girls now. There's cold roast beef in the safe, and cheese and piccalilli and some of that loaf left from this morning. Is that a good idea?'

Hannah sniffed, wiped her nose on the back of her hand, and nodded. Abigail would have to slice the meat because she wasn't allowed to play with sharp knives after what had happened with Sam, but she could put everything on a plate. She went out, yelling for her sister.

Nora flapped out a fresh sheet, rolled it longways, and laid it on the mattress parallel to Harrie's back.

'This is my last set,' she said. 'The rest are dirty. Normally I'd go next door to borrow some, but, well, I don't really like to for this.'

'I've got plenty,' Sarah said. Adam's previous wife, Esther, had left a stock of them in the linen cupboard. She knew how arduous washing all the soiled sheets in the copper was going to be — a chore Harrie normally did. And if it rained, they would take days to dry. 'I'll go home later and get them. And Friday might be able to borrow some old ones from Mrs Hislop.'

Grim-faced, Nora nodded her thanks. 'I just hope to God it doesn't go on that long.'

So did Sarah.

Together she and Nora eased Harrie onto her other side, so she was on the fresh sheet, then smoothed out the rolled-up section. But as they did, more blood oozed through and around the cloths between Harrie's legs and soaked into the sheets. Nora swore quite spectacularly, then folded back the cloths and inspected the contents.

'I think it's come out,' she said after a moment.

Sarah looked. In the folded pads of coarse linen was not a tiny baby as she'd expected, but a lumpy sac-like mass of tissue and blood. 'Are you sure?'

Nora nodded. 'That's what they look like before they've quickened.'

'Really? But why is she so ill? And the blood!' Sarah bent down and sniffed. 'Has it gone rotten?'

'No, there won't have been time for that.'

'Will she stop bleeding now?'

'I bloody well hope so.'

\* \* \*

Friday and Sarah were both with Harrie the next morning when they overheard Nora having a furious row with George. Under the impression that Harrie was suffering some sort of 'women's affliction', George was extremely disgruntled by the fact that his wife intended to pay, from her own purse, the fee for the doctor who would soon be attending. Harrie was the one indisposed, they heard him rant on the floor below; why couldn't *she* pay the cost of the doctor's visit?

'She doesn't have any money!' Nora shouted. 'She's a bonded convict!'

Harrie did have a little, Nora knew — the money she earned drawing flash for Leo Dundas — but George didn't know about that: he thought the only profit being made from that arrangement was the small retainer Leo paid him for Harrie's services.

'Well, that's just too bad!' George bellowed back. 'Doctors' house calls cost a fortune!'

Upstairs in Harrie's room, Sarah muttered to Friday, 'Arsehole. It's Nora's money.'

'But I'm her mistress, George,' Nora responded, loud enough for even the neighbours to hear, 'and you're her damned master. We're responsible for her welfare!'

'Oh, she'll be all right. What does she need a doctor for? And why are those bloody friends of hers here? It's not even nine o'clock in the morning.'

Something broke. A plate?

'Oh, just finish your cup of tea and bugger off to your shop. Go on!'

George didn't know, of course, that Nora would be asking Biddy Doyle for reimbursement, but that was beside the point.

Harrie's bleeding and accompanying pain had eased overnight, but this morning she was so weak she could barely move or speak and was constantly on the verge of passing out. Nora had dispatched Abigail to the Siren's Arms to alert Friday just after sunrise, and they'd decided to send the child out again to fetch a doctor, who was expected any minute now. Sarah had arrived of her own accord.

'Who's the doctor?' she asked.

'A man I've taken the children to once or twice. He's a bit of a bad-tempered old sod, but he knows I can afford to pay, so that should get him out of doors fairly smartly.'

'What are we telling him?'

'That Harrie's having a lot of trouble with her courses.'

The door to Harrie's room opened and Hannah marched in.

'*Hannah*,' her mother said. 'How many times do I have to tell you, knock and wait to be invited! It's very rude to just barge into someone's room.'

Hannah was clutching a handful of flowers that looked as though they might have been pinched from someone's garden. She laid them on the end of Harrie's bed.

Nora frowned. 'Where did they come from?'

'I found them. Is Harrie all better?'

'Not yet, love. That's why the doctor's coming.'

Hannah's eyes went very round and her hand flew to her mouth. 'There's a man waiting outside. With a big black hat on.'

'Oh, Hannah! How long has he been out there?'

'I'll fetch him,' Friday said. 'What's the cove's name?'

'Dr Poole.'

Fed up with standing around in a smelly backyard, Dr Randolph Poole was about to return to his house-cum-surgery in Cambridge Street, and his breakfast, when Friday opened the back door and invited him in. As she stood aside so he could ascend the stairs, she noticed with alarm that he ponged of alcohol. Following him up, she scowled as his hand flew out and clutched at the wall several times to steady himself.

'Keep going,' she said as Dr Poole reached the parlour beyond the landing. 'Her room's in the attic.' She pointed down the tiny hallway, at the end of which were the narrow stairs to the uppermost floor. The doctor tugged at the hem of his waistcoat, tightened his grip on his bag, said 'Thank you,' and lurched off.

With the doctor, Sarah, Friday and Nora all crowded into Harrie's room, and Angus the cat curled up on the rocking chair under the eaves, there was barely space to move. Dr Poole set his bag on the floor, his hat on top of Angus, and stood peering down at Harrie, lying still and pale in the bed. Behind his back, Friday caught Sarah's eye, pointed at him and made exaggerated glass-raising gestures.

'Your daughter, er, Adelaide?' he began.

'Abigail,' Nora corrected him.

'Abigail informed me that your servant is too unwell to attend my surgery, but was unable to tell me what ails her.'

Nora nodded — at eight Abigail wasn't old enough to be told what had happened to Harrie. 'Harriet is suffering from very heavy courses. She bled badly all yesterday, and last night especially. I've been having to change the linen constantly.'

Friday glanced at Sarah again. Their eyes met. Dr Poole was obviously so swattled that if Harrie had just given birth and the baby was sitting up in bed smoking a pipe he probably wouldn't notice. Their secret was likely safe.

'Is she still bleeding?' the doctor asked.

'Yes, though not as much this morning.'

'An improvement, then?'

'Well, yes.'

'Then why have you called me?'

'Look at her!' Friday exclaimed. 'She's so weak she's hardly bloody well breathing! We're really worried. She looks half dead.'

It was true — Harrie's breathing was alarmingly shallow and she was that pale her skin appeared almost transparent. Her eyes were open but she seemed barely able to focus.

The doctor peered blearily down at her. 'Is she prone to this sort of thing?'

'Heavy bleeding?' Nora said. 'Ah, a little.' Though as far as she was aware, Harrie wasn't. Her courses seemed to be as neat and tidy as the rest of her normally was.

'What's her name?' Dr Poole asked. He glanced longingly at his bag, and Friday wondered if his tipple was in it.

'Harriet Clarke,' Nora said.

'Is she married? Had any babies?'

'No and no.'

'Perhaps that's the problem. A baby would fix things. Her menstrual difficulties would no doubt settle if she married and had a baby.'

It was an extremely unfortunate thing for him to say. A prickly silence settled over the room. The doctor noticed it after about half a minute, and looked up to find Friday, Sarah and Nora all glaring at him.

Nora said, 'We were hoping you would examine her, Doctor. If you can't see your way to doing that, please leave. And don't expect the custom of my family at your surgery again any time soon.'

Dr Poole let out a weary sigh. 'Yes. Yes, of course.' He bent over Harrie, and said loudly in her face, 'Miss Clarke, can you hear me?'

Harrie moved her head slightly away from him. That'll be his breath, Friday thought. Nodding weakly, Harrie raised her hand, then let it flop onto the bedcover. Dr Poole lifted the limp wrist and felt for her pulse. He examined her fingernails, peered into her eyes, looked in her mouth and pressed on her gums, and felt around under her jaw with his fingers.

He asked Nora, 'Would you please lower the bedclothes to the hips?'

Nora moved Hannah's flowers and folded back the blanket and sheet — one of Sarah's — and stood back while Doctor Poole prodded Harrie's belly over her shift. Harrie groaned. Then he lifted the bedclothes off the end of the bed and examined her feet, paying particular attention to her toenails.

Finally, he straightened, looked at Nora, and said, 'There is an imbalance of the humours. I note symptoms of disruption of all four — dry and rough skin, split nails, dull hair, bags under the eyes, and she is underweight. Does she have access to adequate nourishment?'

'Of course she does,' Nora said, insulted. 'She eats what we eat.'

'In particular her liver is swollen, a sure indication of a severe deficiency of blood, and of course we are coming into spring, the season corresponding with that very humour. I suspect that coinciding with her menses as it has, this disparity has resulted in excessive bleeding. It seems she is approaching a state of exsanguination.'

'What?' Friday said.

'She is becoming worrying close to bleeding to death. So, clearly, bleeding her is not my preference, though that is what I would normally recommend.'

'I should bloody well think not,' Friday said. 'You'd finish her off completely. You quack!'

'What *do* you recommend, then?' Sarah said.

'Bed rest, gruel and mutton broth, a good general tonic, no bathing in any form for a fortnight, and she should be kept warm.' Dr Poole opened his bag and retrieved a sheet of paper. 'I shall write a receipt for medicants. Take it to the chemist and have him dispense them.'

'Hold on, what are you prescribing?' Sarah asked. The man was mashed. He could be writing out a receipt for anything.

'Preparations for alum boluses to be taken internally to stem the bleeding, enough to last a week. Dandelion tonic for the liver, and citrate of iron for the debilitating effects of blood loss, to be taken in watered wine. And she may, of course, have tincture of opium for menstrual cramps.'

They all stared at him in silence as he got a bottle of ink out of his bag, fumbled a nib into a holder, perched on the end of Harrie's bed and scratched out the receipt, then flapped it in the air to dry. He handed it to Nora, then placed everything back in his bag and fetched his hat, now covered with Angus's white and black fur.

Nora handed him his fee. 'Will you come back if she doesn't improve?'

'If necessary.'

'Well, don't turn up mashed next time. You stink of booze,' Friday said.

Dr Poole examined the fur on his hat, placed it on his head, then opened the bedroom door. 'That makes two of us, doesn't it?'

'That doctor cove could do with a good kick up the arse, turning up drunk like that,' Friday grumbled.

'You're just shitty because he knew *you'd* been drinking,' Sarah said. 'And it serves you right. It's not even nine in the morning.'

'He was a quack anyway. He couldn't even tell what was wrong with her.'

'Maybe,' Sarah said thoughtfully. 'What if he could tell, but just didn't say so? He must see the results of quite a few abortions. They all must, even James.'

'Aren't they supposed to report it?'

'What would be the point? Just because something's against the law doesn't mean it's always a bad thing.'

'That's true,' Friday agreed. 'We could have saved our money, though, and just asked the chemist for everything he prescribed. We don't need a receipt for any of this.'

'Nora's money, you mean,' Sarah said. 'But what if we hadn't got him in, and Harrie had died? He said she was close to bleeding to death. You'd be sorry then, wouldn't you?'

Friday didn't even need to answer that. They stood on George Street outside the gaol, waiting to cross on their way to the chemist, bustling this morning. There were half a dozen [...]ve, and the road was jammed with wagons and [...]h goods either just unloaded or about to be taken [...] voyage. When the harbour was busy, so was the [...]inistrators to the bureaucrats, to the businessmen to the shopkeepers, to the street vendors and the whores.

Friday spotted a gap in the traffic and darted across the street, Sarah right behind her, both hoisting their skirts above the slurry of mud and horse and bullock shit stirred up by the previous night's rain. There was an apothecary on Cambridge Street but his prices were very high, and chemists carried a much larger range of products.

Once across the road it was a short walk south to the chemist near the intersection with Bridge Street. In the mullioned shop window was a display of various-sized carboys filled with emerald, blue, amethyst and red liquid, glittering like enormous jewels. A sign on the footway advertised that the chemist or his assistants would bleed for a penny, and cup or draw a tooth for tuppence. The bell over the door chimed as they entered.

'I love the smell of this shop,' Friday said, inhaling so deeply she snorted.

'You'll turn into a drug inebriate next,' Sarah warned, only half in jest.

The smell was unique — a mix of lavender and iodine and carbolic. A wooden counter ran all the way around the store; in the rear wall a door opened onto a storeroom for bulk raw ingredients such as herbs and minerals. Behind the counter, tiers of labelled wooden drawers and shelves rose from floor to ceiling, the shelves home to many hundreds of glass and ceramic jars and bottles containing a cornucopia of pharmaceutical ingredients. Antimony and arsenic; borax and blistering plasters; calomel and chamomile flowers; dragon's blood and digitalis; Friar's balsam and frankincense; hellebore powder and henbane; ipecacuanha; juniper berries; laudanum, lavender drops and lunar caustic;

myrrh, mercury and milk of sulphur; oxymel of squills; pennyroyal, paregoric elixir, and poppy heads; Spanish fly, senna, snake root and slippery elm; vitriolic acid; worm powders; zinc, etc.

On the counter sat smaller sets of drawers, glass cabinets, two brass beam scales, and five mortars and pestles, three of which were currently in use by the chemist and his two assistants. Also on display were medicinal and cosmetic preparations such as proprietary cordials, ginger beers, tooth powders and brushes, hair powder (scented and plain), flavoured breath pastilles, Castile, Windsor and Naples soaps, smelling salts and smelling bottles (cut glass and plain).

There were already seven customers in the shop, one of whom Friday — to her horror — recognised.

'Bloody hell,' she swore under her breath as she grabbed Sarah's arm.

'Ow. What?'

Friday hissed, 'Shut up!' and inclined her head towards the woman standing at the front of the queue.

Sarah moved so she could see properly, and paled slightly as she recognised Becky Hoddle. 'Shit! Shall we come back?' she whispered.

Friday shook her head, and tilted her hat to such an angle that her face was almost completely hidden. Sarah followed suit, yanking the brim of her bonnet down to her slightly prominent nose and completely covering her eyes. Friday, tired and feeling worn down by worry over Harrie, snorted out a laugh and had to quickly examine a tin of violet-scented hair powder on the counter when customers in front of her turned to look.

'I wonder what she's here for?' Sarah said.

'Medicine for Bella's syphilis,' Friday whispered back.

'Has she got syphilis?'

'I don't know. Probably. She's such an old slag.'

'I'm going up to eavesdrop,' Sarah said.

Friday nodded. She wouldn't get away with it — Becky would recognise her copper-red hair. Sarah, on the other hand, had that knack for making herself look as inconsequential as a mouse when she wanted to.

As the chemist began to stack bottles and packets into Becky's basket, Sarah stepped out of the queue of chattering customers and peered interestedly into a glass cabinet on the counter, carefully keeping her head down. Then, sidling ever closer to Becky, she picked up a jar of skin cream, took off the lid and sniffed appreciatively. By the time she reached a display of rose-scented soap prettily displayed in a basket, she was in a perfect position to listen in on the chemist's instructions.

'Can you read?' he asked Becky.

'Some,' she replied.

'Can your mistress?'

Sarah stifled a snort of derision. By law Bella Shand wasn't Becky Hoddle's mistress — they were both assigned to Clarence Shand, Bella's husband, and Louisa Coutts would be, too. A convict herself, Bella couldn't be anyone's mistress, but Sarah supposed that in practice she was, and no doubt a hard one at that.

'Of course she can,' Becky said.

'I mean, is she still able to read?' the chemist asked. 'People with this condition do sometimes find they can't.'

'I dunno. I s'pose. She got spectacles a while ago.'

'Well, listen carefully while I explain. This one,' the man said, indicating a large brown bottle, 'is tincture of opium for the headaches and the stomach pain. She may have one to two measures per hour, more if the pain is severe. The powders ...' here he tapped a white paper packet sealed with wax '... contain bismuth, tannin and ipecac for the bowel complaint. I've not added extra opium, as that's already been prescribed. The ipecac, however, may worsen the vomiting. The doctor has therefore prescribed an anti-emetic, which is this packet here.' He leant forwards and whispered, but not so quietly that Sarah couldn't hear, 'The big pot contains the hair restoration cream. You can tell your mistress I've doubled the nux vomica this time. The smaller pot is the skin balm. It's a new receipt with chloride of mercury and it's stronger than the last one the doctor prescribed. Tell her to use both every day as usual, but sparingly. And to store the balm somewhere cool, or it will spoil. Do you think you can remember all that?'

'I'll do my best,' Becky said, a trace of sarcasm in her voice.

The chemist gave her a hard look. 'Yes, you do that. Mrs Shand is your employer, not mine.'

Becky lifted the basket off the counter. 'She says to send the account to the house again. Mr Shand will see to it.'

'As she wishes. Good day.' The chemist was already moving on to the next receipt requiring his attention.

Sarah turned her back as Becky swept past, hoping Friday had her head down. Unfortunately, she didn't.

'Bitch,' Becky whispered loudly as she marched towards the door, clearly recognising Friday.

'Slut,' Friday shot back.

The remaining women and one gentleman in the queue stared at her, shocked and open-mouthed.

Rearranging her hat as Becky exited the shop, making the doorbell jangle like mad, Friday glared back. 'What?'

All quickly looked away again. Sarah joined the end of the queue.

'Headaches, stomachache, the shits, vomiting, bad skin and hair loss,' she said to Friday under her breath. 'What does all that add up to?'

'Is that what she's got wrong with her?'

'Sounds like it. That's what all the medicine was for.'

'I don't know. The Black Death?'

'Don't be stupid,' Sarah said. 'She'd be dead, wouldn't she? And if she had the plague, wouldn't everyone?'

Friday shrugged. 'She didn't look sick enough to have all that, last time I saw her. Skinny, yes, but not at death's door.'

'She might be, by now. When *did* we last see her?'

'When we told her about Gellar. Four months ago?'

Sarah nodded. 'Plenty of time to get sick. Plenty of time to die, in fact.'

Friday's eyes lit up. 'Wouldn't it be perfect if she did? That would fix everything.'

'Don't hold your breath,' Sarah said gloomily. 'She isn't going to die just because we want her to.'

'Still, fingers crossed, eh?'

### *October 1831, Sydney Town*

Friday lay on her belly, topless, as Leo bent over her.

'How's Harrie?' he asked. 'I'm hoping she'll feel well enough soon to come and say hello.'

'Well enough to bring you some lovely new flash, you mean,' Friday mumbled, her face squashed against her arm.

'You're a cynical piece of work sometimes, aren't you?' Leo said mildly. 'For your information, not that it *is* any business of yours, I told Nora Barrett that Harrie can have all the time she needs. I'm not desperate for new flash.'

'Did Nora come and see you?'

'She did.'

'Did she tell you what's wrong with Harrie?'

She hadn't needed to, Leo thought, and when I next see my son I'm going to beat the living shit out of him. 'No, and I didn't ask.'

'Women's problems,' Friday said. 'Pretty serious ones. She nearly died.'

Leo went still. Did that mean the abortion hadn't been a success? Had it been botched? It had been over a week and he should have gone to see Harrie, but to be honest he couldn't face it, he felt that ashamed of Mick's behaviour. 'But she's all right now, isn't she?'

Friday propped herself up on one elbow to see his face. 'She's coming right. The quack prescribed a whole lot of shite and it seems to be doing the trick. She nearly bled to death, you know.'

The pigment brush in Leo's hand snapped. He put the pieces aside. 'But everything's fine now? She's as good as new?'

Friday's eyes narrowed and she studied him thoughtfully, and for a second Leo wondered if she'd worked out that he knew. But so what if he did?

'More or less,' she said. 'She's very melancholy, but. She needs something to take her mind off the … everything that's happened.'

'Aye, well, I said not long ago I wanted to start her on the needles, so I believe I will.'

'Good. She can practise on my phoenix.'

Leo grunted. 'You sure you want a beginner's mistakes right in the middle of your back?'

'She won't make mistakes. You've seen how good her drawings are.'

Leo didn't respond; it was a statement, not a question.

'And her needlework's even better. I don't think she'll go wrong just because she's poking needles into me rather than a piece of material. Have faith, Leo.'

Leo wasn't so sure. 'She was a bag of nerves just drawing the outline of the bat on your leg, remember. I was thinking of starting her off on some old bits of parchment.'

Friday waved away his protests and rested her head on her arm again. 'Leo, I said have faith.'

After a few more days resting in bed, Harrie felt well enough to return to her normal duties except for heavy lifting, which Nora insisted on doing for another week. Harrie knew she was underweight and that she'd bled far too much after the … after her visit to Mrs Turner, but physically she was fairly strong. She always had been. She still felt light-headed if she stood too quickly, but expected that a few decent feeds and some more of Dr Poole's tonic would fix that. The trouble was, she had no appetite, and hadn't for some time — well before she'd ever set eyes on Mick Doyle. It was as though someone had turned off the lever inside her that made her want to eat.

Sometimes she had no vitality at all, and craved nothing more than to lie down and sink into a dark and dreamless sleep, but couldn't because the endlessly babbling voices in her head wouldn't leave her alone. At other times, though, she felt galvanised by a wild energy that compelled her to rush around, leaving no surface undusted or unwiped, no article of clothing unfolded, and not a single inch of floor unswept. She liked that state best because she was so tired when she finally did get to bed that the incessant chatter would subside and she could sleep.

But now there was a new voice to add to the clamour — that of a child not born, and who now never would be. She lay awake at night wondering what he or she might have looked like, what colour his or her hair may have been, and who he or she might have grown up to become. She had to know and it was nudging her closer and closer to insanity, and that was terrifying because she realised she possibly didn't have far to go now anyway. Not far at all.

Twelve days after the abortion she visited Sarah and told her she wanted to see Serafina Fortune.

Two days after that, Serafina Fortune said, 'Good evening, ladies,' and stood aside to let Friday, Sarah and Harrie into her little house on Essex Street. 'Nice to see you again.'

'Nice to fleece us again, you mean,' Sarah muttered. She wasn't particularly happy about Harrie seeing Serafina a second time, not after what had happened during their first visit.

Serafina smiled wryly as she closed the door. They all knew Sarah steadfastly professed not to believe in second sight, scrying, ghosts, or indeed anything remotely other-worldly, but Serafina had proved she had the ability to see the past, and, even more unnervingly, the future. Some of her predictions for Sarah had already come to pass — Adam had come home, hadn't he? — and it seemed that several of her prophecies for Harrie had, too. She'd warned that Harrie's mental health could be at risk, and that a pregnancy was a possibility, which they'd all thought was amusing at the time. It wasn't so funny now.

She asked, 'Are you all wanting readings? It's not two-for-three Tuesday, so you'll all have to pay, I'm afraid.'

'Just Harrie this time,' Sarah said, which was what she and Friday had agreed earlier.

'As you wish. Please take a seat at the table.'

As she opened the wooden box containing her assortment of cards, Sarah eyed Friday watching Serafina. Was she admiring Serafina's finely tailored dress and long gold earrings, perhaps? Or was it something else? Her pretty red-gold hair; her striking facial features; her trim but firm-breasted figure? She seemed really quite mesmerised.

Serafina hesitated, then said to Harrie, 'Would you prefer the cards or a straight reading?'

Sarah had wondered if this would happen. During their last visit, she'd *very* reluctantly accused Serafina of having the second sight, suspecting she'd merely been using the tarot cards to conceal her true ability. She'd been right.

'A straight reading, please,' Harrie said. 'Unless you'd rather use the cards.'

'Up to you.' Serafina opened the battered tin in which she kept her money. 'It's your session. The fee's the same as last time, thank you.'

Harrie passed over four one-shilling coins. Serafina dropped them into the tin. 'Is there anything in particular you'd like to know?'

'Yes. I'm not to say what, though, am I?'

Serafina shook her head. She clasped her hands on the table and lowered her eyes without quite closing them. Shifting in her seat slightly, after a long moment she raised her eyes. 'A boy. It was a boy.'

Harrie gasped, then burst into tears, her hands over her mouth. 'Oh! Oh, I wanted him so much! I didn't want to get rid of him, I didn't!'

Serafina lifted a hand. 'Wait. I haven't finished. He was never going to live long. You would have lost him anyway. He would have died at six or seven months of some, I don't know, some sort of constitutional affliction.'

'He wouldn't!' Harrie cried. 'No, he *wouldn't*!'

'I'm sorry,' Serafina said gently, 'but that is what I'm seeing. And he would have suffered.'

Harrie slumped onto the table, her head on her arms, sobbing.

'Shall I go on?' Serafina asked.

'Not if it's more bad news like that,' Sarah said.

'Actually, that was good news, in a way,' Friday said. 'At least the poor little soul was spared the misery.'

'It wasn't a soul, though, was it?' Sarah said, remembering what she'd seen. 'Not really. It was too small.'

'*Shut up!*' Harrie shrieked, and banged her head deliberately hard on the table, the collision of bone and wood making an awful sound.

Friday hauled Harrie upright by her collar and hugged her tightly as she wept and keened. Sarah stared accusingly at Serafina until the tears burning her eyes made her look away.

Serafina said, 'There is good news.' She leant across the table and tapped Harrie's arm. 'Listen to me, girl. I can see how bad things are for you. I can smell the darkness and I can feel your fear and confusion. But that won't go on forever. Things will change. I told you that last time. You'll get what you want. And I can see quite clearly that you'll get what you deserve.'

'You don't understand!' Harrie sobbed. 'I *am* getting what I deserve!'

'No.' Serafina shook her head, her earrings glinting in the lamplight. '*You* don't understand. This will pass. Things will be all right. There'll be a husband, there will be children, and you *will* have family.'

Harrie shoved back her chair and lurched to her feet, her face red and blotchy. 'That's nice, it is, but I don't believe you. I can't. Not ... right now.' And she rushed out of Serafina's house.

'Shit,' Friday said.

Serafina opened her money tin, took out two half-sovereigns and gave one each to Sarah and Friday. 'Here, I can't take your money.'

Friday looked at Sarah. 'What did you give her money for?'

'I came round yesterday afternoon and paid her not to give Harrie any more bad news.'

'Did you?' Friday said. 'I came round last night and did the same.'

Sarah turned to Serafina. 'You took bribes from both of us?'

'Well, you both did offer,' Serafina said. 'But I didn't realise she'd be so ... troubled. So you can keep your money.'

'Was that true about her baby dying anyway?' Friday asked.

Serafina nodded.

'And *was* there more bad news you didn't tell her?'

The answer was yes and when Serafina told them what it was, Sarah and Friday knew they hadn't a hope in hell of doing anything to stop it, because it had probably already happened.

Sarah took Harrie home, but Friday went to her favourite pub, the Bird-in-Hand on Gloucester Street, and got drunk. Not falling-down mashed, but drunk enough, she'd hoped, to numb the dread that pulsed in her belly at the thought of Harrie finding out about Serafina's latest revelation. But it didn't work, so she picked a fight with a loud-mouthed lummocks who kept grabbing at her tits, got punched in the head, and thrown out of the pub with a warning she'd be banned next time.

At about eleven o'clock she staggered home to the Siren's Arms and was about to go up to her room when she decided she wanted to talk to Mrs H. She made her way unsteadily along the alley, fumbled with the latch on the gate at the far end and let herself into the brothel's backyard. As she lurched across the cobbles, her hands out because she knew the clothesline was in front of her somewhere, a figure stepped out of the privy, raised a lantern and demanded, 'Who's that?'

'God, in the shitter again,' Friday boomed, her voice shattering the still night air.

'Oh, shut up,' Lou said.

'You shut up. You're always in the bloody thing.'

They still bitched at each other constantly, but since Rowie Harris had revealed herself to be the mole — the traitorous *bitch* — working for Bella Shand, the venom had gone out of their bickering. Friday, however, could not bring herself to offer an olive branch, and she knew Lou would never get off her high horse to do the same. So here they were, continuing to fire off shots at each other, to the amusement of the other girls and the ongoing exasperation of Mrs H.

Lou lowered her lantern, in an effort to share the absolute minimum of light. 'You go first. You're obviously swattled. Again. I'd hate for you to fall and hurt yourself.'

'No, no, you first. Swine before pearls.'

'Don't you have that the wrong way round?'

'Don't think so.' Friday took two steps, slipped on the cobbles and fell, landing heavily on her side.

Lou gave way to dainty giggles while Friday erupted into her usual raucous shrieks of laughter.

The back door flew open. 'What on earth's going on out here?'

'Friday's fallen over. She's as pissed as a rat again,' Lou said quickly, putting the boot in.

Elizabeth stormed down the steps and grabbed Friday's arm. 'For God's sake, girl, get up! What if the customers see you?'

'Fuck them.'

'You'll be lucky. Not in the state you're in. Lou, help me get her up.'

From the ground, Friday took a wild swing, missing both Elizabeth and Lou. 'Fuck off, I can get up by myself.'

'Good,' Elizabeth said. 'Then get yourself into my office. I want to talk to you. And you,' she said, jabbing a finger at Lou, 'stop spending all night in the crapper.'

'I can't help it,' Lou said. 'I have a delicate bladder.'

'Infected bladder, more like. Make sure you drink plenty of citrate of magnesia in boiled water. Now get back to work.'

While Lou flounced off up the steps, Friday dragged herself to her feet, Elizabeth right behind her. Once inside her office, Elizabeth shut the door and steered Friday towards a chair.

'What's the meaning of this?'

'Of what?'

'Coming over here drunk and making such a racket? You finished work hours ago.'

'I wanted to talk to you. I need some advice.'

'For God's sake, couldn't it wait until tomorrow?'

'No.'

'And why *are* you so drunk? Again?'

'Something's happened.'

Elizabeth gave a weary sigh. 'Friday, something's *always* happening with you. You'll never run out of excuses for getting on the jar, will you? I suppose you were with Molly?'

Elizabeth didn't care at all for Molly Bates, though Molly had been working in the brothel for some time. She felt the girl led Friday astray by encouraging her to drink, though she knew in her heart that Friday was a habitual inebriate. Molly, however, was proving very difficult to fire, threatening Elizabeth with blackmail over her employment of convict girls as prostitutes, an aggravation she had yet to remedy.

'No, me and Sarah and Harrie went and saw Serafina Fortune, then I went to the pub by myself. I felt shitty and I wanted a drink.'

'Why?'

Friday pulled up her skirt and examined her knee; she had a big, weeping graze on her kneecap. 'Why what?'

'Why did you feel shitty?' Elizabeth gritted her teeth. Talking to Friday when she was mashed could be very trying.

'Oh, 'cos Serafina told me and Sarah something horrible about Harrie.'

'But she didn't tell Harrie?' Elizabeth didn't bother asking what Serafina's bad news was. If Friday wanted to tell her, she would.

'She'd already rushed off. She was upset.'

'I don't know Harrie well,' Elizabeth said, 'but would I be right in assuming it was her idea to go to Serafina? About her baby?'

'Serafina said it was a boy, but it would have died anyway.' Friday sighed. 'I don't know. That would have made me feel better. It just made Harrie cry and go a bit unhinged. Have you got any brandy? Can I have some?'

'Haven't you had enough already?'

'I can never have enough.'

'No, more's the pity. You'll drink yourself to death one day.' Against her better judgment, Elizabeth produced a bottle of good brandy and two tumblers from her desk drawer. 'You said you wanted advice. What about?'

'Should we tell Harrie what Serafina told us?'

'Will she find out anyway?'

Friday thought about it, which Elizabeth could see was quite a demanding task, given the extent of her inebriation. 'Probably. But I'm not sure.'

'Then if you're not a hundred per cent sure, keep your mouths shut. Why tell her if she may never need to know?'

'That's true,' Friday said after a moment. 'And clever.' She raised her tumbler. 'You're not just a pretty face, are you?'

'There's no need to be cheeky, young lady.'

Friday gulped down her drink in one go. 'Can I ask you something else?'

'What's that?'

'Who's the dead man in your cellar?'

Elizabeth stared at her, eyes wide in sudden alarm, her throat working as she swallowed. The metal flap in the office door gave a harsh little clang as someone slid the money she'd just earned through the slot and into the basket. Elizabeth started, then rose to collect it. She insisted her girls hand over payments after each customer departed, for their own safety and to keep them from the temptation of slipping it into their own pockets.

Friday watched her as she sat down again, took an age to count the money, and mucked about ticking a column in one of her many ledgers.

Eventually, Elizabeth said, 'What on earth are you talking about, Friday? What dead man? Really, how much have you had to drink tonight?' and poured herself another three fingers of brandy.

Friday pushed her own tumbler across the desk. 'There's a skeleton in a trunk in your cellar.'

'My cellar, under *this* house? Don't be ridiculous.'

'I broke into it, Mrs H, and —'

Elizabeth glared at her, the hand holding the brandy bottle suspended in the air. 'You broke into the cellar? *My* cellar?'

'And the trunk, and I saw it.' Friday grabbed the bottle and filled her tumbler to the rim. 'I don't give a shit what you did. I just want to know if it's who I think it is.'

Elizabeth's face had gone white now. It had been red before. And her hands were shaking badly. She looked really upset. Friday wondered if she was about to have a heart attack.

'What were you doing in my cellar, Friday? *Tell* me!'

'I will, if you tell me who's in the trunk. It's your husband, isn't it?'

Very, very slowly, Elizabeth sat back in her high-backed chair, lifted her hands and placed them over her eyes. For nearly a minute she said nothing, although she did let out a small, barely audible groan. Friday thought it sounded more like the kind of noise you might make if you were relieved, rather than crapping yourself because you were in the shite. But she sort of understood why that might be.

After a while, Elizabeth lowered her hands, and nodded. The little bit of kohl she always wore to enhance her eyes had smudged. 'Yes, it is. It's Gilbert, my husband,' she admitted. 'How does he look?'

Friday took a long sip of her drink. 'Pretty dried out, actually.'

'Yes, he's been there a while.'

'There's a hole in his head. Like from a lead ball.'

'There will be.' Elizabeth frowned. 'I shot him.'

'After he broke your jaw?'

'Yes. I ... I'd had enough.'

'How did you get him down there? He looks like he would have been twice your size. Well, back then, anyway.'

Now that Elizabeth had confessed, the gates opened and out it all came. 'Oh, he was. Gil was a big man. It's extraordinary, really. I've no idea how I've never been caught. It's been a worry, believe me.'

Tell me about it, Friday thought.

'You know, we had our last fight right here in this room. It was a dreadful stormy night with thunder and lightning, well, about two or three in the morning, actually, and he was drunk and very nasty, but not so far gone that he couldn't punch me in the face and knock out two of my teeth. He went through my desk drawers, took all the money the girls had made that night, and walked out the back door. I grabbed my pistol and followed him, and when I got out onto the steps I shot him.'

Friday let out a huge burp, redolent of the gin, cheese and pickles she'd consumed at the Bird-in-Hand. ''Scuse me. And no one saw anything?'

'If they did, they've never said.'

'Then what happened?' This was better than reading the reports on the Court of Quarter Sessions in the *Sydney Herald*.

'I panicked. I'd killed him outright, thank Christ. Blood was pouring out of his head, blood was pouring out of *my* mouth and my jaw was killing me, there was mud everywhere because we didn't have the cobbles down then, it was windy and pouring with rain and as dark as the inside of a coalmine. So I grabbed his feet and dragged him over to the cellar door, which wasn't locked back then, and I opened it and shoved him down the stairs. Then I hauled him across the floor and managed to jam him into that trunk. My *Christ*, he was heavy. And my *back*! I could barely move for days after. I spent the rest of that night praying no one would go down there, though folk never had reason to, and the next day I got Jack to put a couple of locks on the cellar door.'

Friday said, 'When I found him, there was another trunk on top and it weighed a bloody ton. How did you get it up there? You can't have lifted it yourself, surely?'

'Jack did.'

Friday's mouth fell open. Did Jack know his boss had killed her husband?

Elizabeth must have read her mind because she said, 'He doesn't know. I waited two years until I thought the smell would be gone, then I asked him to help me move some old bits and pieces of furniture down there, and while he was at it put the empty trunk on top of the other one. I felt a bit more confident that no one would find Gil after that. Well, not until I'd died myself. It isn't going to matter, then, is it?'

''Spose not. Didn't anyone notice he was missing? What about his ship?'

Elizabeth shrugged. 'I saw in the newspaper it had sailed with a new captain. I suppose they thought ... Well, I don't know what the shipping company thought. Gil *was* known for his drinking, and his temper. He had a drinking mate, William Butler. He came looking for him and when I said I didn't know where Gil was, he went to the police. They came to the Siren's Arms and I told them the same thing, that Gil had just disappeared, and that was the last I heard of it, thank Christ. When did you find him?'

Friday screwed up her face. 'Mid-July?'

'You haven't told anyone else, have you?'

'Er, someone already knew.'

Elizabeth looked horrified. 'Oh my God. Who?'

'Walter.'

'The boy who killed Amos Furniss? Why would he know?'

'Because I hid him in your cellar. He had three days and nights in there before his ship sailed and, well, I suppose he got bored. He told me about it. But he didn't tell anyone else, and he's gone now.'

'But ...' Frowning, Elizabeth ferreted through the enormous bunch of keys on her chatelaine. 'How did you get in? Did you break the locks?'

'Sarah.' Friday knew she didn't need to say any more; Mrs H was well aware of Sarah's lock-picking skills.

'Does she know?'

'No,' Friday lied.

Elizabeth seemed to deflate. She poured herself another drink and sat back in her chair again, her shoulders slumped. 'Well, now you know my darkest secret. You do realise that gives you considerable power over me?'

Friday scowled. She hadn't once thought of that.

'You're in a perfect position to blackmail me.'

Shocked, Friday stared. 'D'you really think I would?'

After a moment — a moment that was *almost* too long but not quite — Elizabeth said, 'No, I don't. I think we're birds of a feather, you and I. And more than that, we're friends. At least, I hope we are.'

Friday said, "Course we are, you silly old trout. But I think you're pushing your luck keeping a trunk full of bones in your cellar. You need to get rid of them. I'll do it, if you like.' She saw herself tossing what was left of Gil Hislop into someone's cesspit one night when the moon wasn't shining too brightly.

'My husband was violent and he was a drunk,' Elizabeth said, 'but that doesn't mean I didn't love him. Yes, I killed him, but he was the only man for me. There's never been anyone else. I loved Gil then, and I still love him now. I want him near me, Friday.'

'Well, I think you're making a bad mistake. What if your house gets raided?'

'Then I'm bound for gaol anyway.'

'But not for the gallows. You'll *swing* if someone opens that trunk.'

Elizabeth remained stubbornly silent. Friday felt like slapping her. She was being a silly, sentimental old woman, and a danger to herself.

'What if we could find somewhere to put him where you could still visit him?' she asked. 'Would that be acceptable to you?'

'I don't see where.'

Neither did Friday. Perhaps Sarah might have some ideas — her mind worked in a clever and twisted way.

'Let me think about it,' she said.

# Chapter Eight

Leo called on Harrie to talk about starting her on the needles. He hadn't seen her for a fortnight, and was shocked when she opened the door to him. She'd lost even more weight and her face, once so rosy, was unhealthily pale. He had wanted to speak with George, but he, apparently, was out, so he settled for negotiating with Nora instead, which was no hardship. She was far more sensible than her husband, considerably smarter, and a lot easier on the eye.

'I can't,' Harrie said after he'd made his proposition.

'Do you not feel well enough yet?' he asked.

'No, it's not that. I'm a lot better now. I walked all the way up to the market yesterday morning and did the shopping.'

'Does it not appeal? I think you'd be very good at it. And of course I'd pay you a fair rate.'

Harrie's heart gave a lurch of hope and excitement — two sentiments that had been in very short supply lately. With better earnings she could send more money home to her mother and siblings, as well as make a bigger contribution to the Charlotte fund. But she was being unrealistic. She couldn't take up his offer — she had responsibilities.

'It's just that, well, I'm assigned to Mr and Mrs Barrett. I can't just go off and work for you. Mrs Barrett needs me here.' She glanced at Nora. 'Don't you?'

'I do, yes. On the other hand, you're not completely indispensible.'

'Oh.' Harrie felt vaguely hurt. She thought Nora had come to rely on her.

Nora smiled. 'Don't look like that, Harrie. We all love your cooking, the children adore you and you're the best assistant sempstress I've had. But I don't think it matters who sweeps the floors or washes the dishes or does the laundry, do you?'

Harrie said nothing — she wasn't sure what Nora was getting at.

'So I might consider employing another girl to do those more menial tasks, which would give you a bit more time to yourself,' Nora went on. 'That is, if you actually are interested in learning to tattoo. I'm not entirely sure it's an appropriate trade for a girl, but Leo seems to be making a mint from it. Perhaps it can't hurt to learn. Do you want to?'

'Yes,' Harrie replied immediately, thinking about the money.

'Well, in that case, go and see what Sam's shouting about. Leo and I have a few details to discuss.'

As soon as Harrie was out of earshot, Nora said to Leo, 'I really don't think the Superintendent of Convicts would approve of his female charges learning to tattoo hairy-arsed sailors, but Christ knows she has to do something to take her mind off ... whatever's been upsetting her. And which started well before she fell ill, by the way.'

Leo opened his mouth to ask whether she was still fretting about the abortion, but changed his mind, deciding it was probably best if he didn't let on that he knew the reason for Harrie's recent ill health. He didn't even like thinking about it himself. After all, for a little while at least, she had been carrying his grandchild. 'She is physically better now, isn't she?' he asked.

'She's coming right, though she really was quite sick. No, she's been out of sorts for a long time. Up here,' Nora said, tapping her head. 'I'm surprised you haven't noticed.'

'Oh, I have.'

'I'm not sure what's going on, though I expect that whatever it is, it's essentially harmless. I mean, I don't have any worries concerning the children or anything like that. If people choose to have conversations in their rooms with dead folk at three o'clock in the morning, who am I to criticise? But I do believe she needs something to take her out of herself. If she comes to you once or twice a week ... er, how often were you thinking?'

'Three times a week, to start with.'

'Three times, then. That should keep her occupied. Busy hands don't give the devil much chance to cause mischief.'

'It sounds like she already has busy hands here,' Leo remarked.

'A busy mind, then.'

'Friday said more or less the same thing, though I've been thinking about starting Harrie on the needles for a while. So, are we agreed?'

'In principle.'

'Good,' Leo said. 'How much will you need to employ another girl to do the basic housework?'

'Why?'

'Well, I'll pay, obviously. I'm the one depriving you of Harrie's labour.'

Nora laughed. 'No, you won't. George'll pay, indirectly. He insisted I go back to work when Lewis was three months old, so I did. George thinks all the money from my business is going into his bank account, but it isn't. I've a bit put aside now. I'll use that. I'm happy to use my savings if it means I get to keep Harrie for what's really important to me, like the kids and helping me with my business, and her company. I've become very fond of her.'

'That's obvious.'

'But you have to promise to look after her, Leo.'

'Of course I will.'

'And don't you dare tell George I'm paying for another housegirl. He'll absolutely spit nails, the mean bugger. If he asks, tell him you're paying as part of Harrie's apprenticeship, all right? I'll tell him the same thing.'

Leo gave her a salute.

Nora grinned.

Harrie's first tattoo lesson the following Monday was a moderate disaster. She was so nervous she stabbed the customer on the tattoo bench with the needles far too aggressively and drew considerable blood, and when she finally got a good rhythm going she lost her perspective and inked well beyond the outline.

'I'm so sorry,' Harrie said, her heart pounding with alarm and embarrassment.

Fortunately the customer was Friday. 'Oh, who cares? Just put a few extra feathers on that wing.'

'As long as you remember to add more to the other one,' Leo said, watching from a nearby chair. 'Or it'll be a bit of a lopsided phoenix. How's your hand?'

'Burning,' Harrie replied.

Leo nodded. 'It will be, till you get used to it. It's the muscles and tendons. Your strength will build up over time.'

'I hope so.' Harrie put down the needles and flapped her hand vigorously to ease the discomfort. 'Am I going fast enough?' Even though it was only Friday and she knew she wasn't going to be doing anything complicated, she'd worried herself close to vomiting that morning and had eaten even less than usual for breakfast, and now she felt quite light-headed. And she felt guilty because she'd left all the dirty dishes for Abigail to do.

'No, you're not,' Leo said. 'How's the pain?' he asked Friday.

'Lovely, thanks.'

Leo snorted. 'It'll take you a while to get up to speed. But you're faster than I expected. That's probably your needlework skills. You're doing well.'

'Excuse me. Good morning.'

They all turned; Harrie let out a little gasp of shock. Standing in the open doorway was a tall Maori man. His face was fully tattooed and he wore expensive-looking European clothing, though his long hair was pulled up in a topknot. His dark gaze settled on Friday's bare white back for a moment, then shifted to take in the hundreds of flash displayed on the walls. For a fleeting, sick-making second Harrie thought he was the New Zealander from Mick Doyle's crew — she couldn't remember his name.

'Morning,' Leo said.

'Is this the premise of Mr Leo Dundas, the esteemed tattooist?' The man's voice was low and cultured, his diction precise.

'Who wants to know?'

'I am Hoata and I am here as emissary of Tumanawapohatu of Nga Puhi.'

Leo launched himself off his chair and across the room, his hand outstretched. 'Welcome! Come in. Good Lord, I'd given up thinking anyone was going to come!'

Friday raised her eyebrows at Harrie, who raised hers back. They'd seldom seen Leo quite so animated. Except for when he was angry, of course. At the moment, though, he seemed delighted.

'Thank you,' Hoata said, and stepped inside.

'Is he here now?' Leo asked. 'In town?'

'He is at Parramatta, staying with Reverend Marsden. He will be pleased to meet with you on Wednesday.'

'Here, or out there?'

'Here.' Hoata glanced around the shop again, slightly disparagingly this time. 'He will bring his wife and his entourage. You will be expected to demonstrate hospitality in the form of refreshments,' he added, and turned towards the door.

'Naturally,' Leo said. 'Er, what time should I expect them?'

Over his shoulder Hoata said, 'When they get here.'

'What an arrogant prick,' Friday said when he'd gone. 'What was all that about? Who's Too-many-thingy-whatsits?'

'Tumanawapohatu is one of the most renowned tohunga ta moko in New Zealand,' Leo said. 'His work is legendary. Only the very privileged are tattooed by him.'

Friday and Harrie looked at him blankly.

'What does "tohunga ta moko" mean?' Harrie asked.

'A tohunga's someone who's an expert in a certain field. In this instance that's moko, though from what I understand it can be all sorts of things.'

Harrie nodded. They'd learnt that the word 'moko' meant 'tattoo' when they'd discovered that Jared Gellar was involved in the trafficking of upoko tuhi, or preserved heads. 'Like you're an expert?'

'Well, if you like, but even more than me.'

'So why's he coming here?' Friday asked.

'I wrote to him in New Zealand and asked if he'd consider meeting with me the next time he visited Sydney. I do get customers wanting the New Zealand tribal tattoos, and some want them done with the traditional chisels, but I don't have that skill.'

'Maori sailors, you mean?'

'No, not usually. They'd rather be tattooed by their own kind because of the ritual involved, so they'll wait until they go home. I'm mostly talking about white-skinned customers. Tumanawapohatu wrote back and said he admired some work I happened to have done on an English whaler living with the Nga Puhi at the time, a cove by the name of John Rutherford, so in exchange for Tumanawapohatu's advice on chisels, I offered to show him the Japanese technique I use. But that was ages ago.' Leo gave a little grunt of satisfaction. 'I'd more or less given up on him.'

'Why does he have to have such a long name?' Friday complained, scratching her armpit. 'And what did that cove mean by refreshments? You're not running a bloody pork scratchings stall.'

'Tumanawapohatu isn't just highly respected — he and his wife are royalty. It's what they're accustomed to.'

'Tough shit,' Friday said. 'Put the kettle on and give them a scone each.'

Leo ignored her and said to Harrie, 'Have you had enough for today?'

'I think so. I need to get home. The new girl hasn't started yet.' She was tired, too, and seeing that Maori man had given her a fright and brought back dizzying snippets of memory from her drunken night with Mick Doyle. She didn't know why — he hadn't really looked like Mick's crewmate, and, after all, she saw New Zealanders walking the streets of Sydney every day. It must be her nerves; she was on edge and filled with a vague sort of dread constantly now.

'Will you come in on Wednesday morning?' Leo asked.

'Won't those people be here then?'

'I doubt they'll be early if they're coming from Parramatta. Anyway, I'd like you to sit in. What about you, Friday? You've got a session booked at eleven.'

'I'll come first thing instead,' she said.

Harrie put on her bonnet, tied the ribbons under her chin, and collected her reticule. 'See you on Wednesday, then.'

'Thanks for doing my phoenix,' Friday said. 'You did a really great job.'

'She did, actually,' Leo said when Harrie had gone. 'Apart from a couple of slight wobbles. I think she might be a natural.'

'A slow one, but.'

'She'll get faster,' Leo said as he sat down, picked up the pigment brush and needles, and bent over Friday's back.

Standing outside the Australian Hotel on George Street after dinner, James looked up at the sky, trying to decide whether or not it was going to rain. Should he walk home to York Street or hire a carriage? The moon was concealed by clouds but he couldn't taste rain on the wind. He thought he'd be safe.

'I bumped into Friday the other day,' Matthew said, stifling a burp. He didn't know what the cook had done to the cream sauce on the fish, but whatever it was had involved quite a lot of curry.

'Did you?' James said, doing his best, Matthew knew, to sound uninterested.

He hadn't brought this up during dinner, but now that they'd eaten and were outside, he could say his piece and hurry off before James could tell him to mind his own business again.

'Yes, on the street.' Actually, it had been when they'd gone to the bank. 'So I took the liberty of asking her if she knew what had upset Harrie so much.' Matthew looked at James. 'You know, the day she came around to your house and slapped —'.

'Yes, thank you, Matthew. It's not something I'm likely to forget.'

'According to Friday, your housegirl, well, your former housegirl, for some reason told Harrie she'd been, er, sharing your bed.'

'What!'

Matthew took a quick step back; James looked ready to explode. 'And apparently Harrie believed her.'

James closed his eyes.

'So now you know,' Matthew said. 'Er, you didn't sleep with her, did you?'

'No, I bloody well did not!'

A couple walking past turned to stare, the gentleman glaring and moving protectively closer to the woman. Matthew tipped his hat to them.

'No wonder poor Harrie was upset,' he said.

'Yes, no wonder,' James agreed tersely.

'You're lucky she didn't knock your head completely off. And I've been wondering whether that had anything to do with your housegirl disappearing. Did you find out where she went?'

'No.' The muscles in James's jaws were so tense, Matthew was worried he might break some teeth. 'And if I ever do, I'll, I'll ... that damned she-devil!'

\* \* \*

Tumanawapohatu and his entourage arrived at Leo's at nine-thirty on Wednesday morning, long before Leo had arranged anything in the way of food or drink. They swept into the shop to find Friday lying naked from the waist up on her stomach on the bench, smoking her pipe, as Harrie bent over her working on the phoenix's feathers. Leo almost gave himself a heart attack leaping out of his chair, shoving down his shirtsleeves and whipping his hair back in a cue. There was nothing he could do, however, about his bare feet.

The group of New Zealanders was ten strong and they filled the room, shuffling around by the door to fit themselves in. All were tall — even the women were well above the average height of an Englishwoman — and some wore European dress while others favoured the long woven cloaks you often saw New Zealanders wearing on the streets of Sydney. The cove named Hoata, Friday noted, first through the door, was giving them that high and mighty look again. Obviously he wasn't happy. Well, hard luck. Who did they think they were? Putting aside her pipe, she turned her back, sat up and slipped her arms into the straps of her shift.

'Good morning, Mr Dundas,' Hoata said. 'Pray allow me to introduce Tumanawapohatu.'

The group parted and a man stepped forwards. He was immensely tall, easily over six feet, Friday guessed, well built and heavily muscled. His skin was quite dark, his hair was cut short, and a bone pendant swung from one ear. His face was heavily tattooed, the deep greenish-blue lines and swirls extending from his hairline all the way down into his mid-length beard. It all looked a bit odd against his beautifully cut coat and trousers, high collar and black silk cravat.

Leo said, 'Welcome, Tumanawapohatu. Thank you for coming.'

Tumanawapohatu bowed his head and said in a rumbling voice, 'Thank you for inviting me, Mr Dundas.'

'This is my assistant, Miss Harrie Clarke,' Leo said.

Harrie looked as though she didn't know whether to offer her hand, curtsy or run away. 'Good morning, Mr Tuna ... Mr Tum ... er.'

'Good morning, Miss Clarke. You may call me Tu.'

'Thank you.' Harrie's face flamed.

'And this is my wife, Mahuika.'

A woman with a startling silver streak in her magnificent long black hair — dressed with a tall comb of bone or ivory — moved to stand beside Tu. The top of her head reached his shoulder, which meant, Friday calculated, that she must be at least five feet seven or eight inches tall. That was huge for a woman! Friday was abnormally tall herself and she was five feet six.

Mahuika's severely styled dress was such a deep burgundy colour it was almost black and appeared to be made of silk, which must have cost a fortune. The neckline was high, the waist neat and the sleeves fitted from shoulder to wrist — none of this silly puffed business that was fashionable at the moment. Friday quite liked it, which surprised her — normally she preferred brightly coloured, low-cut gowns. Mahuika also wore long jade pendants in her ears, and another on a gold chain against her breast.

Her skin wasn't as dark as her husband's, but she looked equally fierce. More so, perhaps. She was very beautiful. Her chin was tattooed with a tracery of delicate whorls and her lips were completely darkened. Friday winced as she imagined how much that must have hurt, especially if it was done with chisels, as Leo has suggested. Stunning, though, and somehow ... erotic.

'Mr Dundas.' Mahuika offered her hand rather imperiously and Leo shook it. She studied Harrie for a moment, frowned, but said nothing.

'And our daughter, Aria,' Tu said.

There was more shuffling and a girl emerged from the group to stand beside him — and Friday's breath was almost torn from her throat. Her heart pounding, she slid off the bench and stood beside it, feeling a fool in her shift and skirt and wishing she were properly dressed.

The girl was absolutely mesmerising. Almost as tall as her mother, her wavy hair fell all the way to her bum and was lusciously thick and gleaming, like black treacle. On each side of her face a lock had been caught and was held at the back of her head with a comb decorated with delicate carved patterns and inset with shiny blue shell. She, too, wore a tattoo on her chin and lips, but her markings were darker than those of her parents, and more precise. Her cheekbones were high and her coffee-bean brown eyes wide and slightly slanted. The dress she wore was the colour of new copper, similar in style to that of her mother's, and hugged high breasts, a very small waist and strong, shapely arms. Jade pendants hung from her ears, too.

Friday could not stop staring. She had never seen anything more beautiful in her life.

'Pleased to meet you, lass,' Leo said.

'And you, Mr Dundas,' Aria replied in a clear, low-pitched voice, and favoured him with a wide and radiant smile.

Friday's heart jolted so violently she felt faintly sick. Aria's teeth were perfect, straight and even, and the canines sharp and dazzlingly white against the velvet darkness of her lips.

Aria turned to Harrie. 'Good morning, Miss Clarke.'

'Good morning, Miss Aria.' Harrie went red again, and blurted, 'This is my friend, Friday.'

Friday's hand gripped the edge of the bench as Aria's gaze shifted to her.

'That's an unusual name,' Aria said, her arched brows raised. 'As in the day of the week?'

'No, it's after St Frideswide, patron saint of Oxford. In England,' Friday added, in case Aria didn't know where Oxford was. 'She was famous for being a virgin and a nun.'

Leo made a snorting noise that turned into a cough, and got out his handkerchief.

Friday shot him a barbed look. 'Not that we have much in common, me and St Frideswide.'

Aria laughed. 'Do you not?'

She had the dirtiest-sounding laugh. Startled, Friday stared at her as ripples of excitement chased up and down her spine. Aria stared back. And Friday knew.

Mahuika stepped in front of her daughter. 'Mr Dundas, we have been travelling for many hours. We came from Parramatta this morning.'

'My apologies,' Leo said. 'I thought you'd be arriving later.'

'He aha te tikanga o to kupu?' Mahuika demanded. 'Haere ki te whakatika kai ma tatou!'

'Do not be so rude,' Tu snapped at his wife.

Mahuika scowled at him.

Hoata moved forwards. 'The refreshments. When I visited previously I requested that refreshments be made available.'

Leo scratched the back of his neck. 'Aye, well, as you can see I've been working. I do apologise. I haven't had time this morning to make arrangements. Also, I don't like to have food in the room when I'm tattooing. I thought we could wait until afterwards, and have a nice cup of tea and something to eat then.' He hadn't planned any such thing at all, but it seemed prudent to suggest he had.

'Is there *nothing*?' demanded Mahuika. 'This is not what I call hospitality befitting of a rangatira's status.'

'Do not complain, wife,' Tu growled. 'The man is simply adhering to the appropriate protocol, and rightly so.'

Leo turned to Harrie. 'Take some money from the caddy and —'

'No, your assistant should stay,' Tu interrupted. 'At any rate, today I planned only to talk. I will demonstrate tomorrow perhaps, and so shall you. For today I will send someone out for refreshments ... to my favourite bakery.' He clicked his fingers, said something in Maori, and two men left the room.

Friday, still trying to get a good look at Aria around her mother, was surprised — and quite shocked — to see the Maori girl staring boldly back at her. Her eyes held an invitation that was very close to a challenge, which Friday found both highly erotic and ... intimidating. Usually she had the upper hand in these situations, but evidently not this time. Aria's dark brows lifted in a question before she followed the men outside. Her heart pounding with anticipation, Friday sidled around the bench, grabbed her reticule and bodice, and, stuffing her arms into the sleeves, crept out after her.

The alleyway outside Leo's shop was empty and Friday's heart plunged into her boots. She ran down the side of the Sailors' Grave Hotel and around the corner onto George Street, and straight into Aria.

On the verge of either shrieking or giggling and wondering why she was being so bloody silly, she blurted, 'Shit! Sorry!'

'It is all right,' Aria said. She gestured disparagingly at the two men walking ahead. 'Come on, I am not allowed to be out of their sight.'

'Well, that's stupid. Why not?'

'Yes, it is stupid. I love your moko.' Aria touched Friday's arm, and just the fleeting weight of her fingers through the fabric of her bodice sleeve made Friday's skin prickle.

'My tattoos? They're nice, aren't they? Leo did them.'

'Mr Dundas?'

Friday nodded. 'I've got one on my leg as well, a bat, and the one I'm getting on my back'll be huge. Harrie's helping with that.'

'It is to be a bird? I saw the wings.'

'A phoenix.'

'I have never heard of a phoenix,' Aria said.

Up ahead the men had stopped. One beckoned impatiently for Aria to catch up.

'Oh, go away,' she muttered.

'It's not real, the phoenix,' Friday said. 'It's mythical.' She frowned. 'At least I don't think it's real. I love your tattoo. Did they use chisels? Did it hurt?'

'Yes, the tohunga used chisels, and yes, it did hurt.'

'Bugger that.'

Aria laughed her dirty laugh again.

'Can I touch it?' Friday asked. Aria's tattoo was beautiful and Friday wanted to trace the intricate lines of the pattern, but more than that, she yearned to touch Aria's smooth brown skin.

Aria threw a quick glance at the men, who had walked on, and nodded.

Hoping her hand didn't stink of pipe tobacco, Friday very gently ran her fingers across Aria's chin, feeling the raised scars left by the chisel. Her own skin thrilled where it touched Aria's, and she wondered if Aria felt the same. She moved her fingers to Aria's full bottom lip — the flesh there felt like a new rose petal.

'No.' Aria took hold of her wrist. 'They will see. We must catch up.'

And so they did, Friday swallowing her disappointment as she hurried beside Aria. It was idiotic of her to hope for anything more, though, in broad daylight in the middle of George Street.

'Where are we going?' she asked. 'To the market?'

'To the bakery in Charlotte Place. The baker there makes very good meat pies and cakes. My father loves them and will think up any excuse to eat them. We always buy food from there when we come to Sydney.'

Friday's heart gave a little leap. 'How often is that?'

'I have visited twice now, but my mother and father come much more often, on business.'

'What sort of business?'

Aria stepped deftly around a pile of horseshit. 'This and that. Markets for our flax and potatoes, usually. This time we are also here to find the graves of several of our children who died some years ago, while studying at Reverend Marsden's Rangihou seminary for Nga Puhi boys at Parramatta. Altogether, thirteen were lost. It was a great tragedy. My mother and father also have some other private business.'

Friday thought it a bit odd that thirteen kids should die while supposedly in the care of Reverend Marsden. The notion of the proud and ferocious Tumanawapohatu being partial to bakery pies, though, was quite funny.

They caught up with Aria's minders on the corner of George Street and Charlotte Place. Aria introduced them as Kahu and Paikea. Both men afforded Friday terse nods of acknowledgment. As they all traipsed along Charlotte Place, she realised she knew the bakery they were heading for, and it did sell excellent pies.

Paikea fell in beside her. 'Are you a married woman, Miss Friday?'

'It's Miss Woolfe, actually. And no, I'm not.'

'Aria is betrothed,' he said pointedly. 'To a renowned chief with much wealth and influence, and considerable prowess on the battlefield and in other areas of note.'

Again, Friday felt disappointment, only this tasted far more bitter. Surely she hadn't misread the signs? She glanced at Aria, who rolled her eyes and gave a very slight shake of her head, making sure only Friday could see. Her spirits took flight again.

Paikea hitched his cloak over his well-muscled shoulder and went on conversationally, 'I note that your moko are very colourful. I have seen the like on white women before, here and in Aotearoa. Of course, those women were whores.' He looked at her, clearly waiting for a response.

Though her fists had clenched, Friday managed to stop herself from driving one into his smirking, brown face. What an arsehole! She had to make a living somehow. What did it have to do with him, anyway? No doubt it was because she fancied Aria, and not him or his mate. Men hated that.

'Paikea!' Aria fired a short, sharp sentence at him in Maori.

He responded, also in Maori. Aria spoke again, then flapped her hand angrily at both men, indicating that they should walk on ahead. To Friday's surprise, they did.

'I am very sorry,' Aria said. 'That was very rude.'

Friday hesitated. Should she tell her? Would it ruin everything? Was there anything to ruin? 'Actually, I am a whore.'

'Yes, I thought you might be,' Aria said. 'You are very beautiful. I expect men pay a lot of money to lie with you.'

Friday suddenly felt so buoyant her feet almost left the ground. She marched up to Paikea, jabbed him in the back and said loudly, 'Did you hear what I just said, Mr Smartarse? I am a whore! So stick that in your pipe and smoke it!'

Paikea didn't break stride, simply exchanged a supercilious glance with Kahu.

The bakery was packed with folk waiting at the counter, but the crowd parted to allow fearsome-looking Paikea and Kahu to be served first. They ordered a ridiculous number of meat pies, pasties, buns and fruit tarts, which had to be packed in layers into a small wooden crate for transportation. In a jubilant yet reckless and slightly dangerous mood now, and not to be outdone by the two men, Friday ordered two and a half-dozen almond cakes — all the bakery had on display.

Irritated by the snail-like pace of the overweight girl behind the counter as she transferred each almond cake to the crate, Friday snapped, 'For Christ's sake, hurry up, we haven't got all day.'

In response, the girl deliberately moved even more glacially. Finally, to the accompaniment of Friday's heaved sighs, she finished mucking about, took Friday's money, draped a square of muslin over the crate, pushed it across the counter, and said at the top of her voice, 'Enjoy your dinner.'

The crowd of waiting customers burst into laughter.

'Don't assume everyone has the same eating habits as you, lardarse,' Friday shot back.

The crowd went, 'Ooooh!' and Aria cackled her laugh.

Friday grinned at her, hefted the crate off the counter and marched out of the bakery.

Outside, Paikea said, 'I will carry the box.'

'Why?' Friday's reticule dangled from her arm and the muscles above the neckline of her bodice bulged. 'I can manage. You and Yahoo can trot along behind.'

'Kahu,' Kahu said curtly. 'My name is Kahu.' He turned to Paikea and said something in Maori so indignant-sounding that Friday smirked all the way back to Leo's.

Everyone was sitting on the floor except Tu and Mahuika, who had commandeered the tattoo chair and stool respectively, and Leo and Harrie, who had brought chairs through from the other room. Spread across the bench was a selection of bone chisels of differing sizes and slightly different shapes, two beautifully carved wooden pots, and a small ceramic container. Tu was speaking while Leo listened intently, and Harrie gazed down at her hands. Friday thought she looked very tired.

'Here,' Friday said to Paikea, 'take the food through to the other room and put it on the table.'

'You take it. I am not a slave.'

'Well, neither am I.'

'You were happy to carry it back here,' Paikea said.

'Friday,' Aria warned quietly.

Across the room Friday could see Mahuika watching them, frowning.

Annoyance flickered across Aria's face. 'Here, I will see to it,' she said, and beckoned to a woman sitting on the floor, who took the crate from Friday.

Paikea made his way around the room until he stood behind Mahuika. He bent and whispered in her ear at length, and Mahuika caught Friday's eye again. This time she scowled — heavily. Feeling the frosty disapproval of the woman's gaze, Friday returned the stare for a moment before looking away. Obviously Aria's mother was an interfering cow, but it probably wouldn't be a good idea to annoy her unnecessarily. She moved towards Leo's parlour-cum-kitchen to see what Aria was doing, but Aria was coming back out.

'Have you laid it all out already?'

Aria looked startled. 'The food? Waiora will do that.'

'Oh.' Friday was surprised. Aria had said it as though she wouldn't even contemplate doing something as domestic and mundane as setting out plates of food.

'Shall we listen to what my father has to say? Whatever else he might be, he is a very skilled tohunga and he is always worth listening to when he speaks of ta moko.'

Now Friday was dying to know what other things Aria considered her father to be. In her experience, no one who said that ever meant well of the person they said it about. It was nice to know it wasn't just English families who bickered, fought and didn't trust each other. She nodded and followed Aria to the front of the room and sat down beside her on the floor.

But as soon as she did, Mahuika interrupted her husband's monologue. 'Mr Dundas, excuse me, why is that ... female still here?' She gestured at Friday with a dismissive flip of her hand. 'Is she not just a customer of yours?'

'Yes, she is,' Harrie spoke up, blushing yet again, 'and she hasn't finished her session. It was booked weeks ago. She should be allowed to stay. She can stay, can't she, Leo?'

Leo contemplated Harrie's worried face. 'Aye, I'd prefer not to turn a valued customer away. I'd rather she stayed.'

Mahuika's mouth puckered in disapproval, but she remained silent.

As Tu talked on, Aria inched almost imperceptibly closer to Friday. At one point she set her hand on the ground, and Friday's heart thrilled as Aria's little finger extended to touch the side of her hand. From the corner of her eye she caught the glorious woman's gaze; Aria winked and Friday ducked her head, hiding behind her hair, grinning with delight.

Tu ended his lecture twenty minutes later by opening the trio of pots. One contained ink made from burnt moth larvae used specifically for moko on the body, another held a very black and therefore highly prized ink for the face, prepared from the soot of the fallen kauri tree, and the third contained bird oil infused with a herbal mulch to treat infected scabs and skin lesions. Friday found it fascinating. She stood up and asked, 'How much do you charge for one of your tattoos?'

'Money?' Tu said in a tone just disdainful enough to be noticeable. 'I do not charge money. For the privilege of receiving my services I am regularly gifted with dog skin and feather cloaks, huia feathers, fine food, weapons, jade, whalebone, beautiful walking sticks, horses. Guns.' This last brought forth mumbles of approval from the audience. 'Do you have guns, white girl?'

'Not on me, no,' Friday replied sarcastically. White girl? She hadn't made a song and dance about him being a brown man.

Mahuika interrupted yet again. 'My husband would not tattoo you, anyway. Ta moko is not for whores, and especially not Pakeha whores.'

Friday thought, well, fuck you, you rude bitch. She wasn't putting up with this, not even to be near Aria. And bugger the rest of her tattoo session for today — she had to leave before she belted someone.

She said, 'Sorry, Harrie, I'll see you next time,' stepped around everyone sitting on the floor and left.

She was almost out onto George Street when she heard, 'Friday, wait!'

She turned to see Aria running down the alleyway, her skirts hitched to her knees revealing shapely calves above button boots, and her long hair flying behind her like a black silk banner.

'I am sorry,' she said. 'I apologise for my mother. And my father. May I please see you again?'

Friday's anger dissolved instantly and a lovely warm feeling spread out from her belly. 'Hell, yes. Better not tell your ma, though. What a cow, if you don't mind me saying so.' A cow? She was razor-tongued bloody old tarleather.

'Of course I will not tell her. Or Paikea. He is my guard.'

'Your guard? What do you need a guard for?'

Aria looked irritated. 'I will tell you another time. Shall I come to you? Where do you live?'

'At the Siren's Arms Hotel, on Harrington Street. It's only round the corner from here. When can you come?'

'I will send a message,' Aria said. 'I must go back.' And she kissed Friday on the corner of her mouth and trotted back along the alleyway, just as Mahuika appeared in Leo's doorway, looking thunderous.

Friday waved gaily at her and walked off along George Street, swinging her arms jauntily and grinning her head off.

Mahuika gripped her daughter's arm. 'What were you saying to that red-headed whore?'

Aria glared at her. 'Goodbye. I was saying goodbye, Mother. You did not have to be so rude to her.'

'Clearly I did. You are forbidden to stray, especially not with some common Pakeha prostitute.'

'Yes. I am sorry.' Aria hung her head. 'You are right. I was only saying goodbye.'

Mahuika loosened the pressure on Aria's arm. 'Good. I am glad you are able to see sense. The girlish freedoms you once enjoyed are behind you. You have responsibilities. You will behave, do you understand?'

'Yes, Mother.'

\* \* \*

That evening, as Harrie sat on the sofa folding washing Abigail had brought in, Nora appeared and said, 'Dr Downey is downstairs asking to see you.'

Harrie sat very still, a pillowslip suspended between her hands. 'Tell him to go away. Tell him I don't want to talk to him.'

'Is that what you really want?' Nora asked.

She wasn't sure what had driven Harrie to squander her virginity on a virtual stranger, but knowing how she felt about James Downey, Nora was fairly confident that something he'd done had been behind it. And as James Downey was a man, she assumed he'd been with a woman. An infidelity was just the sort of thing to push Harrie over the edge in her current delicate mental state. But men were like that. For Harrie to have any sort of future with James, she would have to put it behind her.

'Yes. It is,' Harrie said. She dropped the pillowslip and hurried off towards the attic stairs.

'I'll tell him, then. If you're sure,' Nora said to an empty room.

'God, it's hot this morning.' Sarah fanned her face with one hand and kept a firm grip on Clifford's lead with the other. 'Was it this warm last October?'

'For a few days, it was. Spring's bloody unpredictable here, isn't it? I like it, though. Keeps you on your toes.' In accordance with the warmer weather, Friday was wearing one of her low-cut summer dresses in a startling indigo blue.

Everywhere on the street women had ventured out with nothing more than lightweight shawls over their gowns, and men's hair stuck sweatily to their heads beneath their hats. The heat also had the unfortunate effect of increasing the stink from the open drains and piles of ordure in the streets, attracting growing numbers of flies — annoying harbingers of the infestation that would arrive with summer proper.

'Well, if it's going to be this hot, maybe I won't buy wool after all,' Sarah said. 'Maybe I'll buy all cotton. What do you think?'

'Don't ask me. I don't know the first thing about fabric.'

'No, but you know what colours look nice.'

'Not according to Mrs H, I don't.' Friday laughed. 'She reckons my frocks frighten the horses.'

Sarah laughed as well because it was true — Friday's dresses were quite loud, particularly her summer ones. But they suited her character, and the colours did in fact always somehow complement her fair skin. 'Pity Harrie couldn't come. How's she getting on with Leo?'

'He says she's got a great eye. She has, too. She's doing a lovely job of my phoenix.'

Sarah stepped around a boy sitting on the footway selling bunches of parsley. 'Clifford, stop that! Obviously she's not tattooing you today.'

'Leo's invited some uppity Maori chief to teach him and Harrie how to tattoo the way the New Zealanders do it, him and his high and mighty bloody shrew of a wife. I think they're there this morning.'

Sarah looked sideways at Friday. Though she'd just made a rude comment, she didn't sound irritated. In fact she was in an altogether excellent mood. Something was up. She opened her reticule and took out a piece of paper. 'This is how much fabric Harrie said I should get for each dress.'

'Is she sewing them, or Nora Barrett?'

'Well, I'm paying Nora. I just assumed Harrie doesn't have the time to sew for us these days, though I bet she would if I asked.'

'Time? It's her wits I'd be worried about. You might end up with a dress with four sleeves.'

'Meaning?'

'I was watching her the other day. We were listening to that Maori cove talk about tattooing, and Harrie went into this sort of … trance. And it wasn't even boring, it was more like she couldn't scrape up the energy to stay in the same realm as the rest of us, so she just let go and slid off into another one.'

Sarah swallowed. That was the most frightening thing anyone had said yet about the state of Harrie's mind. 'Has Leo noticed anything?'

'Hell, yes. He's really worried.'

'Is it the abortion, do you think?'

'I think it's everything bad that's happened since we got here,' Friday said. 'I think it's all piling up in her head. Poor love.'

Outside the draper's, Sarah stopped. 'Should we go and talk to James? I mean, he is a doctor. He should be able to tell us what we can do to help.'

'He's half the reason Harrie's unhinged, him and bloody Rowie Harris.'

'But do you really think what Rowie said was true?' Sarah gave Clifford's leash a good yank as she lunged at a passing child. 'Because I'm not so sure it is. I know I didn't like James to start with, but when he came to stay with me while Adam was away, I changed my mind. He's a decent man, Friday. I don't think he did sleep with her.'

Friday made a vulgar noise, startling Clifford.

'Oh, you think all men are bastards, because of what you do,' Sarah said.

'They are.'

'They are not.'

'You're singing a different tune these days.'

'Well, you like Matthew Cutler, don't you?'

'I suppose,' Friday admitted.

'And Adam? And Leo? And Jack at the pub?'

'Most of the time.'

'There you go. James loves Harrie, he really does. I know he does. And he's a good man.'

Friday stood aside to let a pair of matrons into the shop. 'So why won't he help her?'

'You know why. She won't let him.'

There didn't seem to be anything to add to that, so Sarah tied Clifford to a post and they went inside. The shop was long, its dim interior lit with wall lamps illuminating an extensive range — for Sydney — of fabrics stacked on shelves along one wall. There was bolt after bolt of crepe, camlet, calico, gingham, linen, lawn, chintz, muslin, striped cotton, velvet, silk (plain and figured), satin, taffeta, damask, superfine, bombasine, merinoe, kerseymere, flannel, stuff, drab, diaper, blue jean, moleskin, canvas, fustian, duck, drill, and great rolls of silk mosquito gauze (plain and coloured). On the opposite wall deep shelves displayed crepe and silk waistcoats, Norwich and Thibet shawls, straw and fabric bonnets, men's beaver hats and dress shirts, pelerines, stays, house caps (plain and lace), parasols, work trousers and jackets, and a range of readymade children's and infants' wear.

A deep counter ran across the back of the shop for cutting and measuring, and in the centre were arranged tall glass cabinets containing sewing tools, and tables displaying box after box of sewing cottons and silks, edgings, ribbons, lace, tassels and other notions, silk and cloth handkerchiefs, kid and silk gloves, lace and men's collars, buttons, steel and whalebone busks, sheet willow and bonnet wire, split straw, silk flowers, hatpins, men's and women's hosiery, and scarves and veils. Milling around the tables were at least a dozen women, clucking among themselves and picking over the goods like chickens in a yard.

'God, where do I start?' Sarah said.

She wandered towards the more lightweight fabrics — the muslins, cottons, ginghams, calicoes and chintzes — and ran her hand over various bolts.

'Do you want plain or patterned?' Friday asked.

'Oh, plain, probably.'

'Don't be so boring.' Friday indicated a Turkey red floral calico. 'What about this?'

'It's a bit bright.'

'It is not. This, then. The China blue looks really good against your skin. And so does that red. Don't be such a lily liver. Honestly, one day you'll disappear comp—'

Sarah glanced over her shoulder to see what had caused Friday to stop talking — a very rare occurrence. Approaching was an extremely beautiful, big, brown-skinned girl wearing a smart black and silver-striped dress. Her chin was tattooed and she wore a comb of some sort in her hair.

The girl touched Friday's hand. Sarah thought Friday looked like she might faint.

'Mother is up at the counter,' the girl said in a rush. 'Tomorrow morning at your room. I will try to be there by ten.' Then she turned on her heel and hurried back towards the rear of the shop, leaving Friday staring after her.

'We have to go,' Friday blurted, a spot of red blooming on each cheek. 'But we can come back. Is that all right?'

'Why?' Sarah asked. 'Who was that?'

'Um.' Friday panicked. What was she going to tell Sarah? 'Come outside, just for ten minutes? Please?'

'Only if you tell me what's going on,' Sarah grumbled, following Friday out onto George Street.

They collected Clifford and walked fifty yards up the road to lean against the Barracks wall, keeping an eye on the draper's shop so Friday could see when Aria and Mahuika came out.

'Well?' Sarah prompted.

Friday sighed. Her palms were sweaty, and not just because it was hot. 'Her name's Aria. I met her the other day. Her father's the one visiting Leo.'

Sarah said, 'She's very beautiful.'

Clifford growled at a woman walking past. Friday said nothing.

'You fancy her, don't you?' Sarah asked.

'No!' Friday's face heated up again and her skin prickled uncomfortably.

'It's a waste of time lying,' Sarah said. 'I pretty well worked it out a while ago.'

Friday opened her mouth to protest further, but why bother? Sarah knew — she could see it in her eyes. 'God. How did you know?'

Sarah shrugged. 'I'm not entirely sure. I don't know the first thing about, well, girls who like girls. It's just that you've never had anyone special. Anyone at all. But you've got a big heart, so I assumed it was because you couldn't, not because you didn't want someone. You could have had plenty of men as proper lovers, but you never have, so I suppose I eventually decided you must prefer women. And I did get the impression that you fancied Serafina.'

Her eyes burning, Friday struggled to swallow around the lump in her throat. 'And you're not ... angry?' From the corner of her eye she noted Mahuika and Aria emerge from the draper's and walk off in the opposite direction.

'Angry? Why would I be angry?'

'Because I'm not normal,' Friday said. 'Because it's wrong. Because I'm a tribade.' Oh, her throat ached now.

Sarah took her hand. 'You can call yourself what you like, but to me you're just Friday. I don't care who you fancy.'

As Friday wiped tears off her cheeks with the back of her hand, Sarah gave her a hug. Jealous, Clifford squeezed between them and sat on Sarah's feet.

Friday shoved her off. 'Does Harrie know?'

'She's never mentioned it, but I doubt it. You know how naive she is.'

'She'll be so shocked. Or disgusted.' Friday could just imagine Harrie's face when she found out.

'Oh, she will not,' Sarah said. 'She loves you.'

Friday thought about that for a moment. It was nice knowing you were loved. 'She does, doesn't she? She loves you, too.'

'Yes, I know. She was much nicer to me when we first met in Newgate than you were.'

'Well, you were pretty awful.'

'That's true,' Sarah agreed.

'She's held us together, hasn't she? All of us, especially poor Rachel.'

'Do you think that's why she believes Rachel's still here? Because she loved her so much and can't bear to let her go?'

'Christ knows,' Friday said.

'Because I loved Rachel, too,' Sarah said, 'and I've never seen her.'

So did I, Friday thought, and I can't make up my mind whether she's here or not. 'God, poor Harrie. What's she going to be like when she hears about what else Serafina saw?'

'If it's actually happened. It was only a prediction,' Sarah reminded her.

'You just don't want it to be true,' Friday said.

'Of course I bloody well don't. Do you?'

'Hell, no.'

They stood there for several moments in unhappy contemplation.

At last Sarah asked, 'So why did we have to rush out of the draper's?'

'Because Aria's mother was in there. She's taken against me. If she sees me, Aria won't have a hope in hell of sneaking away and coming to visit me tomorrow. But I saw them come out a few minutes ago.'

'Well, you be careful. Those people eat their enemies, you know.'

'Do they?' Friday's stomach clenched slightly. 'Jesus.'

'That's what I've heard.'

'I wouldn't put it past that bloody mother.'

'Do you think we can go back in now? I might get the Turkey

red after all,' Sarah said, flinching as Clifford lifted her leg on the hem of Friday's skirt.

'And the China blue,' Friday said. 'What's the matter? Ah, you little shite!'

With a deep, shuddering groan, Adam gave one final thrust then slowly subsided onto Sarah's slender white back. He moved his hands from her rounded hips and, the muscles of his arms quivering, settled them on either side of her on the mattress to avoid squashing her, and rubbed his face against her tousled sable hair.

'My thighs are going to give way,' she murmured.

'So are mine. They feel like jelly.'

Sarah giggled as he rolled over, taking her with him to fit neatly against his sweat-dampened chest and belly.

'As always, that was exceptional,' he said. 'You're enough to give a man a heart attack, Mrs Green.'

'Oh, don't be stupid, you're as healthy as a horse,' Sarah said.

And he was — healthy, fit, handsome, decent, prosperous (these days), and devoted to her. Sometimes — frequently, in fact — she was awed by her good fortune. True, she was still a prisoner of His Majesty and serving a seven-year sentence, but what did that matter? She'd married her master, and what a master he'd turned out to be.

'Yes, well, right now this horse wouldn't be out of place at the knackers'. It's too hot for sexual acrobatics.'

Smiling, Sarah turned over to face him. 'We didn't have to do it twice.'

'I felt we did, actually.'

Sarah laughed and poked him in the chest. 'That'll teach you.' She snuggled into him, sniffing the faint scent of the sandalwood and lime cologne he always wore. 'Friday told me something this morning. It's a secret. At least, I think it is, though she didn't actually tell me not to tell anyone else. But I'm not sure you count anyway.'

'Thank you very much. Anyway, I bet I do.'

'Oh, you won't tell anyone. She's finally met someone.'

'Well, it's about time. Anyone I know?'

'I wouldn't think so.' Sarah paused. 'Her name's Aria.' Beside her she felt Adam twitch in surprise.

'*Her* name?'

'Er, yes.'

'A girl?'

'Well, obviously.'

'That's interesting.'

'Is it?'

'Well, now that I think about it,' Adam said, 'I'm possibly not as surprised as I should be.'

'Aren't you?'

'She's never had a man friend, has she? Well, not that I'm aware of. Are you surprised?'

Sarah said, 'I did rather think she might be that way inclined. But, you know, it just never really seemed to matter, one way or the other.'

Adam ran his thumb across the curved, silver scar on Sarah's cheek, then stroked and smoothed her hair as though she were a cat. 'I don't suppose it does, as long as she doesn't advertise the fact. I do wonder, though, how she manages to do her job. I mean, all those men.'

'She hates it, you know,' Sarah said. 'Well, when I say she hates it, I know she doesn't get any pleasure from it, and some of her customers she can't stand. You should hear what she says about them. A few she tolerates, though, a couple of her regulars.'

'Then why does she do it?'

'Money. She makes more in a week than we do some months in the shop.'

'Not when we're on the flash, though, I bet.'

'No, maybe not then.'

But they'd been keeping very much on the right side of the law since Adam returned from Port Macquarie. Sarah, however, missed the jewellery rackets, and the thrill of living so dangerously, and she certainly missed the challenge of breaking into houses.

'So what's this girl like, do you know?'

'She's a New Zealander. A native girl. I saw her this morning. She's very beautiful, quite exotic, and even taller than Friday. You should have seen them, Adam: together they look like a pair of Amazons. And Friday's face when Aria was talking to her — she looks like she's bewitched already.'

'And she lives here in Sydney?'

'No, she doesn't.' Sarah was quiet for several seconds. 'And I think that's going to be a problem.'

# Chapter Nine

Grateful that she didn't have to start work until one o'clock, Friday rose uncharacteristically early on Saturday morning, thanks to a clear head from limiting her drinks the previous evening, and got stuck into cleaning up her piggy room. She collected all the dirty shifts, stockings and towels from the floor and sent them down to the laundry, put away everything else vaguely cleanish, returned her hats to their boxes, changed the bed linen, tidied all the cosmetics scattered across the dressing table and wiped the powdery surface. She also returned half a dozen dirty tea cups and a reeking bowl filled with pipe ash to the kitchen, cleared out a sackful of empty gin bottles from under the bed (and the top of the clothes press, the windowsill and behind the chest of drawers), opened the window, and made a quick trip down to the flowerseller on George Street for bunches of violets and sweetpeas to sweeten the air.

At a quarter to nine Jack brought up the tin bath, followed by Ivy from the laundry, labouring under the weight of the first of a dozen buckets of steaming hot water. When the bath was six inches deep, Friday stripped off, stepped in and sat down, sighing as the luxuriously hot water rose to her waist. Normally when she had her weekly bath she lounged around in it, drinking gin and smoking her pipe until the temperature of the water became unpleasant and she was forced to get out, but today she lathered herself with a bar of Mrs H's fancy soap immediately. She washed everywhere but her hair, which wouldn't dry in time and wasn't particularly dirty anyway. Once out and wrapped in a towel, she yanked on the bell-pull to summon Ivy to empty the bath, and sat down at her dressing table.

Staring at herself in the mirror she felt jittery with nerves. Should she put on powder and kohl and lip rouge? Or, being a New Zealander, would Aria not find that sort of thing pretty?

*Shite!* Food! After Mahuika's snide comments the other day, she didn't want to risk insulting Aria by not offering her anything to eat or drink.

Friday ran out of her room into the corridor, her towel flapping, straight into a startled Ivy. 'Quick, go down to the kitchen and ask Jenny to bring up some food on a tray. At exactly a quarter past ten. And a pot of tea. For my visitor.'

'What sort of food?'

'I don't know. Cakes? Have we got any cakes?'

Ivy's long, plain face got even longer as she frowned with concentration. 'Cook did some shortbread yesterday. And a nice madeira cake for Mrs H.'

'That'll do.'

'Mrs H'll go mad if you pinch her madeira cake.'

'Just ask Cook, Ivy, *please*? Tell her Mrs H said I could have it.'

And because Friday had not so long ago saved her from working for a particularly unpleasant master, and therefore she now regarded her with something close to reverence, Ivy nodded and trotted off.

'And don't forget to come back for the bath water!' Friday called after her as she dodged back into her room.

No, she wouldn't wear any make-up. Well, perhaps just the tiniest bit of kohl around her eyes, except her hands were shaking, and there was only one thing that would fix that. She opened a drawer, lifted out a bottle of gin and took a giant swig, closing her eyes briefly as the alcohol burnt its way down her throat. A moment later she felt its familiar, calming warmth spread through her chest and begin to seep into her blood. That was better. She rummaged through the drawer into which she'd dumped her cosmetics, found the kohl and a tiny brush, and expertly applied a thin line around each eye.

Now, what to wear? Something smart? Aria wore lovely dresses. Perhaps one of the gowns Mrs H had commissioned for her when she'd decided Friday didn't look classy enough? She opened her clothes press and inspected them. They were actually very nice, but the problem was they weren't really 'her'. Too conservative, too sober — *too* classy, really. What was the point to pretending she was something she wasn't?

Instead she chose an emerald-green dress cut quite low in the bodice and very fitted at the waist to show off her curves, and with only a hint of puff about the shoulder. She slipped it on over her head and closed the buttons at the side with the usual amount of difficulty, which was why she preferred skirt and bodice ensembles. The fact that she had to breathe in sharply while manoeuvring the buttons made it even harder — perhaps she'd been eating too many potatoes. She yanked her shift down under the dress so the lace wouldn't show beneath the bodice, and slipped her feet into her favourite sturdy black lace-up boots. No, they weren't right, not for indoors. She looked like she was off to work in the market gardens at Parramatta. She kicked them off again, threw them into the back of the press, and shut the door. She had satin slippers for work, but they were silly things and didn't suit her at all. Bare feet would do.

Ivy finally arrived, a bucket in each hand, to empty the bath. Friday looked at the little carriage clock on her nightstand — ten minutes to ten!

'Where have you been?'

'Organising the food, like you said.'

Panicking, Friday grabbed a bucket from her, filled it with cooling bath water and emptied it out the window.

'Jack'll be cross, water all over his yard,' Ivy said, but she was giggling all the same.

'Too bad. Come on, hurry up and help me. She'll be here in a minute.'

'Who?'

'My visitor!' God, Friday thought, Ivy was sweet but sometimes she could be very slow off the mark. Easily amused, though.

At last the bath was empty and Ivy dragged it, with the buckets rattling around inside it, down the corridor.

Friday looked at the clock again. Five past ten. She checked her hair in the mirror, wondered whether she should put it up, decided to leave it down, put her best gold earrings through the holes in her ears, took another large swallow of gin, and crunched some breath pastilles.

Ten fifteen. She sat on the bed, telling herself that if she stayed perfectly still for the next ten minutes, Aria would come.

Ten twenty-five. Friday's neck ached, the disappointment in her belly burnt like bile and her eyes prickled with unshed tears. She wasn't coming.

Someone knocked on the door. Friday flew across the room and opened it.

'I am so sorry I am late,' Aria said. 'It was very difficult for me to get away, and then the man downstairs, Jack? He talked to me for such a long time.'

Friday grinned hugely, thinking she'd give Jack a good kick up the arse the next time she saw him. Randy bugger. 'It's lovely to see you. I'm so pleased you came.'

Aria grinned back. 'So am I.'

Friday ushered her in and closed the door, said, 'Come in, sit anywhere you like,' then winced to herself because there was only one chair, in front of the dressing table. Aria sat on it.

Friday returned to her spot on the bed, then had to get up again immediately because someone else was at the door — Jenny from the kitchen with the food. Friday thanked her, took the tray and set it on the dressing table, inviting Aria to help herself.

'Did you arrange that just for me?' Aria asked.

Already abuzz with nerves, now Friday felt embarrassed. Had she done something wrong? 'Er, well sort of.'

'Because of the other day, at Mr Dundas's?'

Yes or no — which was the right answer? 'Yes.'

Aria burst into her earthy laugh. 'My mother can be an absolute bloody bitch sometimes. She did not have to make such a to-do.'

Friday knew she must have looked surprised because Aria laughed even harder and said, 'Your face.'

'It's just that your English is so proper,' Friday said. 'Far nicer than mine. It sounds funny to hear you swear.'

'The missionaries teach us formal English, everyone else teaches us the swear words. I find they are very satisfying to say.'

'I think so myself. And you don't mind the missionaries?'

Aria shrugged. 'They have been with us since just after I was born. Reverend Marsden's people. We have learnt new ways to farm and how to write our language, but now that Henry Williams is curing our souls we are expected to free our slaves and forsake our old gods. Ha! But Christmas is a good festival. I like the story of baby Jesus in the manger.'

'I like Christmas, too. We give presents. Do you?'

'No.'

'Oh. Would you like tea?'

'Yes, please.'

Friday poured, wondering whether she could sneak a few slugs of gin into hers without Aria noticing. She doubted it, and if she did it openly, Aria would think she was a drunk. 'Your mother doesn't like me, does she?'

'No,' Aria replied bluntly. 'My tribe is Nga Puhi. Since the age of seven I have been betrothed to a rangatira — a chief —'

'Seven! Christ almighty!'

Aria shrugged again. 'It is a union of political advantage. It is just the way of things. His name is Te Paenga and he is from the neighbouring tribe of Ngati Wai.' She smiled. 'As I believe you have noticed, I prefer to seek my physical pleasure with women, and I have, but now that the date of my marriage draws closer, my mother believes I should desist.'

Friday nearly dropped her cup. 'She *knows*?'

'Everyone does. It is not such an unusual thing.'

'And you're not …? No one cares?' Friday couldn't believe it.

'Not particularly. Except for the missionaries. The missionaries think it is evil and depraved. But I do not care what *they* think.'

'And your mother's annoyed because you fancy me?' Friday asked, then nearly died from embarrassment, because what if she'd misread the signs and Aria *didn't* fancy her? What if she only wanted a bit of company?

Aria looked amused. 'Do not worry. I do desire you. A lot. And yes, that is why she is annoyed, and because you are a Pakeha whore. My mother thinks you are the lowest of the low.'

Friday sniffed. 'Well, I'm not that keen on her, either. What *does* Pakeha mean? Is it an insult?'

'It can be. It comes from kehakeha, which means fair, but keha also means stink. And sometimes while people do stink.'

'Oh.' Friday couldn't really argue with that. 'When are you supposed to be getting married?'

'In August of next year,' Aria said gloomily.

'Don't you like him?'

'No. He is forty years old, he is arrogant and cruel, he has ugly feet, and he is far too free with his patero.'

Friday raised a questioning eyebrow.

Aria leant to one side and made a farting noise. Friday burst into giggles, noticed that Aria didn't seem amused, and made a mental note not to let any go in front of her.

'And he is a *man*, Friday. I do not want to have sex with a man for the rest of my life.'

'Neither do I,' Friday agreed wholeheartedly. She eyed Aria, in her fine dress with her glorious hair falling free and her lovely brown skin and full lips, and wanted desperately to jump on her right now, but that would just be crass. A little decorum was probably in order. 'What have you been doing for the last few days?'

'We did not find the graves we were looking for at Parramatta. My father thought they could be located within St John's cemetery, but they were not. Neither were they at Rangihou. It is very upsetting, to not know where the remains of one's relatives are lying, especially in foreign soil. I hope they are found one day.'

Friday asked, 'Honestly, how can you lose thirteen graves?' In London, perhaps, where the dead were buried stacked on top of one another in ancient and overcrowded churchyards, but not in New South Wales, where there was plenty of room to bury folk.

'Not thirteen. Only four died here. The rest passed after they returned, ill, to Aotearoa.'

'Not a good advertisement for the seminary, is it?'

Aria shook her head. 'It is closed now.'

'I'm sorry. That doesn't sound like it would have been much fun for you, poking around out at St John's.' Friday wondered if they'd encountered Rachel's grave. She was buried out there.

'It was not. But my father successfully concluded his business concerning the export of our tribe's flax and potatoes, and he thinks he has found a new buyer for our flour as well.'

'And the other things? You said there was some private business as well.'

Aria hesitated, then set her cup and saucer on the dressing table. 'Can you keep a secret?'

Not really. 'Yes.'

'We are also looking for information regarding my mother's brother, Whiro. Or, I should say, his remains. He was a fierce warrior of much renown and a fine man, and when he died ten years ago his head was preserved, a custom known as pakipaki mahunga. Normally, this is done so that a family may honour an ancestor's memory and be comforted by his presence.'

Friday knew her mouth must be hanging open, and that Aria was probably mistaking her expression for one of disgust. It wasn't, though; it was one of ominously dawning comprehension. This all sounded very familiar.

Aria explained, 'The preserved heads are known as upoko tuhi. To us, these are objects of great elegance, beauty and value.'

Friday nodded. 'I know what upoko tuhi are.'

'Last year the upoko tuhi of Whiro was stolen. It was taken by a Pakeha visiting the Bay of Islands. He was offering fistfuls of money, asking where he might purchase upoko tuhi, but we, Nga Puhi, do not trade in that currency any longer. We have not, since Pomare died in 1826, then Hongi Hika two years after. *They* were the ones bringing shame on all Nga Puhi, raiding the entire countryside and taking many lives, slaves and heads,' Aria said bitterly. She hesitated, then added, her voice heavy with sarcasm, 'At least, my father *says* the trade has ended. I do not know if I believe him. Sometimes I think he is as contemptible as they were.'

'How do you know it was this cove who took your uncle's head?'

'My foolish mother boasted of its supreme quality, but would not show it to him. The Pakeha paid her slave to take it from its resting place, and that was the last we saw of both him and the upoko tuhi of Whiro.'

Friday winced. 'I bet the servant got in trouble.'

'Slave. She is dead,' Aria said flatly.

'Did he have a name, this cove?'

'He called himself Te Kapura. Cheeky swine.'

'What does that mean?'

'It means "the fire".'

Fire. Furnace? Furniss? Friday's heart lurched. 'Was he middle-aged, and really nasty with horrible broken brown teeth?'

Aria gave her a sharp look. 'Yes. Do you know him?'

'I might. If it's who I think it is, his name's Amos Furniss. Well, it was.'

'We have traced him back here to Sydney. We have been told he is in the employ of a very powerful woman. Do you know of her?'

Friday's mouth suddenly went dry. Fucking hell. Could this be a way to finally rid themselves of Bella? 'I do, but we're hardly on good terms. She's a really vicious piece of work. Did you know Amos Furniss is dead?'

'Is he?' Aria's voice was as cold and as uncaring as a steel blade. 'What happened?'

'He was stabbed to death a couple of months ago. And I know that his boss, Bella Shand, *was* arranging to have upoko tuhi stolen from New Zealand,' Friday said, putting the boot in for all she was worth. 'For collectors, I think. And I knew someone who stole four of them from *her*. Jared Gellar. She had him killed. I think Furniss did the deed.'

'Do you have evidence implicating the Shand woman?' Aria's brow furrowed. 'And how do you know such people?'

'It's a long story. It sort of overlapped with something else. I'll tell you one day, I promise. Bella's a convict. She came out on the same ship as we did. But, no, we —' Friday hesitated, realising it might not be a good idea to drag Sarah and Harrie into this. 'I can't prove she was involved. I heard something close to a confession, but that was from Jared Gellar and he's dead and buried. What would your father do if he found out it was definitely Bella behind the theft?'

'It is not what my father would do; it is my mother. And *she* would kill Bella. Or perhaps I would do it myself.'

'Really?' Christ.

'My uncle was a great man. The theft is a gross insult to our family.'

'Would it be enough to tell them what I've told you?'

Aria sighed. 'I think it is too much hearsay.'

'Will nothing I've said help?' Bugger. Friday's vision of nailing Bella was slipping away.

'Perhaps. We will wait. The evidence we need will appear. My family will keep looking. At least now, thanks to you, we have a direction in which to look.'

Friday couldn't stand it — she was gasping. She opened the drawer in the nightstand by her bed and took out a hip flask of gin. 'Do you fancy a drink?'

'No, thank you. I do not drink alcohol.'

'Not at all?'

'No.'

'Oh. Do you mind if I do?'

Aria gave a 'go ahead' gesture. Friday half filled her cup with gin and took an uncharacteristically decorous sip. 'What else have you been doing, apart from shopping with your ma?'

'I have also been shopping with Father.'

'What for?'

'Guns.'

'For hunting and the like?'

'No, for war. Yesterday Father bought sixty new muskets and ordered another one hundred and ten.'

A sip of Friday's gin went down the wrong way and she coughed violently, spraying spit and alcohol across her skirts. Aria moved to sit beside her and firmly patted her back.

'Sorry,' Friday squeaked, blinking furiously and wiping her mouth. She coughed again and cleared her throat. 'I didn't know you were at war. Who with?'

'Other tribes.'

'But … why? Aren't you all the same folk?' It seemed bizarre to get so upset about the theft of some old dried head of a relative, but then happily go around blasting the shite out of your neighbours.

Aria gave her a faintly amused look, then glanced at the clock. 'I have enjoyed talking with you, Friday, but I cannot stay long. I would like to have sex now. Would you?'

*Christ*, yes!

Aria leant in and kissed her. Her blue-black lips were velvet-soft. Friday's belly did a slow flip.

Her nerves jangling, she blurted rudely, 'They're so smooth!'

'What else did you expect?' Aria asked. 'Among my people, dark lips like mine are considered beautiful. And while yours will pale and become thin and indistinct as you grow old, mine will remain defined, a reminder of the lush beauty of my youth.'

'They are beautiful,' Friday murmured, returning the kiss. 'You're beautiful.'

She slipped her hands behind Aria's neck, beneath her hair, to reach the buttons of her dress, and realised there were dozens of the bloody things. Aria turned to allow her better access. Forcing herself to open them one by one and not just tear at them, Friday finally slid the dress off Aria's wide, well-muscled shoulders, revealing, not a shift as expected, but perfect, flawless brown skin.

Aria turned to face her again, and shrugged the dress down to her waist. Her breasts were lovely, full and high and tipped with large nipples the colour of chocolate. Friday sank to the floor, unbuttoned her boots, and slipped them off her feet. She wore no stockings, either, though the lacy hem of a pair of drawers sat just below her knees.

Aria stood, letting the dress fall, and stepped out of it, snatching from Friday a quick, involuntary gasp. She was absolutely magnificent. Unable to stop staring at her, Friday fumbled at the buttons of her own gown, wriggled out of it, tore her shift off over her head, and stepped naked into Aria's embrace.

'You are very, very lovely yourself,' Aria whispered.

Friday gently pushed Aria onto the bed, then climbed on too, knelt over her and kissed her, her palms grazing the brown nipples. Aria moaned and ran her hand down Friday's belly and into her pubic hair. Friday felt close to exploding already, and didn't want to.

She wriggled down the bed and carefully parted the gap in Aria's drawers, breathing warmth onto the moistness between her legs. She felt Aria grip a fistful of her hair. Flicking out her tongue, she began to lick, exploring the sweet folds and crevasses, finding the spot that made Aria twitch and groan, setting up a rhythm Aria matched with counter-thrusts of her hips. Unwilling to wait — *unable* to wait — Friday pressed herself against Aria's leg, rubbing in time, feeling her own climax building. She held on until Aria cried out, her back arching off the bed, then let the pleasure burst and ripple through her.

A minute or so later, her head resting on Aria's thigh, she said when her breath had returned, 'Sorry. That was a bit greedy. I couldn't wait.'

'That is all right. Your elbow is on my hair.'

'Sorry.' Friday moved.

Aria sat up. 'That was extremely nice, thank you. You are very skilled.'

'I was a bit worried. You know, that girls might do things differently in New Zealand.'

Grinning, Aria said, 'No, it is more or less the same.' She cupped Friday's face with a hand and kissed her lingeringly. 'But perhaps we are a little different. Shall I show you?'

'Oh, yes please.'

At midday, Aria looked at the clock again and let out a squawk of alarm. 'Bugger! I must go. My mother will have everyone out looking for me by now!' She slid off the bed, scrambled into her drawers, and put on her boots. Stepping into her dress, she held her hair out of the way and asked, 'Will you close the buttons, please?'

While her fingers were busy, Friday said, 'When do you go back to New Zealand?'

'Tomorrow.'

Friday's heart felt squeezed and for a second she couldn't breathe, which was silly as she'd known Aria's visit to Sydney was only for a week or so. 'So soon?' she said.

'I know. I am sorry. You could come to New Zealand to visit me,' Aria said. 'Not to my home in the Bay of Islands, my mother would not allow that, but we could meet somewhere else.'

'I can't. I'm a convict.' Tears stung Friday's eyes. 'I can't leave Sydney.'

Aria turned and took Friday's hands. 'Then I will see you the next time my mother and father come here for business.'

'She's not going to let you come back, though, is she?' Friday said.

'But I want to see you again.'

'And I want to see you.'

'Then I will try, Friday. I will try as hard as I can.'

Aria glanced at the shingle above the shop door announcing in gold lettering *Adam and Sarah Green Fine Jewellery*, and touched her mother's arm.

'This is it,' she said in Maori.

'And they have the best prices?' Mahuika asked.

'And best quality,' Aria said, though she didn't know if that were true or not. Neither did she care. The expedition to buy jewellery was a ruse, but one she knew her mother wouldn't be able to resist, despite still being angry at her for disappearing this morning. She'd said she'd been bored and had gone for a walk in Hyde Park. Her mother hadn't believed her, but there was nothing to be done about it by the time she'd returned.

'Who recommended this jeweller to you?' Mahuika asked.

'A lady I met walking in the park. A very fine lady. You would have approved of her, Mother,' Aria said, getting in a dig at her mother's snobbery.

Mahuika scowled, but Aria could see she was tempted. No one, in fact, had recommended the shop — Friday had merely mentioned that her friend, Sarah, had been assigned here and had married the jeweller, Adam Green.

They went in. Behind the counter stood the girl whom Aria had seen in the draper's with Friday — Sarah, presumably. She was small (but almost all Pakeha women were), dark and quite attractive in a sleek sort of way, with clever eyes.

'Good morning, ladies. How may I help you?'

If she'd recognised her, Aria thought, she wasn't letting on. Perhaps Friday had told her Mahuika didn't like her. If so, that would be very useful.

'Good morning,' Mahuika said, switching to English. 'We would like to look at gold. Chains and earrings, I think.'

'And perhaps some bangles,' Aria said.

'Are you considering eighteen or twenty-two carat?'

'What do you recommend?' Aria asked.

'Eighteen carat is more durable than twenty-two. It's harder and won't scratch as badly. I'd recommend eighteen carat for a bangle and probably for a neck chain, particularly if you were considering wearing a pendant with it. Twenty-two carat is suitable for earrings, however.'

'Show us some bangles in eighteen carat, then,' Mahuika said, 'wide, not narrow. A selection of long chains also in eighteen carat, and some drop earrings in twenty-two carat. I do not like the short ones that sit close to the ear.'

'Certainly.' Sarah opened the hatch in the counter and unlocked a display cabinet containing bangles and bracelets. She removed a tray, relocked the cabinet and moved to the one containing chains.

'I will take that tray if you like,' Aria volunteered.

'Thank you,' Sarah said.

As Sarah handed it to her, Aria said under her breath, 'I have something for Friday.'

Sarah gave the smallest of nods and opened the next cabinet.

Soon there were five trays on the counter, and Mahuika, laden with gold, was busy admiring herself in the looking glass.

'Have you decided on a bangle, Aria?' she asked, apparently unable to tear her gaze from her own glittering reflection.

Aria made a pretence of dithering. 'I cannot make up my mind.' She slid a snake-quick hand into a pocket, passed Sarah a small, cloth-wrapped parcel, and mouthed, 'Christmas.' Sarah took it and popped it into a drawer.

Mahuika turned around. 'I wish to purchase these earrings, and these three chains.'

'And I would like this,' Aria said, indicating the first bangle she'd tried on.

As Mahuika counted out her money, Sarah found velvet-covered presentation boxes for the jewellery.

'Thank you,' Mahuika said, slipping the boxes into her reticule.

Aria caught Sarah's gaze and held it briefly. 'Yes, thank you very much.'

Friday was in a particularly foul mood, and her behaviour was only making Harrie's headache worse. She and Leo had been working all afternoon on Friday's phoenix, now half completed, and she'd complained the entire time about not being able to drink. Leo didn't allow alcohol during a session, and she'd grizzled and sworn and bitched since midday. It was now almost six o'clock and Harrie, close to tears from the exhaustion of bending over Friday's back and concentrating so hard, felt like slapping her, only she didn't have the energy. She wished Leo had started her on something smaller, but she would have been too nervous to practise on anyone else but Friday, who of course wanted an enormous tattoo.

The design began on Friday's shoulders and ended on one thigh. The bird's outstretched wings spread across Friday's back, the tip of the left wing touching her left shoulder blade, the head on her right shoulder blade, and the tip of the right wing extending beneath her right arm to brush her breast. The long, full feathers of the tail swept down the left side of her back, flicked out at her waist and curved across her right buttock, the longest tail feather ending at the top of the back of her thigh. Between the bird's head and left wing hovered Harrie's trademark bat. The entire outline had been completed, the individual feathers of the body and wings coloured red, green and blue, and now they were colouring the tail feathers orange and red. It would be stunning when it was finished — it was fabulous now — but today Harrie had had enough. Mostly of Friday.

'I think we'll call it a day,' Leo said, looking over Harrie's shoulder.

'Thank God,' Friday grumbled. 'I'm going to *die* if I don't get a fucking drink. It *is* my day off, you know.'

'You didn't have to lie here all afternoon bitching and moaning,' Leo said. 'You could quite easily have gone somewhere else and done that.'

'No, I couldn't. I had an appointment here. It's not *my* fault you've got a stupid rule about not drinking.'

The rule never bothered you before, Harrie thought. In fact, Friday usually loved being tattooed. She got so relaxed she might as well be drunk. 'What *is* the matter?' she asked as she applied salve to the freshly inked areas. 'You've been really horrible today.'

'*Nothing's* the matter.'

Harrie and Leo exchanged exasperated glances.

'Is it because your friend's gone back home?' Harrie said. Sarah had told her Friday had made a new friend, though also that she was worried Friday would be upset now that the girl had returned to New Zealand.

Sliding off the tattoo bench, Friday tugged down her shift and closed the waistband on her skirt. 'Who told you that?'

'Sarah.'

'What else did she say?'

'Nothing. Just that. Oh! I just realised,' Harrie said. 'Was it that girl, Aria? The one who came here?'

'Yes, it was,' Friday muttered. Ferreting around in her reticule for a hip flask of gin, she waved it at Leo. 'Can I drink *now*?'

'You can do what you like now Harrie's finished.'

'Friday?' Harrie persisted. 'Is that why you're upset?'

'It might be.' Friday took an enormous swig and let out a reverberating burp. 'Well, I'm off to the pub. Me and Molly are getting on the jar.'

'Good,' Leo said to her retreating back. 'And don't come back until you're in a better mood.'

In response, Friday slammed the door.

Harrie said, 'She didn't even say thank you.'

Leo shrugged. 'I'm glad to see the back of her. Foul-tempered witch.'

'It's really not like her to be so horrible. Honestly, I don't know what's wrong with her,' Harrie said as she went to fetch fresh cloths to clean her needles.

'I think I might,' Leo muttered. When Harrie returned he asked, 'How's the new lass working out at the Barretts'?'

'Good. Her name's Emma and she's nice and very efficient, though I think Hannah's trying her nerves a little. But Hannah tries everyone's nerves.'

'Assigned?'

'No, she immigrated here. She only arrived last month.'

'And Nora's managed to convince George the lass's pay's coming out of my purse, not hers?'

Harrie nodded. 'We had to tell Emma she's to pretend you're paying her once a week, but I don't think she cares as long as she gets her money. Mr Barrett keeps going on about what a clever deal Mrs Barrett did getting you to jemmy open your purse.' Harrie made an apologetic face. 'I'm very sorry, but he keeps saying you must be more stupid than you look.'

Leo laughed. '*I'm* stupid?'

\* \* \*

Friday and Molly had been in the Fortune of War since seven o'clock and were both swattled. Friday had already thrown up once when she went outside for a wee — not because she'd drunk herself ill, but due to the sheer amount of ale and gin sloshing around in her belly. It had all rushed up and out when she'd bent over to lift her skirts before she'd squatted. How bloody annoying, and what a waste of money. But she had plenty of it in a little cloth purse shoved down the front of her bodice, so she soon filled up again, this time on gin and brandy, never mind the ale. She should have remembered that ale never sat too well in her stomach.

The pub was small and crowded, with only one great table down the middle of the room, low stools and narrow ledges lining the two longest walls, and the serving counter at the far end. The windows were wide open in an attempt to let muggy, rain-tainted evening air into the stuffy interior. In a corner a trio of musicians jammed onto a tiny platform were bashing out tunes on a battered old military snare drum, a fiddle and a wooden flute. There was a severe shortage of seats, and for that reason Friday and Molly began the evening carrying their stools up to the counter so as not to lose them, but the drunker they got, the more complicated this became until eventually they ended up sitting on people's laps.

For the first time in the days since Aria had gone back to New Zealand, Friday felt the painful ache in her chest subside a little. She knew she'd been mean to Harrie and Leo this afternoon, but she couldn't help it. Every time she'd opened her mouth, no matter what she'd intended to say, something nasty had come out. If Leo had let her drink, it mightn't have been so bad, but he hadn't. Even the lovely needles, normally so soothing, hadn't helped.

God almighty, what was she going to do? Getting mashed out of her head tonight was one thing, but even she knew she couldn't stay drunk forever. Well, not this drunk. How was she going to live from day to day not knowing whether she'd ever see Aria again?

The smelly, grope-handed cove whose knee she was sitting on shouted in her ear to shift her arse — he had to go out the back to pump ship. Hoping he'd lose his way and drown in the cesspit, Friday waved Molly over and they both squeezed into his space on the bench. Having grown sick of the inconvenience of traipsing up and down to the counter, they'd both bought bottles of spirits — gin for Friday and brandy for Molly. The bottles were now half empty. Friday's face and mouth were growing numb, and she was fast reaching the point at which she knew she would switch from being an amiable drunk to a deeply unpleasant one.

And, frankly, she was quite looking forward to it. She could do with a bloody good fight.

Molly said, 'Christ, it's hot. I'm seeing double. Are you?'

'Dunno.' Friday closed one eye then opened it again. 'Nearly.'

'Maybe we should have had some supper.'

Friday sneered. 'What for? Just makes you take longer to get drunk.'

'True.' Molly took a long gulp from her bottle. 'You working tomorrow?'

'One till ten.'

'Least you'll get a lie in. I'm on at ten.'

'Mrs H'll bollocks you if you go to work mashed,' Friday said.

'Silly old bitch'll bollocks me anyway.'

Thinking she was about to fall backwards off the bench, Friday made a wild grab at the table. 'Shit! What for?'

'Leading you astray. 'Parantly it's *my* fault you drink too much.'

'Arse.'

'Zackly.'

A bleary-eyed woman sitting across the table leant in and said at the top of her fishwife's voice, 'Hey, you two are whores, aren't yis?'

Molly and Friday stared at her.

"Cos if you are, and I find out my Bill's been with either of yis, I'll scratch your bloody eyes out, I will!'

'Oh, I remember Bill,' Molly said. She turned to Friday. 'Isn't he the cove who reckons his wife's minge stinks like a boatload of fish swum up it and died, and that's why he has to pay to shag us?'

'That's right,' Friday replied. 'That's what he told me, anyway.'

'You bloody pair of sluts!' the woman screeched. 'I hope yis both get the pox and *die*!' And to the noisy delight of everyone else at the table, she grabbed a tankard of ale and threw it over Molly.

With her yellow-blonde hair plastered to her head, Molly shrieked, snatched up a pickle bowl and hurled it at the woman. Pickles went everywhere. The woman retaliated with a glass tumbler aimed at Friday, which missed and hit a man behind her.

Bloody excellent, Friday thought. She leapt to her feet, used the bench to step up onto the table, bent down and hauled the open-mouthed woman to her feet. The crowd roared. Friday dragged the woman along the table, knocking over tankards and bottles and tumblers, then upended her and tipped her onto the floor. A man whose hand Friday had stamped on grabbed her ankle and yanked, sending her crashing to the ground, but a second later she was up again, swinging wildly.

Cursing and wringing ale out of her hair, Molly slipped into the crowd.

Then Friday glimpsed Rowie Harris, lurking near the door. She let out a roar of rage and launched herself towards her, knocking folk in all directions, and managed to grab the back of Rowie's skirt as she tried to dart outside. Hauling her back in and dragging her round by her hair, she ducked as Rowie threw a punch. The blow glanced off the top of her head and she hit back, connecting solidly with Rowie's face. Rowie screeched and her fingernails became cat's claws and their hands were caught in each other's hair and they kicked and bit and Friday managed to bash Rowie's head against the doorjamb with a very satisfying crunch. Then Friday started to choke as someone hauled her backwards by her jacket collar, and she tried to hit out as, to her absolute fury, Rowie stumbled outside and escaped. Friday staggered, bounced off someone else, and used the momentum to throw another punch.

At the other end of the room the publican had come out from behind the counter, having already sent someone to fetch the police. He was sick and tired of drunks smashing up his premises. Forcing his way through the crowd, he shouted in Friday's face, 'You're banned! Get out!'

'And you're an arsehole!' she shot back. 'Get fucked!'

Reluctantly, the publican signalled his barman for help. Between them they could drag her to the door and throw her out, but while the serving counter was unattended God only knew how much he would lose in stolen alcohol.

Friday saw the barman coming — a cove with considerably more height and muscle than the publican — and turned to face him, teeth bared in a snarl, fists up. The crowd cheered her mettle, but also formed a solid wall barring her escape; they were thoroughly enjoying the spectacle, and didn't want it to end. She let loose a punch but the publican blocked it and struck the side of her head with an open hand, and while she was blinking away stars, the barman twisted her arm up behind her back and marched her towards the door. The crowd booed heartily, while the publican raced back to the counter to salvage his stock.

Friday's ear burnt and there was a terrible ringing noise in her head, and now she really was seeing double. Her arm hurt like hell and she was being shoved so violently her feet were barely touching the ground. Where was Molly? Shite, now the bloody police were here. Mrs H was going to kill her.

As a pair of constables hauled her down the steps, slippery now that the rain had started, she shouted over her shoulder, 'Molly! *Molly!*' A constable fumbled at her wrists with a set of manacles and she ducked her head and bit his hand.

But Molly was inside, knocking back a bottle of brandy she'd pinched from behind the counter. Friday would be all right. She'd probably be taken to the Harrington Street watch house, and let out tomorrow morning when she'd sobered up. Or not. Either way, she could look after herself.

Every morning after the brothel closed at one o'clock and the girls had gone, Elizabeth Hislop went around the house closing and locking the windows and doors. Last year someone had tried, unsuccessfully, fortunately, to break into the safe in her office, but she had noticed later that several items were missing from her desk: a lovely silver and ivory pen holder; the tiny silver mesh purse and smelling salts bottle that had fallen off her chatelaine; and a pink topaz, pearl and gold ring, which pinched, so she often took it off. She'd never discovered who'd been responsible, and hadn't decided on a more suitable location for the safe, either, so security in the house was important. The safe held a lot of money overnight, not to mention the bulk of her personal jewellery and some rather sensitive papers.

She was checking the double locks on the front door, and flinching at the muted rolls of thunder accompanying the rainstorm moving east out to sea, when she heard the most hideous caterwauling out on Argyle Street. Peering through the peephole, to her alarm she spied what appeared to be a bundle of wet rags flopping about on the wet road. Good Christ, had some poor soul been knocked down by a carriage?

She opened the door, stepped out, locked the door again behind her and crossed the street. Raising her lantern, she peered down at the sobbing figure on the ground.

Except it wasn't sobbing, it was laughing. And it was as full as a family po.

'Molly Bates! Get up, you drunken tart!'

Molly stopped laughing. 'Who's that? Oh, 's you, y'ol' bitch.'

'Where's Friday?' Elizabeth demanded, knowing full well Molly and Friday had gone out together earlier in the evening.

''S too hot,' Molly said, and retched, though nothing came up. She pushed her sopping hair off her face and started cackling again.

Elizabeth gave her a sharp nudge with the toe of her boot. 'Molly! Where is she? Where's Friday?'

'Dunno.' Molly struggled into a sitting position. 'Watch took her.'

Oh Christ, Elizabeth thought. 'What for?'

'Fightin'.'

'Which watch house?'

'Dunno.'

Elizabeth lost her temper. 'This is *your* fault, Molly Bates.'

Molly waved a dismissive hand and collapsed onto one elbow. 'Ah, fuck off. 'Tis not.'

'It is. I've had a bloody *gutsful* of you, you sneaky little bitch. I *knew* you'd get her in the shit.'

'Get fucked.'

'That's it! You're fired. Go on, piss off. You can come back and clear out your room tomorrow.'

The expression on Molly's face went from drunkenly amused to sly. 'Ya can't fire me. I'll tell the Sup ... Supertend of Convicts what you're doin'. I know a lot about you, y'know. More'n you think.'

Elizabeth itched to plant her boot into the side of Molly's stupid head. 'Do your best! See how you get on!'

'Ah, fuck off.' Molly heaved herself to her knees, then, after much arm-flailing, to her feet. ''S too hot. Goin' for a swim.'

'I hope you drown! And your language is atrocious!'

Seething with impotent anger, Elizabeth watched Molly, muttering to herself, weave off down Argyle Street towards the harbour. Poisonous, foul-mouthed she-devil. Then she went inside, sat in her office and poured herself a whisky. If Friday and Molly had been drinking locally, and they probably had, Friday would have been taken to either the Cumberland Street watch house, or the one on Harrington Street, just around the corner. She would go there soon, regardless of the late hour, and see if she could bribe the policeman on duty to release her. Not that it would do Friday any harm to spend a night in the coop — it fact it might even scare her enough to make reconsider her dreadful drinking habits. Elizabeth sighed. No, it wouldn't. She'd been telling Friday to cut down for ages, and it hadn't made a jot of difference. And Friday was well used to gaol cells — a night in one more wasn't likely to make much of an impression.

She was extremely fond of Friday. She reminded her so much of her own daughter, Amy, whom she'd borne in 1794 at the age of fifteen. Amy had been an inebriate just like Friday, and also like her father, Gilbert. Amy had started drinking young, stealing alcohol from the parlour of the brothel Elizabeth had operated near Covent Garden, and by the time Elizabeth had realised Amy was afflicted with the same curse as her father, it was too late. Gil had been useless, of course, drunk himself, or away at sea for years at a time.

She and Amy had fallen out and at sixteen Amy had gone to live with an awful man who'd beaten her senseless, but supplied her with as much gin as she could drink. By then Elizabeth couldn't help her at all, having been arrested and gaoled in 1811 for brothel-keeping. One night Amy had fought back, stabbed her lover and killed him. She was arrested, tried for murder in 1812, found guilty and hanged outside Newgate Gaol. Elizabeth had been inconsolable. Two weeks after that, utterly undone by grief, she'd been transported to New South Wales, never suspecting she'd one day commit a crime very similar to Amy's.

When she'd taken Friday on, sight unseen, as an assigned housegirl for the Siren's Arms, she'd had no idea she would find in her a living echo of the daughter she'd lost nearly twenty years earlier. They were very similar, Friday and Amy — both wild and headstrong, and both dedicated drunks. Elizabeth had hoped that this time she might succeed in saving someone she cared for very much from her own self-destructive behaviour. But, so far, she hadn't exactly excelled in her goal.

She sipped her whisky thoughtfully as she forced herself to calm down, then looked at the watch on her chatelaine. Twenty minutes to two. Not many folk would be out and about now. She thought a few moments longer, then opened the safe and transferred twenty pounds into a coin purse and put it in a pocket on the inside of her skirt. Reaching for a black and grey Thibet shawl, she draped it over her head and around her shoulders. It was a little unnecessary on such a muggy night, but the colour against her deep charcoal-grey dress was just right. She would merge into the darkness perfectly.

Outside the wind was still brisk, though the rain had stopped, and the half-moon flickered between scudding black storm clouds. It took her less than five minutes to walk to the bottom of Argyle Street then south along George towards King's Wharf. She was taking a small gamble regarding where Molly might have chosen to swim, if in fact she'd got that far, but she thought she was probably on the money. Campbell's Wharf was privately owned and locked at night, as were the wharves at the naval dockyard. She wouldn't have gone to any of the small harbour beaches — they were rocky and littered with rubbish. That only left King's Wharf accessible and within staggering distance.

She saw few others abroad; two of those were sprawled motionless on the ground, and the remainder were locked in violent embrace in shadowed corners. The shore, though, was by no means quiet. A faint racket drifted from the Black Rat Hotel nearby, and the creak of rigging and slap of the sea against the hulls of ships at anchor were clearly audible.

Minutes later, as she stepped onto the planks of King's Wharf, Elizabeth saw she'd been right. At the far end, near a ladder that descended into the sea, lay a small heap — of clothing, perhaps? Tuneless and disjointed singing drifted up to her on the wind. She picked up a discarded boathook and walked slowly out to the end of the wharf, her boot heels ringing hollowly on the planks. The singing stopped.

'Who's there?'

Elizabeth remained silent. She stirred the clothing with her foot: a skirt, stockings and a pair of boots. The silly bitch had gone in in her shift and bodice. Something rolled out of the skirt, glinting in the moonlight as it rattled across a plank. Picking it up, Elizabeth saw that it was a ring, with a pale stone surrounded by small pearls. Thieving cow. She put it in her pocket, leant over the edge of the wharf, and looked down. A pale face floating in the black water stared up at her.

Molly made a splashing dash for the ladder. Just as her hands gripped the rungs, Elizabeth reached down with the boathook, snagged the neck of the girl's bodice, and, leaning all her weight into it, thrust her out and under. Molly struggled briefly, her head thrashing from side to side beneath the water. Her straining hands, fingers outstretched, punctured the surface, but, too drunk to fight hard enough to save herself, she soon stopped. It was very quiet, and very easy.

Crouching now and looking out across the cove, Elizabeth kept her under for another ten or so minutes, just to make sure. There were about a dozen ships at harbour, each one with a single lamp alight on its main mast. They made a pretty sight, rolling on the long, low swell like giant fireflies. Eventually she gave the boathook a twist to tear the barb free, and watched as Molly's body floated face down, arms and legs wide, the yellow hair, grey in the moonlight, spread out around the head like seaweed.

Straightening up, her knees cracking like pistol shots, Elizabeth put the boathook back where she'd found it, wiped her hands on her skirt, and walked away.

\* \* \*

Nothing happened when she hammered on the Harrington Street watch-house door, so she did it again. Finally there were footsteps inside, and a yawning policeman in shirtsleeves opened it.

'Good morning,' Elizabeth said. 'Do you have a girl by the name of Friday Woolfe here?'

'We've got a girl. Don't know her name. She's insensible.'

'What's she done?'

'Drunk, disorderly, assault and biting a constable,' the policeman said, pointing irritably at his bandaged hand.

Elizabeth's heart sank. Drunk and disorderly *might* have seen Friday released in the morning when she'd sobered up, but not assault, and certainly not biting a policeman. Stupid, *stupid* girl. 'Are you alone?'

'Why?' the man asked suspiciously.

Bugger, Elizabeth thought. If he wasn't, that would be two bribes. 'May I see her?'

'Why?'

'I might know who she is.'

The policeman thought for a moment, then crossed his arms. Elizabeth opened her purse and gave him a crown, well over a day's pay. He stepped aside and let her in.

Friday was on her side on the filthy floor of the cell, snoring her head off. Her jacket was torn, a huge bruise was developing on her cheek, her knuckles were skinned and red, and there was vomit on the ground and matted into her rat's-nest hair. Elizabeth could smell her from outside the cell.

'Well? Do you recognise her?' the policeman demanded. 'She wouldn't give her name. Too busy cursing and screaming.'

'Would you be amenable to a bribe for releasing her? I'd make it worth your while.'

'Like hell. The bitch nearly bit my hand off. She can go up in front of the magistrate later today.'

Elizabeth's eyes narrowed. 'I'd make it *very* worth your while.'

'I don't give a shit.' The man raised his hand. 'If this goes poisonous, I'm a dead man. What use will money be to me then?'

'Then good luck trying to get her name out of her when she wakes up.' Elizabeth swept past him. 'And I do hope your hand gets better.'

When Friday dragged herself into consciousness some time after the sun rose, the first thing she did was vomit again, into the bucket this time, the pressure almost bursting her pounding head. Then she turned around, lifted her skirts and, hovering on violently quivering thighs, emptied her bowels into it. The smell was horrific and made her throw up again. She wiped her burning backside with the hem of her shift, stripped off, covered the bucket with the shift, put her skirt and jacket back on, and lay down again, shivering uncontrollably, as far from the bucket as she could get. Her belly hurt, her hands hurt, her arse hurt, her head hurt and she couldn't remember how she'd got there, but all that paled in comparison to the pain of knowing that Aria had gone. Nothing mattered any more. Nothing. If she had a pistol, she'd happily have blown her own brains out.

She heard footsteps, opened her eyes and saw a man's boots on the other side of the cell bars.

'God almighty, you stink.'

Friday said nothing.

'What's your name?'

'Friday Woolfe,' Friday mumbled.

'What? Speak up.'

'Friday Woolfe.'

'Ha! That was easy!' the constable said. 'You'll be up in front of the magistrate this afternoon, then you'll be sorry.'

I'm bloody sorry now, Friday thought. 'What did I do?'

'You bit my bloody hand, you savage bloody cow. And beat the daylights out of a couple of poor judies in the Fortune of War.'

'Will you send a message to Elizabeth Hislop on Argyle Street?' God, it was such an effort to talk. 'Tell her where I am? She'll pay you.'

'Like hell I will.'

Prick, Friday thought, but her heart wasn't in it.

But Elizabeth arrived anyway, accompanied by Jack staggering under the weight of clean clothes, soap and towels, a hairbrush, a boiling-pot filled with hot water, food, plus — thank God! — laudanum, gin and ale for Friday's horrors. And a fat five-pound bribe for each of the constables on duty at the watch house. For that, while one stood guard, they allowed Elizabeth into the cell to empty the filthy bucket, and help Friday bathe and make herself presentable, Friday well beyond caring who the hell was watching. The laudanum muffled her headache and other aches and pains, ale replaced the fluids that had shot out of her mouth and backside, and the gin postponed her dreadful horrors. Nothing, however, could be done about her grotesquely bloodshot eyes.

Jack managed to winkle out of the guard the fact that Clement Bloodworth was the sitting police magistrate; unfortunately, not Francis Rossi, as Elizabeth had hoped. Though she'd used up the favours Rossi had owed her when she had asked him to release Adam Green from Port Macquarie, she'd been expecting she could prevail on his better nature to let Friday off with just a warning, but that wouldn't happen now. She would likely be convicted of assault, and sent to the penitentiary at the Female Factory.

At midday Sarah arrived, Elizabeth having sent word.

'For God's sake, Friday, what were you thinking?' she said, her hands on the cell bars.

Friday shrugged. 'Dunno.'

'Well, what happened?'

'I don't *know*. Me and Molly went to the Fortune for a few drinks, and I can't remember anything else. Ask her.'

'I will. What time are you due at the police court?'

'Dunno.' Friday shrugged again.

Sarah stared at her. 'Look, I know you're upset about Aria, but you can't just give *up*!'

'I'm not.'

'You are. But don't. We need you. Especially Harrie.'

The policeman leaning against the wall made a silly, girlish noise.

Sarah whirled to face him. 'And you can shut the fuck up.' She hated the police, a sentiment compounded since they'd manacled Adam and dragged him into the street for a crime he'd never committed.

'And you can get the fuck out,' he shot back. 'Now. Visiting time's over.'

'No, I haven't finished.'

The man took hold of Sarah's arm and propelled her roughly out the door. Over her shoulder Sarah shouted, 'I'll be there this afternoon! And so will Harrie. Don't worry!'

Friday raised a hand, but she didn't think it would matter who was there to support her. She'd be going back to the Factory for sure, if not the gaol on George Street. And she didn't care.

Sarah knocked on the front door of the brothel on Argyle Street.

When Elizabeth Hislop answered, she said, 'Afternoon, Mrs Hislop. I've just been to see Friday. Thanks for letting me know.'

'Oh, my pleasure, dear. I really don't know how we're going to get her out of *this* one.'

'Is Molly at work? She was with Friday last night. She'll know exactly what happened. Maybe she can speak in her defence.'

Elizabeth nodded. 'I thought the same thing, but I haven't seen her since she finished yesterday evening.'

'Is she still in her room sleeping it off, do you think?'

'I've looked there. No, she isn't.'

'Oh.'

'But I'll talk to her as soon as I see her. She may have slept somewhere else last night. She does that. I am a little worried, though. And annoyed. She was supposed to start work at ten.'

Friday was taken via cart to the police court on George Street just north of the old burial ground, driven through the gate in the high wall surrounding both the court and the central police station, and locked in a cell to wait her turn in the dock. When a court staff constable came to fetch her, she'd fallen asleep, stretched out on the cell's wooden bench, her manacled wrists crossed over her chest. There would be no lawyer to represent her — she was expected to defend herself.

The constable rattled the keys against the cell bars. 'Hoi, you, wake up! Time to go in.'

Friday sat up, yawned, and rubbed her hands over her face. Her headache was nowhere near as bad as it had been in the morning, though she did wonder if someone had broken into her head and stolen her brains. Perhaps she'd overdone the laudanum. She stood as the guard unlocked the cell.

He led her down a corridor, made her wait with him in an antechamber, then escorted her into the main courtroom. The public gallery was full, as she knew it would be. A day at court was always a worthwhile entertainment. She saw, too, that police magistrate Clement Bloodworth was ancient, and looked like a bulldog in a wig.

The constable ushered her up into the dock, reminding her of the last time she'd stood in one, at the Old Bailey in London. That seemed such a long time ago now. She lifted her gaze to the public gallery and immediately spotted Sarah and Harrie, and Mrs H and Jack and Ivy and a few of the girls from work. No Molly, though. And there was Leo, and Nora Barrett! And was that …? Yes, it was — Matthew Cutler. How had he found out? It was nice of him to come, though. Of all of them. She waved, feeling the tiniest bit better.

She cast her eyes more widely and the nice feeling instantly disappeared; there, in the top row of the gallery, sat Bella Shand and Louisa Coutts. Bella, her face pale against the deep green of her high-necked gown, smiled unpleasantly, raised a hand and slowly ran a long-nailed finger across her throat. Normally Friday would have retaliated with a gesture of her own, but today she just couldn't summon the energy. Let the bitch sit there and gloat. She held Bella's gaze for no more than a second, then looked away.

Below her sat the counsel for the prosecution. The Clerk of the Court had a small desk of his own, and in rows on either side were various folk, including police and scribes from the newspapers. Opposite, Bloodworth presided in his elevated perch. Today the jury bench was empty, indicating that no capital or very serious crimes were to be tried.

The clerk stood and read out the charges, which were public nuisance, public drunkenness, violent and riotous behaviour, damage to property, assault of two women, and assault of a constable. Two women? Friday vaguely recalled having a go at Rowie Harris, but who had the other person been? She had no memory of biting the policeman, either. She must ask Molly what had happened to Rowie. Their business wasn't finished.

Counsel for the prosecution called the bitten policeman to the witness box. The constable from the Harrington Street watch house stepped up, his arm suspended in a sling and heavily bandaged from fingers to elbow.

Someone — a woman — shouted from the gallery, 'Charlatan! Shame!'

The questioning began, and Friday lost interest. She had no idea whether the constable was lying or not. She did, however, notice when a nondescript person rose from a side bench and passed a note to the Clerk of the Court, then left the courtroom. The counsel stopped his questioning as the clerk handed the note to the magistrate.

'You may continue,' the magistrate said.

The counsel did, even though it was obvious Bloodworth wasn't listening, too busy cracking the seal on the note. After a moment he folded it and slipped the single sheet inside his robe.

Two male witnesses from the Fortune of War were called, though, to Friday's faint surprise, neither Rowie Harris nor the other woman she was supposed to have assaulted made an appearance.

Finally, the magistrate said, 'Friday Woolfe, do you have anything to say in your own defence?'

'No.'

A few badly stifled groans of dismay came from the gallery.

There was a short, puzzled silence. Bloodworth said, 'Nothing at all?'

'No.'

'Could the truth be that you were grievously provoked by the two women you are alleged to have assaulted?'

'I really can't remember.' Why didn't the silly old shite just hurry up and sentence her?

'Perhaps you feared for your life and it was a matter of self-defence?'

'Look, I just don't know. I was drunk!'

'Hmm.' Bloodworth glanced down at his notes. 'Then in that case, I find the defendant not guilty.'

The entire courtroom was utterly quiet for a moment, then the gallery burst into applause, though there was also a grumble of muttered confusion.

Fully resigned to going back to the Factory or even gaol, Friday's heart was halfway down to her boots before she realised what he'd said. *Not* guilty? That couldn't be right. She glanced uncomprehendingly at the court staff constable.

His face was impassive as he opened the gate to the dock, and gestured for her to present her manacled wrists. 'You're free to go.' She stuck out her hands. He clicked the key into the lock and the manacles fell away. 'Out that way, not through the front door,' he ordered.

Feeling extremely odd, she wandered off in the direction he'd indicated, down another corridor, and outside into the bright sunshine. Nearby was a gate — a guard opened it, and she was out onto George Street, free.

# Chapter Ten

*October 1831, Southern Ocean*

Malcolm Leary had been bored shitless for the past eight weeks, and was almost wishing he'd paid for a passage in steerage rather than a cabin all to himself. At least then he'd have the company of other men to help pass the time. He'd brought two books with him — *Confessions of an English Opium-Eater* by Thomas De Quincey, an inebriate, which had turned out to be bloody boring, and *The Private Memoirs and Confessions of a Justified Sinner*, written anonymously and which he'd thought would be about sex but was instead a whole lot of shite about religion, though there was an all right bit about a murder. He was a very slow and hesitant reader — and the first to admit it — but he was that bored he'd persevered and read them from cover to cover.

The food was all right, better than he'd ever got as a crewman, but the price he had to pay for eating it was the expectation that he'd dine at the captain's table, which was a pain in the arse. The other cabin passengers didn't seem to like him, and he knew why, too — they thought he was rough. Well, he was, and he didn't care. If he wanted to pick his nose or eat off his knife or scratch his balls, he would. He was paying. Sometimes now, though, he took his meals in his cabin, but that only made him feel even more bored and isolated, so he made a point of dining with the rest of them at least three times a week, just to stop himself going mad.

They were in the Southern Ocean now; the westerlies at this time of year had dropped into the high forties and the captain was holding the ship just above the forty-five degree line, so the weather wasn't too vicious. You'd think it was end of days, though, the way the passengers — steerage and cabin — were bleating on. On a few occasions when the captain had dipped below forty-five and things had got a bit hectic, he'd offered to lend a hand on deck. He hadn't even asked for a fee. The captain was running the crew shorthanded, cheap bastard, and hadn't been in a position to say no. That had been marvellous, like the old days before he'd had to retire. He'd lost a fair amount of fettle since then, though, and gained a bit of extra weight. Too much time spent on his arse in Liverpool. By the time he'd come down from the rigging the second time he'd helped out, he was short of breath, dizzy and had a Godawful pain in his side, like you got if you ran for too long, but it went away after a while.

By his estimations they should be off the coast of New South Wales in four or five weeks, depending on the wind. Not long to go now. And when they docked, the first thing he was going to do was buy himself as much rum as he could drink, then a woman, then find Jonah, and together they'd hunt down the foul Bennett.

Friday, Hazel, Sophie, Lou, Vivien and Connie — in fact, the whole afternoon shift — sat in the parlour, staring at Elizabeth in shock.

'Are they sure?' Friday asked, her voice hoarse with dismay.

Elizabeth blew her nose into a lace handkerchief. 'I'm sorry, Friday, I really am. Someone on the shore said they'd seen her quite often in the bar here, and a constable came around asking. I went to the undertaker's and identified her myself. I said she worked for me in the hotel.'

'But how did she end up in the sea?' Hazel wailed.

'Apparently some articles of clothing were found on the end of King's Wharf last Thursday. Boots and a skirt. Molly was only wearing her shift and bodice when she washed up. The constable thinks she went for a late-night swim. He wanted to know if she was fond of a drink. I ... well, I had to tell him she was.'

'She must have gone in on the way home from the Fortune of War,' Friday said. 'Jesus. Bloody hell.'

Elizabeth gave her a pointed look. 'Yes, it's a shocking and very upsetting tragedy, but let it be a lesson to all of you.'

Connie gasped. 'She'll be buried in a pauper's grave! Oh, that's awful! Or was she in a burial club?'

'It doesn't matter,' Elizabeth said. 'I've paid for a good cherrywood coffin with plate and ornaments, a hearse and one, two coachmen, bearers, an attendant, and a plot at Devonshire Street cemetery. She was Church of England, wasn't she?'

Everyone looked at one another.

'Well, she is now,' Elizabeth said.

'No mutes?' Vivien asked.

'No mutes.'

'That's very generous of you,' Lou remarked.

Elizabeth said, 'Yes, well, she did work for me. She deserves a decent send-off. And as she sadly won't need her room any more, I've asked Jack to clear it out and put her things in the storeroom in case her family cares to collect them.'

'She didn't have a family here,' Hazel said.

'Well, perhaps a friend, then,' Elizabeth said. 'It wouldn't be right to just throw them out, would it? Friday, can I see you in my office, please?'

Friday followed her, and sat down as Elizabeth closed her office door. 'Is this still about Molly?'

'No, it isn't. Have you not wondered how you were found not guilty the other day in court? That was quite an extraordinary verdict, you know.'

''Course I've wondered. I still can't remember most of what I did that night, but I must have really gone to town.'

'Clearly.' Elizabeth opened a drawer in her desk and took out a letter. 'This arrived this morning. It's for you.'

Friday froze. Oh God, she thought, not another bloody demand from Bella Shand. Not now. 'Who's it from?'

'I don't know. I'm not in the habit of opening correspondence that isn't addressed to me. But I am wondering if it might have something to do with the magistrate's decision.'

Friday took the letter. Her name was written on the front in a large, flowery hand; on the back were the words, *From an Avid Admirer*. She broke the seal, opened the single sheet and read.

*My Most Charming Miss Woolfe*

*I have had the greatest of pleasures to be a Client of yours several times. I was in the Gallery on Thursday to witness your most Unfortunate appearance in Court. It almost broke my Heart seeing you in the Dock, manacled like a jewelled Butterfly pinned to a piece of card.*

*As I simply could not bear the Notion of your fine, strapping, indeed wondrous, Personage languishing in some filthy, dark Gaol cell for months — if not years! — I made Clement Bloodworth an offer I knew His Crooked Worship would not be able to refuse. And he did not. My Heart soared when you were declared Not Guilty!*

*But may I suggest that one Good Deed very often leads to another? I would be delighted if, one day soon, you would consider visiting me at my Home. I will be in touch when the time is right.*

*Your Most Fervent Admirer*

*L*

'Oh, for God's sake,' Friday said.

'What?'

Friday passed the letter to Elizabeth, who quickly read it.

'It could be worse, you know,' she said. 'God knows how much he bribed Bloodworth. Those weren't exactly petty misdemeanours. It would have taken a lot to get him to so blatantly declare you not guilty.'

'Yes, but what am I going to have to do to pay him back? He could be a complete lunatic! And at his house!'

'Don't be silly. Take Jack. He can wait outside. And Friday, really, anything must be better than time spent in gaol or breaking rocks at the Factory? Be reasonable. It's a small price to pay, surely?'

'Easy for you to say.'

'No, it isn't easy for me to say. But I don't think you realise how bloody lightly you're getting off. People die in that gaol down the street. And they're hanged for not much more than what you did,' Elizabeth said, and burst into tears.

Friday didn't know what to say.

When Harrie returned home from her morning session with Leo, she found she'd also received a letter. Nora told her she'd paid for it, and had left it on her bed.

Harrie hurried up to her attic room, sat in the rocking chair under the eaves, and picked at the seal, already cracked. The wax was cheap and came away easily. She knew who the letter was from and was desperately looking forward to reading it. It was only one page.

*9 July 1831*

*Our Deer Sister Harrie,*

*I have very bad News. Our poor Mother has Died. She Died on the Secend day of July. We could not aford to Bury her, so she is in a Paupers grave. I am sorry, Harrie. We had to find somwhere else to live. Now we have a room in*

*St Giles with two other famlies. Anna is helping Robbie with his barow at Covent Garden, and I am taking in extra sewing. With luck, we will keep out of the Workhouse. The money you send is a big help. We miss you, Harrie.*

*All Our Love,*

*Sophie and Robbie and Anna*

Her mouth open in a silent cry of anguish, Harrie slowly slumped forwards until her forehead touched her knees. Her lungs had locked closed and the pain in her chest was monstrous. Finally she managed to draw in a reedy, whistling breath.

'Rachel!' she gasped. 'Oh, Rachel, help me!'

Presently, a small, cold hand began to stroke her hair.

Harrie was inconsolable. When Nora discovered what had happened, she sent Abigail to fetch Friday. But it didn't matter what Friday, or Sarah, or Leo, said or did, Harrie wouldn't come out of her room for three days. George told Nora he was of a bloody good mind to send Harrie back to the Factory and replace her altogether — with someone reliable and not prone to fits of barminess. Nora told him that would be over her dead body: George stomped off to the pub in a foul mood. Friday told Matthew on the way to the bank about Harrie's news, and Matthew passed it on to James. Forgetting that he had limits and was no longer of a mind to pursue her, James went straight around to the Barretts', demanding to see Harrie, but, at Harrie's instruction, Nora reluctantly sent him away.

On the fourth day, Harrie came out of her room and resumed her duties both with the Barretts and Leo, but wouldn't — or couldn't — smile, and barely spoke. Hannah, normally such a troublemaker, almost turned herself inside out acting the goat in an effort to make her laugh, but nothing worked, leaving Hannah in tears. Harrie was also very distant, and made uncharacteristic mistakes in the house —

burning the supper, putting things away in the wrong place (a leg of mutton in the linen cupboard instead of the meat safe), forgetting why she'd gone down to the kitchen — and, most disturbing of all, answered questions no one had asked. And she was barely eating. Nora was beside herself. Harrie had been behaving oddly before, but her unhinged conduct was reaching new levels.

Sarah and Friday decided that a trip out to the Factory to see Janie and the children would cheer her up. At the very least, they hoped the change of scenery might do something to jolt her out of her strange state. But she refused to go, saying she couldn't face the journey, which was completely out of character. Usually she was desperate to visit Charlotte, Janie and Rosie.

Friday and Sarah went anyway. Elizabeth lent Friday her carriage once again, and early on Sunday morning she and Sarah set out for Parramatta. The weather was good, warm but not too hot, though clouds to the far west suggested there might be rain later in the day. In a basket on the seat was the usual stash of contraband for Janie, including the two pretty, lace-trimmed cotton shifts Harrie had made for her after their last visit.

The trip out was uneventful, except for the usual stops to water the horses. Even Clifford behaved, sleeping most of the way. By the time they arrived at Parramatta it really was quite warm. Jack drew the carriage to a halt outside the Factory gates. Squinting in the sun, Sarah climbed down, Clifford under her arm, set her on the ground and attached a lead to her collar. Clifford hated her lead and shook her head violently, making the exercise as difficult as possible.

'Stop that,' Sarah said. 'It's for your own good.' Though it wasn't: it was for the good of everyone who came within five feet of her.

Cursing, she finally succeeded, looped the lead over her wrist and crossed to the gates in the high outer wall. The porter opened the wicket as soon as she banged on it, which was unusual.

Peering at her, he said, 'Not a good day for visitin'.'

'Why not? It's Sunday.'

He shook his head, making his bristly jowls wobble. 'Got sickness here. Come back another day.'

'What sort of sickness?'

'The bloody flux.'

Sarah swore.

'What's wrong?' Friday asked, just in time to hear her.

'There's dysentery in the Factory,' Sarah explained.

Friday heaved out a sigh of frustration. 'Well, I'm going in. I want to see Janie. I didn't come all this way for nothing.'

The porter shrugged. 'Be it on your own heads.'

'Tell Jack to wait,' Sarah said. 'In case we can't stay.'

Friday returned to the carriage and said to Jack in the driver's seat, 'The porter says there's flux in the Factory and not to go in. Bugger him, but can you wait fifteen minutes, just in case?'

Jack said, 'Rather you than me.' He draped the reins over the footboard, planted his boot on them, and dug around in his pocket for his pipe fixings.

The porter let Friday and Sarah through the wicket, forgetting, or perhaps too distracted, to demand payment for ignoring their contraband. They were halfway to the inner gates when Clifford suddenly lay down, her nose on her front paws.

Sarah gave the lead a gentle tug. 'Get up, girl.'

Clifford wouldn't budge.

Sarah pulled harder. Clifford slid along the ground, her back legs trailing in the dirt. Friday laughed.

Sarah didn't. 'Come on, you hairy little sluggard. Oh, for God's sake.' She grabbed Clifford, jammed her under her arm, marched across to the inner gates, and knocked loudly.

Gladys the portress flipped open the viewing slot, peeped through, and immediately burst into noisy tears. Friday and Sarah looked at each other, mystified. The cover on the slot flapped shut, and the door within the gate opened wide.

'Oh, me dears!' Gladys cried, her eyes red and swollen. 'The calamity of it! It's a blight, it surely is.'

'What is?' Friday asked, panic flaring. 'Glad? What's a blight?'

In an apparent fit of misery Gladys threw her apron over her head. 'The babies! Oh Lord, Janie and the babies! They been taken! And they're not the only ones!'

'Talk sense, Gladys,' Sarah snapped, pulling the woman's apron back down. 'Taken where?'

'To heaven. Home to Our Lord.'

'What?'

'They're dead, Miss Sarah. Oh Lord!'

Friday took a step towards her, then stopped. Utterly stunned, her head rang as though she'd been punched. She shot another look at Sarah, who looked as dumbfounded as she felt, then turned back to Gladys. 'Dead? Janie and the girls are dead?'

Gladys nodded. 'Yesterday morning. The bloody flux. It were so quick!'

Dead? A huge rage boiled up inside Friday, surging from her gut out into her arms and legs. She lunged at the closed half of the gate and gave it three vicious kicks, her breath exploding out of her in a shriek each time she connected. Thinking it was a game, Clifford joined in, darting at the gate and barking her head off. Friday let fly with one final almighty kick, then bent over, her hands on her knees, panting, as her tears began to drip onto the dirt.

Behind her, Sarah stood staring at Gladys in horrified disbelief. 'All three of them? All of them are dead?'

Gladys wiped her eyes and nose on her apron. 'Not little Charlotte. She were taken away. There's no one to look after her, see, now Janie's gone.'

Sarah wanted to slap Gladys. 'Are you saying Janie and Rosie have died ...' her voice cracked and she swallowed '... but Charlotte's still alive?'

Gladys nodded miserably.

'But she's been taken somewhere?'

Again, Gladys nodded. 'To the orphan school. Mrs Dick took her.'

'Jesus Christ!' Friday booted the gate again. Letitia bloody Dick — she'd hated Rachel. It would have given her no end of pleasure to see the poor darling's child dumped in the orphanage. 'When?' she demanded.

'Yesterday afternoon, after dinner.'

Sarah burst into loud and unattractive tears.

Jack appeared, looking alarmed. 'What the hell's going on? I heard screaming.'

'Janie and Rosie died,' Friday said, hiccupping out a sob.

'Your friend and her kiddie?' Jack was shocked. 'Bloody hell. What happened?'

'The bloody flux.'

'Dreadful, it were,' Gladys said, mopping her face again.

'And the other little girl?' Jack asked.

'In the bloody orphan school!' Friday spat, grief-fuelled fury surging through her again. 'How the fuck are we going to get her out?' She gave an almighty sob. 'Sarah? What are we going to do?'

Jack moved to settle a comforting arm around her shoulder but Friday swatted him away. Unoffended, he said, 'What can I do to help?'

'Just wait. We need to talk to Pearl.'

Looking frankly relieved that she hadn't asked him to go inside the actual Factory walls, Jack touched his hand to the brim of his hat. 'Take as long as you like. I'll be outside.'

Gladys took Friday and Sarah through the inner gate and upstairs to the dormitories in the main Factory building to find Pearl, whom they discovered going through Janie's belongings. She looked worn out. Her face was puffy and blotchy, her eyes red, and her hair, normally hanging down her back in a neat plait, was an unbound bird's nest. When she saw them she burst into tears. She might have been paid to mind Janie, but clearly they'd become friends.

'I'm that sorry,' she blurted. 'I couldn't stop them taking Charlotte. I tried, really I did.'

Friday and Sarah each gave her a hug.

'Did you get the letter?' Pearl asked Friday.

'What letter?'

'I sent it yesterday afternoon, soon as I could, to tell you what happened. I had to get someone else to write it. I don't know how to write.'

'She would have missed it,' Sarah said. 'We left first thing this morning. Were you …?' A horrible gob of phlegm caught in her throat and she cleared it. 'Were you with them? Janie and Rosie? When they died?'

Pearl nodded. 'Mr Sharpe let me tend them in the hospital.'

'Useless bugger,' Friday said. 'Why wasn't he tending them?'

'There's dozens sick. We've lost eight this time.'

'Was it … bad?' Friday asked.

'It was for Janie. She were sick for a week. Poor little Rosie were only sick for three days, but she were just a tiny thing. It's the babies and old folk most likely to get taken, though there's mothers gone as well.'

Sarah said, 'Are they still here?'

'Undertaker come and got them straight away, 'cos of the heat. Them and two others.' Pearl swallowed a sob. 'They were buried in St John's this morning. I asked but I weren't allowed to go.'

Friday swore bitterly. If they'd known, they could have been at the graveside.

Pearl looked down at the pile of belongings spread out on the floor. 'I packed what I could for Charlotte. I gave her Rosie's clothes as well, for when she gets bigger. But Janie's things — I don't know what to do with them.'

'Take what you'd like for yourself,' Sarah said. 'I think Janie would have wanted that.'

Pearl looked doubtfully at several items of clothing, and at Janie's good black boots. 'She were a lot smaller than me.'

'Then give the clothes to someone who needs them,' Friday said. 'But you keep the hairbrush and the combs, and the sewing box and the like. And this.' She handed over the basket full of food and gin and bits and pieces intended for Janie and the girls, and placed five pounds from her purse on top of it.

'What's the money for? I don't need paying no more.'

'For taking care of Janie and Rosie,' Friday said, her voice wobbling. 'You didn't have to do that. And for doing your best for Charlotte.' And also for not stealing Janie's things, because you could have, she thought.

Pearl nodded, blinking furiously. 'She were nice, Janie. Decent.'

Yes, Friday agreed silently, her eyes stinging again, she was bloody decent.

'Do you know where the orphan school is?' Sarah asked.

'Just a little ways down the river. Why?'

Friday knew exactly what Sarah was thinking. 'We're going to get Charlotte out. She can't stay there. We made a promise to her mother, and we're keeping it.'

The Female Orphan School was closer than Friday and Sarah had realised, though on the northern bank of the river — which meant they'd have to go all the way back to the bridge in Parramatta township to get back onto the southern bank and the road to Sydney Town — and situated in acres of neatly kept grounds. As they neared the school, they passed paddocks in which grazed sheep and cattle, and, adjacent to the institution, large and well-tended vegetable gardens.

The orphanage itself was unexpectedly big and quite grand, by New South Wales standards at least, and consisted of a central block three storeys high, flanked by lower connecting buildings ending in two-storey wings, all in brick that glowed pink in the sun, fading to pale red in the shade. It looked imposing, like a rich person's country house back in England, Sarah thought, eyeing the place as they drove along the carriageway. A bit grim, though, especially if you were a genuine orphan, or you'd been abandoned. She knew a lot of the girls, however, had mothers in the Factory, or assigned to masters or mistresses unwilling to take on a convict with a child in tow.

Jack brought the horses to a halt outside the main building. The carriage rocked slightly as he jumped down from the driver's seat and opened the door.

'Will I wait? It's just that I need to water the horses. I'll take them down to the river if I can't find a pump.'

Friday and Sarah climbed down. 'We'll wait out here if you're not back by the time we've finished,' Sarah said. 'Can you keep an eye on Clifford?'

Jack made a sour face. 'Must I? She hates me.'

'Hold on, what happens if we have to steal Charlotte?' Friday said. 'We can't run all the way back to Sydney if Jack's not here with the carriage.'

'Oh, don't be so stupid,' Sarah snapped. 'We can't steal her. They'd just take her back and we'd go to gaol for kidnap. Be rational, Friday.'

'Well, have you got a better idea?'

Sarah planted her hands on her hips and stared at the ground. Then she said, 'Yes. I'll adopt her.'

'But ... I thought —'

Sarah's hand went up, palm out. 'Just ... don't say anything. I need to talk to Adam, and I have to find out from the orphanage people first whether I actually can.'

Smothering Sarah in a hug that almost knocked her off her feet, Friday exclaimed, 'You're such a good person, Sarah Green, you really are!'

She was amazed and delighted, remembering the really unpleasant scene on the way out to see Janie and the girls earlier in the year. Harrie had accused Sarah of not wanting to adopt Charlotte, though she was the only one of them who possibly could because she was married, and Sarah had as good as admitted that she didn't want to. It had been so obvious then that Harrie wanted her, but poor unmarried, mentally unstable Harrie would never be allowed to adopt a child.

'I don't know about that,' Sarah said.

'You bloody are.' Friday grabbed her hand. 'Come on, let's go in and see what they've got to say.'

Once inside, Sarah stopped a girl of fourteen or fifteen in a blue uniform hurrying across the foyer, and asked to speak to whomever was in charge.

'That'll be Reverend Duff, the master. Except he's not here. Or do you want to talk to Mrs Duff, the matron?'

'The matron, please,' Sarah said.

A reverend's wife? Oh dear. Friday wished now she hadn't worn such a low-cut dress. She yanked up her bodice as high as it would go.

'This way,' the girl said.

They passed double staircases in the foyer and followed her down a gloomy corridor smelling of cabbage and mutton to a closed door, on which was a brass plaque announcing *Matron E Duff*. The girl rapped smartly.

'Enter!'

The girl opened the door and declared, 'Visitors, Matron, wanting to speak to you.'

'Well, show them in, girl, don't dither!' Matron Duff — presumably — replied.

The girl stood back and made a sweeping gesture with her hand, then hurried off. Sarah and Friday went in.

Matron Duff was a small, plump woman, wearing a navy-blue dress of some stiff fabric, a white house cap, and wire-rimmed spectacles. Her expression was stern, but her cheeks were rosy and her eyes sharp with intelligence. As she looked them up and down, Friday had the uncomfortable impression she'd taken their measure instantly.

'Good afternoon. I am Mrs Edith Duff, matron of this institution. Please sit down. How may I help you?'

'My name is Sarah Green, and this is Friday Woolfe,' Sarah said. 'A little girl by the name of Charlotte Rachel Winter was brought here yesterday, from the Factory. She's twenty months old.'

A frown flickered across Mrs Duff's face. 'Yes. We usually only take girls who have attained the age of two years. However, Mrs Dick was adamant there is no one available at the Factory to care for the girl, and we did not feel we could turn her away. Do you know the child?'

'We do,' Sarah said. 'We knew her mother very well.'

'Such a tragedy,' Mrs Duff said. 'I believe Charlotte's older sister also passed from the same illness?'

Friday shook her head. 'No. Letitia Dick's put you wrong. It was Janie Braine who died yesterday, and her daughter Rosie. Janie was Charlotte's foster mother. Charlotte belonged to Rachel Winter, who died in the Factory having Charlotte. Rachel was transported with us. She was a very dear friend of ours, and so was Janie. Janie was the only mother Charlotte's ever known. And now she's lost her and she's been dumped here.' She tried not to let her grief and anger show, but suspected it had, judging by the matron's raised eyebrows.

'A double tragedy for Charlotte, then.' Mrs Duff clasped her hands in front of her on the desk. 'Though I am still unsure as to how I can help you.'

Sarah took a deep breath. 'I would like to enquire into the possibility of adopting Charlotte.'

Mrs Duff stared at her for a long moment. 'That is a very charitable thought, but am I correct in assuming you are a convict? Both of you?' Her gaze met Friday's. 'You did just say —'

'Yes, we are,' Sarah interrupted.

'And assigned?'

'Yes.'

'Then you must realise that no convict woman would ever be permitted to adopt a child. At the very least not until she has gained a ticket of leave. And even then she would have to be of proven good character.'

'Forgive me, perhaps I may not have phrased my question appropriately,' Sarah said.

Friday worked hard to keep her gob from falling open — Sarah was doing a cracking job of sounding like a toff.

'Go on,' Mrs Duff said.

'I am married to my master, Mr Adam Green. He is a manufacturing jeweller, as I am myself, and owns a salon on George Street in Sydney Town. We have discussed for some time the possibility of adopting Charlotte as our own, but not until she reached the age of four and had to leave Janie and the Factory.'

Really? Friday thought. That was news to her. She suspected it would be news to Adam as well.

'But now, as a result of this untimely tragedy,' Sarah went on, 'obviously we would be more than happy to bring forward our plans. My husband came to New South Wales as a convict, and has a conditional pardon. We are doing very well from our business and feel we could give Charlotte a happy home. Sadly, I am not sure if I can give my husband a child myself,' she added, and began to weep.

The bit about not being able to have babies was bollocks, Friday knew, having taken Sarah to the chemist herself to purchase items to prevent Adam receiving that very gift, but the tears were genuine, and she suspected Sarah was crying again for Janie and Rosie, and for poor, cheated Rachel. Feeling her eyelids burn, she dabbed at her own eyes.

'Again, that is very admirable, Mrs Green,' Mrs Duff said. 'And given the fact that you are married and your husband has a conditional pardon, perhaps a case could have been made for adoption.'

Sarah blew her nose and said, 'I'm sorry? What do you mean, *could* have been made?'

'One moment.' Mrs Duff raised a stubby finger, stood and moved to an enormous set of wooden drawers, each drawer about a foot square. She opened one, flicked through the contents and retrieved several documents folded in half lengthwise and tied with ribbon. Resuming her seat behind the desk, she opened the papers and smoothed them flat. 'These are Charlotte's admission details, which I completed myself, and this is her birth certificate. A child can only be considered for adoption with the permission of both parents.'

'Well, that'll be tricky, won't it?' Friday said. 'Charlotte's mother's been dead for nearly two years.'

'I said both parents, Miss Woolfe. Her father's name is also on the birth certificate.'

Friday dared not look at Sarah. She couldn't have, surely? Why the hell would Rachel have wanted Gabriel stinking bloody Keegan's name recorded on Charlotte's birth certificate?

'May I see that, please?' Sarah asked.

Mrs Duff passed the certificate across the desk.

Sarah read it, then slowly passed it to Friday. The name on the certificate was Lucas Carew.

A big fat tear rolled down Friday's face and plopped onto the paper. Oh, poor, poor Rachel. Lucas Carew had been the lover she'd told everyone she'd eloped with from her home in Guildford — the dashing soldier no one else had ever seen, and who'd abandoned her in London, leading to her arrest. Except Rachel had never truly believed he had deserted her; she'd always thought he'd come back for her. And when Keegan had assaulted her on the *Isla*, she'd somehow managed to convince herself that the child he'd given her was Lucas's. At some stage she must have instructed Mr Sharpe at the Factory to enter the name Lucas Carew on Charlotte's birth certificate, even though Charlotte couldn't possibly have been his.

Mrs Duff said, 'So, you see, Mrs Green, before you could adopt Charlotte, we would need confirmation from this Mr Carew that he is willing to forfeit all paternal rights to Charlotte. Preferably in person, though I realise that could be very difficult. If not in person, then by way of an affidavit if Mr Carew does not reside in New South Wales.'

Christ, Friday thought, we don't even know if he ever existed. And if he did, he could be anywhere now. Dead, even.

Sarah, however, remained calm and lied through her teeth. 'Well, we haven't heard from Mr Carew for some time, but I'll see what we can do.'

Friday thought, that's smart, we can forge something if we have to. 'Could we see Charlotte while we're here?'

'Will she recognise you?'

'Yes,' Sarah said. 'We saw a lot of her in the Factory.'

'Then I'm sorry but I think not. Best to let her settle. She was in quite a state when she was brought in.'

'I'm not surprised!' Friday exclaimed. 'She's just been yanked away from everything she knows. She's too young to understand why she can't be with Janie and Rosie any more. Can we just have a little look?'

'I can assure you our girls here are all very well cared for,' Mrs Duff said.

Sarah asked, 'Is she in a nursery?'

Glancing at a small carriage clock on the desk, Mrs Duff said, 'Yes, it's nap time. All the little ones will be asleep.'

'May we have the tiniest glimpse?' Sarah said. 'I'll feel so much better knowing she's comfortable.'

Mrs Duff hesitated, then said, 'I expect that won't hurt. But, please, you must be quiet. If one wakes and cries, they'll all cry.'

'Oh, of course,' Friday said.

'Good. If you'd care to follow me.'

Mrs Duff led them up to the next floor, the leather soles of her boots squeaking on the polished wooden risers of the stairs.

Behind her Sarah whispered to Friday, 'I'm warning you, don't you dare do anything stupid.'

'When do I ever do anything stupid?'

'Just keep your mouth shut and behave.'

They passed several rooms in which sat groups of girls wearing blue dresses and white aprons, capes and caps. They all turned to scrutinise who was going past.

'Are they at lessons?' Sarah asked.

'Yes, they're learning to read and write so that they may properly understand and benefit from the Holy Scriptures,' Mrs Duff said.

Friday deliberately avoided Sarah's eye, knowing how much she utterly despised anything religious, particularly the Catholic church. She realised the orphan school was run by the Church of England, but suspected Sarah wouldn't even be keen on Charlotte being cared for by Anglicans. They were all pretty much the same to her.

'We also teach them the skills they're likely to need in service, and to manage their own homes when they marry,' Mrs Duff went on.

'Needlework and what have you?' Sarah said.

'Yes, so that they may make their own clothes and linen. We also teach spinning and carding, cooking and baking, how to manage a dairy, and now and then they also work in the gardens. It's useful for them to learn about growing vegetables for the kitchen, and it's also very good exercise. By the time Charlotte leaves here when she turns thirteen she will make an excellent servant, and later on a handy wife.'

'If my husband and I are unable to adopt her,' Sarah reminded her.

'Indeed.'

'And all these girls are the children of convict women?' Friday asked.

'Most of them.'

They climbed a second staircase and traipsed down yet another corridor until they came to a door standing ajar. Mrs Duff cautiously pushed it open, then beckoned to Sarah and Friday.

Peering over her shoulder, which was especially easy for Friday as she was almost a foot taller than the matron, they saw a large room filled with a dozen white-painted baby's cribs. In the middle a girl sat at a small table working on a piece of embroidery. Mrs Duff waved to attract her attention. She put down her needlework and glided over on silent feet.

'Olive, these visitors are here to see Charlotte Winter. Which crib is hers?'

The girl indicated a crib barely ten feet away, containing a small child asleep on her back, her arms thrown above her head, the blanket kicked to the end of the mattress.

Unfortunately, Friday was just then suddenly overcome by a violent attack of coughing. The harsh gasping and hacking blasted around the room and one by one the babies woke up, including Charlotte. Her eyes watering, Friday raised her hand and waved at her.

Startled and disoriented, Charlotte immediately spotted Friday's unmistakeable copper hair and scrambled to her knees, her pudgy little hands gripping the bars of the crib. 'Fwiday!' And then she saw Sarah. 'Sawah! Sawah!'

'Oh dear, I think she's woken up,' Friday croaked.

All around the room little tousled heads were popping up. A child started to cry. Then another, and another.

Mrs Duff glared at Friday.

Charlotte joined in, her mouth opening as wide as a frog's and her voice winding up to a high-pitched wail, her brick-red face in startling contrast to her wispy, silver-white hair.

'It's all right, Mrs D, I know how to settle her,' Friday said, and barged into the nursery.

She bent over Charlotte's crib and picked her up, wrinkling her nose at the astringent whiff of wee rising from the mattress. The back of Charlotte's gown was damp — Friday lifted it to see her soggy nappy sagging halfway down her legs.

'Look at this. Her clout's soaked and she stinks.'

'Yes, well, Olive can't attend to all of them at once,' Mrs Duff said.

'She wasn't even in nappies during the day,' Sarah said accusingly. 'Janie had trained her on the pot.'

Friday cuddled Charlotte and rocked her, but it must have dawned on the little girl that Janie wasn't with them because she started to cry out, 'Mama! Mama!' Her hands full, Friday was unable to wipe away the tears rolling down her face. She looked across at Sarah, who stepped into the room and held out her arms. Friday passed Charlotte to her.

'Oh, you poor little thing,' Sarah said, kissing the top of Charlotte's head. 'We'll get you out soon, I promise.'

Distraught, Charlotte kept crying, her head on Sarah's shoulder.

'I must ask you to leave,' Mrs Duff said. 'The other children won't settle while this one is carrying on.'

Friday turned on Mrs Duff. 'She's not "carrying on", she's heartbroken!'

'I do understand how this situation may be upsetting for you. But Charlotte is a baby. She will adjust,' Mrs Duff said. 'However, someone must care for her, and for now that responsibility falls to this institution.' She held out her arms for Charlotte. 'Now, would you please leave so that Olive may settle the children. Olive, put Charlotte back in her crib.'

'But first you can change her clout and that mattress. It reeks,' Friday said to Olive, who nodded timorously, clearly unsure whether to obey the matron or Friday.

Sarah said, 'I'll be in touch as soon as I hear from Lucas Carew. Thank you for your time, Mrs Duff.' Then she swept imperiously from the nursery.

Friday had to trot to catch up with her, she was marching so determinedly down the corridor.

'I don't think she gives a shit about those babies,' Sarah said once they were downstairs again.

'Probably just run off her feet. Could be worse. She could have ended up in the workhouse.'

'There aren't any workhouses in New South Wales,' Sarah said, yanking the front door open. 'Didn't I tell you to bloody well behave in there?'

Friday followed her outside. 'Christ, what are we going to do about Lucas Carew's name on the birth certificate?'

Jack had parked the landau in the shade of a tree: Sarah waved. 'I'm buggered if I know. If Mrs Duff asks at the Factory, and I bet she bloody does, she'll work out that Rachel was only three months along when we arrived, meaning she must have fallen pregnant on the *Isla*. And that means that, as far as she's concerned, Lucas Carew was either a sailor or a passenger.'

'We might get away with it. She could have got knapped just before we left London.'

'In Newgate Gaol? No, all Mrs Duff has to do is look at the ship's muster to see how long we were at sea, which was eighteen weeks. Rachel wasn't four and a half months along. Sharpe would have put that in his records and he didn't. Harrie told me he put three months.'

Friday was getting lost. 'Which means?'

Clifford came racing across the grass and Sarah scooped her up. 'Which means that if we say Lucas Carew was a sailor on the *Isla*, he's likely to be at sea or Christ knows where by now, and that means we'll have to wait forever until we can produce a forged letter from him saying he's willing to forfeit his paternal rights to Charlotte.'

'Oh.'

'And if we say he was a passenger —'

'Which bloody Keegan was,' Friday interrupted.

'Yes, but we're not telling anyone *he* was Charlotte's father. We were Rachel's best friends. We can't afford to have our names connected with his, not while his murder still hasn't been solved.'

'Christ, no.'

'If we say Lucas Carew was a passenger, that means he's probably, or at least possibly, living here in New South Wales. And Mrs Duff says if that's the case, he needs to give his permission in person.'

'Can't we just say he's dead or something?'

'Maybe. Stop that,' Sarah said as Clifford sniffed interestedly at the smell left on her bodice from Charlotte's wet nappy. 'But then we'd have to produce a death certificate.'

'Would we? Really? Folk die all the time without a death certificate. He might have just disappeared.'

'How did you go?' Jack asked as they reached the carriage.

'Not very well,' Friday said. 'And now I suppose we'll have to tell Harrie.'

Neither Sarah nor Friday said much on the way back to Sydney, their spirits flat, both feeling drained and emotionally battered, and very much as though they'd been robbed of something precious.

By the time Sarah and Friday arrived at the Barretts' later that night, Friday had consumed more than half a bottle of gin, but it hadn't helped her to feel any better.

'I'm not sure, now, if we should tell Harrie,' she said as she climbed unsteadily down from the carriage.

Sarah jumped down after her. 'Neither am I. It might be more than she can bear, after her mother. I think we should talk to Nora first.' She walked around to the driver's seat and offered up Clifford. 'Jack ...'

'No.' Jack tugged the leg of his trousers out of his boot, revealing several small puncture marks on his hairy calf. Sarah really had to squint to make them out in the darkness. 'See what she did? She bloody well bit me.'

'Well, if that's how you're going to be about it.'

'It is, especially if you want me to deliver you home after this.'

Uppity bugger, Sarah thought, walking away, Clifford under her arm.

Friday knocked on the Barretts' back door. When no one answered they thought perhaps everyone had gone to bed — it was quite late, after all — but eventually faint lamplight appeared in the downstairs window and they could hear someone coming down the stairs. Nora opened the door, Lewis, as usual, stuck to her hip.

'Hello, girls. This is late.'

'Yes, sorry,' Friday said.

'Harrie's in bed. She's had another bad day. How was your trip?'

'Awful,' Sarah said. 'We need your advice. It's about Harrie.'

'Oh. Well, you'd better come in, then. Quietly, though, if you don't mind. The children are asleep. That includes George. I'm only awake myself because Lewis won't go down.'

'Can I bring Clifford in?' Sarah asked. 'Jack's outside with the carriage but he's refusing to look after her.'

Nora eyed Clifford. 'Is it house-trained? Will it bark?'

'Yes, she is, and no, she won't bark.'

'I suppose so. Keep it off the furniture, though, please.'

They tiptoed up the creaky stairs behind Nora, her lamp casting tall shadows on the wall, and sat down in the parlour. Clifford turned around three times and flopped onto the rug at Sarah's feet.

'Have you had something to eat and drink?' Nora asked.

Friday nodded.

'Yes, I can tell you have.'

Sarah said, 'We heard some very bad news today. They've had an outbreak of the bloody flux at the Factory. Janie and Rosie —' Her voice broke and she started again. 'Janie and Rosie died yesterday morning.'

Nora's gasp was harsh in the quiet room. 'They died!'

'If we'd arrived an hour or so earlier, we could have attended the burials. They're at St John's.'

'My God! And no one let you know?'

'Janie's friend Pearl sent a letter,' Friday said, 'but I hadn't got it by the time we left this morning.'

'And Charlotte? What about Charlotte?'

Sarah breathed out an enormous sigh. 'Charlotte's been taken to the Female Orphan School. There's no one to look after her now. We went to see her before we left Parramatta.'

'Is she all right?'

Sarah glanced at Friday, who said, 'No, she isn't. Not really. She cried when she saw us and she cried for Janie.'

Nora hoisted Lewis to her chest and rubbed her cheek against his fluffy hair. 'Oh, the poor little thing. She must be feeling so lost.'

'She is. It was heartbreaking,' Sarah said.

'We're getting her out, though,' Friday declared. 'Sarah's going to have a go at adopting her.'

Nora's pale eyebrows went up. 'Really? Can you do that? I would have thought with you being an assigned convict ...' She tailed off.

'Adam has a conditional pardon. Anyway, I'm going to try.'

'The thing is,' Friday said, 'what are we going to tell Harrie? She'll be devastated. Or shall we not tell her anything right now?'

Clifford's ears flicked up and she gave a tiny yap.

'Tell me what?' Harrie said from the hallway leading to the attic stairs.

'Ah, shite,' Sarah muttered.

Harrie moved into the circle of lamplight, her bare feet making no noise on the rug, her hair loose down her back. 'Tell me what?' she said again.

'Go back to bed, love,' Nora said. 'It's late.'

'Why are you here?' Harrie asked Friday and Sarah. 'What's happened?'

'Nothing. We're just having a quick cup of tea,' Friday said, though there wasn't a teacup in sight.

'Don't lie to me!' Harrie said, her voice rising. 'What's happened? I know something's happened. Tell me!'

Friday stood.

Sarah said, 'Friday, no, don't.'

Her gaze darting from Sarah to Friday and back again, Harrie demanded despairingly, 'Is it Charlotte?' She grabbed great handfuls of her own hair and began to tear at it. 'It's Charlotte, isn't it?'

The door to the children's bedroom opened and a little face peered out.

'Close that door!' Nora shouted at Abigail.

Friday rushed at Harrie and gripped her wrists. 'No! It's not Charlotte, I promise. Harrie? It's not Charlotte, it's Janie and Rosie.'

'What about them?' Harrie's eyes were wild. 'What's *happened*?'

'They … well, they died. They got sick and died.'

Harrie opened her mouth and howled.

George charged out of the bedroom he shared with Nora and bellowed, 'What the bloody hell's going on here?'

Over the noise, Friday shouted in Harrie's face, 'Charlotte's all right, Harrie! I promise! She's in the orphanage!'

But the voices in Harrie's head weren't just chattering now, they were shrieking, clamouring for attention, clawing at her brain, demanding vengeance. It was too much. A door slammed shut somewhere inside her, trapping all that she was and everything she'd ever been. The voices had won. She was damned. She was … no one. Her scream built and built in intensity and pitch until even Clifford whimpered.

Horrified by her unnerving response, Sarah yelled at her to stop.

Harrie did, abruptly. She stared at Sarah for a second, her clenched white fists jammed into her temples, then her eyes rolled up and she collapsed on the floor.

'Shit, she's fainted,' Friday said.

But Harrie hadn't fainted. Sarah crouched over her; Harrie's eyes were open and staring, the pupils enormous but unseeing. She rolled away from Sarah, then curled up and covered her ears with her hands.

'What's the hell's going on?' George said a second time, glowering at Harrie on the floor. 'Is she drunk again?'

Nora handed Lewis to him. 'Take the baby and go back to bed.'

'Did you not hear me? I said, is she drunk?'

'And did you not hear me?' Nora said, her hands on her hips. 'I asked you to go away.'

'Don't you speak to me like that in my own house.'

'George, please! For the baby's sake.'

'You'll be hearing about this in the morning!' George barked. 'And get rid of those two,' he added, pointing at Friday and Sarah. But he turned on his heel and marched back into the bedroom, slamming the door.

Friday stood staring down at Harrie. 'Christ, Sarah, is she all right?'

Sarah gazed into Harrie's blank and unresponsive face a moment longer, then straightened up. 'No, she isn't. I think this time we've truly lost her.'

# Chapter Eleven

*November 1831, Sydney Town*

George Barrett poked at the runny yolks of his eggs with his fork, then shovelled one onto a piece of bread, cut it in half and jammed it into his mouth. The new girl Emma had cooked them. He quite liked her — she was pretty, cleaned the house properly and didn't talk back — but she couldn't cook eggs to save herself. Harrie had cooked much nicer eggs, but Harrie, unfortunately, was madder than a sack of ferrets. It was a shame, really. The kids adored her.

He glanced at Hannah sitting opposite him. There was a hole in her slice of bread, she had jam on the handle of her table knife, on her face, on the outside of the jam pot, in her hair, on her pinafore and on her fingers.

'What are you doing to that bread?'

'Putting jam on.'

'Give it here.'

Hannah passed her jammy plate across. George dipped his knife into the jam pot, and spread a dollop across the soft fresh bread.

'Harrie always does it right to the edge,' Hannah complained.

'Well, I'm doing this, not Harrie.'

Nora sat down at the table and settled Lewis on her knee.

'Is Harrie sick again?' Abigail asked, wiping a smear of butter and jam off Samuel's face.

'Yes.' Nora avoided George's eye. They'd had an enormous row the day before about Harrie, and she didn't want another one. George had stomped around insisting he was going to send her back to the Factory, and she'd argued with him ferociously until he'd finally, and very reluctantly, agreed to change his mind. 'She's staying in bed for the day.'

In fact, Nora suspected Harrie could well be staying in bed for the next few months. This morning the poor girl seemed almost cataleptic. She barely moved, she didn't seem aware that Nora was in the room with her, she wouldn't speak, and most distressing of all, she'd wet the bed. Nora had had to strip the damp sheet from under her, spread a piece of oil cloth over the mattress, put on fresh sheets, sponge Harrie clean, and get her into another nightdress. All while the poor thing sat there like a big, brainless doll. She couldn't go back to the Factory like that. She couldn't go anywhere.

'Where's Emma?' George asked, watching Hannah cram her bread into her mouth.

'Downstairs in the washhouse. Why?'

'It's not washing day. Is it?'

'We've got behind. I've asked her to do a bit extra.'

'That'll keep her busy.'

'It will, unfortunately,' Nora said. 'I wanted her to go to the market. Now I'll have to go, and I'm that busy. Hannah, that's Samuel's bread, not yours!'

George asked, 'How long will you be?'

'I don't know, do I? As long as it takes.'

'Who's going to sit with Harrie? She's mad, she shouldn't be left alone.'

'I will!' Hannah declared.

Nora said, 'Sometimes you can be a real bastard, George.'

'Bastard!' Samuel said.

'Just stating the facts.'

'Are you volunteering?' Nora asked.

'Hardly,' George said. 'I'm not a nursemaid.'

'She doesn't need sitting with. Emma will keep an eye on her.'

George eyed his second egg, decided he didn't want it, drank his cup of tea in one go, and pushed his chair back from the table. 'Will you take the kids with you? To the market?'

'Just Lewis.'

George nodded and stood. 'Right then, I'm off.'

As he clattered down the stairs to his shop, Abigail asked, 'Mam, why is Da so grumpy lately? Is he worried about Harrie?'

Nora pulled George's plate across the table, dipped a spoon into the cooling egg and fed it to Lewis. 'That's right, dear.'

'When will she get better?'

'Soon, I hope.'

'Why is she sick?' Hannah asked. 'Has she got the Black Death?'

'No, love, she's just very, very sad, and it's made her ill.'

'If she had a kitten, would she get better?'

'She's got Angus, remember?'

'Oh, yeah, I forgot.'

Nora said, 'Don't say "yeah", love. Say "yes". Now come on, all of you, finish up your breakfasts, we've got a busy day.'

George waited until Nora and Lewis emerged from the alleyway beside the house and passed the window of his shop, plus an extra ten minutes in case she'd forgotten something and came back, then turned the sign on the door so it read CLOSED.

Then he scooted through the house and out to the backyard. Abigail, Samuel and Hannah were playing some sort of game in a pile of sand, though Hannah seemed more interested in teasing the goat.

'You lot keep away from the cesspit, do you hear me?'

They waved, barely looking up.

He found Emma in the washhouse, staring into the depths of the boiling copper.

'Busy?' he asked.

She started. 'Mr Barrett! You almost scared the life out of me.'

'Sorry. Need anything?'

She frowned. 'Er, no thank you.'

'Have you looked in on Harrie?'

'I'm just about to.'

'I'll do that, if you like. I'm going up.'

'Much obliged, Mr Barrett.'

George went inside and up to Harrie's attic room. He knocked. No answer.

Cautiously, he opened the door. She was lying on her side, facing him. Her eyes were open but he didn't think she could see him. That bloody cat of hers could, though. It was crouching on the end of the bed, giving him the evil eye.

'Harrie? It's Mr Barrett. George.'

No response.

'Harrie, I want you to get dressed. We're going for a little ride.'

Still nothing. Shit. Was he going to have to do it all himself? He stepped into the room and closed the door. Treading carefully in case she woke up and had another one of her noisy fits, he approached the bed and laid a hand on her shoulder.

The cat launched itself at him, hissing and clawing at his wrist. George swung at it, knocking it to the floor. It disappeared under the bed. Sucking his wounded flesh as he got down on his knees, George could see it under there, poisonous teeth bared and fur puffed out. Little shite.

He stood and prodded Harrie's arm.

She barely moved. For God's sake. He peeled the bedclothes off, sat her up and swivelled her around so her bare feet were on the floor. Now what? He opened her bureau and found a shift, pulled a dress out of the clothes press, and looked around for her boots. Not stockings, though — trying to get stockings on her would be out of the question.

He looked at her. Christ, this was going to be bloody impossible with her just sitting there like a lump of dough.

'Harrie, wake up, will you?'

Except she wasn't exactly asleep. It was uncanny and deeply disconcerting and the hairs on his arms were all standing up. Holding his breath in case something terrible happened, he slapped her gently across the face. Twice.

She blinked, and seemed briefly to focus.

'Harrie, we're going out. You need to get dressed, all right?'

Nothing. Leaning over her, George eased the nightdress out from under her bum, then lifted it off over her head. Underneath she was naked, and he tried not to look at her. Yes, he had an eye for the ladies, but Harrie didn't fall into that category, and he wasn't a rat who'd take advantage of her while she was so ill. He couldn't help noticing, though, that she was as skinny as the handle on a yard broom, and that her full bust and rounded hips had almost disappeared. He felt a brief but genuine pang of sorrow for the bright, cheerful girl she'd once been.

He put the shift on her, then followed with the dress, a much trickier proposition. Eventually he got it over her head and eased her arms into the sleeves, then helped her to stand up. When she let out a loud burp, he nearly had a heart attack. Could you still burp when you were in a trance? Obviously you could. After his heart had slowed down he spent what felt like hours fucking about trying to do up all the buttons, gave up and left half of them undone, slipped her boots on her feet, tied the laces, and draped a shawl around her shoulders.

Worried now that Emma would appear, he took Harrie's arm and guided her down the stairs to his shop, where he collected his satchel, then outside onto the street. Tucking his arm into hers as though they were out for a leisurely stroll, he walked her to the stables up on Cambridge Street and, sweating profusely now but resolute, paid over the odds to hire a horse and gig with the minimum of fuss. Where they were going was far too far to travel on foot.

It took them much of the day to get there, but, to George's relief, Harrie slept most of the way. Or, at least, he assumed she'd slept. After an hour of sitting on the seat next to him, staring blankly ahead, she'd curled up and put her hands over her ears. He'd checked a few times and once her eyes had been open, and twice they hadn't. She hadn't said a single word to him, though she'd muttered on and off as though she'd been talking to someone, which had been quite off-putting.

When he'd stopped for his dinner he'd been worried, not that she might run away, but that she might just wander off, so he'd taken his plate of food and tankard of ale outside and eaten it in view of the gig. She hadn't wanted anything to eat or drink. Well, she'd not responded when he'd offered. And neither had she responded to his question about her need to use the inn's privy, which he'd regretted later when she'd peed on herself and the gig's seat.

The sun was beginning to slide down the sky by the time they reached their destination. By then, Harrie was truly, deeply asleep. George had to shake her quite hard to wake her. When he helped her down from the gig she fell over — he'd forgotten she hadn't been off the seat all day and he looked around, worried anyone watching would think he'd pushed her. He picked her up and half walked, half carried her through the gates.

The building was disappointingly ordinary, given that it had once been a courthouse — he'd been expecting something much more grand. In fact, it was little more than a two-storey oblong box with a chimney at each end and windows on both levels. He hoped he was at the right place. Propping Harrie up with one arm, he banged on the door.

It was opened by a cove wearing navy-blue moleskin trousers, an unbleached cotton shirt and a brown waistcoat.

'Is this the Liverpool lunatic asylum?' George asked.

'’Tis.'

'I've got a new patient for you.'

'You'll be wanting to speak to Mr Plunkett, then. He's the superintendent. He does the admitting.'

'Well, can you fetch him?'

'Hold on.'

'Can I bring her in? We're tired. We've travelled out from Sydney.'

The man shrugged, opened the door wider, then walked off.

George sat himself and Harrie down on a pair of hard wooden chairs in a moderately spacious foyer. Presently a second man appeared, carrying a clipboard and dressed, far more elegantly than the first, in pale trousers, a well-cut coat and waistcoat and polished boots. He offered a neatly manicured hand.

'Good afternoon. I'm Thomas Plunkett. I'm the superintendent here. I'm told you've brought us a new patient?'

George stood, wiped his palm on his crumpled jacket, and shook Thomas Plunkett's cool, dry hand. 'Yes, this is Harriet Clarke. She's … not well.'

The superintendent glanced at Harrie. 'It's very nice to meet you, Mr Clarke. I'm sorry about your wife.'

'Oh, no, my name's George Barrett,' George said quickly. 'Harrie's my servant. We got her from the Factory.'

'Ah. A bonded convict?'

'That's right.' George opened his satchel. 'These are her assignment papers.'

'Thank you.' The superintendent wrote down a few details and gave the papers back. 'Keep these. You'll need them. So the government will be paying?'

'Er, yes.'

'And what seems to be the problem?'

'Well, she's mad. Demented.'

'Mad in what way, Mr Barrett?'

'She won't speak to anyone, she won't eat, she won't get out of bed, she has these terrible screaming fits, and she talks to herself. And, er, she's incontinent.'

Mr Plunkett wrinkled his nose. 'Yes, I'd noted that. Screaming fits, you say? She seems quiet and really rather docile at the moment.'

'Well, yes, at the moment,' George admitted.

'Do you know of any possible reason for her indisposition?'

'She's had a lot of bad news lately. But that doesn't excuse the fact that my wife and I need a servant who can perform her duties, and Harrie can't. Not any more.'

'Mmm,' Mr Plunkett said. 'Melancholia, perhaps, with a touch of mania. I'm not the medical expert, of course. Well, we'll admit her, and Dr Ashton can examine her in the morning and make a full diagnosis. Will you want her back if she can be cured? She may be here some time.'

'No. I'll get another girl.'

'In that case a letter will be sent to you, which you should take to the Factory with her assignment papers, to prove that she's been unsuitable. That should clear the way for you to obtain a replacement in a timely fashion.'

'Very good.' George put on his hat. 'I'll leave you to it, then.'

'No,' Harrie said, her voice eerily flat.

Startled, the two men looked at her.

The superintendent turned to George. 'I thought you just informed me that she couldn't speak?'

'She doesn't, most of the time.' George gripped Harrie's hand and pulled her up off the chair. 'Come on, Harrie. You need to go with Mr Plunkett.'

Thomas Plunkett beckoned to someone standing in the shadows — an attendant, who trotted across the foyer and took hold of Harrie's other arm.

'No!' Harrie cried, and let loose a wild howl.

George dropped her hand as though it were on fire, and made a dash for the door, Harrie's shrieks ringing in his ears. He glanced behind him just once, to see her being dragged across the floor, struggling and kicking, her skirts up around her thighs, and then, thank God, he was outside.

He sat in the gig, his head down, breathing deeply. That had been more unpleasant than he'd expected. But he'd had to do it. He had to get rid of Harrie. It was the only way to stop Nora paying Emma's wages. He knew she was because the money she kept hidden in the linen cupboard was going down each week by exactly the amount Emma was receiving. It wasn't right — Nora was his wife, and that money was his. It was Leo bloody Dundas who wanted Harrie to work the extra hours in his tattoo shop, so Dundas should be paying to replace her. And there'd been no point to having it out with Nora because she just would've run rings around him, or completely ignored him, like she always did.

But it was worse than that, much worse. George spat over the side of the gig, the thought, as usual, filling his mouth with bile. Dundas — with his muscular bloody arms and flat belly and flashy gold teeth — had been around at his house seeing Nora when he wasn't home. He knew because the nosy old mot next door had come into the shop one day full of glee and told him. Nora and Dundas! God, the thought was killing him! He couldn't bear it if he lost her. And if Harrie were gone, there'd be no connection with Dundas any more. To hell with the piddly retainer he was paying so she could draw her pictures — forfeiting that was nothing compared to the prospect of losing Nora. So Harrie had had to go.

Which was a shame in a lot of ways because she was great with the kids, and Nora thought the sun shone out of her arse, but she was sick and she really should be in the asylum. Perhaps he'd done her a favour.

He sat up. Yes, he had, actually. Now that he thought about it, he had done the right thing.

He flicked the reins and headed off to find a pub with decent food and a comfortable bed for the night.

Nora knew even before she was properly awake that George still hadn't come home. It wasn't the first time, of course, but on those previous occasions Harrie hadn't also been missing. She knew he'd taken her — Hannah had seen them. She'd crept up the stairs behind her father and hidden behind the sofa (thank God for her sneaky little ways) and watched him lead her down from her attic room; then she had hung out the window and seen them going up the street. To hire a carriage to drive out to the Factory? But why hadn't he come home last night? The return trip to Parramatta was long, she knew, and could be arduous, depending on the weather, but it was certainly achievable in one day. So where the hell was he?

Wherever it was, when he eventually did come home she was going to absolutely kill him.

Without looking at the clock, she knew it was barely past dawn. She got out of bed, dressed quickly, washed her face, dragged a brush through her hair and went out to the parlour to stoke the fire for the kettle. The kids would be awake soon — she would trot around to the Siren's Arms then.

'Well, where the fuck is he, then?' Friday demanded.

'How the hell should I know?'

'He's your bloody husband.'

'Not for much bloody longer,' Nora said through gritted teeth.

'Christ!' Friday ran her hands through her hair, and swore again as her fingers caught in the knots.

'I did have one horrible thought,' Nora said. She'd had an unpleasant hour or so pondering this. 'He could have taken her to the asylum.'

'Oh, Jesus.' Friday was horrified. 'That would just … that would kill her!' She reached under the bed and felt around for the bottle of gin stashed there, and took a long swig. 'But why there? Why not the Factory?'

'I don't know, but it's the only reason I can think of for him not coming home last night. It's a longer trip because of the distance and the bad road. Do you have to do that? It's not even eight o'clock yet.'

Friday ignored her. 'So what are we going to do? How the hell do you get someone out of a place like that?'

'I really don't know. If that's where she actually is. As soon as my noble husband turns up, I'll find out and I'll let you know.'

'You'd better,' Friday said, stifling a burp.

Nora lost her temper. 'Look, you, don't you go ordering me around.'

'Well, she's my friend.'

'She's my friend, too,' Nora shot back, 'and my responsibility. Which is why I'd rather be out looking for her than sitting around getting swattled. And belching and farting like a pig.'

Friday banged her gin bottle on the nightstand. 'You've got no bloody idea, have you? My friend drowned the other day, someone I … cared about a lot's left me, Janie and Rosie are dead and Charlotte's in that poxy orphanage, and I've been worried sick about Harrie and a whole lot of other things. You just don't know.'

'Oh, boo hoo. Life isn't easy for anyone, girl. Now pull yourself together. Harrie needs you.'

Stung, Friday said, 'And how do we know your stupid, selfish bloody husband hasn't murdered her? Eh? Have you thought of that?'

'He hasn't because he doesn't have the balls. I know him. Now get up, get dressed and go and tell Sarah what's happened.'

Friday glared at her, but as soon as Nora had gone she burst into tears. This was all just too much. She wanted nothing more than to drink herself senseless, pass out and hope that when she came to, someone else had fixed everything. But it never worked like that, and she knew it.

\* \* \*

James opened the door, his hat on and his doctor's bag in his hand. He looked startled and more than a little alarmed to see them. 'Oh. Hello. I'm just on my way to the surgery.'

'Harrie's missing,' Sarah said without preamble. 'We think George Barrett's taken her either to the Factory or to Liverpool asylum.'

He stared at them. 'Harrie? To the asylum? But ... why?'

'Because she's gone completely unhinged,' Friday said. 'Barking. And George wants to get rid of her.'

James dropped his bag. It contained a heavy pharmaceutical text, a bottle of brandy and an assortment of medical implements, and landed on the ground with a loud bang. Both Friday and Sarah jumped.

'When was this?'

'Yesterday. You have to help us, James. Please,' Sarah implored. 'We have to get her back.'

'I had no idea she'd deteriorated so much.' A suspicious frown creased James's face. 'Or has she? I wouldn't put it past George Barrett to get rid of her just to avoid the burden of her care.'

Friday said, 'No, she really has, and you'd have known it if you'd gone to see her.'

'Look, I damn well tried and she refused outright. I could hardly force my way into the Barretts' home, could I?'

'Some bad things have happened, James,' Sarah said. 'They've pushed her over the edge.'

'Well, of course I'll help. But which is it? The Factory or the asylum?'

'Don't know,' Sarah said. 'Harrie and George went missing yesterday morning. George isn't back yet and that makes Nora think he took her out to Liverpool, not Parramatta, because Liverpool's a longer trip. We're waiting for him to get back.'

James checked his watch. 'I'll get through my patients as quickly as possible and try to finish by two o'clock, then I'll meet you two at the Barretts'. Can you manage that?'

'Shite. I have to start work at one,' Friday said. 'Will you come and tell me what happens? Or send a message?' she asked Sarah.

'I'll need to talk to Adam,' Sarah said. Then she shook her head. 'No, bugger it, I'll be there, James.'

George arrived home at half past two, tired from getting up so early and with a sore arse from sitting on the hard seat of the gig for two days straight. He was also dreading what Nora was going to say about what he'd done, but that couldn't be helped. Once he fired Emma and got a new girl from the Factory — one who worked full time, for free, and only in the house — she'd see what a good idea it was. And he wouldn't have to worry about Leo Dundas any more.

As he trudged up the stairs to the parlour, he noticed the absence of noise in the house. Usually the kids were making a hell of a racket, but not today. Nora hadn't been in her shop, either. A horrible thought occurred to him and his stomach clenched into a hard, painful ball — was she so angry at what he'd done that she'd taken the kids and gone? But she couldn't. The kids were his — any magistrate in the colony would uphold that. He stepped onto the landing and nearly fainted with relief when he saw her sitting on the sofa.

'Nora.'

'Where the hell have you been? And where's Harrie?'

He sat down beside her. She stood up and moved away.

'Where are the kids?' he asked.

'Next door. I said, where's Harrie?'

'She was sick, love. I took her to a place where they can give her the best care possible.'

'Where?'

George knew his voice sounded shaky, so he spoke louder to control it. 'The asylum at Liverpool. The superintendent there says she has mania and melancholia. She's really very poorly.'

Nora's fists clenched and her face looked drained of blood. George had never seen her so angry. 'You fat, selfish sod,' she hissed. 'I'll never forgive you for this.'

'We'll get a new girl.'

'I don't want a new girl. I want Harrie! And that's not the point. You dumped her as though she's a piece of rubbish, just because she's ill!'

'Everyone else does it.'

'No, not everyone, George. Just mean, greedy bastards like you.'

'I am not greedy. Anyway, she's never going to get better. Anyone could see that.'

James stepped out of the children's bedroom. George almost shat himself.

'That's not true, Mr Barrett,' he said. 'With the right treatment, care and rest, Harrie could very well recover.'

'Who the hell let you in here?' George blustered, his heart pounding violently as the doctor strode across the floor and loomed over him. He'd forgotten about how keen James Downey was on Harrie.

'I did,' Nora said.

'I have a proposition for you,' James said. 'Permit me to buy Harrie's assignment papers from you. She will then become my responsibility.'

George snatched with both hands at the unexpected chance to make some money. 'Ten pounds. No, fifteen! Fifteen quid and you can have them.'

Nora marched over to the sofa and booted him in the shin. 'A shilling, George. We'll transfer Harrie's papers to Dr Downey for one shilling.'

'One piddling bob! What if I refuse?'

'Then I'll leave you.'

'Not with my kids, you won't,' George said, defiantly staring up into Nora's face. Noting her expression, however, he immediately regretted his comment.

'Then I'll have more. With another man,' Nora replied, her voice as cold as a snowy January day in London.

Oh God, George thought, his heart racing now and his palms suddenly sweaty. She meant Dundas. He knew it. He dug Harrie's assignment papers out of his satchel and handed them to her. She fetched a nib and ink and signed them, then he did, followed by the doctor; the shilling was handed over, and Harrie was in effect assigned to James Downey.

'One more thing,' James said.

'What?' George muttered.

James punched him full in the face, knocking him backwards onto the sofa, which he slid off like a half-empty sack of spuds until he came to rest on the floor, blood trickling from his nose.

'You deserved that,' Nora said.

Sarah, who'd been sitting on the Barretts' stairs, her ears flapping madly, sprang to her feet when James came pounding down.

'Jesus, did you hit him?'

Wincing, James flapped a set of grazed knuckles at her. Sarah's opinion of him rose even further.

'Did you hear all that?' he asked.

'Some of it. Not the beginning.'

James opened the back door. 'Would she really have left him?'

'Not sure but I doubt it. She'd never leave her kids. What are you doing now?'

'Riding out to Liverpool.' James looked at the sky.

'Will you make it before dark?'

'I can find somewhere to sleep if necessary.'

'You will bring her back, won't you?'

'I won't be leaving without her.'

On the street they parted ways — James to fetch his horse from the stables, Sarah to tell Friday what had happened. She hurried down Gloucester Street, ducked down a lane into Harrington then turned into Argyle, almost running by the time she reached Mrs Hislop's front door. She banged the knocker hard until Mrs Hislop answered, looking faintly irritated.

'I need to talk to Friday. It's urgent.'

'Hello, Sarah. I'm afraid she's upstairs with a customer.'

'Five minutes? Please? It's about Harrie.'

'Well, come in. I'll just check in the book to see how long she'll be.'

As Elizabeth disappeared into her office, Sarah darted silently past the door and up the stairs. Opening the first door she came to, she apologised and shut it again, quickly. The second room was empty, but she found who she wanted in the third.

Completely naked and with her hair tumbling down her back, Friday was sitting astride a reclining pale, trim and equally naked man.

'Oh, hello,' she said as Sarah stepped in and closed the door.

'He's back,' Sarah said. 'He did take her to Liverpool.'

Friday's lip curled. 'God, what an arsehole.'

'I know. But James bought her assignment papers off him, for a shilling. And then he punched the shit out of him.'

'James did? Bloody hell.'

'Don't mind me,' the customer said.

Friday patted his chest. 'Sorry, Ralph. Won't be a minute.'

'He's on his way out to Liverpool now, to bring her back.'

'Thank Christ for that,' Friday said.

'Well, that's it,' Sarah said. 'I'm off back to work.'

Ralph Kidd looked up at her with bright blue eyes and asked lazily, 'Why don't you stay and join us?'

Sarah glared at him. 'You couldn't afford me,' she said, and opened the door and stalked out.

Ralph grunted. 'Which one of your fascinating friends was that?'

'None of your business.'

James rode all that afternoon and as far into the night as he could before he feared that both he and his horse might collapse with exhaustion. When he came to a tavern — particularly unwholesome, as it turned out, but choices were few on the road south-west — he overpaid for a stable for his mount and a flea-ridden mattress for himself. While scratching at large red welts all over his body the next morning, he reflected he might have done better to sleep in the hay with his horse. He declined the tavern keeper's offer of an overpriced breakfast of ale, bread and a lump of cheese resembling an old piece of dried-out soap, and rode on until he found an establishment advertising better fare for a much lower fee. He rode for miles and miles, sometimes not seeing another soul, until he finally reached Liverpool at eleven o'clock in the morning.

He wondered if it might be quicker to take a boat back to Sydney along the Georges River, and if so, whether any vessel could accommodate his horse. Then again, any such journey would terminate at Botany Bay, the mouth of the Georges River, which would mean a further trip overland to Sydney Town, or by sea around to Port Jackson and Sydney Cove, which may in fact be too physically and mentally demanding for Harrie.

He rode in through the gates of the Liverpool lunatic asylum, and around to the rear of the building to find someone to take care of his horse. That achieved, he returned to the front door, knocked and was greeted by a porter in civilian clothing — a convict, he assumed. He was aware that almost all the staff at the asylum were unpaid bonded convicts with no training relevant to their positions, except for the superintendent, Thomas Plunkett, who had previously superintended the men's convict barracks at Parramatta, and the doctor, Edwin Ashton, and one other official whose name he didn't know.

As Harrie was a convict herself, the New South Wales government was obliged to pay for her care in the asylum — if she was staying, but she would not be staying. The government also paid the fees of free paupers. Any free settlers with means unfortunate enough to find themselves in the asylum paid seven shillings per day, or their guarantors did. The asylum had moved from Castle Hill north of Parramatta several years earlier, as the premises there had apparently been entirely unsuitable — decaying, overcrowded, and too far from Sydney for regular inspection. Of course, Liverpool was even more distant from Sydney, and James had been told that the old, abandoned courthouse was hardly in better condition than the farm buildings had been at Castle Hill.

While he waited for Dr Ashton, he inspected the ceiling of the foyer, which appeared to have been given a rudimentary sweep with a brush followed by a quick coat of white paint, entombing flies or some other insect in the emulsion. Someone in the building was shouting, and someone else was weeping rather manically. He knew that the treatment of the insane had improved markedly over the past forty years, particularly in the context of the asylum, thanks to the implementation of an enlightened theory of ethical and humane management. But the success of most public health treatment regimes depended on the money spent to support them, and the welfare of mental patients, in his admittedly limited experience, had never been at the top of any government's priority list. He'd been to Bethlem at Southwark in London several times to visit a mentally deranged aunt of his deceased wife, Emily, and had been appalled at the conditions in which the poor woman had been living — and Bethlem was supposed then to have been operating according to a philosophy of moral treatment. He couldn't see that this asylum would be any better, and had, in fact, heard that it most definitely wasn't.

He stood as a man strode towards him. 'Dr Downey? Good morning. I'm Dr Edwin Ashton. How do you do?'

James shook his hand. 'James Downey. I'm here concerning a patient admitted the day before yesterday, a Miss Harriet Clarke?'

'Yes. Property of …' Dr Ashton consulted a sheet of paper. 'A Mr George Barrett. He brought her in.'

'Actually, no. She's assigned to me now.'

Dr Ashton's scruffy eyebrows went up. 'Is that so?'

'It is.'

'Do you have the papers with you? One must apply a certain level of rigor to these things.'

'Yes. One must.' James handed over Harrie's assignment papers. It was obvious that Edwin Ashton was bursting to ask why he'd taken on responsibility for a mentally ill convict girl, but was far too polite.

'Well, that all seems to be in order.' Dr Ashton returned the documents. 'Thank you.'

'I take it you've made a diagnosis regarding Miss Clarke's condition?'

'Saw her yesterday.'

'And what conclusions have you drawn?'

'Unfortunately, Mr Barrett provided little information regarding the patient. In fact, he was rather keen to leave the premises as quickly as possible. But I gather there was quite an unpleasant scene at the time. I had, therefore, to make the diagnosis without much of a history. I take it you know Miss Clarke?'

'I do.'

'How long has she been unwell?'

'I'd say probably up to a year,' James said. 'Initially not as unwell as she is now, of course. I believe the illness has progressed exponentially over a matter of five or six months.'

Though Harrie must be in a dreadful state for Barrett to have dumped her here, he thought. Sarah had filled him in on the events concerning the death of Harrie's mother, and Janie and Rosie

Braine, and the transfer of Charlotte to the orphanage. Any one of those would have upset Harrie dreadfully, but all together, no wonder she'd lost her mind.

'Are you familiar with nervous disorders and maladies of the mind, Dr Downey?'

'Not intimately. It isn't my field. I'm a general physician, although I was a naval surgeon.'

'But you have some knowledge?'

'Of course.'

'Are you aware of any tragedies that may have befallen Miss Clarke?'

God, James thought, where do I start? 'She has lately suffered several bereavements, including that of her mother. Also, a small child she adores has recently been sent to the Female Orphan School, and she is constantly worried about her younger siblings left alone in London.'

'And was she perfectly healthy before the onset of the disorder? She didn't suffer any accidents involving the head? Illnesses?'

James thought back to the way Harrie had once been — capable, calm, loyal, cheerful, and soft and rounded like a little robin — and almost burst into tears. 'No, no accidents, no illnesses. She was a normal happy young woman. Well, as happy as possible, given she'd recently been transported.'

'So no evidence of organic cause. Good. Thank you. The history complements my diagnosis admirably.'

'Which is?'

'At first I assumed hysteria, which is, as I'm sure you know, the nervous disorder to which females are most prone. However, after examination I decided on severe melancholia, likely to be the result of prolonged exposure to calamitous or mournful circumstances, interspersed with episodes of periodical but acute mania. Though I was also considering, possibly, romantic disappointment as a cause for the melancholia. Has she been disappointed in love?'

'Er, I wouldn't know.'

'You should read Dr Alexander Morison's *Outlines of Lectures on Mental Diseases*. Consultant at Bethlem, talks about hysteria, melancholia and romantic disappointment. Very informative. Miss Clarke hears voices, did you know that?'

'Multiple voices? Not just one?' James was thinking of Harrie's belief that she could talk to Rachel's 'ghost'.

'Well, it's difficult to get much out of her at the moment, as she's barely communicative —'

'Is she not talking at all?' Oh, bloody hell, James thought. Why had he not insisted on seeing her? How could he have let her down so badly?

'The odd word, perhaps. But from observation I gather she hears endless chattering in her head. Sometimes, however, it appears to be just one person. On occasion she says the name Rachel out loud, as if in conversation.'

So she hadn't gone away. 'And your prognosis?'

'On admittance she lapsed into an episode of really rather violent mania and had to be fitted with a restraint.'

'Good God, a straitjacket?' James was horrified.

'Only until she settled, which she did after a liberal measure of laudanum. She spent the night comfortably, though she refused food this morning.'

'Your prognosis, man,' James said more tersely than he'd meant to. 'Will she recover or not?'

'Oh, I think so. In time, though possibly quite some considerable time. Patients with reactive nervous disorders, as opposed to organic, often do recover. We have a very comprehensive and moral treatment plan here. We follow, more or less, the regime of Philippe Pinel. Have you read his book, *Treatise on Insanity*? Most enlightening. We provide nourishing food and good, sound laudanum-assisted sleep at night, we insist our patients partake in chores, crafts and daily walks — those who are capable, of course —

and we take considerable care to separate our less acute patients from our idiots, syphilitics and those with criminal tendencies.'

'Are you saying, then, that what Miss Clarke needs is good food, plenty of sleep, rest and something to occupy her?'

'Essentially, yes.'

'I can provide that,' James said. 'Please arrange for her release. I'll be taking Miss Clarke home today. Now, in fact.'

'Oh. Well. Do you not even want to see her first? You might be inclined to change your mind.'

'I won't,' James replied quickly, suddenly alarmed that for some reason he might be prevented from taking Harrie home. That wouldn't be the case, of course — Dr Ashton worked for the New South Wales government, which surely would rather not pay for Harrie's care — but still, the idea filled him with a panicky terror. Ashton seemed competent enough, but he'd put Harrie in a damned straitjacket!

'That's entirely your prerogative, of course, as her master,' Dr Ashton said. 'Mr Plunkett, the superintendent, will have to sign her release papers, but I'm willing to transfer her medical care to you.'

'Excellent.' James felt himself relax. 'Thank you. Now, if you'd kindly show me to, er, wherever she is.'

He followed the doctor along a gloomy, smelly corridor, past several closed doors from behind which came thumps and muffled wails, and up a staircase to the next floor and through a set of locked doors. His nostrils were immediately assaulted by the stink of urine, and worse. So much for Dr Ashton's insistence that his patients received moral treatment, fresh air, calming rest and restorative distraction. The light was a little better up here, though the large windows at each end of the corridor had been reinforced with bars. At one, a woman stood as still as stone, staring down at the property next door, her hands stiff by her sides, the tendons in her neck rigid. Farther along, an elderly man shuffled the length of the corridor muttering to himself, his head down, one arm out, his hand touching the wall as though he were afraid he might fall. When James drew level with him, he saw he wasn't old at all, just stooped and prematurely completely grey.

James and Dr Ashton passed an open area, a sort of parlour in which several sofas and armchairs were arranged around a fireplace. James looked in and regretted it, seeing only blank and lost faces. In a chair a young woman sat and rocked what he feared must be an imaginary infant, while a man knelt on the floor, knocking his head persistently against the wall. Dr Ashton broke away to attend to him, helping him to his feet and sitting him on a sofa.

James swallowed. Christ, he couldn't leave Harrie in a place like this. He wondered where the warders were.

'This way,' the doctor said.

They came to a room, the door of which was ajar. The small window was barred and the furniture consisted of a single iron bedstead, a small chest of drawers, and a wooden chair. Harrie was lying on the bed, dressed, apparently dozing.

'Was she given laudanum this morning?' James asked.

'No.'

James moved closer. Harrie's face was pasty white, her lips dry and flaking, and there was a sore in the corner of her mouth. Her hair had lost all its lustre and she was so thin that the bird-like bones of her hands, tucked under her chin like a child's, were visible through the skin.

'Harrie?' he said gently.

Nothing for a long while, then her eyelids flickered and opened. 'James?' Her voice sounded like the wind in dry grass.

'It's all right now, my dearest. I've come to take you home.'

As Harrie gazed at him, a tear welled from one eye and trickled slowly across her nose.

Sarah lay in Adam's arms, having just finished telling him about James's rescue of Harrie from the asylum the previous day. Now, she had a question for him she was almost too afraid to ask, and was dreading his answer. But she couldn't put it off any longer.

'Adam?'

'Mmm?'

'You know how Charlotte's been sent to the orphanage at Parramatta?' He was aware, of course, that she and Friday had visited her the day they'd discovered that poor Janie and Rosie had died. She'd come home extremely upset and had talked of little else.

Adam gave her a sympathetic squeeze. 'Poor little thing.'

'Well, the matron there, some do-good reverend's wife called Mrs Duff, implied that it might be possible for Charlotte to be adopted. She didn't say it outright, but she did imply it.'

'After you asked her, you mean?'

Sarah winced inwardly — she might have known he'd see right through her. 'Well, I might have mentioned it, yes.'

Adam propped himself up on an elbow so he could see her face. 'Adopted by you?'

'Maybe.'

'But, love, you're an assigned convict. Would that be allowed?'

'I'm married to you, and you have a conditional pardon. So, yes, apparently it might be allowed.'

'Do you want to adopt her?' Adam asked gently. 'According to you, you don't even like children.' He smoothed her hair. 'Though Friday tells me they like you.'

Sarah kept silent, waiting.

'I know she's Rachel's daughter, and how much Rachel meant to you,' he went on. 'To all of you. But it's a responsibility, a child. It's not like bringing Clifford home. You know, a few mutton bones and a kick up the bum when she pees on the rug.'

Sarah sat up, her back against the headboard. Right now she needed not to be distracted by the closeness of Adam's inviting body. 'I want to know, what do you think? Do you want to adopt her?'

Adam sat up beside her, rearranged the sheet over their laps, fussed about, sighed, and said, 'No, I don't, Sarah. I'm sorry. It's got nothing to do with whose child she is. I just don't want to share you with anyone. Not for a while, anyway. It's bad enough with that bloody dog.'

Sarah lifted his hand and kissed it, so relieved she couldn't speak.

James installed Harrie in Rowie Harris's old room at his cottage, and rallied everyone he could think of to help. He asked his business partner, Dr Lawrence Chandler, to thoroughly examine her, not because James believed he himself wasn't up to the task, but because he was worried about accusations of impropriety. Not being an expert on nervous disorders, Lawrence couldn't confidently confirm Dr Ashton's specific diagnosis, but he did consider that as well as being mentally disturbed, Harrie was very undernourished, likely somewhat anaemic, and mentally and physically exhausted. He advised plenty of good food, nourishing tonic, sleep and rest. Which, James told him, was pretty much what Dr Ashton had said.

Sarah and Friday arrived to thoroughly clean Harrie's new room — and James's cottage, which had gone somewhat to the dogs since Rowie had disappeared — bringing with them new linen, and all of Harrie's things from her old room at the Barretts', including Angus. Friday had a word with Elizabeth Hislop, who had a word with James, and on the third day, Elizabeth's girl Ivy moved in with Harrie to keep her company day and night, sleeping on a mattress on the floor of her room, which allowed James to return to work. As Ivy wasn't a particularly inspired cook, Elizabeth arranged to have nourishing meals sent over from the hotel kitchen four days a week, and, after Sarah talked to Adam's friend Bernard Cole, Bernard's lovely wife, Ruthie, happily agreed to provide her famously girth-increasing meals and homemade baking the other three. This left Ivy time to spend with Harrie during the day, and when she was busy with housework, Sarah and Friday sat with her whenever they could get away from work. James, of course, dedicated every evening to her, except when he was called out. Matthew also came around, to read to Harrie, to hold her hand while she slept, and to listen patiently for hours to James blaming himself for the terrible state into which she had slipped.

Nora and her children were also frequent visitors, the kids desperate to see her and bringing her little gifts — a cotton handkerchief embroidered with Harrie's initials from Abigail, biscuits 'made' by Samuel and Lewis, and a paper twist of lemon drops from Hannah with one lemon drop left in it. Leo Dundas called, too, on the fourth evening, with an enormous bunch of flowers from the market that must have cost the earth, and a message from Serafina Fortune saying she was very confident that Harrie would get better. Friday, who was there at the time, didn't bother to ask Leo how Serafina had known about what had happened.

James stopped Leo as he went to leave. 'Mr Dundas, may I have a word?'

Leo almost said, 'It's a free country,' but, actually, New South Wales wasn't. He didn't feel like talking to James Downey. Any cove who'd behaved as pompously and arrogantly towards Harrie as Downey had in the past didn't deserve respect, even if he had just dragged her out of a lunatic asylum. But he probably did deserve a hearing. 'If you like.'

'I must confess I hadn't realised until recently that Harrie had been working for you,' James said. 'I was under the impression she'd been solely assigned to the Barretts. But Friday tells me she draws designs for you, and has lately done some tattooing. Some arrangement you had with George Barrett?'

'Actually, it was an arrangement I had with Harrie. George Barrett only thought he was profiting from the deal.'

'Yes, well, Harrie is now assigned to me, so I'm afraid that will all have to stop.'

Leo stared James in the eye. They were the same height, so it wasn't difficult. 'You think you own her now, do you? Just because your name's on her papers?'

'Of course not. It has nothing to do with ownership. Bonded convicts aren't slaves.' James's voice was frosty. 'I have taken over responsibility for Harrie's welfare and I mean to see that she receives the best care possible. I don't feel that tattooing sailors in some little shop down on the waterfront is in her best interests.'

'Have you talked to her about this?'

'Not yet. The time isn't right.'

'Well, when it is, I suggest you do,' Leo said. 'She enjoys her work, she's good at it, and she very much appreciates the money. Which, I gather, she uses to support her friend's daughter in the Factory, and her brother and sisters at home. She won't want to forfeit that.'

'Perhaps not, but we'll cross that bridge when we come to it.'

'No, you won't. But she'll have to.' Leo's bearded chin went up. 'Do I take this to mean I'm not welcome here?'

James hesitated, but only for a second. 'Friday tells me Harrie is very fond of you, Mr Dundas. My aim is to surround her with all those who care for her, and from whom she might draw love and support. So yes, you are welcome.'

Perhaps not such a shit after all, Leo thought grudgingly. Still a stuffy bugger, though. 'Thank you.'

James gestured at the tattoo on Leo's forearm. 'Royal Navy?'

'Slightly long story. Started off merchant, got pressed, sailed the world for a few years, saw the Battles of Cape St Vincent and the Nile, then eventually got out. My choice.' He'd deserted, in Japan, but what did it matter if he admitted it to James Downey now? Downey wasn't in the Andrew any more, either.

'It's a hard life,' James said. 'I'm glad I'm out.'

'It is, and so am I,' Leo agreed.

'Though I do miss the sea,' James admitted.

'Aye, she gets in your blood.'

Loitering unobtrusively by the hearth, fetching hot water from the kettle for another pot of tea, Friday smiled to herself, pleased that it seemed James and Leo were no longer circling each other like a pair of feral dogs. Silly buggers.

And what of Harrie herself? After about a week, she slowly started to improve. She began to talk again — and to real people, not just to those only she could hear — she ate a little of everything that was put in front of her, she ventured out of her room to the parlour and helped Ivy to peel late apples to stew for breakfast and plums for preserves, and she walked in the garden, pulling weeds when she had the energy. But she was never, ever left alone. She desperately wanted to go to Parramatta to visit Charlotte, but James — and Friday and Sarah — said no. James insisted that she drink tonic three times a day, rest whenever she felt even vaguely tired, which was much of the time, and gave her laudanum at night so that she slept without dreaming.

To her enormous relief, the endless chattering of voices in her head faded, giving her a sort of peace for the first time in months. But Rachel abandoned her, too, during the day at least, and she couldn't swim hard enough against the velvet tide of laudanum that lulled her to sleep at night to know whether she came to her then. Harrie missed her. She started to put on a little weight, colour came back into her face and the sores on her mouth and her body began to heal. By the end of November she was starting to look like the old Harrie.

But she wasn't the old Harrie, even though she'd improved vastly, and everyone knew it, not least James.

# Part Three

# And Drown the Wakeful Anguish of the Soul

# Chapter Twelve

*December 1831, Sydney Town*

On the first day of December, in the evening, while Harrie, James, Ivy and Friday sat in the parlour with the front door open to let in the last of the day's breeze, Harrie told James she wanted to go back to work.

'But you don't have any work,' James said. 'You're assigned to me now, and I don't expect you to do anything. I don't want you to do anything.'

Harrie looked at him beseechingly. How was she going to say this? She didn't want to hurt his feelings, but sitting around doing nothing was fraying her nerves. That awful sensation of dread was worming its way back into her belly. She desperately needed something to keep her mind occupied and all the bad things … out.

'I'm so grateful to you for bringing me back from Liverpool, I really am, and I'm feeling so much better, but I can't just sit here idly. I need to keep busy. I don't want to think all the time, and I do, when I'm idle. And I do have work, James. I have a job at Leo's.'

'I'd really rather you didn't go back to that,' James said firmly.

Friday nudged Ivy. 'Why don't we go and tidy Harrie's room?'

They left, but once outside, huddled just beyond the back door, listening avidly.

James said, 'There's no need for you to work, Harrie. I can give you everything you need.'

'No, you don't understand,' Harrie insisted. 'I have to make money to send home to Robbie and Sophie and Anna, and Leo paid me very well. And we might need money for Charlotte until we can get her out of that awful place.'

As she said this, she was engulfed by a wave of grief and need so savage she literally saw stars. Poor little Charlotte had been in the orphanage for nearly a month, all by herself, and it was heartbreaking. They had to rescue her. But Friday and Sarah didn't seem to be doing much to help her at all, apparently content to let her languish there, frightened and alone. Oh, Friday said they had a plan, but no matter how many times Harrie asked, Friday wouldn't say what it was. She was to concentrate on getting better, according to Friday, not worry about Charlotte. They were excluding her, and Harrie didn't know why. Couldn't they see what was so obvious, that she would be the best mother for Charlotte? She was feeling vastly better now, and she loved Charlotte as dearly as she loved Rachel. And even though sometimes her yearning for Charlotte felt like a fever, growing ever more consuming by the day, and a little tiny part of her did wonder now and then just how truly recovered she really was, it didn't matter. All that mattered was Charlotte.

'I can give you money,' James said. 'God knows I'm not short of funds.'

'I don't want you to give me money. I'm not your wife. I can earn my own!' Harrie's heart pounded alarmingly. Would he also give her money so she could contribute to Bella Shand's next blackmail demand?

James slipped off the mourning ring he'd worn for the past two years and dropped it into his pocket. 'Then be my wife, Harrie. Marry me. Please.'

Outside, Friday and Ivy gawped at each other, eyes huge with delight.

'No. I can't,' Harrie said flatly. 'I'm sorry, I just can't.' She couldn't look at him, unable to bear the disappointment on his face. She wanted to weep. She wanted to die. He'd finally asked her, and she couldn't say yes because of what she was and what she'd done.

'Shit,' Friday cursed.

'I want to go back to work for Leo,' Harrie said again, desperate to get away from the subject of marriage, desperate to stifle her own bitter disappointment.

'I'd really prefer that you didn't,' James said, his voice stiff with dejection.

'Why not?'

'It's not an appropriate thing for someone like you to do.'

'Someone like me? A mad convict girl?'

'You're not mad. You're recovering from a nervous disorder.'

'If I did it anyway, would you send me back to the Factory?'

'No.'

'Would you throw me out of your house?'

'No.'

'Would you stop being so nice to me?'

'Of course not.'

'What would you do?'

James sighed. 'I'd worry, Harrie. I always do.'

Harrie went back to work for Leo on the fifth day of December. They agreed that she should work three mornings a week, drawing designs onto customers and tattooing some of the easier outlines. If she coped with that, Harrie hoped after a month or so to also work part time for Nora, who had asked her if she could assist her some afternoons with her sewing. Paid, of course, out of Nora's own purse, and to hell with George. Emma, Nora had told Harrie, had left, afraid of what might happen to her if she, too, fell foul of George, and a new girl had arrived from the Factory. Her name was Tilly, she was pleasant and a moderately competent domestic, and Hannah had bitten her twice.

Ivy was to stay on with Harrie and James for another six weeks, but when Harrie was feeling fully fit she would take over the domestic duties at James's cottage and Ivy would return to the Siren's Arms.

Everything, Friday said to Sarah one day, looked as though it was getting back to normal, and now that Harrie was living in James's house, surely she would give in eventually and agree to marry him?

'I wouldn't bet on it,' Sarah said. 'She might not be a raving lunatic any more, but I don't know if she'll ever make peace with her guilt over what we did to Keegan.'

Friday got out her pipe and tamped tobacco into it. 'You know, if I'd known it was going to turn out like this, I wouldn't have let her come with us.'

'No. Neither would I.'

'But she really wanted to, didn't she? She was so angry. And she really put the boot in. I think she kicked him harder than you and me put together. So why the hell is she so haunted by it?'

'I think,' Sarah said, 'she had to because she needed to see the scales balanced. She thought it was a terrible injustice. And it bloody well was. But finding out that poor Rachel's brain burst because she had a disease and not because of what Keegan did to her really knocked her sideways.'

'But Rachel might have been all right if she hadn't had Charlotte. And that was definitely Keegan's fault.'

'I know, but Harrie isn't seeing it like that. And she's suffering for it now because, frankly, she's a better person than you and I will ever be.'

'Do you think so?' Friday said, unoffended.

'Well, don't you?'

'Yeah, I do, actually.'

Harrie and Leo were at work when a customer, a tar by the look of him, came in requesting a tattoo. For a change there was no one booked, so Leo sat him in the chair. The man reeked of alcohol, was unsteady on his feet and seemed short of breath, clearly suffering from the horrors.

'Royal Navy or merchant?' Leo asked conversationally.

'Merchant, retired,' the man said, wiping sweat off his brow. 'You?'

'Both. Got a name, have you?'

'Malcolm Leary. Just got into port last night, had a few rums, a woman. Old habits die hard. Beg your pardon, girl,' he said, nodding at Harrie. 'She your good wife?'

'My assistant. She works the needles and draws damned good flash.'

'Is that so? There's a novelty.'

'Got anything in mind?' Leo asked.

'Already got plenty of ink, so just something small, a memento of me visit. But maybe something a bit different, like?' Malcolm Leary gazed around at the flash on the walls, and eventually pointed to an image of a vicious-looking, stubby little dog-like animal with a wide-open mouth full of sharp teeth. 'What the hell's that?'

'They're called devils. Ferocious little buggers.'

'You only get them here?'

'Down south in Van Diemen's Land.'

'That'll do,' Malcolm Leary said. 'On top of me wrist here.'

Trying not to breathe in through her nose, Harrie sat down next to him and drew the image onto his skin with Indian ink, then used blotting paper to carefully soak up the excess.

'Happy?' Leo asked.

Malcolm nodded, retrieved his handkerchief and wiped his gleaming face yet again. 'Bloody hot here, isn't it?'

Leo took his place on the stool and prepared pigment and his needles. 'In summer it is. Is that a Liverpool accent?'

'It is. Ever been there?'

'Often, when I was at sea. What brings you to New South Wales?'

'I'm looking for someone. Me older brother, Jonah Leary. Convict. D'you know him?'

'Can't say I do.'

'What about you?' Malcolm looked at Harrie.

She shook her head.

Malcolm belched, made a pained face and rubbed his chest. 'Beg pardon. Cheap rum. Jonah was sent here in 1825 on a seven-year sentence, so his time's nearly up. Where am I likely to find him?'

'Could be anywhere in the district.' Leo dipped his brush into a tiny pot of black pigment, touched the needles against it, and went to work. 'Likely he's got a ticket of leave by now, and holding down a proper job. But if you're not farm folk, I'd say he's still in town.'

Malcolm was silent for a while, except for the rasp of his heavy, accelerated breathing. At last he said, 'I asked in the pub last night. The Black Rat? I'm lodging there. Bit of a shithole but the ladies are friendly. And they say you're the best tattooist in town. Is that right?'

Leo shrugged.

'Me brother Jonah has a tattoo,' Malcolm went on. 'Unusual. Me other brother Bennett had something similar. Being an artist of note, I was thinking you might have heard of Jonah.'

'No, can't help you.'

Malcolm gripped Leo's hand. 'Stop a minute and I'll show you what I'm talking about.'

He stood, unbuttoned his heavy shirt and slipped it off, releasing a sour waft of stale body odour and revealing a fish-white belly hanging over the waistband of his trousers. Then he turned, arms elevated. On his back was a tattoo extending from just above his shoulder blades to his waist. It was obviously some years old as the ink had spread and faded slightly, and sparse patches of dark hair obscured the lines in places, but it was clear that what he wore on his skin was a map. It had been expertly executed and was very detailed, but lacked street names and gave no indication of what the map represented.

He faced Leo and Harrie again. 'Like that, but not exactly the same. Nice piece of work, eh?'

Leo agreed that it was.

'So have you ever seen or heard of someone with anything like this?'

'I would tell you if I had,' Leo said. 'I'd certainly remember it. It's a map of part of a town or city, isn't it?'

Malcolm didn't answer. He bent to retrieve his shirt and sat down. But instead of straightening, he stayed bent, his head down. Then he let out a grunt, followed by a low moan.

Leo stared at him for a second, then grasped his shoulders and pushed him upright. The man's sweaty face was scarlet, his teeth bared in pain. His right hand flapped about helplessly, then settled on his naked left breast, squeezing the flesh there until it whitened around his fingers.

'The map on me back,' he gasped. 'Find Jonah and give it to him. Please.'

He grimaced again, his eyes seemed almost to bulge from his head and he slumped sideways in the chair, a dribble of thick yellowish spit trickling from his slack mouth.

'Bloody hell,' Leo said into the silence. 'I think he's slipped his cable.'

A terrible stink rose off Malcolm Leary then, and Harrie stepped well back, fanning the air in front of her face, which didn't help at all.

Leo held his nose and eyed Harrie. 'Are you all right, lass?'

She nodded. It had given her a fright, but she'd seen folk die often enough. She felt curiously flat. Detached.

'That's all I need,' Leo muttered. 'A bloody dead body covered in shite in my shop. Go and get a sheet off the cot in the other room, there's a good lass.'

Harrie did as she was told. Leo laid the sheet over Malcolm Leary's body, making sure to cover his face.

'We can't leave him there,' Harrie said.

'I do know that, lass. He's in my good tattoo chair and I've got a customer coming in at ten, not to mention he'll start to go over in fairly short order.'

'Should we fetch the undertaker?'

Leo sighed. 'Not yet. The cove expressed a dying wish, and I can't deny a man that. Especially one who's sailed the same seas I have. I suppose I'll have to look for this bloody brother of his.'

'But you said you didn't know him.'

'I don't, but he shouldn't be that hard to find. I'll ask around the pubs tonight.' Leo had a bad feeling about this: something to do with the way the dead man had said his final words. 'I'll put Mr Leary in my kitchen, for now. Christ.'

Leo asked everyone he knew — a fair number of folk — but learnt nothing of Jonah Leary that night, or the next morning, which was extremely unfortunate as his dead brother was really starting to stink. But still he couldn't bring himself to call in the undertaker, not until he'd executed Malcolm Leary's last request. Finally, he did what he should have done in the first place, and what he suspected Leary had been alluding to with his dying breath. He made a trip to the chemist for a few necessary items, then, back home again, tied a peppermint oil-infused cloth around his face, unwrapped Leary's now grey, greasy and expanding corpse, turned it over, and carefully flayed the map off its back with a very sharp knife.

There was no blood, of course, the heart having stopped beating, but the smell was nauseating and the feel of the thin layer of skin as it came off — far too easily — made his gorge rise. He gently lowered the piece of skin into a large jar filled with a mix of ethyl alcohol and formalin, and watched as it floated around and finally settled near the bottom like a grotesque sort of manta ray. If Jonah

Leary — if he ever turned up — wanted his dead brother's tattoo dried, he could take it to a tanner himself.

He put the jar aside, rolled the corpse again in its sheet, washed his hands and arms thoroughly with lye soap, and went down the street to speak to the nearest undertaker. He'd had enough of harbouring a dead body in his house. The flies had already arrived, and the rats wouldn't be far behind.

Friday was sitting in the brothel's salon, filing her fingernails, chatting to Hazel and waiting for her next cully to arrive, when Mrs H stuck her head around the door.

'Friday, can I talk to you? In my office?'

'Ooh, what have you done now?' Hazel asked.

Friday stifled a sigh. It was probably about the state she'd come home in last night. Again. She trudged down the hall expecting an earful, but when she entered the office she found herself looking at an old man sitting in the good chair next to Mrs H's desk.

'Friday, I'm sure you'll remember Mr Lucian Meriwether,' Elizabeth said. 'He spent some time with you … When did you say you last visited our establishment, Mr Meriwether?'

'In September and October of 1830, encounters I have never forgotten.'

Mr Meriwether pushed himself to his feet with the aid of a silver-topped cane, grasped Friday's hand and kissed it. 'Miss Friday, I'm absolutely delighted to see you again. You look as charming as ever.'

Friday had certainly forgotten ever meeting him. Silly old shit. He must be sixty-five years old at the very least. He was as bald as an egg on top, the remaining strands of his white hair smoothed back at the sides — though at least he wasn't wearing a wig. They always made her sneeze. His beeswax-coloured face was wrinkled, jowly and disconcertingly kind-looking; he had pouches beneath his eyes, and he wore expensive Waterloo dentures. Hunch-shouldered, he was tall and had a pot belly, and obviously plenty of money as his cutaway jacket was of very fine cloth and his off-white trousers, hugging slightly bowed legs, of best kerseymere. A heavy ring set with a dark red stone glittered on his right hand, and a thick gold watch chain looped between a button and a pocket in his waistcoat. Definitely not short of a bob. She wondered if he'd tipped her well.

'Lovely to see you again, Mr Meriwether.'

'I've been in London for some months,' he said, resting his hands one on top of the other on the head of his cane. 'I only arrived back in New South Wales on the fourteenth of October. Just in time to attend your unfortunate appearance in the police court.'

Friday's heart sank. 'Oh. Was it you who —?'

'It was indeed,' Lucian replied, 'and let me say it was a great honour and a privilege to be able to assist you.'

God, Friday thought wearily, now he's here to claim privileges of his bloody own. Still, shagging a decrepit old man for nothing was better than going to gaol. Just. 'I'm ever so grateful for your kindness and generosity, Mr Meriwether. I truly am.'

Lucian waggled his fingers dismissively. 'It was the least I could do.'

Elizabeth said, 'Mr Meriwether has a proposition for you, Friday.'

Here we go.

'Mr Meriwether has a certain peccadillo,' Elizabeth went on, 'and it is his desire that you might accommodate him.'

Friday stared at her. What the hell was a peccadillo? 'I don't do animals.'

'Tastes, Friday,' Elizabeth said. 'Mr Meriwether has slightly unusual tastes.'

'Yes. I enjoy being whipped,' Lucian said.

Oh, was that all. 'I've never done any of that, myself,' Friday said.

'Would you care to learn?' Lucian asked. 'I do hope so. I've thought of little else while I was away, even while I was visiting the flogging brothels of Covent Garden and Marylebone. Mrs Berkeley — have you heard of her? — has invented a marvellous new flogging machine. Accomplished though she is, it was your magnificent muscles flexing and your titan's hair flying as you wield the whip that I couldn't help imagining.'

Friday knew she had no choice but to learn. She owed Lucian Meriwether. 'Would you want sex as well?'

'No, you don't understand, the flogging is the sex,' Lucian said eagerly. 'At least, for me it is.'

Actually, that sounded like quite a good deal. Perking up, Friday said, 'I'd be very pleased to accommodate your peccadillo, Mr Meriwether.'

'You would need to come to my home, however. I hold a position of some authority on the board of the Benevolent Society. It would not do for my private proclivities to become public knowledge.'

'What about Mrs Meriwether?'

'Mrs Meriwether, God rest her soul, passed on several years ago. There is only me at home now, and my driver and a servant.'

Friday turned to Elizabeth. 'We don't have any whips, do we?'

'I'll have to talk to Minnie Thompson. She caters to that sort of thing.'

'Could you arrange for some lessons as well, Mrs Hislop?' Lucian asked. 'I'm sure you realise there is a very specific art to flogging. Naturally I will pay any costs associated with that, above and beyond payments to Miss Friday.'

Friday blinked, surprised and pleased to know she would be getting paid. And then she thought, lessons? How hard can it be, whacking the shite out of someone with a whip?

'Of course,' Elizabeth said. 'When would you like your first appointment with Friday?'

'Let's say in three weeks?' Lucian smiled with his bright, slightly ill-fitting teeth. 'I don't mind if she's a bit rough around the edges. I really don't think I can wait any longer than that.'

\* \* \*

Standing outside James's cottage, surrounded by the busy nocturnal sounds of early summer, Friday blew a mouthful of pipe smoke at a cloud of voracious mosquitoes and said to Sarah, 'She's going to be so angry we went without her.'

'But you know what would have happened if she'd come with us.'

Friday did. Poor Harrie would only have become dreadfully upset at the sight of Charlotte in her little orphanage gown, standing up in that crib, her hands wrapped around the bars, red-faced and shrieking to be picked up. It had been upsetting enough for her and Sarah. This time, Mrs Duff had only allowed them to visit the nursery while the babies were awake, which made Friday wonder, did the poor little things do anything but sit around in that room? Did they not get to toddle about, or play on the floor, or go outside in the fresh air? Sarah had asked Mrs Duff, and she'd said yes, they did, but you just didn't know, did you, unless you saw it with your own eyes? And this time the old boot had told them they were forbidden to touch Charlotte, so Friday had had to pretend to faint in the corridor, and while Mrs Duff's back was turned Sarah had ducked into the nursery and picked her up.

'I'm pretty sure we've buggered our chances of going back,' Friday said. 'Well, at least of getting anywhere near Charlotte. She'll be watching us like a hawk now, that woman.'

Sarah nodded. 'I'm glad I never said anything to Harrie about adopting her. It would have been cruel to get her hopes up and then have to tell her that Adam said no.'

'D'you think she would have been happy about it? If you had adopted her?'

Sarah waved a mosquito away from her face. 'I don't know. Probably not.'

'You didn't really want her, though, did you?'

'I did so.'

'Are you sure?' Friday said. 'Because that day when you and Harrie had that tiff going out to the Factory, and you said in the end you would adopt her, I sort of felt it was only to settle her down.'

Sarah looked uncharacteristically guilty. 'Oh, I suppose it was, really. Look, I love Charlotte, I do. But it wouldn't just be me, would it? It'd be Adam, too. And it isn't what he wants.'

'Or you.' In the moonlight Friday noted that Sarah's expression was rapidly changing from guilty to shitty.

'Look, Harrie's desperate to have Charlotte. She'd make a much better mother than I would. She's getting better, she's gone back to work, and if she stopped being such an idiot about James, she could *have* Charlotte. I mean, he's asked her to marry him, for God's sake. He's far more likely to impress the bloody Duffs than Adam and I are. And Harrie's said no!'

'You know why she won't marry him.'

'Well, it's time she got past that,' Sarah declared.

'Well, what a stupid thing to say. You know she can't. You're the one who said she's still suffering because she's a better person than you and me. Not everyone's as tough as you, you know.'

'You are.'

Friday considered how often she'd cried — and drunk — herself to sleep since Aria had gone, and thought, no, I'm not, Sarah. I'm nowhere near as tough as you.

'Oh, it's you two,' a voice said.

Friday almost leapt out of her skin, and whirled to face the sound.

James appeared out of the shadows of a wattle bush. 'Sorry. I heard talking. I came to see who it was.'

Fucking hell. Friday shot Sarah a glance. Had he heard any of that?

'We've come to see Harrie,' she said.

'Well, come in, then,' James said, slapping at a mosquito. 'You'll get eaten alive out here.'

\* \* \*

The bamboo curtain rattled as someone entered the shop.

Leo said, 'Be with you in a few minutes.'

Harrie looked up from her work, eyed the man briefly, then focused herself and reapplied the needles. She only had half an inch to go and the outline would be complete. The customer, a sailor, had chosen one of her designs — a small version of an angel with bat wings — and when the swelling from the outline had settled in a few days, and providing there was no infection, Leo would start on the shading.

At last she finished, wiped away the blood and applied some salve. The sailor thanked her and paid, and left the shop gingerly shrugging into his canvas jacket.

The stranger sat himself down in the tattoo chair. He looked faintly familiar, though Harrie couldn't think why, and was a little above average height for a man, dark-haired, rough-shaven, thin but obviously very fit. He wore a workman's clothing — trousers, shirt, jacket, boots — and a hat, which he took off and set on his lap. She thought he was probably about thirty-five.

'You need to book if you're wanting a tattoo,' Leo said sharply.

'I don't,' the man said. 'The name's Jonah Leary.'

'Ah.' Leo crossed his arms. 'I've been on the lookout for you.'

Wiping down her needles, Harrie nodded to herself. So that's where she'd seen an echo of those facial features — on Malcolm Leary.

'So I've heard,' Jonah Leary said.

'Look, I'm sorry to tell you this,' Leo said, 'but your brother's passed on.'

Jonah Leary looked faintly disbelieving. 'Is that so? How would you know? Me brother, both me brothers, are living in England.'

'No, I'm afraid at least one of them was here in Sydney last week.'

Stony-faced now, Jonah Leary said, 'Which one?'

'Malcolm.'

'And?'

'He'd come in for a tattoo, obviously. He was sitting in that very chair, and, well, he had some sort of seizure and died.'

Leary cocked his head. 'Who says it was me brother?'

'He did. He told us he'd come to New South Wales to look for you. He showed us a tattoo of a map on his back. Asked if we'd seen you — another cove with ink like his.'

Leary was suddenly listening very hard.

'Just before he died,' Leo went on, 'he asked us, he asked me, to find you and give it to you.'

'What, exactly, did he say about it?' Leary demanded.

'Nothing. Nothing at all. Just that he wanted you to have it. I put the word out but nobody seemed to know anything about you.'

'I been working out Parramatta way. Where's me brother now?'

'He died a week ago. It's been hot. I had to fetch the undertaker.'

Jonah Leary was out of the chair in a flash, fists clenched, but Leo was even faster, darting between Harrie and their visitor, a knife suddenly in his hand.

'Settle down. I'll have no temperamental behaviour in my shop.'

Reluctantly, Leary sat. 'Where's he buried? You had no right to do that. Burial's a job for next of kin.'

'We had no choice.' Leo went to the cabinet that held his books and papers and took out the jar containing Malcolm's skin. 'I took it off him before the undertaker arrived.'

Harrie glanced at the jar then quickly away. She hadn't known he'd done that. Thank God she hadn't been here when he had.

Leary took the jar, held it up to the glow of a Sinumbra lamp, and shook it to make the skin unfurl in the solution. After a minute or two of intense study, he lowered the jar to his knee. 'You did a good job.' He stood and walked to the door, where he turned, nodded once and said, 'I'm obliged to you for salvaging it for me.'

'I thought you wanted to know where your brother was buried?' Leo said.

'No need, now. I've got what I wanted,' Leary said. 'What was the name of the undertaker?'

'Brownlow and Son. Up the street.'

Leary nodded again and walked out.

Harrie said, 'God, how heartless.'

'I'll say,' Leo agreed. 'Not a lot of love lost there, I suspect. Not from his side, anyway. Lucky we've seen the last of the bugger.'

Jonah Leary wasn't happy. He tucked the jar containing his brother's skin awkwardly under his coat so passers-by wouldn't gawp, and returned to deposit it in the room he'd rented for a couple of nights at the George Inn on Market Street. Then he strode purposefully back along George Street, keeping an eye open for the premises of an undertaker called Brownlow, which he located not far from the gaol.

Peering through the window, past a display of wooden and black crepe-covered coffins, he saw that the cove behind the counter was occupied with a woman in black weeds snivelling into a handkerchief, and waited until she'd finished carrying on. He raised his hat and held the door open for her as she left, then went in himself.

'Brownlow, is it?' he asked, approaching the man.

The cove looked him up and down. 'Mr Lionel Brownlow, undertaker, yes.'

'I'm told you buried me brother a couple of days ago: Malcolm Leary.'

Lionel Brownlow looked blank for a moment, then said, 'Oh, yes. The man who died while being tattooed,' in a tone that implied that he considered getting a tattoo was the same as being voluntarily sodomised. 'The tattooist called us in. Most, er, unfortunate.'

The tattooist had also, Mr Brownlow recalled, paid a bribe of two pounds to secure his silence as, under the Murder Act of 1752, it was a criminal offence to interfere with any corpse other than that of an executed murderer, and that particular corpse had been neither entirely whole nor fresh from the gallows.

'Where're his things?'

'His effects?'

'His clothes, his purse. The things he had with him.'

'The trousers we had to, ah, burn. They were soiled. I believe we have everything else. In cases such as this we keep items for three months. One moment, please.' The undertaker disappeared out the back, returning almost immediately with a cloth-wrapped bundle.

Leary took a folding knife from his pocket, startling the crap out of Mr Brownlow, flicked it open, and cut the string. Grasping one end of the cloth, he gave it a yank, dumping everything on the counter. There were a pair of boots, socks, a jacket, a shirt, a waistcoat, a neckerchief, a flattened hat, a pipe and fixings, and a purse, all accompanied by a powerful waft of meat gone over. No room key. That was odd. His brother must have been staying somewhere. Leary opened the purse.

'Is this all the money there was?'

Mr Brownlow looked at him as though he'd farted. 'I have no idea. We never interfere with a deceased person's effects.'

'What was he buried in?'

'A shroud. I'm afraid your brother was buried as a pauper, in the Devonshire Street cemetery.'

Leary put the purse in his pocket. 'Just the shroud? Not with any other possessions?'

'No. What you see here was all he had on his person.'

Waving his hand over the pile of clothing, Leary said, 'You can keep all this. I don't want it.'

There was nothing here. Shit.

'You may wish to consider making a contribution towards the costs of your brother's burial,' Mr Brownlow suggested, but Leary was already halfway out the door.

\* \* \*

In Friday's opinion, Minnie Thompson's brothel on York Street wasn't half as nice as Mrs H's. It was smaller, for a start, but then Mrs Thompson's girls only catered to a very specific sort of customer. It was dramatically decorated in dark colours and heavy fabrics, with furniture of rich rosewood and paintings everywhere depicting naked women. Also, there was no salon and only two work rooms, both upstairs. Friday was in the largest, having her first lesson. The walls of the chamber were papered with a pattern of black lilies on an oxblood-red background, swathes of heavy black velvet framed the windows, and the floorboards were polished to a high sheen. There were no hooks and pulleys in the ceiling with which to hoist customers, the likes of which Friday had seen in several of London's flogging brothels, but there was a set of wrist irons bolted to a wall, an iron bedstead and mattress draped with oilcloth, a sort of wide leather stool over which a body could be bent for flogging, and a glass-fronted cabinet displaying assorted whips, birches, straps, paddles, manacles and ropes, and beautiful little cut crystal bottles containing smelling salts. If Mrs Thompson's house were ever raided, Friday thought, she'd be for it. On the other hand, perhaps she was immune; she could just see Clement Backhander Bloodworth creeping in through the back door, quivering with excitement.

At the moment, one of Mrs Thompson's girls, named Violet, was bent naked over the stool, and Friday was practising her whipping on her. Violet enjoyed being flogged, and was paid extremely well by the men who visited Mrs T's house for allowing them the privilege to do so. She felt, however, that Friday hadn't quite got the hang of it, and that she was also holding back.

'Well, I don't want to hit you too hard,' Friday said.

Though the sight of Violet's bare and lushly round bum presented over the stool really was quite appealing, the idea of thrashing her silly with the whip wasn't. Violet, however, was proving to be physically very tough, belying her appearance. Her name suited her. She was fair-haired and very pale-skinned, and had genuinely violet eyes with mauve shadows beneath them. She looked imminently bruisable, and Friday imagined some men would thoroughly enjoy laying into her.

'You're not supposed to beat the living shit out of 'em,' Mistress Ruby said, puffing on her pipe and taking a swig from her tumbler of gin. 'That's not the point. You're supposed to "tickle" 'em with the very end of the thong, so it's just painful enough to drive 'em mad with excitement. You don't want to send 'em home lookin' like a side of raw beef. 'Course, some coves want you to go real hard, and that's fine, long as they say so first. But there's more skill needed when you're going soft.'

Mistress Ruby's name, Friday had discovered, really was Ruby — Jones — and she was a bonded convict originally from Wales. Ruby was about four feet ten inches tall, stocky and well muscled; and she could wield a whip like a professional bullocky. Her very long hair was dyed the colour of pitch except for a single white stripe, had the texture of straw, and was piled up, making her look as though she had a badger dozing on her head, though she said she usually wore it down when she was working.

She was the only professional flagellant in Sydney Town, and Friday had been wary of meeting her, aware of just how vicious the jealousy among women in the sex trade could be. She and Molly had had a nasty fight with a handful of tarts from Nellie McShera's bawdyhouse in the Black Rat Hotel the year before. But she'd been pleasantly surprised by both Ruby's and Violet's open and generous natures. As far as Ruby was concerned, Sydney was no different from London: it was full of Englishmen, and Englishmen were always wanting someone to beat and humiliate them. Another female flagellant hanging out her shingle wasn't going to make much difference to her.

Friday laid the whip on the floor and flexed her right arm. Whipping was hard work and her shoulder muscles were aching. She was sweating heavily, too, and had already stripped down to her skirt and shift, the tattoos on her bare arms gleaming. It didn't help that the day was warm and the drapes across the windows were stifling the meagre breeze.

Ruby put aside her pipe and drink. 'I'll show you again. It's a bit like pullin' your punches. Pay attention to my wrist this time.'

She picked up the whip handle, the leather thong trailing on the floor like a skinny black snake, positioned herself behind Violet, and raised her arm. A crack rent the air; the thong flew out and connected with Violet's buttock, once on the left, then again on the right, leaving two marks like slashes of crimson wax on the pale flesh.

'See?' she said, and handed the whip to Friday.

Friday made sure she was grasping the handle in the manner Ruby had demonstrated, widened her stance for balance, raised her arm, let fly and took two candles out of the brass ceiling candelabra.

'Shit. Sorry.'

'The wrist action was better,' Ruby said, 'but your aim was way off. And it's more of a sideways flick than an overhead one. Have another go.'

Friday did, and succeeded in hitting Violet this time, but on the back of her calf, making her swear.

'Bloody hell,' Friday said. 'I can't do this. Not to a girl. It might be different if I was walloping the hell out of some arsehole cove.'

'No, you're gettin' there,' Ruby said encouragingly. 'It takes time. It's not as easy as it looks. And it's not to do with anger. You have to remember that.'

Violet stood up, her face red from dangling over the stool, rubbed her stinging calf, then stretched and shook out her arms. 'Do we need to get a man, do you think? Will all your customers be coves?'

'I've only got the one.' Friday fetched her bottle of gin from her reticule. 'I'm learning this just for him.'

Violet and Ruby exchanged amused glances. 'We wondered why Mrs T agreed to let us teach you,' Violet said as she pulled on a robe. 'We're not bothered, but we thought she'd be worried all our cullies'll go galloping down to Argyle Street if they hear there's a new flagellant in town. But if you've only got the one, who cares?'

Ruby said, 'Wouldn't matter, anyway. Like I said, there'll never be a shortage of coves wanting their arses whipped. What are you going to call yourself?'

Friday took a staggeringly large swig from her bottle and wiped her mouth. 'Dunno. Friday, I suppose.'

'No, you need a special name, to add to the theatre. You know, Mistress or Madame Something-or-other. Then the cove can go, "Mercy, Mistress Ruby, please don't beat me," or, "Whip me, Mistress Ruby, I've been a bad boy," dependin' on whatever gets him goin'.'

'You use your normal name,' Friday said.

Ruby said, 'That's not the point.'

Friday thought about it. Unsuccessfully. 'Dunno. What do you think?'

'Why don't you ask him?' Violet suggested, peeling an apple with a fruit knife, the skin coming off in one long, curling piece.

'That's a good idea. And what am I supposed to wear? Anything special?'

'Well, he obviously fancies you,' Ruby said, 'so somethin' that plays up what you've got. But it's the pain and submission he'll be after, not so much your body. Is he askin' for actual sex?'

'No.'

'Well, a lot of 'em don't. He'll still make a mess, but at least it won't be all over you. How old is he?'

'Ancient. Easily in his sixties.'

'Jesus, girl, you'd better have the smelling salts ready.'

Friday turned to Violet. 'I don't understand it. How can you actually like being flogged? How can anyone? Doesn't it hurt?'

'Yes, and that's the point. That, and knowing someone else has complete control over me.' Violet pointed at Friday's tattoos with her fruit knife. 'How can you tolerate that? That must hurt like a bastard.'

'Well, yeah, but it's a good sort of pain. Intense. After a while I sort of float off and nothing seems to matter any more. It's like being mashed, but without all the fighting and having to suffer the horrors the next day. I can't explain it.' She faltered, because she couldn't. 'You've got no idea.'

'And you've got no idea what it's like being flogged,' Violet said, but she didn't say it nastily.

Ruby peered into the bowl of her pipe, then sucked vigorously on the stem to get it going again. 'Sounds to me like it's two sides of the same coin.'

'Do you like what you do?' Friday asked her. Violet obviously did.

'I don't give a shit either way. But the money's good, and I never have to lift my leg for anyone. Can't ask for much more than that.'

'Never?' Friday said, astonished. 'But what if they ask for it?'

'There's two other girls here that do that side of things. I just do the flogging and the like, though sometimes we'll work together. But I never even have to touch the buggers.'

'Really?' Friday thought that sounded fantastic.

Unfortunately, Leo and Harrie hadn't seen the last of Jonah Leary. He appeared again the following Monday, sidling in the door just as their first customer of the morning walked out.

Leo swore under his breath, and gestured at Harrie to position herself to run out of the shop if things became unpleasant.

'What do you want now?' he said. 'Our business is finished.'

Leary shook his head. 'No, it isn't. I want to know exactly what me brother told you about the tattoo you took off him.'

'I already told you.'

'I don't believe you.'

'You can believe what you bloody well like. He said nothing at all, other than to find you and give it to you, which I've done.'

'You said he showed it to you.'

'Aye, he did. He said his tattoo was like yours, and showed me. He thought I might know you, because of it. I also saw it when I flayed it off him. Obviously.'

'What else did he say about it?'

Leo's fists curled. 'How many times do I have to say this? Bugger all! And I didn't ask anything, either.' He leant towards Leary. 'Do you know why? Because I don't give a shit.'

Leary didn't flinch. 'Did he give you another tattoo?'

'What?'

'Another one, like the one you took off Malcolm. Preserved. Did you keep that one for yourself?'

'What the fuck are you talking about?'

'Me and Malcolm had another brother,' Leary said tersely. 'By the name of Bennett. I was thinking, Malcolm might have had Bennett's tattoo with him.'

In the hope that it would satisfy the ghoulish bastard and get rid of him, Leo made a concerted effort to remember exactly what Malcolm Leary had said. 'He showed me his tattoo, said you had one like his, and mentioned that another brother had something similar. I think he did say the name Bennett.'

'Said what about him, exactly?'

'Just that he had a similar tattoo,' Leo said, his temper ratcheting up a level. 'That's it. For Christ's sake, does it matter?'

Leary gave Leo a foul look. 'Yes, it bloody does. Did me brother say where he was lodging?'

'A pub called the Black Rat.'

'Did you steal the key to his room?'

'No, I did not! Now get the hell out of my shop!'

Leary stood motionless for a moment, then said, 'If I find out you've lied, I'll be back, and you'll bloody regret it.' He glared at Leo, took a good hard look at Harrie, and left.

His next stop was the Black Rat Hotel. Having got the publican's attention, he informed him that Malcolm Leary was dead and that he had come for his brother's belongings. He had to show his certificate of leave to prove his surname was Leary, but eventually he was shown to the room Malcolm had rented, a poky, rancid-smelling little chamber with mouldy walls far inferior to Leary's modest accommodation at the George Inn. His brother must have been short of brads. But then, he'd never been any good at managing his money. Useless bugger. At least he'd had the decency to die in the presence of someone who knew how to wield a flaying knife.

He went through his brother's sea bag, and found a change of clothes, eleven pounds, four shillings and tuppence hidden in a rolled-up sock (which he pocketed), a comb, a razor and a strop, and a half-empty bottle of rum, then turned his attention to the room itself. There was nothing under the thin, damp mattress, or in it, and the battered chest of drawers was empty. There appeared to be no secret compartments in the walls, and although several of the floorboards were loose, none could be levered up. Just as he was leaving, it occurred to him to look under the chest of drawers, and there it was, a small cloth-bound ledger, the cover tacky with cobwebs, the first two dozen pages filled with his brother's poorly formed and misspelt handwriting.

He sat on the bed by the dirty window to read it. It was a diary of sorts and although most of the entries chronicled Malcolm's clearly deathly boring voyage to New South Wales, it was the first few pages that caught his eye. Some cove in a pub on Dock Road back home in Liverpool had apparently told Malcolm that Bennett had been transported.

Leary closed the ledger and tapped it on his knee thoughtfully. So Bennett was actually here. It wouldn't be too hard to guess what his crime had been. It was odd that he hadn't encountered him, but he wasn't necessarily in Sydney Town, he supposed. He could well be in Van Diemen's Land, or even on Norfolk Island. Obviously he should now be hunting down Bennett himself, rather than looking for a tattoo flayed off a dead man. He slid the ledger into his pocket.

Back downstairs again, just to be sure, he asked the publican if there was a strong box for lodgers' valuables.

The publican laughed. 'The types that stay here don't have no valuables.'

'Has anyone been in that room since me brother's been gone?'

'Not to my knowledge.' The publican wiped the serving counter with a filthy rag. 'There's only the one key and Mr Leary had it.'

'He didn't have it,' Leary said, but he was inclined to believe the man — the money, after all, had still been there. 'Right. I've cleared out his things. I'll be gone, then.'

'Just you hold on. Your brother owed me a week's rent.'

Leary snarled, 'Don't tell me you didn't charge him in advance.' The publican glared at him. Leary stared unblinkingly back, his face frozen in an icy glower. Then his hand shot out and he grabbed the man's shirt front and yanked him halfway across the bar. 'I know you did, so don't fuck with me.'

The man nodded vigorously, then, in case that was the wrong response, shook his head for good measure. Leary let him go and his feet found the floorboards again. Tentatively, he rubbed the back of his neck where his collar had dug into his flesh. 'My mistake.'

'Yes, it was.'

Outside in the sun and heat once again, Leary ambled the few yards down to the waterfront and hurled his brother's bag into the sea.

He hadn't found what he was looking for yet, but that was all right. He'd just have to look harder.

# Chapter Thirteen

Harrie had done an awful thing, but she'd had to, and it would be worth it. This morning she'd gone into James's purse while he'd been in the privy and stolen three five-pound notes. It was a crime possibly worse than the one that had seen her transported to New South Wales, but she hadn't been able to think of any other way to achieve her aim. She'd earned a little money since she'd been back at work, but some of that had gone into the Charlotte fund — which she supposed would all go towards paying Bella Shand, now that Charlotte was in the orphanage — and the rest she'd sent home to Robbie and Sophie and Anna. She couldn't just ask James for the money, not after her performance the other day about not being his wife, and she knew he wouldn't give it to her anyway, when he found out why she wanted it. And neither would Friday or Sarah. Or Leo. In fact, she suspected no one would, because they all thought they knew what was 'best for her'. But they didn't. Only she knew what she really needed.

When James had come out of the privy she'd told him she had to go to Leo's early, and left the cottage as quickly as possible before he could lecture her. He never missed a chance to go on about her working for Leo, and she couldn't face it this morning, and anyway it would only slow her down. Also, she was frightened he would look in his purse and see that the money was gone. So she'd almost run up York Street, the ribbons on her bonnet flapping and her skirts catching around her ankles, to the stables on Market Street. She felt sick about behaving so sneakily and treating him like that, but he'd left her with no choice. And neither had the others.

She'd thought about purchasing a seat on the Sydney to Parramatta stagecoach, which also delivered the mail, but discovered that it stopped and started endlessly and took nearly all day to get to Parramatta, and she needed to be back home by nightfall, so as to cause James the minimum of worry. In the end she hired a very expensive four-seat phaeton drawn by a two-in-hand. She felt as though she were being horribly irresponsible, and knew she could have saved money by hiring just a two-seater, but she had no idea how to drive a carriage herself, and in a two-seater she would have had to sit next to the driver, which she couldn't tolerate. Not at the moment. This way she could sit by herself behind him, thinking her own thoughts in peace and preparing herself.

As it turned out, she needn't have bothered wasting the extra five pounds on the second bench seat, as the driver said barely a word to her during the entire trip, except to point out the location of the facilities when he stopped halfway at a coaching inn to water the horses. And she already knew where they were from previous trips. She bought herself a jar of lemonade, and cheese, pickles and a bread roll in the dining room, and picked at the bread while the driver disappeared into the bar. He must have knocked back a fair bit of ale, because he certainly reeked of it by the time the phaeton was brought around again. It had improved his mood, though, as when she asked him to raise the hood to keep the sun off, he obliged with something she almost recognised as a smile.

When they reached Parramatta, they rattled across the bridge on Church Street and headed back in the direction from which they'd just come, this time following the northern bank of the river, to the Female Orphan School. She knew exactly how to get there even though she'd never been: she'd known since the day Charlotte was born and Rachel had died.

The driver drew up on the carriageway outside the entrance to the forbidding-looking building, its small, high windows looking blankly out across the fields, and asked her how long she'd be. When she told him probably only about an hour, he complained that that wouldn't give him time to go into town to the pub, but cracked his whip irately and headed back along the carriageway, almost knocking a man off his mount in the process, looking for somewhere to water the horses.

Harrie stood outside the front door, taking deep, slow breaths, trying to calm herself.

'Rachel?' she whispered. 'Are you here?'

She waited, reaching out with all her senses, looking for the tiniest sign, but there was nothing. Well, then, she'd just have to do this herself. She knocked and when no one came, she went in.

Stopping a girl in a blue uniform, she asked to see the superintendent and was taken to meet matron, who introduced herself as Mrs Duff. Harrie didn't like her on principle.

'And you are …?' Mrs Duff asked.

'Harriet Clarke.'

'Delighted to meet you, Mrs Clarke.'

Harrie didn't bother to correct her. And even though fear of the matron's potential response was making her dry-mouthed and dizzy, she might as well come right out and say it. 'I'm here about Charlotte Winter. I'd like to know what it would take for me to adopt her.'

Mrs Duff's eyebrows went up. 'She's a popular little girl, isn't she?'

'Yes, I understand my friends Sarah Green and Friday Woolfe have been out to visit.'

'Indeed. Unfortunately, Miss Woolfe is no longer welcome here. She has proved to be somewhat of a disruptive influence. But that isn't what I meant. I was alluding to the fact that Mrs Green has already made enquiries into the possibility of adopting Charlotte herself.'

A poison-tipped dagger plunged straight into Harrie's heart, and she couldn't stop herself from crying out.

Mrs Duff half rose from her chair. 'Mrs Clarke, are you all right?'

With one hand pressed over her mouth, Harrie weakly waved away the matron's concerns with the other. 'I'm sorry,' she mumbled. 'It's just that … no, I'm fine, thank you.'

'Are you sure?'

'Yes, thank you.'

How *could* Sarah? Harrie thought. How could *they*? They knew how much she wanted Charlotte. Had they waited until she was really ill, thinking she wouldn't know? But why? She couldn't understand it. Why would they be that cruel to her?

'Mrs Green was to attempt to locate Charlotte's father, Lucas Carew,' Mrs Duff said. 'However, I'm not sure how far she's progressed regarding that matter. She and Miss Woolfe were out here the other day, and Mrs Green didn't mention it.'

'Lucas Carew?' Harrie stared at her. Lucas Carew wasn't Charlotte's father.

'Yes. It is Mr Carew's name entered on Charlotte's birth certificate.'

Harrie had never seen a birth certificate for Charlotte. Janie must have had it. But for the purposes of adoption, wasn't it irrelevant who Charlotte's father had been? 'Why does the father have to be located?' she asked.

'Providing he's still living, he must be given the opportunity to forfeit all paternal rights to his daughter. I did advise your friends of this.'

'What if he isn't living?'

'Then we'd need to see a death certificate.'

Harrie drew in a deep breath, her belly churning. 'Mrs Duff, I should tell you that Charlotte's mother, Rachel Winter, was a very close friend of mine. I was present when she died, when Charlotte was born, and I'm very experienced at caring for children. I can provide references. What if I'd like to adopt Charlotte?'

For a fleeting second, Harrie could hardly believe she was saying such things, that she was competing with Sarah and that the prize was Charlotte. She was suddenly filled with shame, and a surge of self-disgust so bitter and sharp she thought she might be sick. But a moment later it had gone, and all she could think of was Charlotte's pale, silky-soft skin and the smell of her hair.

'That would depend, Mrs Clarke, in the first instance, on any response from Charlotte's father, and in the second, who Reverend Duff and myself consider to be most suitable as guardians — Mr and Mrs Green, or you and your husband.'

Harrie felt herself collapse like a failed soufflé: all of her — her shoulders, her ribs, her hopes, her spirit and her future.

'May I see her?' she whispered. Then, to her mortification, she started to cry. She dug around in her reticule for a handkerchief, but couldn't find one.

Mrs Duff studied her for a moment, then opened a drawer in her desk and passed her a handkerchief with perfect creases ironed into it, stood and tugged on the bell-pull behind her chair. When a girl appeared, Mrs Duff said, 'Will you kindly bring Charlotte Winter down from the nursery?'

The next few minutes were the longest Harrie could remember. When Charlotte arrived in the girl's arms, pink-faced and sweaty as though she'd just woken, and wearing a plain white smock and a little cotton bonnet, it was all Harrie could do not to snatch her away and sprint for the door. The moment Charlotte saw Harrie she stretched out her chubby little arms, cried, 'Hawwie!' and started to bawl.

'I do hope that child isn't developing a speech impediment,' Mrs Duff said.

Harrie took Charlotte off the girl and hugged her to her chest, pressing the child's cheek into her own neck and murmuring against the top of her head. Charlotte stopped crying immediately, though Harrie had started again. She walked slowly around Mrs Duff's office, joggling Charlotte very gently and rubbing her back. Charlotte started up a tuneless humming, apparently content now, her eyes open, one hand gripping Harrie's collar, the other arm flopping bonelessly.

'Is she happy here?' Harrie asked, her voice cracking. She took Charlotte's bonnet off and smoothed her hair.

'I believe she's settling,' Mrs Duff said. 'There are other children here just a little older than she is. She's a bright child. When there are opportunities to join in she does.'

'Is she eating?'

'Better than she would have in the Factory. What does your husband do, Mrs Clarke?'

Harrie took a deep breath and forced herself to say it. 'I'm not married.'

'Ah. Then I'm afraid we couldn't possibly consider allowing you to adopt Charlotte. You do understand we have a responsibility to the children under our care here?'

Harrie nodded, unable to speak.

Mrs Duff tactfully busied herself with some papers for the next five minutes while Harrie wandered around cuddling Charlotte, but eventually she announced it was time for the baby to go upstairs. When Harrie gave Charlotte back, she felt as though she were tearing off the deepest of scabs.

She asked Mrs Duff where her driver might have taken the horses for water — the river — said thank you, and saw herself to the door.

Outside, the sunshine almost blinded her. She hadn't realised how gloomy it had been indoors. If only it was that easy to walk away from her own darkness.

As she trudged down the carriageway towards the river, a figure on horseback emerged from a stand of trees on the far side of the lawn, and trotted towards the orphanage.

\* \* \*

Harrie hurried along York Street, stumbling and tripping, so tired she could barely pick up her feet, but going as fast as possible in the hope she'd get home before James. He usually arrived back from the surgery at around six o'clock and she thought, with luck, she might just beat him.

She staggered up the gravel path to the cottage, put her key in the door and pushed it open.

Sitting in the parlour, staring at her grim-faced, were James, Matthew, Friday, Sarah, Leo and Nora. And Angus.

'Where the hell have you been?' James exclaimed, springing to his feet.

Harrie's heart sank so low she felt like she was falling down a hole. 'Out.'

'Out where?'

Harrie could see by his face he was angry, but he seemed frightened above all else. She knew this would happen. 'Parramatta. The orphanage. I had to see Charlotte. I had to.'

'By yourself?'

She nodded.

'For God's sake, Harrie!'

James took two strides forwards, stopped, raised his hands to his head in voiceless frustration and relief, then grabbed her in a ferocious hug, squashing her face against his shoulder.

Friday, Sarah and Nora looked on approvingly, Leo examined the ceiling, and Matthew stared at his hands.

Then, just as quickly, James let her go, perhaps remembering he had an audience. He pecked her on the cheek and stood back, his hands gripping her upper arms.

'We've been looking everywhere for you,' James said. 'All day, all of us.'

'I'm sorry.'

Leo said, 'You didn't come to work this morning, lass. I was worried so I closed the shop and went to your man's surgery and had a talk.'

'We had a good idea where you might have gone, though,' Friday said. 'Didn't we, Sarah?'

Sarah nodded. 'Didn't stop us walking round the cove and checking all the beaches and under the wharves,' she said crossly.

'I'm *sorry*,' Harrie said again.

Nora left her seat, took Harrie's hand and led her back to the table. 'Sit down, love. I'll make another pot of tea.'

James sat, too. 'Matthew took a day off work to help us look, and so did Mrs Barrett. We've been up and down George Street, all round the Rocks, in the market sheds, to Hyde Park twice, everywhere.'

Exhausted, bitterly disappointed about Charlotte, and overwhelmed with guilt at having put everyone out, Harrie gave way to bad temper. 'Well, what for? Friday just said she knew where I'd gone. You didn't need to send out a search party. Why not just wait until I came home?'

'We were worried, Harrie,' Matthew said. 'You haven't been yourself.'

'Haven't I? Then who have I been?'

'Christ knows,' Friday muttered.

James said, 'That's enough. She's been very ill.'

'But I'm not ill now, am I?' Harrie pointed an accusing finger. 'I'm getting better and I know what you've been up to, Sarah Green.'

Sarah looked startled. 'What?'

'Don't pretend you don't know,' Harrie said. Was she going to lie about it, even now? 'Mrs Duff told me.'

'Told you what?'

'Harrie, love —' Nora began, but Harrie ignored her.

'You tried to get Charlotte!' she said. 'You told her you wanted to adopt her! Well, you can't. She's mine! Do you hear me? Mine.'

Shocked, everyone stared at her.

Seeing their dismayed and saddened faces, Harrie realised she'd lost control. Horrified, she put her hand over her mouth.

Gently, Friday said, 'But, Harrie, you wanted Sarah to have Charlotte, remember? You had a go at her when she said she didn't think she could.'

Harrie nodded, though to be honest she couldn't remember whether she'd said that or not.

Sarah said, 'Harrie, listen to me. We did ask Mrs Duff about it the first time we were there, the day we found out Janie and Rosie had died, and I did talk to Adam about whether we might adopt her, but he said no.' She paused, let out a wobbly sigh, then said, 'And I feel bloody awful about that because I'm glad. I could have wiped her bum and fed her and cuddled her and all that, but I'm not the one who should be her mother. You are, Harrie, even if you are barmy. Of all of us, you've always been the mother.'

'But I can't have her!' Harrie wailed. 'I'm not …'

She didn't finish. Everyone was deliberately not looking at James, trying to spare his feelings. She couldn't face him, either. She couldn't face any of them. He was her master, she was living under his roof, he'd asked her to marry him, and she'd refused him.

She'd ruined everything.

### *Christmas Day 1831, Sydney Town*

On Christmas morning James and Harrie walked over to St James's Church in King Street for the ten o'clock service, the first Harrie had attended in months. Being a Sunday, Sydney's churches were all packed. After they returned home Harrie made eggnog, not particularly nice in the summer heat, and James plied her with embarrassingly expensive gifts, fully aware he was attempting to buy his way to her heart, but beyond caring. He gave her a gorgeous silk and wool Norwich shawl, a solid silver filigree nosegay holder and luxury rose-scented soap. She gave him a Christmas cake she'd baked a few weeks earlier, with ingredients he'd paid for. He also gave her a kiss on the lips — relatively chaste, but still, the closest he'd come to making an outright physical advance. And she let him, because she didn't have the energy to stop him. Also, she wanted him to, because despite her refusal to accept his proposal of marriage, she loved him. As well, he hadn't mentioned the money absent from his purse, and she felt guilty. She hoped he hadn't noticed, but suspected he had, and had chosen to ignore it. Typical James.

Friday, who'd taken advantage of Mrs Hislop's traditional early closing of the brothel the previous night to go out and get horribly drunk, dragged herself out of bed in a terrible state at eleven o'clock. She'd been sick on her pillow, which she couldn't remember doing so she must have been asleep — lucky she hadn't drowned in it. There was spew on the sheets, and on her, and in her hair, and she'd still been dressed but her purse was empty, though she'd gone out with nearly ten pounds. Christ knows what had happened to it. She couldn't have spent it all on drink. Could she? She looked at the clock and realised she was meant to be at Sarah's and Adam's for Christmas dinner at half past one, and couldn't face it. There'd be too much noise and she couldn't bear the thought of food. Shuffling downstairs, holding her pounding head, she perched on the bog for fifteen minutes, shitting out of one end and vomiting into a bucket from the other. How many times had she sat in here like this? She cleaned herself up and plodded back to her room. Feeling vile, unloved and desperately lonely, she undressed and went back to sleep.

Elizabeth Hislop, as had been her habit for the past six years, locked herself in her office for the morning with an iced Madeira cake and half a bottle of premium whisky, and wept bitterly as she remembered the love of her life, whose dry and brittle bones lay barely yards beneath her feet.

Sarah and Adam woke reasonably early. Sarah needed to ready the meat for roasting — beef, not the usual mutton — in time to get it into the camp oven over the fire, make dough for several loaves of bread for the second oven, and prepare the vegetables. She'd thought about sending her dough up to the bakehouse, but so, probably, had everyone else, along with their Christmas roasts, and had decided she was more likely to get everything onto the table on time if she did it all herself. Bernard and Ruthie Cole, and Harrie and James, and Friday would also be coming for dinner, and Ruthie was bringing the plum pudding and custard, sugar plums, and something she called a raspberry caudle pie. Harrie was bringing shortbread and crystallised fruit for afterwards, and James the Christmas 'spirit'. Being thoughtful, he'd already checked with Sarah regarding what meat she planned to serve. Nobody knew what Friday intended to contribute.

While Sarah worked in the kitchen, Adam wandered happily around the garden in his shirtsleeves with scissors and a folding saw, picking roses, dahlias and, Sarah's favourite, freesias, for the table. How anyone could have a traditional Christmas while it was so bloody hot, he told Sarah, he didn't know. How he could have one at all when he was Jewish, she didn't know. Before their guests arrived, she gave him a beautifully cut and exquisitely tailored coat in black kerseymere with silk lapels, and he gave her a rivière of small but perfectly graded sapphires to match the earrings he'd gifted her on their wedding day.

At the Barrett house the children were up early, in particular Hannah, who was thumping around in the parlour at a quarter past five, though an irate Nora told her to get back into bed and not get out again until at least seven. At eight the whole family went along to morning service at St Philip's Church, then returned home to prepare for Christmas dinner, which Nora was cooking with Tilly's help. Nora had forgiven George — barely — even though his selfish behaviour had robbed both her and the children of Harrie's company and the important role she'd had in the family. Harrie, she hoped, would work with her again soon, but now that she was assigned to James Downey, the children wouldn't see her anywhere near as often as they'd like. Especially Hannah, who had cried and cried for her and still suggested they visit her several times a day.

Nora knew there'd been more to George dumping Harrie at Liverpool asylum than him simply wanting a servant who wasn't mentally unstable, and when she'd threatened to leave him, he'd looked terrified, as though he'd really believed her. Which was silly: she could never leave, not if it meant losing her children. But he'd refused to admit what had been upsetting him, no matter how hard she'd tried to winkle it out of him. He was an idiot sometimes, and bad-tempered and selfish, but the children loved him and in his own way he loved them. She could do a lot worse.

Leo spent Christmas morning in bed with Serafina Fortune in her little house on Essex Street. In between episodes of very satisfying sex, Serafina listened patiently to Leo talking about how much he missed Walter and how he hoped he was all right, and how worried he was about Harrie. Serafina, who knew a few things about Harrie, assured him that she would be, eventually, and told him not to worry. She admired the diamond, emerald, amethyst, ruby, sapphire and topaz 'dearest' ring he'd given her for Christmas, tilting her hand so it sparkled becomingly in the lamplight, told him again how much she liked it, then rolled onto her belly to expose the Japanese tattoo extending from her shoulders down her very shapely back, over her buttocks and to her knees. It had taken Leo over a year to complete, and he was particularly proud of it. She gave him a stunning piece of scrimshaw — whaling scenes depicted on a flawless sperm whale tooth capped with silver.

Matthew had invited his fiancée, Sally Minto, to Christmas dinner at the home of the Vincents', the family with whom he boarded, but she'd declined, terrified she'd commit some awful gaffe such as use the wrong knife. Sally was an assigned convict and the Vincents were well-to-do free settlers; she'd be far more comfortable with supper that evening at the table of her employers, who were bakers and ex-convicts, she said, where it wouldn't matter if she spilt her peas. Matthew could appreciate her point of view, but wondered, and not for the first time, whether in marrying her, he was condemning himself to a life of drinking grog, eating muffins and pickled eggs from street vendors, and singing along to a fiddle and tin whistle in the pub of a night. It was deeply uncharitable of him, he knew, but he couldn't help himself.

Finally he'd suggested that they go to the Australian for their Christmas dinner, though Sally nervously confessed she found even a smart hotel intimidating, but in the end she'd agreed. Nothing had gone wrong — well, he'd knocked over the bottle of port he'd bought to plug the gaps in their rather stilted conversation — and she'd acquitted herself admirably, he thought, looking very pretty if slightly plump in her best dress. She must be taste-testing a few too many of the macaroons they made at the bakery. He gave her a Norwich shawl, similar to the one James had bought for Harrie, and she presented him with a book by James Fenimore Cooper he hadn't read yet called *The Water-Witch*, which he thought was a really thoughtful gift. She said she'd gone into the bookseller's on George Street and asked what was the latest thing from England or America, and James Fenimore Cooper had been recommended. But she'd had to rush off from dinner early, to be at work in time to open for folk who wanted their Christmas meat and loaves cooked, leaving him to sit in the Australian with another bottle of port to drink all by himself. Which he did.

At Sarah and Adam's, no one was left sitting alone. By the time everyone found a seat, the table was laden with food. Ruthie Cole, as usual, had brought more than just puddings, and there was barely enough room for everything. The floral centrepiece — initially attempted by Adam then rescued by Harrie — had been moved to the sideboard, leaving the table gleaming with silver candlesticks, cutlery, the best cruet set, and two drinking glasses each. Sarah's roast beef had turned out beautifully, which was gratifying as occasionally her meat dishes were prone to quite spectacular failure. Friday hadn't arrived, but Sarah expected she wouldn't be far away. Unless she'd gone out last night and got mashed, in which case she might not turn up at all.

As Adam stood to carve the roast, Sarah glanced at Harrie, wondering if she, too, was recalling the scene the previous April when it had been Jared Gellar doing exactly the same thing, usurping Adam's place in the house while Adam languished at Port Macquarie. Gellar had got meat juice on his white trousers, and had made some idiotic remark about Sarah laundering them. Harrie gave her a sad little smile, so yes, she must be. Bernard and Ruthie had been there that night, too, and Friday, and they'd all gone to great lengths to scare the crap out of Gellar by convincing him that Rachel's ghost was haunting the house. Harrie had 'summoned' her, and had done an extraordinary job of acting as though she really were talking to an invisible ghostly presence.

Adam announced, 'Plates, please,' and served the sliced beef.

The vegetables were passed around next, then Ruthie's spring tart, followed by the meat sauce, and James went around with the wine pretending to be a waiter, except that Harrie said she would rather have lemonade.

Then Bernard stood to make a toast. Raising his glass in a chubby hand, he said, 'Here's to folk we're really quite happy aren't with us any more.'

Sarah laughed. So he was remembering, too.

Then James said solemnly, 'And here's to those we wish still were.' He gazed down at Harrie. 'Rachel Winter, and Janie Braine and her daughter Rosie.'

He looked sad, and Sarah suspected he might also have wanted to say, and my late wife, Emily, but hadn't, because of Harrie. Which was very thoughtful of him.

Then it was Adam's turn. 'And here's to the coming year. May it be a lot less eventful than this one was.'

They all went, 'Hear, hear!' and drank.

And then they ate. Sarah was already feeling stuffed as she brought the puddings to the table, but had some raspberry caudle pie — which was delicious — and two sugar plums anyway, and then felt positively bilious. Clearly, so did everyone else, except perhaps for Harrie, who only pecked at her food. She spied both Adam and James surreptitiously undoing the buttons on their trousers, and Bernard, whose belly bulged over his waistband at the best of times, let out a belch so hearty it almost extinguished the candles.

'I wish Friday was here,' Harrie said.

Sarah said, 'So do I.'

Blotting his mouth with a napkin, James asked, 'Where is she?'

'Probably in bed with the horrors,' Sarah said. 'They don't work late on Christmas Eve. No doubt she went out. I might just pop down and see if I can rouse her. I could do with a quick walk. I'm stuffed. Do you mind?' she asked Adam as she pushed back her chair.

'You won't be long, will you?'

'Shouldn't think so.'

He rose and pecked her on the cheek. 'Just don't expect any sugar plums to be left when you get back.'

Sarah grabbed her reticule. 'Couldn't manage them if they were. I'll be back soon, I promise. Come on, girl,' she said to Clifford, who was hiding under the table gobbling a lump of plum pudding Bernard had deliberately dropped to her. Candied peel, which she'd spat out, and crumbs were scattered all over the floor. 'Oh, no, who gave her that?'

Silence.

Then Ruthie said, 'Oh dear, that had rather a lot of prunes in it.'

Sarah dragged Clifford out and scooped her up. She blinked, custard stuck on her snout. 'She can't have cakey things. Sugar makes her even more bad-tempered. And that's got brandy in it. Where's her lead, Adam?'

Clifford barked and snapped at passers-by all the way down George Street, so Sarah left her tied up in the shade of the Siren's Arms stables.

Inside, she met Elizabeth Hislop on the stairs. 'Is that your dog making all that noise?'

'Yes, sorry. She's a bit over-excited. Someone gave her plum pudding.'

'Oh dear. I hope it hasn't eaten the sixpence.'

Sarah hadn't considered that. 'Is Friday in?'

Elizabeth sighed. 'She's in her room, sleeping off last night. I despair of her, I really do.'

'She was supposed to be having Christmas dinner with us. I was hoping I might get her out of bed.'

'Good luck,' Elizabeth said as she continued down the stairs.

Sarah knocked on Friday's door. When there was no response she pushed, found the door open and went in. The drapes were drawn, the room, stiflingly hot, reeked, and clothes were strewn all over the floor.

'Friday, wake up.'

The lump in the bed stirred and mumbled. All Sarah could see was a mass of copper hair sticking out from beneath the sheet. The pillow was on the floor, a disgusting, lumpy, brownish-yellow stain across it, beside a tray on which sat a pair of teapots. There was an empty teacup on the nightstand, next to a flask of gin with its cork out. She bent to feel the teapots. Both were almost empty, but still faintly warm. At least she'd had something to drink.

'Friday, it's Sarah. Wake up!'

'Go away.'

'No. Wake up.'

'No.'

Sarah grasped the sheet and yanked it off. Friday was naked, curled on her side. Her hand flew up to hide her eyes.

'Bugger off.'

'No. It's Christmas, Friday. You were supposed to come to my house.'

'Shut that bloody dog up.'

'I'll bring her in here if you don't get up,' Sarah threatened.

'I can't. I'm sick.'

'You mean you've got the horrors. Now sit up, come on.'

'I can't. My head hurts.'

'Have you got any laudanum?'

Friday waved an arm vaguely in the direction of the dressing table. Sarah looked in the drawer, found the bottle and twisted the cork out of the neck, producing a sharp, high-pitched squeak that made Friday flinch and hunch her shoulders. She raised her hand to receive the bottle, but Sarah withheld it.

'Not until you sit up.'

'Fuck's sake,' Friday muttered as she crawled laboriously up the bed and turned over, her back against the bedhead. 'Where's my pillow?'

'You've spewed on it.' Sarah fetched her the cushion from the dressing table chair, and gave her the laudanum. Friday took several sips, and chased them with a long swallow of gin. And then another. Then she pulled the sheet up over herself.

'And your hair looks like rats are living in it,' Sarah added.

Friday sighed, but said nothing.

'Honestly, Friday, what are you doing?' Sarah asked, her hands on her hips. 'This is killing you. And if it doesn't, it might as well, because in a couple of years your looks'll be gone, and so will all your money.'

'I don't care.'

'Yes, you do.'

'I don't.'

Sarah opened the window, leant out and shouted, 'Clifford! Shut up!' She turned back to Friday. 'You do care. Is it because of Aria?'

Friday said nothing. She took another swig of gin.

Sarah said, 'Look, I know it is.'

'I really loved her,' Friday said at last. 'I *really* loved her. I do love her. And every time I think about not seeing her ever again, I feel like dying.'

Sarah thought that sounded a bit dramatic, but when she considered the awful, yearning desperation she'd felt when she'd imagined Adam never coming back from Port Macquarie, perhaps it wasn't.

'Well, maybe this'll cheer you up,' she said, passing her Aria's cloth-wrapped package from her reticule.

'What is it?'

'I don't know, do I? It's not for me, it's for you. It's from Aria.'

Her mouth open so that she resembled a startled, pasty-faced fish, Friday looked from the parcel, to Sarah, and back again to the parcel. 'Did she send it by post?'

'No, she left it with me before she went back to New Zealand.'

'With you?'

'Yes,' Sarah said with exaggerated patience. 'She asked me to give it to you, today. From her. But you didn't turn up, did you?'

Friday turned the parcel over in her hands. It was oblong and wrapped in a very fine cream linen handkerchief, and secured with a length of lilac satin ribbon. She squeezed gently — whatever was inside was flattish, and mostly hard.

'Are you going to open it, or just play with it?' Sarah asked. A thought occurred to her. 'Do you want some privacy?'

'No. Stay.'

Friday pulled on the satin ribbon and the bow unravelled. She put the ribbon aside — to save, Sarah suspected — and unfolded the linen. Inside was a sealed letter, and a very beautiful hair comb made of ivory or bone, Sarah couldn't tell which without a closer look, decorated with intricate carving and inset with a disc of purple-blue abalone shell. With it were two feathers about eight inches long, glossy black tinged with green, with white tips.

'This is her comb,' Friday said, pressing it against her lips and blinking hard. 'She was wearing it the first time I saw her.'

'What do the feathers mean?'

Friday looked at them, then sniffed one. 'I don't know.' She picked up the letter, glanced at Sarah, then broke the seal.

Sarah went to the dressing table and rummaged through the drawers again. She found a toothbrush and a tin of tooth powder (and another bottle of gin; God, she had it stashed everywhere), put them aside, poured cold water from a jug into a basin, and fetched a facecloth and a clean towel from the clothes press. Behind her she heard a stifled sob, and said without turning, 'Are you all right?'

'Yes,' Friday replied in a thick voice. 'It's good. It's a good letter.'

Busying herself tidying Friday's collection of cosmetics and creams and lotions, and wiping up spilt powder and pipe ash, Sarah waited until Friday had finished reading and quietly crying.

'I'm all right now,' she said after a few minutes.

Sarah sat on the end of the bed. 'How's your head? Is the laudanum starting to work?'

Friday nodded, but gingerly.

'Good. Then why don't you get up and have a wash, including your hair, it's disgusting, and come back to our house? Harrie and James are there, and Bernard and Ruthie. You like them.'

'Is Harrie being mental?'

'No, she's good today. Come on, it's Christmas. We're all waiting for you so we can swap presents.'

'Is there one for me?'

'Of course there is.'

'Have you got any gin?'

Sarah stifled a sigh; she knew more alcohol was the only thing that would help Friday through the horrors. 'Yes, we've got some gin.'

* * *

Jack took Friday to her first appointment with Lucian Meriwether in Mrs H's around-town gig. Mrs H had gone to some lengths to cater to Mr Meriwether's particular needs, which she felt was warranted as he was paying a premium, and had purchased a very costly whip and a pair of manacles, had consulted with Minnie Thompson regarding the best local softwood for use as a birch (willow, soaked in brine), and had commissioned a costume for Friday.

This consisted of a deep navy-blue satin corset, reinforced with extra whalebone so Friday didn't burst it when she was letting fly with the whip, a (silly, in Friday's opinion) pair of fitted, knee-length drawers in the sheerest lawn dyed a matching colour, which she was tempted to toss out of the gig because she just knew they'd stick annoyingly to her arse as soon as she started to sweat, and a pair of buttoned ankle boots in dark red kid leather with ridiculous heels two inches high, making her a towering five feet eight inches tall. She hated stays because they squashed her guts and only conceded to wear them for work — and these had been made to lace really tightly, giving her a waist of a mere nineteen and a half inches — and she disliked drawers even more because the edges around her crotch always managed to sneak up her crack, unless the things were so baggy they gaped. (Though she had to admit it had been fun getting in between the edges of Aria's.)

And the mask! Mrs H had said that when she'd been a madam in London the flagellants had worn masks, therefore Friday should wear one. Friday had asked her what was the point, when her arms, back and one calf were covered in highly distinctive tattoos and Mr Meriwether knew bloody well who she was anyway, but no, it added to the mystery, apparently. It was stupid, and she felt a fool wearing it.

Halfway along Cumberland Street she said, 'Stop the gig.'

Jack glanced at her. 'Why?'

'Just stop for a second.' Friday reached beneath the seat and hauled out the case containing her costume and other paraphernalia.

The mask, an absurdly frothy concoction of black cock and blue peacock feathers, lay on top. Spotting a trio of scruffy young lads chucking stones at a cat trapped up a tree, she leant out of the gig. ''Oi, you lot, come here.'

Two shot off, but one stood his ground. 'It's just a dumb tibby!'

'Never mind the cat. I've got something for you.'

The boy sidled closer, ragged trouser bottoms flapping around thin, dirty ankles, ready to run if necessary. 'What?'

Friday passed him the mask. 'A Christmas present.'

Jack rolled his eyes.

'What is it?' The boy fingered the shiny feathers.

'A mystery mask. For balls for nobs and that. It's worth a bit. You could sell it down the market.'

The boy grinned and put it on, looking like a strange hybrid of starved sparrow and peacock. 'Ta!' He ran off, flapping his arms and making cawing noises.

'Mrs H'll have your guts for garters,' Jack said as he flicked the reins.

'Well, it was stupid.'

Lucian Meriwether lived in a substantial one-storey sandstone house towards the smarter end of Princes Street, in fact not that far from Bella Shand's brothel, Friday realised, as they drove past it. Mr Meriwether's residence appeared welcoming, at least from the outside. A verandah ran along the front and down one side, cream-painted shutters flanked the windows and a low wooden fence separated the property from the street. A garden filled with a profusion of brightly coloured flowers, uncommon in a Sydney summer, bordered the fence and there were roses, too, in smaller round beds in the browning lawn. Mr Meriwether had said his wife was dead — she wondered who did the gardening, and how he managed to keep the plants watered, especially at this time of year.

'How long's the session?' Jack asked.

'Two hours.'

'Christ, your arm'll drop off, and so will his arse.'

'It's not two hours of solid flogging. I'm supposed to be having afternoon tea as well.'

'La de da.'

'Oh, shut up.'

'Will I wait?'

'No. Go back to the Siren and do some work.'

Jack snorted. 'Who made you my boss?'

'Well, you'll only melt sitting out here in the heat.'

'That's true. Do you need a hand down?'

'No.' Friday scrambled inelegantly off the gig and adjusted her hat. Jack passed down the case. 'Four o'clock, thanks, and don't be late. Christ knows what I'm supposed to talk to him about.'

'You'll manage. Think of the money.'

Friday opened the hand gate and crunched up the gravel path to the front door, wondering, too late, if she should have gone around the back. Mr Meriwether might not want his neighbours to see what sort of visitors he was receiving. Still, she looked reasonably respectable today. More or less. She knocked on the green-painted door.

It was opened by an austere-looking middle-aged woman in a brown dress, a white apron and a plain white house cap. 'Miss Friday?' At Friday's nod, she said, 'Mr Meriwether's expecting you. Please follow me.'

The woman led Friday, not to a bedchamber as she'd been expecting, but into a study, its walls lined with shelves stacked with more books than Friday had ever seen. Lucian Meriwether sat at a desk beneath the room's single window, assorted cut blooms scattered before him. Several had been carefully arranged on a piece of card, which in turn was aligned on a rectangle of shellacked wood about a foot long and eight inches wide. A brass screw pierced the wood on each side.

Mr Meriwether glanced up. 'Ah, Miss Friday! Lovely! I shan't be a moment.'

Friday watched, fascinated, as he laid another piece of card over the blooms, then took a second of piece of wood, this one decorated with a floral marquetry pattern, and settled it over the screws. She suddenly realised, as he fitted a pair of bolts and tightened them, that he was pressing flowers! What a strange hobby to interest a man! Especially one who liked to be battered with whips. Still, it took all sorts, she supposed.

She asked, 'What do you do with them?'

'I put them in albums. The very best specimens, I frame.'

'I'll be going out now, Mr Meriwether,' the woman in the brown dress said. 'I'll just fetch my bonnet and basket.'

'Yes, thank you, Mrs Wright.'

Friday heard her clomp down the hall towards the back of the house, clomp back again, then open and close the front door.

'Off to the market,' Mr Meriwether said. 'Doesn't entirely approve.'

'Oh well.'

'Though she understands that a man has certain needs. And she certainly values her position here. She's been with me for years, since well before my wife died. A good woman, Mrs Wright.'

'I'm sure.'

'And she's left us a very nice afternoon tea. All I have to do is boil the kettle.' Mr Meriwether put aside the flower press. 'Well, shall we get down to business? I can't tell you how much I've been looking forward to this.'

This was all feeling rather odd to Friday. According to Mistress Ruby, she was supposed to be assuming a position of uncompromising dominance over Lucian Meriwether, and here he was, talking about putting the kettle on. Was she doing it wrong? Already?

'Er, am I supposed to be kicking you up the arse or calling you rude names or something? Is that what you'd like?'

Mr Meriwether gave a little smile. 'Not really, thank you. I've tried that and I've found I don't have a specific need to be humiliated. I simply enjoy the pain, which I would like you to administer. I have never forgotten your magnificent physique, and I was thrilled to see when we met again the other day that your beautiful hair is even longer.'

Friday had racked her brains since that meeting, and still couldn't remember Lucian Merewether as a customer, but he must have been. Of course, there'd been so many. Perhaps it was the alcohol, eating holes in her memory. 'And do you want to call me by a special name? You know, like Mistress Whiparse or something?'

Mr Meriwether laughed out loud, almost losing his dentures. 'No, no. Miss Friday is perfectly adequate, I feel, don't you?'

Friday shrugged. 'Up to you. I've got a costume. Shall I wear it?'

'Is it revealing?'

'Quite.'

'Yes, please.' Mr Meriwether reached for his cane and stood. 'Now, if you'll give me a moment, I'll go and prepare myself. I'll be in my bedchamber. You may dress in here. Feel free to close the drapes.'

He hobbled out. Friday leant across the desk; there were bushes and a tree outside — no one would see her getting changed. She opened her case, took off her dress and shift, and stepped into the despised navy-blue drawers. But at least they sat neatly on her waist, having been made to fasten at the front and back with buttons instead of ties. Knowing she wouldn't be able to bend without passing out once she got into the corset, she sat down next to put on the boots, her bare bum poking out of the gap in the drawers as she did so. The boots fastened, she dropped the button hook back in the case and lifted out the corset. The lacing was at the front, otherwise she couldn't close it by herself. She loosened the grosgrain ribbons, shrugged it on over her head, swearing as she caught an earring, and wriggled it down into place, the hem sitting over the waistband of the drawers. She made sure none of her waist-length hair was caught under it, then started tightening the laces, bottom to the middle, top to the middle, bit by bit, until finally it was tight enough and the shape was sitting correctly on her. She hoped Mr Meriwether hadn't died of old age in his room.

She swore again as she realised that her whip, birch and manacles were still in the case on the floor. Dropping to all fours to avoid bending at the waist, she grabbed them, and heaved herself up again. Bloody hell, this was ridiculous.

Taking as deep a breath as the stupid stays would allow her, she walked out into the hall, the high heels of her boots clacking on the floorboards. 'Mr Meriwether? Where are you?'

'I'm in here, Miss Friday!'

Following the sound of his voice, Friday found him stretched out face down on his bed, a double four-poster, fortunately without a canopy to interfere with the whip. He was naked, except for a pair of knee-length black silk hose. His skin was white and alarmingly fragile-looking, his legs thin and his flanks concave, though his torso was soft and barrel-shaped.

He gasped when he saw her. 'Oh, I say. What an absolutely charming ensemble! And you have some new tattoos. Stupendous! And the colour of that corset against your hair. Delightful!'

Friday turned and raised her arms so he could appreciate the full glory of the phoenix rising up her back out of her stays.

'Bravo, my dear! Bravo!'

'What would you like?' she asked. 'I've got a whip, a birch and manacles.'

'Manacles, please. And the whip, of course.'

Having had four lessons now from Mistress Ruby, Friday knew what to do. She manacled Mr Meriwether's left wrist to a bedpost, then walked around the bed and manacled his right wrist to another, leaving him helpless. She wondered what would happen if she just abandoned him. Poor Mrs Wright would certainly get a fright when she came back. She moved to the end of the bed, swung her arm a couple of times to limber up and gave the whip a few practice cracks.

'No,' Mr Meriwether said. 'Not there. Come around to the side here, so I can see your magnificent personage.'

Friday did as he asked, checking the ceiling for candelabra. Nothing — it was all wall sconces in Mr Meriwether's bedroom, fortunately.

'Are you ready?' she asked.

'Oh, yes.'

Friday lifted the whip, flicked her wrist and brought the thong cracking down on Mr Meriwether's skinny backside. He jumped and moaned simultaneously, his face creased in apparent ecstasy. She kept going, establishing a measured rhythm, which he matched, grinding his elderly hips into the mattress. After about ten minutes, it occurred to her that it didn't matter that she was using a whip on him — he was still an old man and old men usually took forever to ring their chimes. Also, she was sweating like a pig and her right tit was falling out of the corset, and while Mr Meriwether might think that was fun, it was bloody uncomfortable.

A few minutes after that her shoulder began to feel as though it had caught on fire, so she changed hands, a bit worried because she wasn't as accurate with her left. And then she missed, getting him on the inside of his thigh. He cried out, but pumped even harder. She aimed for his back, then, a bigger target, planning to move back to his bum when she swapped hands again. His arse looked like it needed a rest anyway. It was bright red and she'd broken the skin in one or two places. She could see a thin trickle of blood running down his flank and another disappearing between his cheeks, and wondered if that was supposed to happen. Who knew there'd be this much to whipping someone?

Come on, come on, she said to herself, glancing at the ornate clock on the mantel above the fireplace. Both shoulders hurt now, and she could absolutely murder a tankard of ale. She changed hands again, noticing that she'd developed a blister on her right palm. For God's sake, this wasn't supposed to be hurting her!

'Oh, hurry up, you stupid old shit!' she exclaimed, and brought the whip down with an almighty, zinging crack across Mr Meriwether's bum.

He spasmed violently, his back bowing, chest and feet off the mattress, and let out a long, loud groan. Then he collapsed, his face buried in the pillow.

Friday stared down at him, wondering for a very unpleasant moment if he'd had a heart attack. It'd be a bit of a problem if she'd killed him. 'Mr Meriwether? Are you all right?'

He turned his head and opened an eye. 'I've never been better, my dear. That was truly invigorating. And you were magnificent.'

Friday grunted and tucked her breast back into her corset. 'Your arse looks a mess. There's blood.'

'Truly, a small price to pay. Why don't you go and get changed into your street clothes and put the kettle on, while I tidy myself?'

Sighing, Friday freed him from the manacles, collected her gear and clacked back to the study in her noisy boots. She should have known she'd be the one to end up making the tea. By the time she'd changed, packed her things in her case, found the kitchen at the back of the house and boiled the kettle, he'd also dressed, and appeared in the kitchen.

'There you are,' he said. He opened a cupboard and indicated a tray on which sat a cake, a plate of biscuits and various tea things. 'Would you mind carrying the tray through to the study?' He waved his cane. 'I'm afraid I can't. A damned nuisance, this.'

'You go through,' Friday said resignedly. 'I'll bring it all.'

She dumped tea leaves into the pot, plonked it on the tray and carted it down the hall. Mr Meriwether had cleared some space on his desk and moved a chair closer to his.

'Please, sit down,' he said when she'd deposited the tray. 'Do you take milk? I think Mrs Wright bought some yesterday, but it goes off so quickly in this weather.'

Friday shook her head. 'Sugar, though.'

'Cake?'

'Yes, please.' The cake looked delicious, and so did the biscuits. Obviously Mrs Wright was a good cook.

Shovelling cake into her mouth, Friday feared that the next fifty minutes would crawl past and she'd have to stifle her yawns, but she was pleasantly surprised. Mr Meriwether showed her his pressed flower albums, and some of his books filled with illustrations of strange animals and plants from all around the world. Prior to his retirement, he told her, he'd been a natural historian with a particular interest in botany and birds, and had gone on many expeditions to exotic locations such as India, the Bahamas, the Mosquito Coast, Jamaica, Guiana, Dominica, Gibraltar, Tangier and some of the British-owned territories in North America. Friday was astounded to hear that his wife, Florence, had accompanied him at times, as she couldn't think of anything worse than traipsing through mud, or a jungle, or across a desert, or a mosquito-infested swamp, just to look at a boring little plant, and said so. Mr Meriwether said yes, actually, he wished that Florence hadn't, because she'd contracted malaria, which had severely weakened her constitution. On physicians' advice they'd immigrated to New South Wales for the warmer weather, but it had been too late — ultimately Florence had died from her illness. And he'd been lonely ever since.

Friday's eye was caught by a row of glass domes on a shelf, under which were forever captured an assortment of stuffed birds. Most were small and brightly coloured, like jewels, but under one dome was a pair about the size of crows with gleaming black plumage and orange wattles. One had a short, stout ivory-coloured beak while the other had a long narrow beak that curved downwards. Their tail feathers looked familiar — long and tipped with white.

'What are those?' she asked.

'The black specimens? Striking, aren't they? They're huia birds, native to New Zealand. Curiously, they mate for life. Very highly prized by the Maoris, too. They view them as sacred. Only those of high rank are entitled to wear the feathers or skins. I'm told they're occasionally given as tokens of esteem, respect and love.'

Friday felt a warm glow spread though her chest, and a burst of goodwill towards Mr Meriwether. She decided she didn't mind keeping him company, as long as he was paying for her time — which he was, and very handsomely, too.

At five minutes to four he withdrew his watch and said wistfully, 'Oh dear, I see my treat is coming to an end. But what a delightful way to finish the year. Thank you, Miss Friday. I trust you will be back soon?'

'When would you like to see me?'

'In a fortnight? I'll send word.'

'As long as you give me plenty of notice. I'm usually quite booked up.'

'I've no doubt you are.' Mr Meriwether took her hand and kissed it. 'Will you forgive me for not seeing you to the door? I'm afraid I'm feeling a little, er, battered.'

'I can see myself out,' Friday said, standing. 'Have a nice New Year, Mr Meriwether.'

'A happy New Year to you, too.'

Closing the front door behind her, she hurried down the path, pleased to see Jack waiting on the street in the gig. She slid her case under the seat, hoisted her skirts and climbed up, settling herself beside him.

'How'd it go?' he asked.

'Bloody hard work, actually. Afternoon tea was nice.'

'Mrs H says to remind you you've got a customer at half past four.'

Friday hadn't forgotten. 'Well, get a move on then.'

But something caught her eye as they neared Bella Shand's establishment, farther south on Princes Street — Bella's distinctive midnight-blue curricle emerging from the carriageway at the side of her house.

Friday grabbed Jack's arm. 'Stop!'

'Now what?'

'Just do it, Jack.'

Sighing heavily, he did.

Friday squinted to pick out the driver of the curricle, who appeared to be wearing a dress. It looked like — it was! Louisa Coutts. Louisa drove the curricle onto the street and parked in front of the house. A moment later, Bella appeared from the shadows, her hand at her brow as though shielding her eyes from the sun. And she was carrying a cane. She crossed the shallow verandah running along the rear of the house, which faced the street, descended the three steps, and walked unhurriedly to the curricle. She wasn't limping, merely using the cane a little for support. She seemed perhaps a hint slower than usual, but alert as ever, her back straight and her head held high. Friday's heart sank.

Louisa jumped down from the curricle and helped Bella to climb up onto the seat.

'Go,' Friday urged Jack. 'I want to see her up close.'

Jack flicked the reins and the gig moved parallel to Bella's vehicle. Friday leant out past Jack and stared. Slowly, so slowly, Bella turned her head. She wore a hat with a brim that cast a shadow across her features, but Friday could still see her face. She was as thin as usual, her nose as prominent as a shark's fin, but, disappointingly, there was no evidence in her features of some terrible, life-sapping disease. Her eyes remained twin pools of glittering jet, rimmed, as usual, with the kohl she favoured, and full of her sharp, detestable intelligence. The ringlets of her wig gleamed in stark contrast with her white-powdered skin, and long, heavy gold earrings visibly stretched her earlobes. Friday noted with satisfaction that neither the slash of red lip rouge nor the deep purple of Bella's expensive dress and matching silk scarf at her throat complemented her pale complexion. But then, she never seemed to wear colours that suited her.

Bella sneered, her curled upper lip revealing yellowing teeth and, Friday was sure, a new gap at the side. Good job.

'Slag,' Bella mouthed.

'Bitch,' Friday responded, and raised two fingers.

Knowing Friday, and what would surely happen next, Jack gripped the reins and urged his horses forwards. Mrs H would kill him if he didn't get Friday back to the brothel on time, or if he delivered her late and with a black eye.

But instead of berating him as they tore off down the street, the horses' hooves scattering gravel, Friday sat beside him, deep in thought.

'What?' he asked.

'She might not be dying, Jack, but her teeth are falling out and she's using a cane. I suppose that's better than nothing.'

'Is it?' He had no idea what she was talking about.

'Yes. It is.'

# Chapter Fourteen

*January 1832, Sydney Town*

Harrie saw him coming and tried to get away by weaving through the crowd in the market shed and ducking out the door at the far end, but she wasn't fast enough. He caught up with her just as she got outside, and grabbed hold of her basket, almost tugging it from her grasp. She thought of screaming at the top of her voice in the hope that folk would think she was being assaulted, which in a way she was, but was loath to draw so much attention to herself.

'Wait, stop,' he said. 'I want to talk to you.'

She stood perfectly still, eyes cast down, hoping that if she said nothing, eventually he would go away. This had been a mistake, coming to the market by herself — a terrible one — just as James said it would be.

'Can you hear me?' Jonah Leary said loudly, as though she were deaf or slow. 'It's Mary, isn't it?'

'No, Harrie. Please let go of my basket.'

He did. 'That's a strange name for a girl.'

'Please go away.' Bands of panic tightened around Harrie's chest. 'I don't know anything about another tattoo, and neither does Leo. So leave me alone. Leave us both alone.'

Leary nodded gravely, giving every indication of seriously considering her request, then leant towards her, as though he were about to share a confidence. Harrie stepped back; if he was, she didn't want to hear it. 'Granted, I might have made a mistake about the second tattoo,' he said. 'It turns out me brother, Bennett that is, could be here in Sydney after all. Hale and hearty, I mean. And if he is, me other brother Malcolm wouldn't have had bits of him tanned or floating in a jar, would he?' He smiled. 'So, I'll ask you this. Do you know Bennett Leary?'

'No!'

'You've never heard of someone with a map tattooed on his back?'

'Only your brother, Malcolm.' Oh, why will he not believe me? Harrie thought. Could he not see she was telling the truth?

'Then ask everyone you can think of. You work for a tattooist. I'm betting someone with an eye for tattoos will have seen or heard of him.'

Harrie looked wildly around. No one was watching them. The way Leary was standing now, one hand casually on his hip, hat dangling from his fingers, a smile on his face, was giving the impression that they were having a nice, friendly conversation in the sunshine. But they weren't. Couldn't anyone see?

Summoning all her courage, and praying her voice wouldn't wobble, she said, 'No, I won't. It's nothing to do with us. He's your brother. You find him.'

Slowly, Leary shook his head, though his smile never slipped. 'Oh dear, what a shame. I was hoping I wouldn't have to do this. I'm that sorry.' But he didn't sound sorry, not at all.

Harrie's legs suddenly didn't want to support her. 'Do what?'

'That little girl you're so fond of in the orphanage. Charlotte? I know how upset you'd be if something bad happened to her.' He paused for a second, watching her, then added, 'You would be, wouldn't you? Very upset.'

Harrie's heartbeat roared in her ears and her throat was suddenly as dry as old bones. 'How do you know about Charlotte?' she whispered.

'It's surprising what five shillings will buy.'

Not Mrs Duff, surely? Harrie thought, horrified. 'Please, don't hurt her. She's only a baby.'

Leary put his hat back on. 'I won't have to, will I, if you find out where me brother is.'

'But I told you, I don't know him! I don't even know where to start!'

The smile finally left Leary's face. 'Then talk to your boss. *He's not stupid.*'

He walked off, leaving Harrie staring at the ground, her fists clenched, hot tears welling in her eyes. He'd threatened Charlotte, and she didn't know what to do. And he'd implied that she was stupid. She wasn't stupid.

Was she?

Forgetting about the shopping, and convinced that Leary was following her, Harrie went straight down to Leo's and told him what had happened.

Furious, Leo said, 'But how did he find out about Charlotte in the first place?'

'I don't know!'

'Did he follow you out to Parramatta, do you think?'

'No, I would have known. Surely?'

Leo frowned. Over the past four or five months, there'd been times when Harrie wouldn't have known who was in the room with her, but he didn't say as much. 'And he suggested that something bad would happen to her if you don't track down this Bennett?'

Blowing her nose on one of Leo's enormous handkerchiefs, Harrie nodded. 'He'll do it, too. I know he will. Look how little he cared about his other brother.'

'Aye, lass, I hate to say it, but I think you might be right.' Leo patted her shoulder in a manner he hoped would be comforting. 'I also think it might be time to tell that man of yours about everything that's been going on.'

Harrie froze. 'Everything?'

God, Leo thought, she looked so frightened. But then, Jonah Leary was a bloody frightening cove. 'What harm can it do? This business with Leary isn't your fault. Tell James what's happened. He might be able to help.'

'How?'

'I don't know. And neither will you until you talk to him about it.'

Leo splayed his hands and looked down at the words HOLD and FAST tattooed across his fingers. He did know how James could help; it was obvious to everyone — including, no doubt, James — except for Harrie herself. Poor, sad, unwell, stubborn and bloody exasperating little Harrie.

Deliberately changing the subject, Harrie said, 'What if we do find Bennett Leary? We can't tell his brother. We don't even know where he's staying.'

'Yes, we do. The George Inn, on Market Street.'

'How do you know that?'

Leo tapped his nose. 'Anyway, *we* are not looking for Bennett bloody Leary.'

'We have to! Char—'

'No, you won't be doing anything. I'll do a bit of asking around. Go and talk to your man.'

'He's not my man.'

Leo sighed. 'Harrie, why are you making this so hard for yourself? Talk to him, go on. Be a good lass.'

But that's the problem, isn't it? Harrie thought. I'm not good.

\* \* \*

Leo had deliberated all day over what he was about to do. If it turned to shit, there could be bloody serious consequences, but if it worked, his plan could go a long way towards getting rid of Leary.

Turning off George Street into Market, he pulled his hat lower onto his forehead against the stiff but warm evening breeze gusting up the hill from Darling Harbour, bringing with it dust and grit from the street and the smell of the sea, cesspits, and a nearby tannery. The sun had only just dropped behind the hills on the far side of the harbour, forcing him to squint against the line of liquid flame burning along the horizon, until a bullock team hauling a precariously overloaded wagon crested the hill rising from Market Wharf and blocked the fiery glare. The skinny little bullocky, arse off the seat and his whip cracking like a musket going off, shouted and swore, urging the beasts over the summit, breath shooting from flaring nostrils as though they were a team of lumpy, misshapen, shitting dragons.

Leo watched from the footway, unconsciously leaning with the bullocks, urging the loaded wagon up and over until at last they made it, to cheers and applause from the open windows of the George Inn at his back. He turned and went in.

The publican confirmed that Jonah Leary had been renting a room upstairs for the past week and had just paid for another, and no, he didn't know if he was in or not. Leo thanked him, had a quick look around the public room to see if he could spot Leary among the drinkers, couldn't, and made his way up to the first floor.

Clearly the publican was the parsimonious type, Leo thought, as although sconces were attached to the walls, the candles themselves were missing. He walked to the end of the corridor, his boots making a hell of a noise on the uncarpeted floorboards. Which was fine — he had no intention, after all, of sneaking up on Leary.

Reaching the farthest door, he knocked purposefully.

'Who is it?' a voice called.

'Leo Dundas.'

The door opened slightly; Jonah Leary peered out. 'Have you found him?'

'No. But I've been thinking about how you could get a heads up on whether you will find him.'

Scowling, Leary opened the door another few inches, keeping, Leo noticed, his boot firmly wedged behind it. 'What?'

'I know a woman who reads the cards. She has a very good reputation. She can tell you what your future holds, and maybe even where your brother is. She can at least tell you whether he's definitely here.' Leo spread his hands and shrugged. 'I mean, he might not be. He might be in Van Diemen's Land. You don't know. There's no point any of us looking for him if he isn't in Sydney, is there?'

Leary gave him a long, suspicious look. 'What's her name?'

'Serafina Fortune. You've heard of her?'

Leary nodded and asked, as though sensing a trap or a swindle, 'How well do you know her?'

'She reads the cards for me every six months or so,' Leo said truthfully, but not quite answering the question — Serafina did poke around in his future now and then, though of course he saw her a lot more frequently than every six months. Anyway there was no trap. He hadn't spoken to her at all about Leary. Either the cove's brother was in Sydney or he wasn't, and if he was, hopefully Serafina, with her fey and alarming gift, would be able to discover where, then Leary would leave him and Harrie alone.

'Where is she, this Fortune woman?'

'Essex Street.'

Leary shut the door. Five minutes passed and Leo thought his plan had failed before it had even got under way. He swore under his breath and turned to leave, but then Leary emerged from his room dressed for the street.

'We'll go now.'

Disconcerted, Leo said, 'You don't have an appointment. It's after hours.' Serafina was likely to tell him to fuck off if she wasn't in the mood for reading the cards without warning.

Leary dug in his pocket and flapped a ten-shilling note in Leo's face. 'I don't need an appointment.'

Arrogant prick, Leo thought. 'I should warn you, I gather she's not known for her good temper.'

'Neither am I,' Leary said, and strode off down the corridor.

Leary said little as they walked down to Essex Street, except to recount the experience of an acquaintance, a convict with a ticket of leave, who had engaged Serafina Fortune's services to find out whether he would marry a woman over whom he was lovesick — Leary's sneering interpretation of the situation — and whom he'd been avidly courting. Serafina had apparently read the man's cards and told him he had a choice; he could either forget about the woman, or marry her and live under a long shadow of misery. The man had dumped his sweetheart, which had been fortunate as she'd been carrying some other cove's brat. That was how he'd learnt of Serafina Fortune's talents.

Hoping that Serafina was in a reasonable mood, because quite often she wasn't, Leo knocked on the blue-painted door of her cottage. She took so long to open it that he thought for a minute she might be out, despite the light in the window. When she did, he shook his head once, almost imperceptibly, as she gazed at them in silence, hoping to convey via the tiny movement that she was not to let on how well they knew each other, and fairly confident that she'd understand. Perhaps she was expecting them anyway. Who knew, with her?

'Good evening, Miss Fortune,' he said. 'We're sorry to disturb you. This is Mr Leary. He'd like a reading, if it's not too much trouble.'

'Mr Dundas,' Serafina said, her expression inscrutable. She turned her attention to Leary, taking her time assessing him. 'Mr Leary. The fee is six shillings after hours without an appointment.'

Leo bit his lip. She never charged more than four.

'Six! Christ,' Leary said.

'If that's beyond your means ...' Serafina stepped back, her hand on the door.

Leary said, 'No, wait, I'll pay. But I'll expect me money's worth.'

'Oh,' Serafina said, 'I'm sure you'll get that.'

Inside she sat him down at the oval table, turned up the lamp positioned in the centre, and opened the wooden box that held her cards. While Leo made himself comfortable at the far end of the table, she took her money tin out of the box, unlocked it and looked at Leary expectantly. 'Fee in advance, if you don't mind.'

With obvious reluctance, Leary gave her his ten-shilling note. She placed it in the tin, handed him four shillings in change, and locked it again.

'Do you have a specific set of cards you prefer?' she asked.

'Dunno. Never done this before,' Leary said. 'I've heard about you, though. I'm looking for —'

'Hush!' Serafina raised a long-fingered hand. 'Please say nothing about yourself or what you seek, Mr Leary. The cards will do that.'

Leary sat back in his chair hard enough to make the legs scrape on the floor, and folded his arms belligerently across his chest.

Serafina took a pack of cards from the box and shuffled them expertly. Then she set them before Leary, asked him to touch the pile, shuffled again, cut the deck and laid out five in the shape of a cross.

'This is a general reading reflecting where you've been and where you are now,' she said.

'I know where I am. Sydney Town.'

'I mean where you are in your life,' Serafina said, not looking up but making it very clear by her frosty tone that she knew he was being a deliberate smartarse. 'The next spread I'll do will answer the questions you have.'

Leaning back in his own chair, Leo looked at Leary through half-closed eyes. The man was frightened, or at least visibly on edge. Sweat had popped out on his forehead and his leg was fidgeting under the table. Was it Serafina and the cards unnerving him, or was he worried he'd discover his brother wasn't in Sydney after all? Or something else altogether? Leo shifted his gaze to Serafina, staring intently down at the spread. He knew the cards were just a prop. She had the sight and could see the future, and the past, by just letting her mind drift. It scared the shit out of him, actually.

'Mmm,' Serafina said at last. 'A port city. Not London. Bristol? Liverpool? Liverpool, I think. You come from a large family, more sisters than brothers. Four sisters? And — forgive me for being blunt — you're all as crooked as they come. What were you transported for, Mr Leary?' She glanced up: he was staring at her, his eyes comically round. 'Your father is dead. Your mother is a strong woman, a matriarch. And very, very smart. Perhaps even smarter than you realise. There isn't a lot of trust in your family, though, is there? You certainly don't trust anyone. You're always looking over your shoulder. But then, you'd need to, in your line of work. Your brothers ... oh, I see one has recently passed over. Did you know that?'

Leary nodded.

Leo was surprised; Serafina wasn't pulling her punches. He knew that normally she didn't pass on bad news to customers, unless they specifically asked to be told.

She looked at the cards again, and frowned. 'I'll come back to the other brother. This one ...' she tapped a card illustrated with ten brightly coloured pentacles '... is interesting. It represents the accumulation or laying away of wealth over a period of time. Did your family, or a member of your family, make an investment of some sort at some time in the past?'

Leo, who knew Serafina very well, noted the tiniest of smirks on her lips, but doubted Leary had. Obviously not wanting to give anything away concerning his financial affairs, Leary said nothing.

'If so,' Serafina continued, 'it may be about to come to fruition.' She studied the cards a moment longer, then her gaze lifted and settled on a point somewhere behind Leary's head.

Leo knew she was seeing far, far beyond the confines of her little house and anything the cards might be telling her now, and the hairs on his arms rippled.

'Streets,' she said. 'A tapestry of old city streets running down to the dirty river. Saints in the fields. The bewigged on one side and the poor on the other. Oh, the dirty little children. Books and coffee and a long, long strand. The market and churches with graveyards and spires made tiny. Oranges and lemons, ringy bells at —'

Leo slammed the flat of his hand on the table, the sound a pistol crack in the little room, his gaze on Leary, whose mouth had fallen open, an expression of shock on his face. He shot an angry, fearful glance at Leo.

Serafina started, and blinked. 'What?'

Leo was horrified. Had she been seeing the location disclosed by all three of the Leary brothers' tattooed maps? Or even worse, the secret they revealed? Whatever that was, it was plain Leary wanted it very badly. If he suspected she had seen, she could be in real danger.

'You drifted off,' he said, forcing himself to sound calm.

'Did I?'

'What did you just say?' Leary demanded.

'When?'

'Just then, about rivers and churches.' Leary waved his hand angrily. 'What did you mean?'

'I really don't know,' Serafina said. 'Sometimes these things just come to me. They come through me. I'm barely aware of what I'm saying. Do you know what it means? It's your reading.'

Leary remained silent.

Leo stared at him; Leary glared back. It was clear from his clenched jaw and the vein pulsing in his forehead that he did have a good idea of what Serafina's vision meant, but also that he was furious that Leo, and probably Serafina, had shared it. It occurred to Leo that Leary might think he'd brought him here to deliberately delve into his secrets for his own gain. Shit.

Serafina gathered up the cards, shuffled them once more, asked Leary to think of the question he wanted answered, and laid a spread of seven.

She frowned again.

'Your brother's here,' she said.

'Which one?'

'The one who still lives.'

'Bennett?'

'The cards don't give names,' Serafina said.

Leary stood to lean across the table. 'Where? Where is he?'

Staring intently at the spread, Serafina said, 'In Australia somewhere.'

'Where?' Leary's hand shot out and grabbed Serafina's wrist.

Leo leapt out of his chair, knocking it over with a clatter. 'Hoi! Get your hands off her!'

Unperturbed, Serafina calmly dug the fingernails of her other hand into the flesh of Leary's palm until he let go. 'That is not going to dispose me to tell you anything further. Either sit down or get out.'

Leary glared at her for a moment, then tugged at the hem of his jacket and resumed his seat.

'I can't tell you exactly where,' Serafina said. 'The cards are not that specific. Sydney, perhaps. Van Diemen's Land? But I can tell you he's not incarcerated, and by that I mean not behind bars or in irons.'

'So he could be assigned?'

Serafina shrugged.

'Or have a ticket of leave?'

Nothing from Serafina this time.

'I need more than that if I'm going to find him,' Leary snapped.

'When was he transported?' Leo asked.

Leary started, as though he'd forgotten Leo was there. 'I don't know. I haven't seen him for ten years.'

'Could he be free by now?' Leo said.

'I doubt it. He'd've got fourteen years, or even life.'

Serafina gave him a thoughtful look. 'Really? Why do you think he was transported?'

Leary's face hardened. 'None of your business.'

'Well, at least now you know he really is here in Australia,' Leo said.

'Only according to a didikai fortune teller.'

'Excuse me.' Serafina's voice was icy. 'I have no Romany blood in my veins whatsoever.'

'And that being the case,' Leo went on, ignoring both Leary's and Serafina's comments, 'you can stop terrorising Harrie Clarke.'

'I can't see why I should,' Leary said. 'I still don't know where the fuck my brother is.'

'And neither does Harrie, so leave her alone. I mean it. She hasn't got a clue. You're wasting your time.'

Leary stood. 'Well, we'll see about that.' And he left, banging the door behind him.

'What an arsehole,' Serafina said. 'Thank you very much, Leo. I can do without customers like that.'

Leo let out an enormous sigh. That hadn't quite gone the way he'd wanted it to. 'I'm sorry, love. I was hoping you'd be able to tell him exactly where his sodding bloody brother is, and get him off Harrie's back. And mine.'

'I can't see everything, you know. I'm not that good. The brother is in Sydney, though. I did see that much.'

'Well, let's hope Leary buggers off for six months on a wild goose chase,' Leo said. 'Did you recognise what you saw? The business with the oranges and lemons?'

'Pretty much. It was a map. Of London, and detailed, but a little blurred. I've been there myself, and so, probably, have you.'

'Don't tell me,' Leo said, alarmed. 'I don't want to know.' He hesitated. 'Was there something else you didn't tell him?'

Serafina nodded. 'In the second spread, concerning his brother. They're more or less for show, the cards, you know that, but they do tend to reveal some interesting things. Leary got the Magus, in conjunction with two other specific cards, which signifies a reversal pointing towards the Empress. Harrie's friend, Friday Woolfe, got the same reading. Very unusual, and very odd. I can't say I know what it means. And I can't "see" what it means, either. I've never come across it before, and I've no idea what connection there might be between Leary and his brother, and Friday. If there is one at all.' She rubbed her mouth thoughtfully and made a face. 'And when I "saw" Leary's brother, I didn't, not really. I had a sense of him, but I couldn't see his features at all, and often I can. It was almost as if he's ...' She thought for a second. 'I don't know how to describe it, I really don't.'

Leo scowled. It all sounded very strange. But it was Serafina's field, not his, and the less he had to do with it the better, as far as he was concerned. 'What sort of investment did Leary's family make? Could you see?'

Serafina laughed. 'Someone did a robbery. A big one. There's quite a stash hidden away.' Her brow furrowed slightly. 'Or at least I think there is.'

Ah, Leo thought, so that's what the maps mean. Bloody funny place to put them, though — tattooed onto actual people.

'Be careful, Leo,' Serafina said. 'That Leary's dangerous.'

'Don't fret, love.' Leo stood and pushed his chair under the table.

'And don't bring him back. I won't have him in my house again.'

'Fair enough. I'd better go. He might be lurking outside, checking to see whether I come out or not. I told him we're barely acquainted.'

Serafina raised her face for a kiss. 'I mean it. You need to take care.'

And Leo took heed, because he knew she'd seen his future.

\* \* \*

While Leo was escorting Jonah Leary to Essex Street, James was trudging home from work even later than usual. There had been a backlog of patients this afternoon, due to a thirteen-year-old girl giving birth in the surgery. Her mother had brought her in, seeking a diagnosis and cure for the large and painful 'growth' in the girl's belly. Lawrence Chandler had taken one look at her, clutching her abdomen and howling her head off, understood the situation, and had barely got her skirts out of the way before the baby crowned. The mother, also belatedly realising what was going on, had laid into her daughter mid-delivery; Lawrence had shoved her out of the way, after which the mother had punched Lawrence, who had been forced to shout for James. When James had come running and hauled the mother out of the room, Lawrence had locked the door and finished delivering the baby. Unfortunately, the girl had torn due to her diminutive size and the speed of the baby's exit, and the repair had taken Lawrence some time. James had seen as many of Lawrence's patients as he could, but still, they hadn't closed the surgery until after six-thirty.

As always, James hoped to be greeted by Harrie's smiling face, though often he was disappointed. Sometimes she was relaxed and calm and approaching cheerful, but usually she wasn't. Some days he wondered if she was ever going to get well, but he knew that what ailed her could take months, even years, to heal. Still, he was prepared to wait.

She'd been living in his house for a little over seven weeks now. Technically he was her master, and he felt deeply uncomfortable about the dynamic that created between them, but apparently he was the only one who did. Harrie seemed quite happy to ignore his legal status in their relationship, going off to tattoo for Leo Dundas whenever she felt like it, when in theory she should be working in a domestic capacity at home. He was the one, however, who'd suggested she find herself something to occupy her mind, though he hadn't meant tattooing hairy sailors, and he genuinely didn't want her to feel in a position of servitude towards him. Lately, though, she'd begun to do a bit of housework and prepare meals, and a damned good cook she was, too. He suspected she was taking on some of the domestic duties around the house because she felt guilty — he knew she constantly felt guilty about something or other, and he wished she wouldn't — and he wondered if she was also bored, which must surely be a good sign.

He'd been very, very careful not make any advances towards her, apart from a hug or two and that single but delicious kiss on her lips on Christmas Day, and it was killing him. He'd loved her constantly and passionately for more than three years, no matter how she'd looked or where her mind had taken her, but now that her figure was filling out again and the roses had returned to her cheeks, he was in agony living in her presence, every day watching the way her body moved and smelling her scent and her hair. In his somewhat sweaty dreams she acquiesced — very happily — to his advances, and their physical union was as exciting and as satisfying as he'd always imagined it would be. But in the light of day he would never pressure, or even expect, her to sleep with him while they remained unmarried. Though she'd turned down his first proposal — admittedly made on the spur of the moment but heartfelt all the same — he understood why. She was still ill, and possibly she hadn't quite forgiven him for what had happened after Rachel Winter died. But he was prepared to make many more proposals. As many as necessary, in fact, until she said yes.

He opened the front door and was greeted by the smell of something very tasty cooking. A pie? He hoped so. He loved homemade pies, and Harrie was very good at them. Harrie herself was standing at the bench at the back of the room, sleeves rolled to her elbows, looking out the window, washing something in the basin. The table had been laid for supper; Angus was sitting on the end of it, his backside on the white tablecloth, cleaning his face with a paw.

James dropped his bag and closed the door. Harrie turned, and saw him and Angus at the same time.

'Shoo!' she said, flicking water at the cat.

Angus glanced at her, blinked slowly, then strolled across the table, hopped down onto a chair then the floor, and meandered across to James's armchair, where he made himself comfortable.

James stifled a sigh. Angus was moulting, and if he tried to unseat him, the cat would ensure — deliberately, he suspected — that he ended the manoeuvre covered in black and white fur. He removed his coat and took the other chair instead.

'How was your day?' he asked Harrie.

She looked tired. Tired, distracted and apprehensive. She pulled a chair out from the table and sat down, facing him.

Without preamble she said, 'I have to tell you something.'

By the time she'd finished, he was cursing himself for not noticing that she'd been even more distressed than usual over the past week or so, but most of all for not putting his foot down about her working in that damned tattoo shop. If he had, this couldn't have happened. He felt sick with fury at the thought of Harrie being actually physically threatened and was appalled by the events she'd described. And also, to his regret, a bit disappointed, as he'd quite liked Leo Dundas.

'Why didn't you tell me when it first started?'

'Because you would have told me I couldn't work for Leo any more.'

'What difference would that have made? I made it clear I didn't want you to work for him, and you did anyway.'

Harrie looked down at her hands.

'So what's the real reason?' he prompted.

'I don't know. I think … I think it didn't really matter when it was just Leo and me. I don't think I cared. But now he's threatened Charlotte, and it does matter. He walked straight into the orphanage and managed to find out all about her.' Harrie's hands clenched. 'What's to stop him from doing that again and just walking out with her?'

'Well, it damned well matters to me, you getting dragged into something as dangerous as this. This Jonah Leary sounds like a madman. And what's Leo Dundas doing about it? It's his fault you're involved.'

'It is not Leo's fault. And he's doing as much as he can to get rid of him. It was Leo who said I had to tell you.'

Surprised, James looked at her. 'Was it?'

'He said you might be able to help.'

Though his heart was beating wildly, James took a few moments to brush a clump of fur off his trousers. He had her now, if he wanted her. And he most certainly did. But would she hate him if he did it this way? He wanted her to give him her love freely, not to agree to marry him under duress. But what if she never did agree, and he missed out? Wouldn't this way be better than not at all?

He breathed in deeply through his mouth then exhaled through his nose in an inadequate attempt to calm his nerves. 'I *can* help, Harrie. If you consent to marry me, I can adopt Charlotte. I'll be her father. We'll bring her here and she'll be safe.'

Harrie's face lit up and just for a second all the long, long months of pain and fear and confusion fell away. Then she burst into tears. James hoped they were tears of happiness, but soon saw that they weren't.

'What's the matter?'

'Her real father,' Harrie sobbed, wiping tears off her cheeks with the heel of her palm. 'Lucas Carew, I mean, on her birth certificate. How will we prove he's dead?'

James moved to stand behind her, and laid a gentle hand on her shoulder, not daring to do more. 'I'll think of something. Don't worry.'

They stayed like that for a while.

Eventually, Harrie said, 'Yes. I will marry you,' and lowered her head so her cheek rested on his hand.

It was a start, James thought. It was enough.

After Harrie had gone to bed, James sat down at the writing desk in his room and wrote a long letter to his late wife's sister, Beatrice Penfold, who lived in London. He told Beatrice that he was marrying again, that his intended, Harrie, was a convict, and he thought Beatrice would like her. And that Emily would have, too. He also mentioned that he and Harrie were adopting a child, but he hoped there would be plenty of children of their own in time.

He also asked an enormous favour of Beatrice. To help her accomplish what he wanted, he included in his letter a signed permission for Beatrice's husband to access James's account at the London branch of the Bank of England. He also suggested she contact his old navy friend Victor Handley, whom he knew would be more than capable of executing what could possibly be the less than savoury, perhaps even dangerous, aspects of the task.

It would all take a while, but in the end it would be worth it. He hoped.

Cursing, Matthew slipped and slid in the gravel, on his way down the hill to visit Sally Minto. The sun had set half an hour earlier and the sky was filled with chittering, squeaking bats, roiling around the fig trees near the quarries on the slopes rising above Windmill Street. He hoped he wouldn't get shat on — bat shit was terribly corrosive and he was wearing his best clothes.

Last night, for the first time ever, James had paid him a visit at his lodgings on Princes Street. Initially, Matthew had thought something awful — something else awful — had happened to Harrie, but James, being the decent sort he was, had come to tell him in person that she had finally accepted his proposal of marriage.

Which, actually, had been pretty bad news, as far as Matthew was concerned, because it meant there was no hope left for him. But they were meant to be together, Harrie and James, and there wasn't a lot else to be said about it.

So now he was on his way to ask Sally for her hand. He'd prevaricated and prevaricated, but there was no reason now for them not to marry — except for that tiny but vastly irritating voice in his head that kept asking him whether Sally really was the right girl for him. He conceded that perhaps she wasn't, not quite, but he was lonely and he wanted a wife, and he most certainly needed someone in his bed. She was physically attractive, reasonably bright, a good cook, and he was fond of her, even if she hadn't let him sleep with her despite his increasingly persistent advances. He was permanently employed at the Office of the Colonial Architect, had money in the bank now and could afford to buy his own house if he wanted to, and wasn't entirely unattractive (and he had a lion tattoo on his arm), and was therefore a bit of a catch, even if he did say so himself. They would both gain from the marriage.

Arriving at the Lavertys' bakery at the northern end of Kent Street, below the looming hill on which perched Fort Phillip, Matthew went around to the back of the building. Clamping his handkerchief over his mouth and nose against the Godawful stink of the cesspit in the yard, he knocked on the door. The Laverty family, and Sally, lived in the two-storey house attached to the rear of the bakery, itself a one-storey building organised around a massive, domed oven that baked dozens and dozens of loaves at any one time. The heat during the summer was appalling, and it leached into the house despite the double brick wall separating dwelling from bakehouse. Matthew knew he'd be sweating within minutes of entering.

Mrs Laverty came to the door. 'Oh. Good evening, Mr Cutler.'

'Good evening, Mrs Laverty. Warm, isn't it?'

'Very.'

Matthew smiled nervously. Lately, he'd detected a faint air of disapproval emanating from Mrs Laverty, though he wasn't convinced it was directed specifically at him. Or perhaps it was — maybe she'd guessed he would eventually propose to Sally, and didn't want to lose her. She was assigned to them, after all. God, that was something he hadn't thought of. What if his application to marry Sally was turned down by the governor?

'Is Sally at home?'

'Yes. Come in. I'll fetch her.'

Matthew waited in the narrow hallway at the bottom of the stairs, hat in hand. Through a doorway into the parlour he could see Mr Laverty sprawled in an armchair in his shirtsleeves, his slippered feet up on a footstool, asleep. As you would be when you got up regularly at four in the morning to start work, Matthew thought. Three of the Laverty children lay on the floor, playing some sort of game, while the two older girls were clearing the supper table.

Sally appeared at the top of stairs. 'Matthew. I wasn't expecting you.'

'No. I thought I'd just drop by. I'd, well, I'd like to ask you something.'

Mrs Laverty eased past Sally, descended the stairs and went into the parlour.

'Where can we talk?' Matthew asked. He thought, certainly not in Sally's room — Mrs Laverty wouldn't be happy with that. The parlour was too crowded, and the yard smelt like a privy. Hardly romantic.

'Here,' Sally said. She came down and sat on the bottom riser. 'This will do, won't it?'

Not really. 'Would you like to go for a walk?'

In the parlour the younger children shrieked; their mother told them off.

'It's too hot for walking,' Sally said.

It's bloody hot in here, too, Matthew thought, as sweat trickled down his sides beneath his best linen shirt. He sat beside Sally. This close he could see tiny beads of perspiration on her forehead and upper lip, and smell the sweat that had soaked into her clothing.

'Busy day?' he asked.

'Quite. We ran out of eccles cakes before dinner.'

'Did you?'

'Mmm.'

Matthew's palms suddenly got even sweatier. 'Sally?'

She turned her head towards him.

'We've been walking out for a while, haven't we?'

'A year,' Sally agreed.

'I'd like …' Matthew stopped and cleared his throat. 'Sally, I'd be honoured if you'd become my wife.'

Deathly silence, both from the parlour and from Sally.

Matthew grabbed her hand, opened the back door and led her outside.

Sally pinched her nose shut. 'It really stinks out here.'

Refusing to give up, he towed her out onto Kent Street, where the air was a little fresher, and turned her to face him. She was still holding her nose; he pulled her hand away. 'Will you, Sally? Marry me?'

She wouldn't meet his gaze. 'Oh, I can't, Matthew.'

Shocked, Matthew stared at her. 'Why not?'

'Because, well, you're a swell and I just roll out dough. And I'm a convict.'

'I'm not a swell!'

'You are. You'd soon get tired of me.'

'I would not!'

'You would,' Sally insisted. 'I'm sorry, Matthew, I can't. I can't marry you, and I can't see you any more.' And she spun around, her skirts whirling, and ran off.

'Sally! Wait, stop!'

But she didn't. Matthew stared after her, his heart thumping with disappointment and humiliation, feeling an absolute fool and wondering how it had gone so wrong so quickly. How utterly, in fact, he'd misjudged her feelings for him. He waited in case she came back, and the longer he stood on the street the more stupid he felt, and the less inclined he also felt to knock on her door again. After ten minutes he walked away, heading for home, confused and with his confidence severely bruised, but more or less resigned to his fiancéeless state.

At the sound of boots crunching on gravel, his heart leapt and he turned — and saw not Sally but Mrs Laverty, trotting after him through the gloom, the untied ribbons of her bonnet flapping.

'Mr Cutler, wait, if you please.'

Matthew wondered what she could want.

'I couldn't let you go without telling you,' Mrs Laverty said, puffing from exertion. 'She's a minx, that girl, and if you want my opinion, you've just had a very lucky escape.'

'I beg your pardon?'

Mrs Laverty fanned her pink face with her hand. 'I couldn't help overhearing what you said to her. No, I'll speak the truth, I was eavesdropping. I don't know if you're aware, but Sally's with child. Now, tell me if this is none —'

'What?'

Mrs Laverty gave a knowing nod. 'Well, that's that question answered, isn't it? Yes, she's been stepping out with another. The lad who delivers the flour, to be precise. I'm assuming the babe is his?'

'It certainly isn't mine!' Matthew knew damned well it wasn't. But why some common, ignorant delivery boy, and not him?

'If she'd said yes to you tonight, I'd have throttled her,' Mrs Laverty said. 'I just wanted you to know, in case you were feeling let down. You're a nice gentleman, Mr Cutler, and you deserve someone better. Someone from your own class.'

Matthew gathered together the torn remnants of his pride. 'Thank you for informing me, Mrs Laverty. I appreciate your concern.'

She patted his arm. 'Go and have a nice life. Good night.'

As Matthew traipsed miserably up the Windmill Street hill feeling cuckolded and sorry for himself, he realised that, if you left out the business of her shagging the flour boy, the reason Sally had turned him down echoed his own doubts about marrying her, but from the opposite perspective. Perhaps Mrs Laverty was right — perhaps you shouldn't marry outside your own class.

James and Harrie, though, were very shortly about to do exactly that. It wasn't quite the same, Matthew knew, because Harrie was different. Yes, she was a convict, and from the working classes, but James always said she should never have been condemned for stealing to support her family. Matthew agreed. Harrie wasn't like Sally — she was virtuous and gentle and the most caring of souls.

If Harrie were my wife, Matthew thought, I'd treat her like a piece of silk.

But she wasn't.

# Chapter Fifteen

James had hand-delivered his and Harrie's marriage application the day after she'd accepted his proposal, together with a discreet payment to the clerk to hurry the matter along. As Harrie was a convict, the new governor, Richard Bourke, had to approve the marriage, but James didn't foresee any problems and there were none. He also raced along to Sarah and Adam's and picked out a red-gold bethrothal ring set with an orange citrine and two small diamonds for Harrie. He would have preferred all diamonds but didn't think he could afford them, given his future plans. Sarah and Adam were delighted when he told them his news.

As soon as approval was received, in a very speedy matter of days, the banns were published for the first time at St James's Church on the eighth of January. After they'd been published twice more on consecutive Sundays, James and Harrie could be married.

On that same Sunday, they travelled out to Parramatta to the Female Orphan School. Mrs Duff greeted Harrie with her usual courtesy, though she was quite disconcerted when Harrie introduced James as her fiancé.

'I'm very surprised that you didn't mention your betrothal during your last visit, Miss Clarke,' the matron said across her desk, looking at Harrie over the rim of her spectacles. 'You simply stated that you were not married.'

'I wasn't betrothed then,' Harrie said, twisting her lovely new ring nervously. 'It's a recent development. We're to be married in a few weeks. Aren't we, James?'

'Yes, we are,' James said, amused by the vaguely scandalised expression on Mrs Duff's face. Was she shocked because he was choosing to marry a convict? He supposed he might have been once, too.

Harrie said, 'And that means we can adopt Charlotte, doesn't it? As Dr and Mrs Downey.'

'I must advise you that the committee would take a very dim view of a marriage of convenience,' the matron said, 'just so you can adopt this child.'

James crossed his legs. 'And I must advise you, Mrs Duff, that I take a very dim view of remarks of that nature. Miss Clarke and I have known each other for several years and I hold her in the very highest regard. I can assure you that our impending nuptials are genuine.'

Mrs Duff peered at him. 'And you're a doctor of ... what?'

Cheeky old bat, James thought, then instantly regretted his lack of goodwill — she no doubt had a very demanding job overseeing the welfare of the orphanage's children, and he certainly didn't blame her caution. She could hardly hand over babies to just anyone who walked through the door.

'I was a surgeon in the Royal Navy for some years, but I now practise medicine privately in Sydney. I operate a surgery with my business partner, Dr Lawrence Chandler. You may be aware of his charitable works?'

A flush crept up Mrs Duff's neck. 'Oh. Er, yes, I have heard of Dr Chandler. Fallen women, I believe? Very commendable.'

'Yes, that's him. And as charity begins at home, it is my wish to adopt Charlotte Winter. I understand that Harrie has explained how familiar she is with Charlotte? She knew her mother very well, you know, and the woman who fostered her.'

'Yes, she did mention that,' Mrs Duff said.

'As I've said,' James went on, 'I'm a professional man, my income is very satisfactory, I own a house, and I believe Harrie and I can give Charlotte everything she needs. And, of course, at the same time save the state some expense by providing a home for her.'

'Yes, I'm sure.' Mrs Duff shuffled some papers around on her desk. 'There is, unfortunately, the matter of Charlotte's natural father. We can't release her without his consent, or evidence of his demise if he has indeed passed on.'

'I think you'll find that isn't a problem.' James stood, said, 'One moment please,' and left the matron's office.

Harrie smiled at Mrs Duff then looked down at her hands until James returned a minute later, with Matthew in tow.

'Mrs Duff, allow me to introduce Lucas Carew, Charlotte's father.'

'Afternoon, ma'am,' Matthew said, coming to a shuffling halt just inside the door and removing his cabbage-tree hat.

His beige duck trousers didn't quite meet the tops of his battered boots, revealing several inches of pale shin — more each time he scratched his backside — and his dark blue fustian jacket had seen far, far better days. Beneath the coat he wore a collarless cotton shirt, worn thin from multiple launderings. His hair was unbrushed and he'd let his beard grow for two days. He looked a yokel, and James reflected anew on the truth of the aphorism, *Clothes maketh the man*.

'Oh,' Mrs Duff said. 'You found him?'

'He left the sea last year, apparently,' James said. 'Didn't you?'

Matthew nodded, and said in an accent distinctly unlike his own, 'I got a wife and kiddies on shore. Well, common-law, like. It were too hard not seeing them, so I threw it in.'

'You were a sailor?' the matron asked.

'Not in the Andrew, like. I just signed on and off, mostly convict ships.'

'And is that how you, er, met Rachel Winter?'

Matthew lowered his head and mumbled, 'Aye, it were. On the *Isla*.'

Mrs Duff gave a satisfied little nod. 'Can you prove you were a crewman on the *Isla* at the time that Rachel Winter was transported?'

'You'd have to ask Josiah Holland,' Matthew said. 'He were captain. I'm a tar, all right, but.' He shrugged out of his jacket, undid the top three buttons of his shirt — to Mrs Duff's alarm — and bared his upper right arm, revealing the lion and peony tattoo.

Astonished, James stared. What hidden depths Matthew had!

Mrs Duff seemed not quite able to look, focusing intently on the wall several feet from Matthew's arm. 'Yes, thank you, Mr Carew, that's enough. Do you have some means of identification?'

Matthew put his jacket back on, dug in a pocket and handed her some papers, a forgery obtained via Leo's contacts and paid for by James, after considerable soul-searching. It was the sort of shady endeavour in which he'd never imagined himself becoming involved, but he'd decided he was willing to do it if it secured Charlotte's adoption and made Harrie happy.

Mrs Duff glanced at the papers, and gave them back. 'And you're not in a position to take the child into your own family?'

'I didn't even know I had another kiddie, till the doctor here come along and told me.'

'That doesn't answer my question, Mr Carew.'

''Course I'm not,' Matthew said. 'The wife'd have me guts for garters. Anyway, we can hardly afford the ones we got.' He shrugged. 'Sorry.'

Mrs Duff pushed her spectacles up her nose. 'So you're prepared to relinquish all your paternal rights to your daughter?'

'Where's the blonde girl? Her mother?' Matthew asked, which James thought was an inspired touch.

'Unfortunately, she died when Charlotte was born,' Mrs Duff said.

'Oh? Shame. Well, I do relinquish me rights then. She'll have a better life with the doctor and his good wife than she ever would with me.'

'And has Dr Downey offered you compensation for making such a sacrifice, Mr Carew?'

'No, missus, he hasn't.'

Mrs Duff fixed Matthew with a long, hard look; Matthew's return gaze never wavered. At last she stood, opened a drawer, withdrew a sheet of paper and asked him to sign it.

'Thank you, Mr Carew. Your business here is now concluded.'

Matthew nodded, jammed his cabbage-tree hat back on his head and left the office. James sat down again in the chair next to Harrie, whose hands, he noted, were shaking.

'I take it this means we may begin the adoption process?' he asked.

'The matter will have to go before the committee, of course,' the matron said. 'But I see no impediments. All we really need now is to see your marriage certificate.'

James breathed a silent sigh of relief. Harrie beamed at him, her face transformed.

'There is one other matter,' he said. 'It has been brought to our attention that approximately two and a half weeks ago, someone came here and managed to obtain information relating to Charlotte.'

Mrs Duff frowned. 'Who?' Then, 'You were here two and a half weeks ago, weren't you, Miss Clarke?'

'Not me,' Harrie said. 'It was a man. We're obviously worried now she could be in danger.'

'Danger? What are you talking about? No one enters this institution without the knowledge of either myself or Reverend Duff.'

'But someone did, Mrs Duff,' James said. 'Evidently, a stranger wandered in here and ascertained from your staff that my fiancée was visiting one of your charges, a baby girl by the name of

Charlotte Winter, and you're saying you don't know anything about it. That wouldn't look very good on page two of the *Gazette* or the *Herald*, would it?'

Mrs Duff said nothing, but her lips, already rather thin, had compressed into a flat, colourless line.

'How might that have happened?' James went on.

Reaching behind her, Mrs Duff yanked on the bell-pull. A girl of fourteen or so appeared in the doorway. 'Daisy, you were on reception duty the week before Christmas, weren't you?'

'Yes, Matron.'

'Do you recall a man here then, asking about Charlotte Winter?'

'No.' Daisy's face flushed scarlet.

With practised ease, Mrs Duff let the silence draw out. 'Are you sure?'

More silence. Daisy's eyes glittered with unshed tears.

'Daisy!'

'He gave me five shillings!' she burst out.

'You accepted a bribe? You wicked, wicked girl, Daisy Miller!'

'I'm sorry, Matron, I'm sorry!' Daisy wailed. 'I've never had that much money, ever!'

'It's all right,' James said.

'No, it is not,' Mrs Duff countered, rising swiftly to her feet.

Harrie asked, 'What did he look like?'

Daisy dabbed at her eyes with the hem of her apron, earning a slap on the arm from Mrs Duff. 'Not quite as tall as the gentleman,' she said, nodding at James. 'Dark hair, sharpish nose, mean face. I didn't like him.'

'That sounds like Leary,' Harrie said.

James asked, 'What did he want to know?'

'He wanted to know who the lady'd been to see,' Daisy said, indicating Harrie. 'I wasn't going to tell him, really I wasn't, but then he showed me the money and said I could have it. But when I went to take it he said I had to tell him how old Charlotte was and what she looked like and where she slept.' She choked back a sob. 'So I did. I'm so sorry!'

'Daisy Miller!' Mrs Duff had gone almost purple in the face. 'No dinners for you for the next two weeks, and an hour of prayer three times a day for a month! Where are the five shillings now?'

God, James thought, that was a bit harsh. And so was the prohibition on dinners.

'In my drawer.'

'Go and fetch them.'

Daisy trotted off; James could hear her crying all the way up the stairs.

'Do you see now why we're concerned for Charlotte's safety?' he asked.

'Quite. Rest assured that no one will be permitted into the orphanage without good reason, and certainly not near Charlotte. I'll endeavour to have your application put before the committee as quickly as possible. If it is approved before you and Miss Clarke are married, then so be it. I feel that, given the unusual circumstances, such haste is warranted. You, of course, will then be responsible for the child's welfare.'

'Of course.' It was obvious to James that Mrs Duff was quite keen to see the back of Charlotte, now that 'Lucas Carew' had renounced all claim to her and there was some question over her safety. Who in her position would want a potential kidnapper running amok through wards of helpless children?

'Who is this man Leary?' Mrs Duff asked.

James said, 'With all due respect, Mrs Duff, that's our business.'

'Just please don't let him in here,' Harrie begged.

'Well, of course not,' Mrs Duff said, and wondered whether she should speak to the senior constable at Parramatta.

\* \* \*

Friday was visiting Lucian Meriwether. She'd had the horrors that morning and had been out of sorts, and had whacked him rather too energetically, so now he was sitting gingerly, favouring his left buttock, his right liberally smeared with a soothing salve. She'd apologised and offered him a discount, but Mr Meriwether had waved it off. He understood she was a novice, he said, and these things happened. And why had she been in a foul humour?

'Had a headache,' Friday muttered, pouring the tea.

'Ah. Too much libation last evening?'

'Could've been.'

'Perhaps you should consider modifying your drinking habits.'

Oh, for God's sake, not you as well, Friday thought. 'I think I might've had a bad brew.'

'Anything else bothering you?'

'Oh, I don't know. Just everything.'

'Oh dear, the dreaded everything,' Lucian said, selecting a homemade Naples biscuit. 'I find, when I have an attack of the everythings, the best thing to do is to deal with those matters over which I have control. The rest, I leave to fate. The trick is to know which matter goes into which category.'

Friday suspected Mr Meriwether had just given her some very useful, if slightly cryptic, advice, but right now she couldn't be bothered unravelling it. 'Someone I know, someone really important to me, has gone away, and I don't know if she's ever coming back. She probably isn't.'

'Ah.'

Friday didn't look at him, but she knew a loaded 'Ah' when she heard one. Had he realised? She'd only said it because he was a man of the world and she had an idea he wouldn't give a rat's arse whether she preferred men or women. And it made no difference to their professional relationship. Anyway, she was starting to like him. He was easy to talk to.

'Have you been drowning your sorrows?' Lucian asked. 'Is that how you arrived in the police magistrate's court?'

'Sort of. Er, this is a rude question, but how much did you have to pay old Bloodworth to get me off?'

Lucian brushed crumbs off his jacket. 'Not as much as you might think. He is, as they say, "in my pocket". Can you keep a secret?'

''Course I can.' Amused, Friday realised that Mr Meriwether was an old gossip.

'I was visiting Bella Shand's establishment one day when I entered the wrong chamber, and who should I accidentally interrupt, in flagrante delicto with one of Mrs Shand's mollies, but Clement Bloodworth.'

Trust bloody Bella to be offering male prostitutes, Friday thought.

'He saw me, and of course I saw him,' Lucian went on. 'Naturally, Clement would prefer that his predilection for pretty boys remain out of the public domain, so since then he's been in my debt. Try a Naples biscuit, my dear. They're very good.'

'Have you been blackmailing him?' Friday took a biscuit.

'No, although I could have, I suppose. Everyone's extorting money or favours from someone in this grubby little town.'

Unnerved, Friday gave him a sharp look. He couldn't be making a sly reference to her, surely? 'Even rich people?'

'Especially rich people, my dear.'

'I wonder if Bella's blackmailing him?'

'I've no doubt she'd like to. A very unpleasant woman, Mrs Shand. Her girls are rather attractive, however.'

'But you don't know if she is?'

Lucian placed a rout cake on his plate and inspected it. 'Mrs Wright puts currants in these. I prefer them plain, but there's no changing the way she does things.' He bit into the cake and said through his mouthful, 'Not to my knowledge, she isn't. But she very easily could, quite apart from her knowledge of his sexual preferences. As you're well aware, he's the assistant police magistrate — the last man who should be visiting a brothel.'

'If she did, he could just have her arrested for running a bawdyhouse, couldn't he?'

'Yes. So she won't blackmail him, and he won't arrest her.'

'Oh.'

'Also, Clement has an insurance policy, something else he has over Mrs Shand.'

Friday forced herself to stay calm, though her pulse was suddenly racing. 'Really? What's that?'

Lucian shifted uncomfortably in his chair and carefully unstuck his trousers from his backside. 'Don't quote me, and I do mean that, but an acquaintance of mine has it on very good authority that Bella Shand was, and probably still is, masterminding the trafficking of Maori artefacts. Preserved heads? Do you recall? It was in the newspapers. It's illegal now.'

'I remember seeing something,' Friday said, trying to sound only vaguely interested. She poured herself another cup of tea, hoping like hell that Mr Meriwether wouldn't notice her trembling hands. 'What sort of authority are we talking about? Would you like more tea?'

'Thank you, my dear. His own, actually.'

'A friend of Bella's? Or of Mr Bloodworth's?'

'A business associate's of Mrs Shand's. Nothing more, I'd say. His name's Clayton. Dr Neville Clayton.'

'Never heard of him.'

'Possibly you wouldn't have. Calls himself an ethnologist, a scholar of the natural history of man. Interesting fellow. Educated at Oxford but lives in Sydney for now. I believe he's out here on a collecting spree.'

'Collecting what?'

'Oh, you know. Primitive weapons and art, people's heads.'

'But you don't know him well?'

'Not really. I've met him at soirees once or twice.'

'But why would he tell you that about Bella, if he hardly knows you?'

'He didn't. He did some business with Clement, and Clement told me.'

Christ, was she ever going to get to the bottom of this? 'What business?'

'You seem very interested in the matter,' Lucian remarked. 'May I ask why?'

Friday shrugged and broke a Naples biscuit in half. 'No real reason, I suppose. It's interesting, all this gossip about stolen heads.' She manufactured a shudder. 'It's eerie. Like a ghost story. I love a good ghost story.'

'Yes, well, mind you keep it under your hat,' Lucian said. 'I shouldn't really be telling you all this. But I will. Clayton commissioned Mrs Shand to obtain some heads for him last year. When they arrived from New Zealand they had to come through Customs and Excise, like everything else does. This was just after Governor Darling's declaration in April, banning their importation. So, to get them past Customs, he wrote to Clement citing essential anthropological research and what have you, and requesting his help.'

'And offering a hefty bribe?'

'Naturally. Clement saw to everything and the shipment of heads entered the colony without official detection. Unfortunately, Clayton was somewhat indiscreet in his correspondence and he actually named Bella Shand, together with another fellow whose name I've forgotten.'

Friday bet it was Jared Gellar.

'Clement rather prudently kept the letter,' Lucian added, 'and Mrs Shand knows he has it. Well, that's what he told me.'

Friday thought Clement Bloodworth sounded like as much of a chatterbox as Mr Meriwether. 'I wonder where they are?' she said. 'The heads, I mean.' She envisaged a bag full of them, including possibly that of Aria's uncle, Whiro, stuffed under Neville Clayton's bed.

'According to Clement, Clayton sent them on to England almost immediately. Or some of them, at least. I don't know. One would probably have to ask Dr Clayton that himself, and given that trade in such artefacts is now forbidden, I wouldn't expect a straight answer from him, would you?'

Shite. But at least there was real evidence now to prove that Bella had been involved in trafficking heads, and that would definitely make Aria happy.

All Friday had to do was find a way to tell her.

To Nora Barrett's great delight, Harrie asked her to make her wedding dress. Nora was busy with her own work, and was in fact behind with orders now that she didn't have Harrie to assist (though she hoped that would change soon), but decided her customers could wait. She had waited long enough for James and Harrie to stop playing absurd games and finally accept that they belonged together, and she wasn't about to pass up the opportunity to contribute to Harrie's wedding day. Harrie, of course, had offered to pay, but Nora had told her not to be so silly, the dress was a gift.

The fabric was very fine cream muslin lined with lawn, with a modest neckline, a Vandyke collar of silk ending in a point at the fitted waist, and puffed sleeves narrowing at the elbow. The hem was decorated with a deep border of lace. Harrie, and Nora, would have preferred embroidery, but that would have taken months to complete, and they only had three weeks. As it was, Nora would be up late every night to finish the dress in time. There were also dresses to be made for Hannah and Abigail, whom Harrie had chosen as flower girls, which had made Nora cry.

'You are putting on weight, aren't you?' she said through a mouthful of pins during Harrie's second fitting. 'A good thing, too. You were far too thin there for a while.'

Her arms out so she wouldn't stab herself in the armpits, Harrie said, 'I think I'm nearly back to my normal shape.'

'Well, not quite. I can still see your backbone. Is it happy weight?'

'Mostly.'

Kneeling, Nora said, 'Hold still. What do you mean "mostly"? What is there not to be happy about?'

'Oh, I don't know.' Plenty, Harrie thought. I've still done what I've done. There's no changing that.

'Give yourself time, love. You've been extremely poorly. But you're marrying a very decent man, you know. Aren't you happy about that?'

Harrie looked down at Nora under her arm, popping a row of pins out of the waist seam, and smiled, looking for a moment like her old self. 'Yes, I am. I'm very happy about that. I wondered for a few days whether I'd done the right thing, but I think I have.'

'Of course you have, you silly girl. Stand straight.'

'What if he can tell, though?' Harrie felt her face burning.

'Tell what?'

'That I'm not … that I've already … you know.'

'That you're not a virgin? Oh, don't worry about that. Once isn't going to make much difference, not to a man on his wedding night.'

'And what if I can't have my own babies?'

Nora sat back on her heels. 'Now stop that. You don't know that.'

'But after —'

'Stop it! Anyway, you'll have Charlotte in a week or so. And you can thank James for that, as well. There's not many men who'd take on someone else's child, you know.'

'Charlotte's Rachel's, not mine,' Harrie said after a moment. 'I didn't have anything to do with Charlotte's father.' Sometimes she got quite muddled about that; everything got jumbled in her head and from time to time she caught herself thinking that Charlotte really was her child. But she wasn't.

'Yes, I know, that's what I said,' Nora said, repinning the waist seam. 'James is being extremely generous.'

Yet again, Harrie wondered what Rachel felt about her becoming Charlotte's mother. She'd asked her — begged her — to say something about it, but since James's proposal there'd been nothing from Rachel but an ominous silence.

A fat, shiny blue fly landed on Harrie's face and crawled across her cheek. She flicked it away. But it kept coming back.

Harrie was worried that the clothes Pearl had sent to the orphanage with Charlotte might have disappeared, so, in anticipation of their application to adopt her being successful, one morning James gave her a purse full of money to buy whatever she might need. When he'd arrived home from work that night, Harrie had shown him little gowns and capes, soft bonnets and tiny shoes, and wool and fabric for knitting and sewing projects. She'd also bought yards and yards of diaper for napkins, crossly explaining that Charlotte had been close to pot-trained in the Factory, but had gone notably backwards in that department. The next day the crib had arrived, plus an assortment of child-sized bed linen, and a high chair.

On Tuesday the seventeenth of January, James received a letter from Mrs Duff advising him that their request to adopt Charlotte Winter had been approved. She was therefore available to collect at any time forthwith.

Taking a day off work and throwing the surgery into chaos, but knowing that his signature would be required on the adoption papers, he and Harrie hired a carriage and drove out to Parramatta the following day to pick up their daughter. Harrie exhausted herself weeping all the way out, mostly from relief that Charlotte hadn't been kidnapped by Jonah Leary, and she and Charlotte, now just six and a half weeks short of her second birthday, dozed much of the way home.

Another passenger shared the carriage on the return trip — fourteen-year-old Daisy Miller from the orphanage. James had felt sorry for her, and when Mrs Duff had confirmed that the girl had been trained to cook, launder and sew, and was accustomed to handling infants and children, he'd decided she would make an ideal domestic servant and companion for Harrie. Harrie, however, had been horrified by the idea when James had mentioned it as they'd set out. What if the girl took another bribe from Leary? Or even worse — simply handed Charlotte over to him? James countered by pointing out that Daisy was unlikely to accept a bribe if she was paid well, which she would be, and that she knew what Leary looked like, which could only be an advantage. He also suggested that Harrie shouldn't be so hard on her — she of all people should know that people did irrational things when they were unhappy — to which Harrie grudgingly agreed.

When they arrived home, James's cottage suddenly seemed too small. Harrie had not yet moved into his bedchamber, and wouldn't until their wedding night, and the crib in Harrie's outside room meant there was barely space on the floor in there for a mattress for Daisy. Also, Charlotte, tired and hungry, was bawling her head off, her cries seeming to pierce the very core of James's brain; he could see he would have to look into purchasing a larger house sooner rather than later.

Apart from the crying, however, she was very sweet. When she'd first been born he'd thought she'd looked like a little monkey, though of course he hadn't dared say so, but she was a lovely-looking child now. She was very much her mother's daughter with her silver-blonde hair and elfin face, though she did have her father's very dark brown eyes. He hoped, prayed in fact, that she didn't also have his character.

The next morning, before work, Friday paid Harrie a visit. While she bounced Charlotte on her knee, making her giggle hysterically, Harrie poured the tea.

'What are these red spotty things?' Friday asked, indicating Charlotte's neck.

'James thinks they might be flea bites.'

'From the orphanage?' Friday was disgusted. 'Christ, you'd think they'd wash the bedding now and again, wouldn't you? Did they?' she asked Daisy.

'The mattresses got aired every six months, but never washed. There were fleas everywhere. And ringworm. I was always scratching.'

'Are those flea bites on your face?' Friday asked.

'Pimples.'

'You want to get witch hazel onto those. That'll dry them out.'

'James has recommended a lotion,' Harrie said.

James, James, bloody James, Friday thought uncharitably. She didn't know why. Yes, she did. She was jealous. Sarah had Adam and now Harrie had James. Why couldn't she have Aria? It wasn't fair. 'Has Sarah been around yet?'

'She sent a note to say she'd visit tonight.'

Friday broke off a piece of cake and fed it to Charlotte. 'I know who'll be really happy you've got her back: Rachel. Does she know?' She glanced at Harrie, looking for a reaction.

Harrie wouldn't meet her gaze. 'I haven't seen her lately.'

Friday supposed that was a good sign. She felt mean, now. It hadn't been a very nice thing to say. What a bitch she was. She'd only said it because she wanted someone else to feel as miserable as she did herself. She knew Harrie would be feeling guilty about finally getting Charlotte. Oh, why was she being so bloody horrible?

'I'm sorry, Harrie. I shouldn't have said that.'

Ashamed, and ducking her head so she wouldn't have to look at Harrie, she gave Charlotte another piece of cake and put her on the floor. Charlotte immediately dropped the cake, let out a terrified wail and flung out her arms to be picked up again.

Harrie scooted around the table and snatched her off the floor. 'I forgot to say, she hates to be put down. You can't leave her alone.'

'God, that's going to wear thin, isn't it?'

'Well, how would you feel if you'd been left to cry for hours and hours in a puddle of your own wee? It'll take her a while to understand she isn't going to be abandoned again.'

Friday could see the logic in that. Harrie sat down with Charlotte on her lap, enfolded her in a hug and rocked her. The child's huge dark eyes gazed at Friday as though she'd done something unforgivably cruel to her, which made her feel like an absolute shit. She made a funny face and waggled her fingers. Charlotte smiled tentatively, then giggled, then held out her arms. Friday took her, relieved beyond measure. 'Who's Aunty Friday's good little girl, eh? Is it you?' she said as she cuddled her.

Charlotte nodded and stuck her thumb in her mouth.

Over the top of the child's head, Friday said, 'Fucking hell, Harrie, you might be taking on a lot more than you'd bargained for.'

'Language, please,' Harrie said, so primly that Friday gave one of her loud hoots of laughter.

'It's a bit late for that, isn't it, given where she's grown up so far?'

'No, it isn't. And I do know what I'm taking on, thank you.' Harrie paused. 'I have been thinking, though. I'm not sure if I should, well ...' She tailed off.

'Should what? Spit it out.'

'Have one myself. If I can, that is.' Harrie glanced uncomfortably at Daisy. 'After, you know, what happened.'

'A baby? Now?'

'Mmm. At least, not while Charlotte's so young. So I was wondering if you could —'

'Tell you how not to?' Friday interrupted.

Harrie said, 'Er, Daisy, would you go outside, please?'

'Why should she?' Friday looked Daisy up and down. 'How old are you?'

'Fourteen.'

'Have your courses started?'

Daisy nodded.

'Do you know how to keep yourself out of trouble?'

'No. But I don't need to know, honestly I don't.' Daisy looked terrified, as though she were about to get into awful trouble.

'Well, you will one day,' Friday said. 'She might as well stay, Harrie. You could be doing her a huge favour.'

Daisy's face glowed bright pink — almost as red as Harrie's.

'All right, but don't —'

''Course not.' Friday had no intention of mentioning Harrie's past business. Or of saying anything that would frighten Daisy. She nearly smiled, and had to stop herself in case Harrie took it the wrong way; here she was again, handing out advice, the same as she had before Sarah had married Adam. For women who were really quite smart in lots of other ways, her dear friends were as thick as two short planks when it came to keeping themselves out of that sort of trouble. Of course, she had been, too, when she was young.

She passed Charlotte back to Harrie and, for the next half-hour, talked about the different methods a woman could use to avoid catching for a baby. She personally favoured the use of a sea sponge soaked in lemon juice with a few drops of quinine, but there were other ways, too. Poor Daisy's eyes nearly popped out of her head, which, Friday supposed, is what happened when you spent years being raised in a place run by religious types. She also went over what you could do to end an unwanted pregnancy, more for Daisy's sake than Harrie's, as Harrie, of course, already knew.

'So get yourself along to the chemist and stock up. I'll come with you, if you like,' she said in summary.

She agreed with Harrie, and thought it would be better for her and James to wait until Charlotte was a little older before they had a baby of their own, if they could avoid it. Not that it was any of her business either way. And as for Harrie's fear that she wouldn't be able to get pregnant, Friday suspected that was all it was — fear.

'I can manage, but thanks for the offer.' Harrie turned her cup around in its saucer. 'It's sad, isn't it?'

Friday waited patiently.

'I'm marrying a nice man —'

'Nice!' Friday interrupted. 'He's more than nice.'

'A lovely man, then. And I've got a lovely little house with a garden. And cake.' She gestured at the half-eaten lemon cake. 'All the things Rachel wanted. And I've got her daughter. All she got was a really short life, transportation and that devil Keegan. It doesn't seem fair, does it?'

'That's because it isn't fair,' Friday agreed. 'Lots of things aren't fair.'

'I wish she was here. Alive, I mean.'

'So do I.'

Charlotte had fallen asleep. Harrie kissed the top of her head and said, 'I feel —'

She didn't finish, but Friday knew her very well, and understood perfectly what she was feeling.

Harrie and James were married at ten o'clock on the morning of the twenty-third of January, a Monday, at St James's Church. In attendance were their daughter Charlotte Downey, wearing a dear little dress in the same fabric as her adoptive mother's wedding gown, Daisy, Friday, Sarah and Adam Green, Matthew Cutler, Dr Lawrence Chandler (who'd hired a locum to manage the surgery for the day), Leo Dundas and his companion Serafina Fortune, the Barrett family (including a contrite George), and Elizabeth Hislop. To complement her gown, Harrie wore flowers in her hair, and a rope of perfectly graduated pearls, another gift from James.

Afterwards everyone squashed into James's cottage for a wedding breakfast catered by the Siren's Arms Hotel kitchen —

Elizabeth's wedding gift. When Harrie threw her bouquet of cream roses and maidenhair fern, Serafina, Friday and Elizabeth all stepped smartly out of the way: Serafina because she had no intention of submitting herself to the whims of some man, not even Leo; Friday because she would never marry; and Elizabeth because marrying again meant her fortune would automatically become the property of her husband, and bugger that. Daisy caught the bouquet, and stood giggling and blushing.

Friday, missing Aria particularly keenly, got drunk and threw up in the front yard then passed out in the fuchsias, where Hannah Barrett found her and poked her repeatedly with a stick to see if she was dead. When she didn't stir, Hannah went inside and told everyone that Friday had died in the garden. Between them, Adam and Matthew got her on her feet and back into the house, where Nora made her drink two cups of tea and eat a wedge of chicken pie, after which she vomited again, this time in the backyard. In the end, Harrie and Sarah put her to bed in the outside room with towels and a bucket.

'Has something upset her, do you think? Is it me?' Harrie asked Sarah.

'You? Why would she be upset with you?'

'Because James and I have got married.'

'No, I don't think it's that.'

'She was upset when you and Adam were married.'

'No, she's always thought you and James should be together.' Sarah hesitated. She didn't want to cast a shadow across Harrie's day, but it was about time someone told her. 'Friday met someone a few months ago, visiting Sydney. But they couldn't stay. She's heartbroken.'

'A man?' Harrie asked. 'Or a girl?'

Sarah was really quite shocked. 'How did you know?'

'I didn't, really. Not for sure. It was that girl from New Zealand, wasn't it? The lovely-looking one?'

Sarah nodded.

'I thought so. Oh, poor Friday. That's so sad.'

'Really? I thought you'd be revolted or angry, or something,' Sarah said. 'You were so sure Friday wasn't that way inclined when we first met in Newgate. You tore a strip off me for suggesting it, remember that?'

'Yes, but that was a long time ago. I've changed since then. Lots of things have changed.'

'I suppose they have.'

'Is that why she's been getting so horribly drunk lately?' Harrie asked.

'I think so, but also because she *is* a horrible drunk. She's a souse, Harrie, and she'll drink herself to death one day.'

'I know. It's an awful worry.' Harrie gave a little smile. 'I have to say, though, it's nice to be well enough to worry about someone other than myself.'

If you say so, Sarah thought.

By three o'clock Harrie and James's guests had all gone. Jack had arrived in Elizabeth's landau to whisk away all the dirty serveware, glasses, cutlery and flatware — Elizabeth insisted that a newly married woman shouldn't have to clean up after her own wedding celebrations — and Daisy had swept the parlour floor, wiped down all the surfaces, and scrubbed the rug in the outside room where Friday had missed the bucket. Friday herself had been taken home in the landau holding her head, moaning, spitting out the window and demanding gin to forestall her horrors.

At five o'clock Daisy boiled several pots of water over the fire and prepared a bath for Charlotte, who had fallen asleep in James's arms, barely waking when Harrie took her to undress her. She had raspberry jam on the front of her beautiful little muslin dress, and a blob of chocolate cream near the hem, but, to James's private relief, Harrie merely passed the garment to Daisy and suggested she soak it in cold water, then try white vinegar on the jam and the 'hard' soap on the chocolate. He'd been harbouring a slight concern that, given the requirements of her past assignments, Harrie might have developed rigid methods of managing children and everything that came with them, but it appeared not. In the days since Charlotte had arrived she'd been fairly relaxed about when the child had her sleeps and what have you, as long as Charlotte was happy. He was aware, however, that the soiling of a best garment was always the ultimate test, and Harrie had just passed it with considerable aplomb.

Though he and his first wife, Emily, had been childless, his sister-in-law Beatrice and her husband had produced a great tribe of them, and Beatrice raised her children with a casual but loving hand. James had always thought that if he was ever lucky enough to have a family, he'd like to emulate Beatrice's style, and now it looked like he could. But, really, in what other manner would Harrie mother children? She was such a gentle, kind person herself.

The child seemed to have settled in very well, given the upheaval to which she'd been subjected and the fact that she'd recently lost Janie Braine, the woman she'd believed to be her mother, not to mention Rosie, her 'sister'. She was in reasonable health, though she had a severe rash, no doubt from wearing a wet napkin for too long, and flea bites. Nothing that couldn't be remedied fairly easily, but still, it was distressing.

At six o'clock Daisy prepared a light supper, washed the dishes, then took herself and Charlotte off to bed, leaving Harrie and James alone in the parlour. James had a small glass of brandy, though he thought he'd probably had enough to drink today already, and Harrie was sipping a cup of tea. They were both nervous, acutely conscious of what was coming next.

'It was a good day, wasn't it?' James said.

'Perfect.' Harrie smiled at him. 'Charlotte enjoyed herself.'

'But did you? It was your day.'

'Oh, James, of course I did. It was everything I'd thought it would be.'

'Does that mean you had thought about it? Before I proposed to you?'

Harrie felt her face redden. 'I never expected that we'd marry. I never assumed anything.'

'No, that isn't what I meant.' James swirled his brandy around in his glass, not meeting her gaze. 'Harrie, I'd like to know ...' He stopped, then started again. 'I need to know, would you have eventually married me anyway, if it hadn't been for Charlotte? I suppose what I'm asking you is do you love me?'

Harrie said, 'James, no matter what else has happened, it's always been you.'

She put aside her cup and saucer and went and sat in his lap.

When Harrie awoke the next morning, for a disconcerting moment she didn't know where she was. The sunlight slanting through the gap in the drapes was on the wrong side of the room, and the bed seemed strange. Then, with a jolt, she remembered — she was James's wife now. At the same time she realised what the low ache between her legs must be: the after-effects of last night.

Making love with James had been extremely nice. She couldn't compare it with her one other sexual encounter because she couldn't remember that, for which she was grateful. James had been passionate yet gentle and considerate, and his body was lovely — strong and clean and manly. When she'd seen him naked she'd been so overwhelmed with jealousy at the thought of him with Rowie Harris that she'd had to ask. He'd got quite angry then, and called Rowie a poisonous little slattern, and she'd wondered if she might have spoiled everything, but the moment passed.

They'd not slept until well after midnight. She'd dreamt, then, of the London street where she'd lived all her life, of her mother, and of Rachel. She had thrown her wedding bouquet, and Rachel, wearing a white dress draped like a shroud and her silver hair falling to her waist, had caught it. She'd laughed in delighted triumph, but then the laughter had turned to shrieks of rage and Rachel's beautiful features had disintegrated into a rotting, mouldering mask and she'd hurled the flowers back in Harrie's face and accused her of letting her die in the Factory so she could steal Charlotte. Harrie had cried that it wasn't true but no words would come out of her mouth, and Rachel had roared that she wanted Charlotte back, and Harrie had struggled to fight her way to the surface of the dream like a swimmer drowning in a sea of treacle. She'd lain half awake for a few minutes in the dark, sweating and panting, then slipped under again, grateful to find that this time Rachel hadn't followed her.

Now, she half sat up and glanced across James's sleeping form at the clock on his nightstand. A quarter to seven. James stirred and opened his eyes. Seeing her, he smiled and touched her cheek, clearly unaware that his sandy hair was sticking up all over the place.

'Good morning, Mrs Downey.'

'Hello, husband.'

'Are you well?'

'A little tender.'

James made an empathetic face. 'Er, yes. So am I. It's been quite a while.' Turning slightly pink, he added, 'I hope you, er, thought it was worth it.'

'I did. I ... it was lovely.'

Catching sight of the clock himself, he groaned and sat up. 'Damn, I'm supposed to be at the surgery at eight.'

Harrie threw off the bedclothes. 'And I need to get Charlotte ready. I'm taking her to work.'

James frowned. 'Work?'

'Yes. Well, I didn't go yesterday because we got married, so I thought I'd go today instead. And if Charlotte comes with me,

Daisy can get on with the laundry, which also didn't get done yesterday. Leo won't mind.'

James wasn't just frowning now, he was outright scowling. 'But I thought, I'd assumed, that once we were married, you'd stop.'

Harrie had never intended giving up her job, and in fact planned to take on even more work, with Nora. She couldn't stay at home, even if she wanted to. She couldn't expect James to support her siblings, and no doubt there'd be another blackmail demand soon.

'Well, I'm sorry, James, but you've assumed wrongly. I have to work. I need to.'

'Why?'

'I need the money.'

'What for?'

'To send home to Robbie and Sophie and Anna. They depend on me.'

James got out of bed and pulled on his trousers. 'I can give you money for that. How much do you need?'

'No!' Panic laced with dismay surged through Harrie as she thought of the lies she would constantly have to tell him, together with a bright anger at his assumption that he could fix everything. 'You can't just take control of me and tell me what to do.'

'But you're my wife now.'

'Yes, but I'm not … I'm not like Emily. I'm not saying she was weak or silly, but I'm just not the same class of person she was. She was a lady of leisure. I've always worked.'

'She wasn't a lady of leisure. She was always running around organising things, serving on this board and that committee. It's not so much … God.' James sighed. 'It's not the fact that you work, Harrie, it's what you do.'

'For Leo?'

'Yes. Tattooing tars in a poky little room beside the Sailors' Grave pub, to be precise. It's so, well, it's beneath you.'

Said like that, Harrie supposed it did sound ... common, though in her eyes her work was a form of art. It's just that her art was applied to living skin, rather than canvas. And it wasn't beneath her: she was common. She eyed James, waiting for him to go on, as no doubt he would.

'I know how you feel about what you do, and Friday tells me you're very good at it, but not everyone appreciates tattoos. You know as well as I do that it's a specific sort of person who gets them.'

'Like Friday?'

'Er, yes, though I was thinking more of sailors and the like. And sailors don't have a particularly good reputation, do they? And neither, by association, will you if you carry on with it.'

Harrie could see now where James's argument was going. 'And you're worried that that will reflect on you?'

'More on the practice, specifically. How can I expect my patients to heed my advice on cleanliness and sober habits if they think I condone my wife jabbing needles into dirty, smelly sailors? Anyway, it's not safe. Look at this business with Jonah Leary.'

Harrie realised with a jolt of fear that he did have a point; what if Leary turned up at Leo's while she had Charlotte there? 'Is it just the tattooing you don't approve of?' she asked.

A knock came at the bedroom door, and Daisy called timidly, 'Excuse me, sorry, it's me.'

James slipped on his shirt. 'Come in.'

Accompanied by the sound of grizzling whimpers in the background as she opened the door, Daisy said while staring fixedly at her boots, ' Excuse me, Charlotte's up. She wants Harrie.'

Harrie fetched her and brought her in. Charlotte's face was flushed and she was being very clingy. 'She feels very hot to me.'

James felt the child's forehead and cheeks. 'It's a warm morning. Plenty of fluids today, I think. I'm not sure what you mean by "just" the tattooing.'

'I do understand what you're saying, you know,' Harrie said. 'Before I started on the needles, I drew flash for Leo. Those are the tattoo designs. Would I still be able to do that? He's always paid me well for those.'

'Could you do that from home?'

'Well, I'd need to drop them off when they're finished, but, yes, I could.'

James considered for a moment, then grinned. 'I think that's a reasonable compromise, Mrs Downey, don't you?'

Relieved and pleased, Harrie smiled back. She'd raise the issue of working for Nora later — surely he couldn't object to that? 'Yes, I do. I'll tell Leo today.'

Now that the possibility of Leary snatching Charlotte had once again been raised, Harrie saw sinister shadows lurking everywhere on the way down George Street. Her nerves weren't helped by Charlotte herself, who insisted on being put down and allowed to walk — although, actually, she ran, in all directions, and quickly. Harrie had to go into the nearest draper and purchase a length of twine to tie around her middle, a trick she'd employed with Hannah Barrett, also an expert escapologist. Once Charlotte was forced to slow down, she went very slowly, examining everything she encountered — each stone, blade of grass, spider and lump of dog shit. Harrie doubted they'd reach Leo's by dinnertime.

When they finally did, at a quarter to eleven, Charlotte wanted to do a wee. Harrie had been working very hard to get her to use the pot again, so Leo had to be prevailed upon to fetch his, so as not to disrupt her training.

'What's wrong with the lass's nappy?' he grumbled. 'It's what they're for, isn't it?'

'I can tell you've never washed four dozen stinky clouts,' Harrie said.

'Why would I? How was the wedding night?'

'None of your business.'

Leo grinned and tamped tobacco into his pipe. 'It was a good do. I enjoyed myself. So did Serafina. I suppose you're here to hand in your notice?'

'I am, actually. I'm really sorry. How did you know?'

'I imagine fellows like your James aren't too keen on the missus working, never mind working in a job like this. Am I right?'

'Something like that.' Harrie peeped into the other room; Charlotte was off the pot and wandering around. She hoped it was only a wee she'd done. 'Hang on a minute.'

Yes, a small one. Harrie emptied the pot out the window, put Charlotte's nappy back on her and carried her into the tattoo room.

'It's just the tattooing he objects to. He's happy for me to carry on doing the flash. Is that all right with you?'

'Can't say I'm not disappointed, with you having such a good eye. How do you feel about it?'

'Well, if it makes him happy. He's a good man.'

'Happy,' Charlotte said, clapping her hands.

'Aye, he is that,' Leo agreed. 'And worth keeping happy, I'd say. As for the flash, the more you can draw the better. Which reminds me; now that I'm not being forced to pay that magsman George Barrett a retainer, I think it's about time you had a pay rise. Would an extra guinea per series suit you?'

'Oh! That's a lot. Are you sure?' Harrie was delighted. 'Thank you very much.'

Leo waved away her thanks. 'Friday'll be disappointed. She's got plans for something new on her leg now the phoenix is finished, and wanted you to do it. Still, can't be helped. Perhaps you could draw something new for her.'

'I'll talk to her, shall I?'

Leo nodded, and amazed Charlotte by sucking on his pipe and puffing smoke from the side of his mouth. 'I heard something the other day, about Jonah Leary. I've been keeping an eye on him.

I didn't mention it yesterday because, well, it wasn't the day for it, but a mate told a mate who told me he's gone to Van Diemen's Land.'

'Looking for his brother?'

'Must be.'

'For how long, I wonder?'

'Well, there's thousands of convicts down that way, so it could be months. Let's hope so.'

Enormously relieved to hear that Leary was no longer in Sydney, on the way home Harrie still couldn't shake off the unnerving sensation that she and Charlotte were being followed. But every time she turned to look, all she caught from the corner of her eye was the barest glimpse of long, silver-blonde hair.

# Chapter Sixteen

*February 1832, Sydney Town*

Sarah and Adam were just about to sit down to supper when someone knocked on the back door. Growling and barking, Clifford darted across the dining room, poised to pounce.

'Pretend we're not home,' Sarah said, buttering a slice of bread.

Adam got up from the table, his napkin still tucked into the open neck of his shirt.

'Only me,' Friday announced as he opened the door.

Disappointed, Clifford retreated to her basket. Friday was a frequent visitor and had long ago stopped being terrified of her.

'Have you eaten?' Sarah asked. 'We're just having supper.'

'Not hungry, thanks.' Friday pulled out a chair. 'Wouldn't mind a drink, though. What have you got?'

'Tea.'

'Anything else?'

Sarah rolled her eyes. 'Red wine and brandy. No gin.'

'Brandy'd be good. Ta.'

As Sarah went out to the parlour to fetch it, Friday asked Adam, 'How's life in the jewellery business?'

'Good. Plenty of money to be made if you're selling what people want, and we are. How's life in the prostitution business?'

Friday made a disparaging face. 'Plenty of money to be made if you're selling what people want, and I do.'

Adam laughed and speared a round of cucumber with his fork. 'Sounds like you need a change of profession.'

'You could be right.'

Sarah plonked the brandy decanter on the table and sat down. 'Don't drink it all, please. It wasn't cheap, that one. What are you talking about?'

'I think Friday's fed up with her job,' Adam remarked.

Sarah said, 'You're always fed up with your job.'

'I know.' Friday poured herself a generous drink. 'Well, most of it. Mr Meriwether's all right, I suppose. I don't mind doing that.'

Adam said, 'Is he the old goat with the whips?'

Friday frowned at Sarah. 'That was supposed to be private. It's business.'

'Sorry.' Sarah went pink. 'Anyway, you shouldn't have told me if it's private.'

'Oh, who cares?' Friday waved a dismissive hand. 'Anyway, I'm here to talk about Harrie. I'm worried.'

'So am I.' Sarah moved her plate aside.

'She seems all right to me,' Adam said.

'But you don't know her like we do. She still seems … what's the word I'm looking for?' Sarah looked at Friday.

'Haunted?'

'That's it. Or maybe even "hunted". That feels closer. She should be happy now but it's as though she can't rest, as if something's driving her to … well, I'm not sure what. And I think she might be losing weight again.'

'I wonder if Rachel's back. She said she isn't,' Friday said doubtfully.

'Oh God, don't start that bloody ghost business again.'

'Come on, Sarah, even you weren't sure. The bat?'

Adam, who'd stopped eating, looked from Sarah to Friday, and back to Sarah again. 'What bat?'

'Oh, it was something that happened when Gellar was here. Nothing important. Not now, anyway.'

Friday, who'd been slouching in her chair, sat up straighter, took a humongous gulp of her drink and rubbed the back of her neck. 'I have to say something. I said a bit of a mean thing to Harrie the other day. I sort of asked her if she thinks Rachel knows she's got Charlotte.'

'Oh, for God's sake, Friday!' Sarah said. 'You know how guilty she feels about everything. What did you do that for?'

'I don't know. It was just before the wedding and I was feeling —'

'Jealous?' Sarah shot a meaningful look at Adam, who was busy staring intently at his half-eaten supper. For a while, he'd also suffered the effects of Friday's jealousy.

'It slipped out,' Friday said. 'I didn't mean it. I said I was sorry.'

'Too late then. You'd have already put the idea in her head!'

'If it wasn't already there. You know what she's like.'

Looking hugely confused, Adam said, 'Are you talking about an actual ghost? Because you don't believe in them. I know you don't.'

'No,' Sarah said. 'But Harrie does. She's the one who thinks she can see Rachel. But she can't really. It's part of her illness.'

'I didn't believe her when she said she hadn't seen her,' Friday said. 'You know what a rubbish liar she is. I think we should talk to James. Because if she does think she's back, she could be getting really sick again.'

When Friday got back to the Siren's Arms, Elizabeth told her a letter had arrived for her; she'd put it under her bedroom door. Friday raced up the stairs and along the hall, fumbling in her reticule for her key. Could it be from Aria? If it was, she'd never drink, or swear, or say another mean thing about anyone ever again. She unlocked the door and threw it open, and there the letter lay.

Snatching it off the floor, she sat on her bed and scrabbled at the seal, but already her heart was sinking. The letter's condition was far too good for it to have come all the way from New Zealand. And then she knew what it must be.

'You scabby, fucking old bitch,' she said out loud as she unfolded the single sheet, the disappointment of it making her dizzy.

> *To Friday Wolfe, Sarah Morgan, and Harrie Clark*
> *You didn't think I'd forgotten, did you?*
> *£250. If you don't want to feel the hangman's rope around your worthless necks, be at the stable yard of the Harp and Angel on York Street, this Sunday night at six o'clock. Someone will be waiting for you.*
> *B*

The rotten, bloody cow. She *still* couldn't spell their names right, and didn't she know Sarah and Harrie were married now? She must do.

This was Bella's third demand, and each time the amount went up. They had the money — they hadn't heard from her since they'd paid Rowie Harris, so it had been accruing in the bank — but that wasn't the point. After this, they would have paid her six hundred pounds: a fortune, and not even a small one, for most folk.

Today was Monday. There'd be plenty of time during the week to ask Matthew to withdraw the money. He was a good man, Friday reflected. He never pried, and never asked what the money was for.

Bella had been smart this time choosing a public meeting place just on dusk — even smarter than she usually was. Amos Furniss had been murdered and robbed, and Rowie Harris had been thumped; they'd both met Friday in a lonely part of town late at night. This time there'd be folk around, otherwise known as witnesses. Whoever collected the money on Sunday — no doubt either Louisa or Becky — would be fairly safe from attack, which, as far as Bella was concerned, meant they wouldn't lose it.

Friday put the letter aside and fetched her gin from the dressing table, noticing with a start that the bottle was nearly empty. She'd only opened it the night before. She'd have to get a couple more. Bella's demand was bloody annoying, but, to be honest, it felt like just one more stinking turd on the great, steaming heap of shit her life was becoming. She hated her job, nobody had murdered Bella yet, Harrie still wasn't right, and most achingly painful of all was the gaping hole left in her heart by Aria's absence. Except for the gift at Christmas, she'd heard nothing from her. Either she couldn't get a letter past her mother, a possibility Friday, perversely, was praying for, or everything she'd written in the note accompanying her gift had been lies, and Friday could hardly bear to think of that.

She opened another drawer and took out the note, which she kept carefully wrapped in the linen handkerchief with the comb, feathers and the lilac ribbon, and read it for at least the hundredth time.

*My beautiful Friday,*
  *Here are my precious huia plumes. They are my right to wear as befits my status as a princess of high rank. You are my* princess.
  *Our time together was so short, but I will never forget it. I will never forget you, and I will do everything I can to come back to you. You live forever in my heart.*
  *Aria Moehanga Te Kainga-mataa*

No, Aria hadn't been lying when she'd written that. Friday suspected Aria never told lies. But to have heard nothing at all was agony. After making Leo give her Tumanawapohatu's address in New Zealand she'd written half a dozen letters of her own, and still there had been only heartbreaking silence.

Perhaps she should go and see Serafina Fortune again. Serafina had said she'd find love with someone tall, dark and strong, and that must be Aria, surely? But is that really what she'd said? Or had Friday only dreamt that?

It was getting hard to tell, these days.

Sarah and Friday stood outside James's surgery, hogging the shade under the eaves of the small porch and staring out at the other patients suffering in the stark, bright heat of the gravelled front yard. Sarah had taken an hour off work and Friday hadn't yet started. The morning was almost unbearably warm already, the heat made worse by a thick, hot wind. In the west enormous sepia and white clouds drifted across the sky, and the smell of smoke tainted the air.

Friday pulled out the neck of her bodice and blew down it. Sweat was trickling down her sides and her shift stuck clammily to her skin.

'He does know we're here, doesn't he?' Sarah asked.

Friday nodded. 'He's got someone in there, but he saw me and waved when I banged on the window.'

'Christ, it's hot.' Sarah took off her bonnet and used the brim to fan her face. 'We got bugger-all sleep last night. And the mosquitoes! The Tank Stream's full of them. We had to shut every single window. It was murder.'

'At least you haven't got the horrors. I can't decide whether to spew, shit or pass out.'

'Well, whose fault's that?'

'Oh, shut up.'

'Shut up yourself. Have you been to the bank yet?'

Friday stifled an acidic burp. 'Tomorrow.'

'You haven't told Harrie, have you?'

'No. Have you?'

'No, and I don't think we should. Not at the moment.'

A window opened and James stuck his head out. 'Come on, in you come.'

Friday and Sarah scooted through the door of the surgery and down the narrow hallway, passing a deathly pale, glassy-eyed and profusely sweating man with his arm in a sling. The fingers poking out of it were swollen and a greenish-black colour. The stink was appalling. Friday retched, clapping a hand over her mouth.

The smell wasn't any better in James's office.

'Christ almighty,' Friday said as she sat down, dug a handkerchief out of her reticule and applied it to her lower face.

'My apologies,' James said as he lit a candle infused with oil of lavender. 'My last patient — you may have passed him in the hall? I've just sent him off to the hospital. The poor fellow pricked his finger on a rose bush and now has a gangrenous hand and forearm, and will most certainly lose the arm. And, I expect, his life. You wanted to talk to me? I assume it's about Harrie, or you would have come to the house.'

'Yes, it is,' Sarah said. 'How do you think she's getting on?' She made a fist and rapped on her head, as though she were knocking to be let in.

For a moment, James said nothing. 'I don't know,' he answered eventually.

'Because we don't think she's doing very well at all,' Friday mumbled through her handkerchief.

Sarah said, 'Put that away. We can't hear you.'

'I can't. I'll be sick. The smell.'

James wafted the air above the candle towards her. Friday stuffed the handkerchief up her sleeve and breathed through her mouth. 'We thought with being married and getting Charlotte she'd come right, but she hasn't.'

'She's a lot better than she was,' James said.

'Yes, she is,' Sarah agreed. 'But she's not the way she used to be. She's still not the old Harrie, is she?'

James sighed heavily. 'No, she isn't.'

Friday thought he looked incredibly sad.

'You must have an opinion, though?' Sarah said. 'You live with her.'

James let out another sigh. 'This isn't a medical opinion, it's just ... my personal observation. I feel as though some sort of essential spark within her has been extinguished.'

Friday and Sarah exchanged a glance; he'd described it perfectly.

'But the physician at the asylum,' James continued, 'said it could take quite some time for her to recover, so we shouldn't expect miracles.'

'We're not,' Friday said. 'Except I think she's seeing Rachel again.'

James seemed almost to flinch. 'Has she told you that?'

'No. I did ask her, but she denied it. But I know her. I know when she's lying.'

'*Is* it happening again?' James said to Sarah.

That's right, Friday thought. Ask Sarah, because I can't be trusted to tell the truth.

'If Friday thinks she is, she probably is,' Sarah said. 'Friday knows her as well as I do, and I know Harrie bloody well. We both do.'

Friday felt so overcome with gratitude her eyes stung.

'How would I tell?' James asked. 'What should I look out for?'

'She might talk about her,' Sarah said. 'She did, to us. And Nora Barrett said she used to hear her talking to someone in her room, at night.'

'I haven't heard anything like that, I'm sure I would have. What do you think it means?'

Friday said, 'Well, Rachel turned up when Harrie started getting sick, didn't she?'

'Did she?'

'Yes. So *we* think she comes when Harrie's worried. Or frightened.'

James said, 'But I just don't understand what it is she's so worried about! I mean, we have Charlotte now, and she told me that Leary fellow's left Sydney, so it can't be that.'

'She worries constantly about her brother and sisters in London,' Sarah said. 'Especially now her mother's died.'

'Yes, well, that's understandable. That's why I —' He stopped.

'You've what?' Sarah demanded.

James said, 'Damn. I wanted it to be a surprise.'

Friday leant forwards, almost setting her hair on fire over the lavender candle. 'Oh, go on, tell us.'

So he did, after extracting sworn promises from them that they wouldn't breathe a single word. They grinned at him like fools.

'You're such a sweetie, James,' Friday said.

Sarah agreed.

Blushing fiercely, James said, 'I really am at my wits' end. I'll do *anything* to try to make her happy.'

'Will you tell us if she says anything about Rachel?' Sarah asked.

'Why? I mean, yes, of course I will, but why?'

Sarah thought for a moment before she spoke. 'Well, she has Charlotte, and now Rachel might have come back.' She paused for emphasis. 'Charlotte, and Rachel. Do you see? We're wondering if the two things are connected in Harrie's head. And we're worried.'

Alarmed, James asked, 'Do you think she might harm Charlotte?'

'Hell no, we're worried about Harrie,' Friday said. 'She might be feeling guilty. Christ, she's *always* feeling guilty.'

'Guilty about what?'

Friday rolled her eyes. 'For being Charlotte's mother, when Rachel can't. Even though it's something she really wants.'

James nodded. 'So what, exactly, are you telling me?'

'Keep a close eye on her,' Sarah said bluntly. 'A *very* close eye.'

\* \* \*

The weather had cooled a little by the following Sunday, but the stable yard behind the Harp and Angel Inn still wasn't a pleasant place to be on a warm summer's evening. A carriage had arrived only fifteen minutes earlier and the yard reeked of horse sweat and swarmed with flies buzzing manically between the fresh shit on the ground and the inn's evil-smelling privies. Sarah and Friday sat on a pair of upturned barrels, keeping out of the way of the small crowd of travellers milling about, waiting for their luggage to be handed down from the roof of the carriage. The horses had already been unharnessed and led into the stables.

'I wonder where they've come from?' Sarah said.

'Who cares? Where the fuck's Becky?' Friday was on edge because it was now a quarter past six and no one had appeared to collect the money.

'I bet it's Louisa.'

'I'd have thought Becky'd be more trustworthy, from Bella's point of view. She's meaner.'

'Louisa's bigger.'

'That's true. It'd better not be Rowie again,' Friday said. 'I'll kill her.'

They sat there fanning at sluggish flies for another five minutes until, finally, Louisa *and* Becky appeared in the back doorway of the inn, followed, alarmingly and very unexpectedly, by Bella herself.

Friday and Sarah stood as the trio approached. Bella, as usual, was splendidly attired in a high-necked, claret-coloured taffeta dress and a black, wide-brimmed hat. She must be roasting under all that, Friday thought, and the colour against her white skin made her look like death. She was using her cane, and her arms below the puffed upper sleeves of her dress were as thin as ever. As usual her face was plastered with paint, her eyes dark and her cheeks heavily rouged. In comparison, Louisa and Becky wore hardly any cosmetics at all, and Friday noted with satisfaction that Louisa was getting really quite fat.

Friday stepped forwards and demanded, 'Where's Rowie Harris?'

Bella smiled widely but unpleasantly. 'Gone.'

'Gone where?'

'How should I know?'

'Did you kill her?' Not that Friday cared if she had.

'Me?' Bella looked shocked. 'I'm a businesswoman, not a murderer.'

Friday snorted. 'My arse. Where is she?'

Bella shrugged. 'I've no idea. She'd served her purpose, she wanted to go, and I let her.'

'She had a ticket of leave,' Friday said. 'She can't move out of the district.'

But after their fight in the Fortune of War, perhaps Rowie really had left town. She doubted it, though. More likely she was rotting at the bottom of some cesspit. Either way, Friday was satisfied. Gone was gone.

Bella rapped her cane smartly against a barrel. 'Enough. I'm not here to talk about Rowie Harris. You owe me money.'

'We don't *owe* you anything,' Sarah snapped.

As if in a pantomime, they all froze as a man staggered past, listing due to the weight of his travelling case. Risking letting go of the handle with one hand, he politely raised his hat. Sarah, Louisa and Becky nodded in reply, but Friday and Bella glared at him. Disconcerted, he hurried through the doorway into the inn.

'You do, if you value your lives,' Bella said.

'When is this going to end?' Sarah demanded.

'Never!'

'Why the hell not?' Sarah took a step forwards. 'What have we ever done to you?'

'Ask her!' Bella burst out, pointing a beringed and bony finger at Friday.

'Me?' Friday was astounded. 'Why me?'

Bella's mouth was set in a grim slash of red lip rouge and she'd squeezed her eyes shut. After a moment she opened them, took a deliberately deep breath in and then out through her nose as though calming herself, and said, 'Becky. The money.'

Becky stuck out her hand. Sarah withdrew the bag containing the two hundred and fifty pounds and dumped it on her palm. Becky dropped it.

'For God's sake, you clumsy cull, pick it up!' Bella ordered, whacking Becky's skirts with her cane.

Louisa snatched up the bag and shoved it under her jacket.

Bella said, 'Do say hello to your mad little friend from me, won't you?' then turned and led the way back inside the inn.

'Bitch!' Friday shouted after them.

Bella responded by lifting her cane and, without looking back, jabbing it violently into the air.

Friday stomped back to the Siren's Arms, swearing and muttering and elbowing folk off the footway. By the time she slammed the door to her room, she was in such a rage half the windows on the top floor rattled in their frames. She rummaged in a drawer for a bottle of gin, knocked back a gargantuan swig, then kicked off her boots and lay on her bed, seething and imagining hideously drawn-out and painful deaths for Bella. *Her* fault? Why was it *her* fault Bella was persecuting them?

When a furious knock came at the door she barked, 'What!'

Elizabeth swept in. 'Was that you making all that noise?'

'Might've been.'

'What's the matter?'

'Nothing.'

'Well, it's obviously not nothing, is it?' Elizabeth said, her hands parked on her hips. 'I heard your door slam all the way downstairs in the kitchen. What's happened?'

Friday took another drink and snapped, 'We've just handed over yet another bloody lot of blackmail money, that's what.'

Sitting on the end of the bed with a rustle of taffeta, Elizabeth said, 'You can't keep doing this.'

'Oh, why not? We've been having such good fun.'

Elizabeth slapped Friday's bare foot. 'That's enough of that. I'm only trying to help. Why won't you tell me who it is? There'll be something I can do.'

'There isn't.'

'Tell me anyway. You'll feel better for it.'

Friday stared at the manufacturer's initials embossed on her gin bottle for almost a minute. Then she said, 'She says it's *my* fault she's blackmailing us.'

'Who says that?'

Friday went on, 'Sarah asked her what we'd done to deserve it, and she said to ask *me*. But *I* didn't do anything bad to her. Well, not till after she started in on us, I didn't.'

'Friday — bad to who?'

'To Bella bloody Shand!'

Elizabeth looked horrified. 'My God, Bella Shand's blackmailing you?'

Friday nodded. 'Yes, the whoremongering old bitch.'

'But ... why?'

It would be such a relief to tell her. Friday was so very tired of keeping secrets. And she knew Mrs H wouldn't tell anyone else. She couldn't — Friday knew where *her* secret was buried.

'If I tell you,' she said, 'you have to promise not to mention a word of it to a single soul. Not even Sarah and Harrie. If they find out, they'll kill me.'

'Oh, Harrie wouldn't, surely!' Elizabeth said.

Friday noted she wasn't shocked at the idea of Sarah killing someone for revealing a secret, and nearly smiled. 'I don't mean they'll *actually* kill me. They'll want to, though.'

'Christ almighty, Friday, what on earth did you do?'

Her heart thumping now that she was so close to confessing, she took a deep breath and said, 'It wasn't just me, it was the three of us. That cove found beaten to death in Phillip Street the year before last? In May? No, April. Gabriel Keegan? Well, me and Sarah and Harrie did that. We killed him.'

As Elizabeth gaped at her, Friday wondered whether she might have been smarter to say she'd killed Keegan by herself, and left Harrie and Sarah out of it. But it was too late now.

'Can I ask why?'

'He was Charlotte's father. He was the one who beat the shit out of Rachel on the ship and made her pregnant. If he hadn't, she wouldn't have died in the Factory giving birth. It wasn't right. He had to pay for what he'd done.' There was no point telling Mrs H what had really killed Rachel — that would only complicate things.

'How did Bella find out?'

'Don't know. She must have seen us. Or maybe Amos Furniss did. He was working for her by then.'

'Oh, Friday,' Elizabeth said.

'She'd've been delighted. I can just see her face. She hated us on the ship. Me, especially. And, no, I *don't* know why.'

'And presumably she's been threatening to tell the police about the murder if you don't pay her?'

Friday nodded.

'Because you'd most certainly hang for that.'

'Yes, we do know that. Bloody Rowie was working for her, too, you know.'

'Rowie Harris?' Elizabeth was aghast. 'Working for Bella Shand?'

'Yes, while she was here. I'm sure she was spying on me.'

'I got that bloody little tart a job with James Downey!'

'*And* she told Harrie she'd been lifting her leg for James. So Harrie went out and got drunk and —'

'Threw herself at the first handsome young cove she saw,' Elizabeth said. 'And look what happened. What a tragedy that was. *Had* she been shagging the doctor? Rowie, I mean?'

'I doubt it. James is such a boring old fart. And he wouldn't have wanted to ruin his chances with Harrie.'

'I've a good mind to tell Rowie Harris exactly what I think of her,' Elizabeth said. 'And she won't enjoy it, I can assure you.'

'Good luck finding her. She's disappeared.'

'Since when?'

'The end of July? I think Bella might have done away with her.'

Elizabeth's arched brows rose. 'Really? You think so? So she's a murderess as well?'

'I'm pretty sure she's killed at least one person I know of, and ordered the death of another, if she didn't do it herself. And that's not counting Rowie.'

Elizabeth brushed a loose thread off her skirt. 'Well, we're hardly any better, are we?'

'Not really. Are you bothered?'

'I killed in self-defence,' Elizabeth said.

'I didn't. I did it for revenge. But I thought it was justified. No, I'm not particularly bothered, and Sarah gives even less of a shit. She can be pretty hard-hearted, Sarah.'

'I'm sure.'

'Harrie's bothered, though,' Friday said. 'I think the guilt of it's partly what made her go insane.'

'The business with the abortion can't have helped.'

'No, it didn't. And she's still eaten up with guilt, even though me and Sarah've told her a thousand times Keegan deserved what he got from us.'

'He did deserve it.'

'I know. Poor Rachel was so young, and while she *was* quite cunning in some ways she really didn't have a hope in hell against him. Filthy, arrogant, violent *bastard*.'

'Your Rachel wasn't the only one, you know.'

'The only one what?'

'The only young girl to fall foul of him.'

Friday frowned. What was Mrs H talking about? She hadn't even met Keegan. 'What do you mean?'

'If I'd known about this, about what you've just told me, I could have told you ages ago. You know Nellie McShera, who has the brothel down by the Customs House?'

'I do. Her girls are all jack-whores and barrack hacks.'

'That's true. She also offers, or should I say used to offer, very young girls, around the age of eleven or twelve.'

'Really? What a bitch.' Friday was disgusted.

Elizabeth made a disparaging face. 'Yes, well. The year before last, in January I think it was, so that would have been before your poor friend died, he beat one of Nellie's younger girls so badly she never recovered.'

'He *killed* her?'

'Nigh on knocked her brains out.'

'How do you know that?'

'Nellie called a quiet meeting of brothel owners. She never said outright that he'd killed one of her girls, just that he was a rum cove with heavy fists and we might want to think twice before letting him into our houses. A couple of the other madams said he was known to them and he'd already done a bit of damage. But Nellie told me later that's what he'd done, that he'd killed her girl. Can't say any of us were too upset when he turned up dead. So, you see, he did deserve it.'

Friday was thinking about the time frame. 'Bella Shand wasn't at that meeting, was she?'

'I don't think she'd opened her establishment by then. She doesn't come to our meetings anyway. Not all the madams do.' Elizabeth reached for Friday's gin, then put the bottle back on the nightstand, evidently thinking better of it. 'You're going to have to do something, love. You can't keep paying her forever.'

'Don't you think we've thought about it?'

'I'm sure you have. She'll bleed you dry. I don't personally know her but some of the other madams do, and they say she's evil.'

'She is. She's a bloody witch,' Friday said. 'I'd kill *her* if I could get away with it.'

Sarah and Friday were keeping something from her: Harrie knew they were. But she was frightened to ask them what, in case it was a bad thing. She couldn't tolerate anything else bad. She was teetering on the edge as it was. Pretending she was getting well was so exhausting — even more exhausting than actually being sick. The night before she'd dreamt of Keegan again. He'd chased her down the streets of London, his face all smashed and crooked, shouting something she couldn't understand. She'd run and run, looking for a place to hide, but everywhere had been too small — she hadn't been able to squeeze herself in. So she'd had to keep on running and he'd kept coming, shouting his incomprehensible words, gradually getting closer and closer ...

She must have been making noises of her own because James had woken her, shaking her gently and saying her name. Then he'd cuddled her and told her not to worry because everything would be all right, but it wouldn't. She knew it wouldn't. And this morning at breakfast Rachel had been sitting at the table and she hadn't said a single word; she'd just watched Charlotte throw her bread and egg everywhere and the terrible look of longing on her face had broken Harrie's heart. Unable to bear it she'd closed her eyes, and when she'd opened them again, Rachel had gone.

It was quiet now. Daisy had gone out to get a few things for supper and James wouldn't be home from the surgery for a couple of hours at least. In the morning Harrie had taken Charlotte to visit Nora and the Barrett children, and in the afternoon she'd worked on some new flash for Leo. She missed going to the tattoo shop three times a week, but James was a lot happier with the new arrangement. Charlotte was sitting on the carpet playing with a doll Friday had bought for her. It had a head of varnished papier mâché with beautifully painted eyes, lips, cheeks and hair, a body of stuffed kid leather and carved wooden limbs, and wore a tiny, exquisitely made evening gown of silk. At the moment, Charlotte was holding it by one foot and inspecting its miniature cotton drawers.

Harrie, in an armchair before the hearth, was folding washing. The next time she glanced up, Rachel was sitting in the chair opposite, watching Charlotte.

'You must miss her so much,' Harrie said.

Rachel remained silent for some time. Then: 'It's as though my heart's been torn out.' Her voice was hollow and distant.

Harrie rolled up a pair of James's socks. 'Are you lonely?'

'No, I'm not lonely.' Rachel turned her head towards Charlotte again, her silver hair shifting in a shimmering wave.

'Bum, Mama.' Charlotte had the doll's drawers off now.

'Bottom,' Harrie corrected.

Rachel said, 'She calls you "Mama".'

Harrie felt the tea towel she was holding slip from her fingers and fall into her lap. Here it was — the confrontation she'd been dreading. There was a disconcerting moment of thinking that she, too, was falling, that all the strength was draining out of her limbs, then the sensation passed and the fear receded as another emotion swept through her. When she recognised it, she wanted to laugh. It was relief.

'I'm so sorry, Rachel. I know she's not mine.'

'No. She isn't.'

'I do love her, though.'

'I know that.'

'I love you, too.'

'I know.' The corners of Rachel's mouth flickered in a smile. 'You loved me more than my own mother did. You *were* my mother, Harrie.'

Harrie wiped her face with the tea towel, her tears washing away the corrosive and poisonous guilt she'd carried for so long. Her sadness was draining away like an ebb tide, and already she could feel a sense of calm flowing through her.

'So,' she said. 'What will we do?'

Rachel leant forwards, her small, white hands on the armrests of the chair. 'You already know. Don't you?'

And Harrie nodded. Because she did.

That night, in bed, when the house was quiet and still and nothing stirred outside except for Angus creeping sneakily through the undergrowth in the garden, Harrie whispered to James, 'Are you asleep?'

'Not quite.'

'Can I say something?'

James rolled over and cuddled behind her. 'My dearest, you can say anything you like.'

Harrie was silent for several long seconds. James took the opportunity to sniff her hair; he loved the scent of the soap she used.

Eventually she said, 'It's just that, well, I can't remember ever saying this to you, and I want to.'

James couldn't see her face, but he thought she might be blushing.

'I love you, James. Very much. I really do.'

His heart swelling with love to such an extent that he didn't think he could speak, James held her even more tightly.

The following Sunday, another warm and sunny day, Sarah, Friday, Harrie and Charlotte, and Daisy went for a picnic in the Domain, which had recently been opened to the general public.

Sarah thought it would be interesting to see the exotic trees and plants imported by various botanists of note. Friday said she didn't give a shit about trees, but a day out would be nice. However, she wasn't traipsing all the way to the end of Anson's Point just to sit in Mrs Macquarie's stupid chair. That sounded like far too much hard work.

As they passed through the gate at the end of Bent Street and into the Domain, Sarah asked, 'Should we eat first or have a look around?'

'We should probably eat,' Harrie said, Charlotte slumped in her arms, red-faced and sweating. 'Or at least have something to drink. I think Charlotte's over-heated.'

'She does look a bit hot,' Sarah agreed. 'Shall we find a nice cool spot under some trees?'

'What about down by the shore?' Friday suggested, even though it meant another walk of at least ten minutes. 'It's always cooler by the water.'

Harrie nodded. 'Then we can watch the ships. She likes the ships.'

So off they went again, Friday carrying Charlotte now, Sarah lugging the picnic basket and Daisy with the rug folded under her arm.

Harrie hummed to herself. It was lovely here with all the pines and trees and plants she'd never seen before, and the wide-open, grassy spaces perfect for children to run around on, though the grass was suffering quite badly from sunburn. From here, they couldn't see Mrs Macquarie's Road way over on the eastern side behind all the trees, but there were smaller roads and they passed several gigs and quite a few folk out walking. Harrie waved.

She felt good, the deep sense of peace that had come from talking to Rachel still with her. Also, she'd woken with a feeling of expectation and it had been building all morning. Something was going to happen today — something momentous.

'She's not too heavy?' she asked Friday. Charlotte had her head on Friday's shoulder, but she was awake, keenly watching everything around her — a mangy feral cat crouched beneath a bush, wallabies in a stand of trees, birds wheeling in the sky.

'No, she's fine.'

'Ships!' Charlotte cried suddenly as Sydney Cove came fully into view.

'Clever girl,' Harrie said.

Sarah pointed at a copse of trees some yards back from the shore. 'What about down there? That looks a nice shady spot. And it's private.'

As soon as Daisy spread out the rug, Friday handed Charlotte back to Harrie, collapsed onto it and yanked off her boots and stockings.

'Bloody hell,' she complained, examining her bright pink toes, 'my feet look like lumps of Turkish Delight.'

'Well, why did you wear those heavy boots?' Sarah said.

'Because I always do.'

Harrie settled Charlotte on the rug in the shade, took off the child's cotton bonnet, fluffed up her hair, and removed her little kidskin shoes. 'There, that's better, isn't it? Would you like a drink?'

Charlotte nodded vigorously. 'Lemerade.'

'I'm going to wash my feet,' Friday announced. 'They stink.'

Daisy giggled as she unpacked plates and cutlery from the picnic basket, looking for the bottle of lemonade.

Friday wandered off towards the water's edge. '*Fish!*' Charlotte shrieked after her, making her almost leap out of her skin. The coarse grass felt nice on her bare feet. It petered out into sand, which formed a tiny curved beach barely five yards wide, bordered by slabs of rust-coloured rock tilting into the sea. The waves were nothing to speak of, not even a foot high, slapping onto the grainy sand with such a beguilingly insistent rhythm that Friday, tired from a late shift at work, felt she could easily lie down and sleep for an hour. She hitched her skirts above her knees and waded in, sighing as cool water washed over her hot feet and splashed up her calves.

She paddled about in the shallows for a few minutes, then retraced her steps, getting sand all over her nice clean soles. Returning to the others, she saw that Daisy had laid out the picnic.

'This looks good.' She sat down cross-legged beside her. 'Did you cook all this? I can't cook to save myself.'

Daisy blushed. 'Oh, no. I only made the chicken pie and the bread. Mrs Downey made the lemon cheese tarts and Mrs Green made the biscuits. I don't know who made the sausages. The butcher, I suppose.'

Friday nodded. 'Very nice. What have we got to drink?'

'No gin,' Sarah said.

'That's all right. I brought my own.' Friday fished in her reticule and pulled out a hip flask.

Pointing to the food, Charlotte said, 'Cake, Mama.'

'No, you can have a sausage first. Or would you rather have some pie?'

'Cake.'

'That's sweet,' Sarah said. 'How long has she been calling you "Mama"?'

Harrie said, 'A week or two.'

'Did you tell her to?'

'No, she just said it one day.' Harrie cut a small slice of pie and gave it to Charlotte. 'It is sweet, but it gave me a shock. She can't have forgotten Janie already, surely?'

'I doubt it,' Friday said. 'But I suppose, in her little two-year-old head, the one who does the cuddling and putting to bed and what have you is the one who gets called Mama, and that's you now, isn't it?'

Harrie sat back on her haunches. 'But I'm not her mother, am I?'

Sarah and Friday exchanged uneasy glances.

'I saw that,' Harrie said, and laughed at their worried faces. 'Don't worry. I know I'm not, but it really doesn't matter. I honestly think everything's going to be all right.'

Sarah asked suspiciously, 'All right in what way? What do you mean?'

Cutting a loaf into slices, Harrie said, 'I understand everything a lot better now. I know what I need to do to make sure I'm at peace with all those things that were making me ill.' Noting Sarah's doubtful expression, she added, 'Truly, I do. I haven't felt this calm and relaxed for a long time.'

'Really?' Friday grinned. 'Well, that's good, isn't it?'

Any response Sarah might have been going to make was drowned out by an ear-piercing squeal from Charlotte pointing at the feral cat, which had followed them and was now hungrily eyeing their picnic.

'Angus!' she announced in delight.

Friday said, 'That's not Angus, love, that's some other dirty old cat.'

'Angus isn't dirty,' Harrie protested.

'You know what I mean.'

Before anyone could grab her, Charlotte scrambled to her feet and made a dash for the cat, treading squarely on her slice of pie. The cat saw her coming and, not unexpectedly, streaked off through the undergrowth. Charlotte, her focus solely on her disappearing target, fell over. She sat up, noticed the lump of chicken pie stuck to her foot and held up her leg with both hands.

'Pie, Mama!'

Friday roared with laughter. Daisy and Sarah giggled themselves silly and even Harrie laughed. Friday and Sarah stared at her — it was the first time they'd heard her really laugh in ages.

Daisy got to her knees, but Harrie, giggling, said, 'It's all right, I'll get her.'

She carried Charlotte back to the rug. Although most of the pie had detached itself by now, the child's foot was coated with dirt, twigs, and chicken and mushroom filling.

Examining the mess, Harrie tutted and said, 'Oh dear. Now I'll have to rinse her off. Can someone finish slicing the loaf?'

'God, that was funny.' Friday dabbed at her eyes. 'That was the sort of thing that kid of Nora's would do. Hannah? You should meet her, Daisy.'

'No, she shouldn't,' Sarah said, reaching for a sausage. 'She's a menace.'

'An entertaining one, though. She's certainly got character.'

'Like Clifford, you mean?'

Harrie was almost down to the sand when Rachel appeared, just above the low waves about twenty yards out into the harbour. And even though she was quite a long way away, Harrie knew she would be able to hear every word Rachel was going to say. She stopped a few feet from the water.

'Who's that?' she asked Charlotte.

Charlotte gazed out towards the waves, squinting against the millions of diamonds sparkling off the sea's surface.

Harrie said, 'That's Mama, isn't it?'

'Mama.'

'It's time to give her back, Harrie,' Rachel said as she swayed and shimmered, her flowing hair dissolving into the midday sun.

'We have to go now, sweetie,' Harrie told Charlotte. 'Wave bye-bye.'

She turned so Charlotte could see the others under the trees. Friday was looking, then so were Sarah and Daisy. Beyond them, on a narrow carriageway winding among the Domain's trees, the sun glinted off the lacquered door of a midnight-blue curricle.

Charlotte raised a chubby arm. 'Bye-bye,' she whispered.

Harrie waved, too. Goodbye. I love you, Friday and Sarah. And James. This is for the best.

She waited until the others had turned away, then walked into the sea. It wasn't cold, and Charlotte wasn't heavy, and Rachel was waiting for them, her arms open wide. And then the water was up to her waist, floating her skirt and freeing her legs, then it was to her chest and Charlotte was crying and clinging tight, and Rachel was still hovering ahead of them like a blazing angel in a church window, and someone was shouting and the ground beneath her boots changed from sand to hard, slimy rocks, and she lost her footing and slipped under. But something tore like fire at her head and she popped back to the surface again, her ears full of water, and she was being dragged on her back by her hair and one arm and couldn't get her feet on the ground. Her eyes stung, she couldn't see. Where was Charlotte? Oh God, she'd lost hold of Charlotte! She thrashed and kicked out and tried to scream but got a mouthful of seawater and choked on it. Something hauled on her skirt and she rolled over, and she was out of the water and scraping face down across sand and grass, coughing and coughing, and then she stopped, retching. She tried to say Charlotte's name again and it wouldn't come out, then a blurry, dripping wet Sarah was crouching in front of her, hugging Charlotte, who was screaming herself blue in the face.

Harrie coughed again and someone thumped her across the shoulders and she vomited. Hands pulled her into a kneeling position and she leant to one side, coughing, retching and spitting until it was all out. She blinked furiously — her eyes finally cleared of seawater and tears, and Friday was beside her, drenched and white-faced, her hair plastered to her skull. She caught sight of Daisy standing over by the picnic rug under the trees, her hands over her mouth.

'What the fuck were you doing, Harrie?' Sarah demanded furiously. 'How *could* you?'

Harrie burst into sobs. 'You don't understand.'

'No, we don't. You could have *drowned* her.'

'No, I was giving her back. To Rachel. To her real mother.'

Sarah thrust Charlotte at Harrie. 'For fuck's sake, Harrie, *you're* her real mother. Rachel's dead.'

'Sarah!' Friday said, alarmed. 'She might —'

Sarah sent her a swift warning glance. 'I know what I'm doing.'

'No, you *don't* understand,' Harrie said again, sobbing and gathering Charlotte in her arms, gently joggling her without even realising it. 'She was out there, waiting for us.'

'She was *not*. That's just a lot of shit in your mind. You conjured it, Harrie. It's not *real*!'

'But I *saw* her. I see her all the time!'

'Harrie, do you really think the Rachel we loved — *our* Rachel — do you really think she'd want you and Charlotte to drown? To *die*? Well, do you?'

Put like that, the answer was obviously no, and the realisation hit Harrie like an extremely sharp slap in the face. She glanced down at Charlotte, whose cries were settling to whimpers now, and hugged her until she squirmed.

'I thought ... I thought if I gave her back, I'd stop feeling so guilty,' she said into the top of Charlotte's wet head.

'Why do you have to feel so bloody guilty about everything?' Sarah demanded. 'Christ. Who made you responsible for the entire bloody world?'

*Am* I responsible for the entire world? Harrie wondered. Really? 'No one did,' she mumbled.

'*You* did, that's who. So stop it. It's the guilt that's making you sick. The only people you're responsible for are you and Charlotte, because she's your daughter now. And that's it.'

Hitching in a deep breath, Harrie said, 'But it isn't just Charlotte. It's easy for you to say all that about responsibility and guilt, Sarah, you're as hard as nails, and I've tried so hard, I really have, but truly, I *can't* live with what we did to Gabriel Keegan.' She spat out more seawater. 'I just can't.'

'Wait a minute.' Sarah stood, flapped out her dripping skirts, took Charlotte from Harrie, squelched away to the picnic rug and handed the baby to Daisy.

Returning, she said, 'I told her it was a silly accident. We don't want her telling all of bloody Sydney Dr Downey's wife tried to commit suicide and drown her daughter, do we?'

Harrie went on as though Sarah hadn't even moved. 'We killed Keegan for nothing. I can't forgive myself for it and I'm tired of pretending I can.'

'But he deserved it,' Sarah said.

'But he didn't *kill* her, and that's what we did to him.'

Friday said, 'He did kill another girl.'

There was a short, ringing silence.

Sarah stared at her. 'What?'

Friday suddenly realised the magnitude of the words she'd just spoken. But it was too late now. It had been too late for a whole week. 'He killed someone else. Another girl.'

Sarah was giving her a *really* evil look. 'How do you know that?'

This was it, Friday thought, as a great, painful lump swelled in her throat. This was the point at which their friendship ended.

'Mrs H told me. Mrs McShera, another brothel owner, told her. Keegan beat the life out of one of Mrs M's girls. They covered it up.'

Both Harrie and Sarah were staring at her now.

'When?' Sarah demanded.

'Not long after we got here. A few months before Rachel died, it would have been.'

Sarah's face had gone incredibly hard and mean. 'When did you find this out?'

'A week ago.' Friday felt sick.

'Then why didn't you *tell* us?'

'I don't know! I didn't want … I didn't want you to think I couldn't keep my mouth shut,' Friday said. 'I was going to tell you. I was! When the time was right. I didn't know Harrie was going to do this today!' She shot a panicked glance at Harrie, and saw that her eyes were filled with the most awful hurt. And something else. Relief? Oh, please God, let it be relief.

Harrie staggered to her feet. 'So even though he didn't kill Rachel, he'd murdered another girl?' Her eyes were huge and she was trembling. 'He really *was* a killer?'

'You useless, selfish, drunken bloody bitch!' Sarah shouted. 'You could have saved Harrie from today. She nearly bloody *drowned*, Friday! *Charlotte* nearly drowned!'

Then Sarah hit her, a full punch in the face with a closed fist. Friday fell back on the grass, shocked wordless.

'Fuck off,' Sarah said, looming over her. 'Go on. Go and drink yourself stupid somewhere else. We don't want to see you any more.'

Friday tried to get up, stood on her hem and fell over again. Finding her feet, she trudged across to the picnic rug, one hand over her bleary, throbbing eye, collected her boots and walked away.

James had spent the afternoon with Matthew, then had supper with him at the Australian. Matthew had been out of sorts since Sally Minto had spurned him, and Harrie supposed James might be feeling the smallest bit guilty because he was married now. Anyway, she knew he was going to be late, so there had been more than enough time for her, Daisy and Charlotte to get home that afternoon, clean themselves up, rinse their clothes in the copper and hang them on the line. Entire dresses weren't usually washed, they were normally just sponged, but James wouldn't know that and was unlikely to remark on gowns flapping in the backyard if he looked out the window tomorrow morning. She could never, ever tell him what she'd done.

Charlotte and Daisy had been asleep for hours — poor Charlotte had been exhausted and Daisy not much better. She was bone-tired herself, but had remained up after they'd retired so she could sit quietly for an hour in the armchair, waiting for Rachel. But Rachel hadn't come. Had Sarah been right? Harrie wondered. Had she only ever been a figment conjured by her sick and chaotic mind?

Harrie didn't think so.

By the time James finally did arrive home, she was in bed herself.

Sliding under the sheet beside her, he said, 'I thought you'd be asleep by now, after your day in the sun.'

Harrie shook her head. 'How was your supper?'

'Same as usual. The gravy was too salty.'

'And Matthew?'

'He'll survive. He's lonely, though. We really must find him a nice girl. How was your picnic?'

'It was nice. The Domain's very pretty. Sarah and Friday had a fight.'

James's eyebrows went up. 'Anything in particular?'

'Friday told us something she should have told us a little while ago.'

'Anything that matters? Do I need to know?'

'It did matter, but no, you don't.'

'Did it upset you?'

Harrie examined the end of her plait. After a moment she said, 'It did at first, yes. A lot. But now, I'm pleased she told us.'

'Have you forgiven her?'

'I didn't feel like it, but I have. Of course I have. How could I not forgive Friday?'

'Good girl.' James patted her leg. 'You don't want to fall out, the three of you. Not after everything you've been through together.'

'No. And James?'

'Mmm?'

'I really think I'm getting better. I really do.'

James took her hand and kissed it.

'I really do. And I think everything's going to be all right,' Harrie said, and when she looked at her husband she saw the beginnings of tears in his eyes.

\* \* \*

Sarah and Adam were halfway up the stairs on their way to bed when someone hammered on their back door.

'Oh, for God's sake,' Adam said. 'At this hour?'

Sarah took the lamp off him. 'I'll get it.'

She made her way downstairs and through the dining room. Leaving the chain on, she opened the door, raised the lamp and peered out. A dishevelled figure sat on the porch steps, reeking of tobacco smoke and alcohol.

Friday peered up at her through one eye, the other swollen shut.

'Please don't hate me, Sarah. I can't do this by myself.'

Sarah stared at her for a long moment, sighed, then slipped off the chain, opened the door and held out her hand.

# Author's Notes

The snippets of poem I've quoted at the beginning of parts one, two and three of this story are from John Keats's 'Ode to Melancholy', written in 1819.

The Female Orphan School at Parramatta was a real place, but Matron Duff and her husband are fictional. Reverend Charles Wilton and his wife Elizabeth were the actual superintendent and matron at the time, though they resigned in December 1831 and were replaced by Lieutenant Alexander Martin of the Royal Navy and his wife Sarah.

In August 1801, Governor Philip King, concerned about Sydney's numerous neglected, abandoned or orphaned children, opened the town's first female orphan school in a two-storey waterfront house on George Street, purchased from Captain William Kent for 1,539 pounds, seventeen shillings and thruppence, and initially accommodating thirty-one girls aged between seven and fourteen. King blamed the girls' destitution squarely on their convict parents, and while not all convict women were as compassionate as Harrie, Sarah, Rachel and Friday, many, of course, were, but found themselves trapped in a cycle of poverty and servitude that rendered them incapable of caring for their children.

The girls were taught to sew and spin, and some to read and write, though in 1812 Governor Bligh gave evidence to the British Select Committee on Transportation implying that education was not a priority at the orphanage, and that it had become little more than a training school for domestic servants and a clothing factory.

The orphanage was initially run by a committee of worthies appointed by the governor, including Reverend Samuel Marsden and other clergy, surgeons, and government officials and their wives. In March 1826, the management, care and superintendence of the Female Orphan School, and the Male Orphan School that opened later, became the responsibility of the Clergy and School Lands Corporation, and from 1833 they continued under the control of the Colonial Secretary.

Almost from the outset it was clear that the George Street premise was too small, and plans were made to build a much bigger and more grand institution at Arthur's Hill, Parramatta. This opened in 1818 when a hundred girls (ages five to eight only) moved in on 30 June, leaving the George Street property to become Sydney's first Male Orphan School. When girls turned thirteen, they were found positions as apprenticed servants in 'good homes'. A bit like kittens and puppies. If a girl married and had behaved extremely well during her apprenticeship, she received a cow as a dowry.

Religious instruction was essential to the girls' training, they were seldom allowed out of the orphanage, and parents who did want contact with their daughters were forbidden access.

By 1829, the orphanage was home to one hundred and fifty-two girls (fifty-two over the limit), including Indigenous children from the Blacktown Aboriginal Settlement, and the admission age had been lowered to two. In 1823 the Male Orphan School relocated to Liverpool, then again in 1850 to the Parramatta Female Orphan School facility, where the boys' school amalgamated with the girls' school to form the Protestant Orphan School. The school closed in 1886 and reopened two years later as Rydalmere Psychiatric Hospital under the control of the Department of Lunacy. The original Female Orphan School building had fallen into disrepair by the 1960s but was restored and is now part of the Parramatta campus of the University of Western Sydney.

Speaking of lunacy, Harrie was lucky to go mad during an era of enlightenment as far as treatment of the mentally ill was concerned. Until the latter decades of the eighteenth century, management of the insane was, on the whole, barbaric. The mentally ill were scorned and ridiculed, and hidden away in filthy, dark asylums, where they were isolated and constrained with manacles and chains, whipped, let of their blood, shocked and starved, as portrayed in many depictions of the London lunatic asylum Bethlem (Bedlam).

Towards the end of the eighteenth century, a movement emerged in Europe that focused on a more 'moral' and holistic approach to the treatment of the mentally ill. This included the banning of chains (though not straitjackets), and the concepts that the mentally ill would respond better if they had access to fresh air, sunlight and meaningful activities. Most importantly, moral treatment embraced the idea that many people suffering mental illness could actually recover.

While in theory this movement was a vast improvement on what had come before, in practice being a patient in a mental asylum in the nineteenth century still would have been rather dire, whether the asylum was state-run or private. The Liverpool Lunatic Asylum, where Harrie is dumped by George Barrett, was managed by the state, and staffed mainly by convicts, who had little or no training regarding how to manage mental patients, which is why I only left her there for a day or two.

A note on distances: it was pretty well impossible to find out how long it would take to drive a cart or ride on horseback from Sydney to Liverpool in 1831, so I had to make a bit of an educated guess.

Another note, this one on Christmas: the one the characters celebrate is a little more modern than it should be in the 1830s. Then, people were probably still giving gifts on the traditional New Year's Eve — and only small ones, like sweets and trinkets — and not sitting down to a lavish Christmas dinner. That didn't really come into fashion until Victorian times, i.e. after 1837. But that didn't work for the story, so I tweaked it a little.

# Bibliography

The more I write in this series, the fewer books I need to buy. Which is a shame, really, because I like hunting down and purchasing books. I bought a few, though. *Bedlam: London and its mad* (Simon and Schuster, 2008), by Catherine Arnold, was particularly useful when it came to the description, diagnosis and treatment of Harrie's mental health issues. I also found a beautiful copy of Terence Lane and Jessie Serle's *Australians at Home: a documentary history of Australian domestic interiors from 1788 to 1914* (OUP, 1990) in a Newcastle second-hand bookshop for *much* less than the $912 for which I saw it advertised on Amazon. Entries in this inspired Biddy Doyle's house, and it will come in very handy for *A Tattooed Heart*, in which there is more house-breaking to be done. Thanks, Indigo Books!

*Victorian Pharmacy: rediscovering forgotten remedies and recipes* (Pavilion, 2010), by Jane Eastoe, was useful, as were *Millers Point: the urban village* (Halstead Press, 2007), by Shirley Fitzgerald and Christopher Keating (Sally Minto, of course, lives at Millers Point), and *True Blue: 150 years of service and sacrifice of the NSW Police Force* (HarperCollins, 2012), by Patrick Lindsay. This is the first history of the NSW Police I've come across, it weighs a ton and I had to cart it all the way home from Sydney on the train. But I can't complain because I got it for free.

One book I couldn't have done without is *Mau Moko: the world of Maori tattoo* (Penguin, 2007), by Ngahuia Te Awekotuku with Linda Waimarie Nikora. This award-winning study is, in my opinion, the definitive work on Maori tattoo, and was invaluable to me, in particular regarding issues surrounding upoko tuhi.

I also revisited *Illness in Colonial Australia* (Australian Scholarly Publishing, 2011), by FB Smith, and Frank Bongiorno's *The Sex Lives of Australians: a history* (Black Inc., 2012) — another award-winning book — for information on self- and assisted abortion. In the days when attempts at contraception regularly failed, abortion was frequently a last resort for women wishing to terminate a pregnancy. It was a dangerous and illegal practice, which, without resort to penicillin to treat infections, often had horrific consequences.

# Acknowledgments

As always, thank you to publisher Anna Valdinger at HarperCollins Australia for remaining constantly enthusiastic about this series, and to publishing director Shona Martyn, and the team at HarperCollins in general. Thanks again also to freelance editor Kate O'Donnell — another great editing job, and some excellent ideas for the next book. My agent, Clare Forster, also deserves thanks for her sterling efforts and encouragement.

More thanks are due to my writing group Hunter Romance Writers for their endless support; my friend and colleague Ngahuia Te Awekotuku for further advice on moko; Mary and Bridget Nicholls again for the continuing lend of Clifford; and, as always, my husband Aaron, for never-ending tolerance, understanding and good cooking.

# A Tattooed Heart

BOOK FOUR

*Deborah Challinor*

1832: Convict girls Friday Woolfe, Sarah Morgan and Harriet Clarke have been serving their sentences in Sydney Town for three years. For much of that time they have lived in fear of sinister and formidable Bella Jackson, who continues to blackmail them for a terrible crime.

Each of them has begun to make a life for herself, but when Harrie's adopted child, Charlotte, is abducted and taken to Newcastle, the girls must risk their very freedom to save her.

But is Friday up to the task? Will her desperate battle with her own vices drive her to fail not only herself, but those she loves and all who love her?

In this final volume of a saga about four convict girls transported halfway around the world, friends and family reunite but cherished loved ones are lost, and an utterly shocking secret is revealed.

**Read on for a sneak peek at *A Tattooed Heart* …**

*July 1832, Sydney Town*

Friday Woolfe, Sarah Green and Harrie Downey were about to cross George Street when the funeral procession approached on its way to Devonshire Street cemetery, stopping traffic, demanding attention and respect from all. It was an extremely grand affair, but then it would be: Clarence Shand had been a very wealthy man.

Leading the cortege were six grim-faced mutes walking two abreast, the brisk winter wind snatching at trailing hatbands and the black crepe draping their tall staffs. Then came the hearse, a jet-lacquered vehicle enclosed by costly plate glass etched with gold, and drawn by four gleaming horses as dark as night and bedecked with ostrich plumes. The widow, Mrs Bella Shand, sat alone and resplendent in black bombazine and a veiled hat in the mourning coach following the hearse.

'It's not fair,' Friday said bitterly from the footway. 'It should be bloody Bella in that coffin, not faggoty old Clarence. And look at all those mutes. They'd have cost a fortune.'

As well as the half-dozen mutes leading the procession, ten more walked alongside the hearse and Bella Shand's coach, bedecked in black cloaks, hats, sashes and gloves, all provided by the undertaker. Contrary to their job description, these mutes weren't without voice — they wailed and howled, demonstrating their grief for Clarence Shand, a man whom, in all likelihood, they'd never met.

Sarah said, 'Adam heard he died of a heart attack.'

Friday snorted. 'I bet bloody Bella poisoned him.'

'No, it was a heart attack,' Harrie said. 'James was saying last night he knows the doctor who signed the death certificate.' She lowered her voice. 'Apparently he died at Bella's brothel. With a boy.'

Sarah laughed. 'Whoops. That's a bit embarrassing.'

'Only if it gets out,' Harrie said.

'Well, it has, hasn't it?' Friday smirked. 'We know.'

Sarah said, 'It won't get out. Bella knows who to pay off and she can certainly afford to now. Christ, look at all these carriages.'

The cortege was still passing, though now it consisted of approximately twenty carriages occupied only by drivers, as it was not the fashion for the wealthy and upper classes to attend funerals in person. To send one's empty vehicle was considered tribute enough.

It was Sarah's turn to smirk. 'Poor Clarence,' she went on. 'She's really let him down and I bet she doesn't even realise it.'

Friday frowned. 'How?'

'Well, all these carriages mean Sydney's rich folk are paying Clarence their respects, which I suppose is nice for Clarence, but she's lowered the tone by hiring all these mutes. No truly classy funeral would have this many. Two, maybe, but this is just vulgar. Her pedigree is showing.'

'Eh?'

'You know, her roots. You can tell where she really comes from. The bottom of the heap.'

'Oh.' Friday thought about that for a moment. Ever since they'd had the misfortune to know her, Bella had had money, and, these days especially, she spent a lot of it on her appearance and surrounding herself with expensive things. Friday had almost forgotten she belonged to a criminal underclass not renown for elegance or style. 'I suppose. Silly bitch. Well, I'm going to the burial ground. I want to see where Clarence gets planted.'

'You mean you want to gloat at Bella,' Sarah said.

'Doubt it. She won't give a shite about Clarence going belly up. More chink for her.'

'Well, keep out of sight. If she sees you, it'll only remind her she hasn't put the screws on us lately.' Sarah took her watch from her pocket. 'Christ, I need to get back to work. Adam'll be wondering where I am. I said I was only coming out for an hour.'

The last empty carriage went past, the crowd dispersed and the stalled traffic began to move once more.

'I need to go, too,' Harrie said. 'Charlotte threw an almighty tantrum when I left the house without her. She'll think I've abandoned her.'

'I thought she was growing out of that?' Sarah said.

'She has. We're into the terrible twos, now.'

'Rather you than me,' Sarah said with heartfelt sincerity.

Harrie smiled. 'Oh, I think it's quite sweet, really.'

'Only you'd think a shrieking, spitting, bad-tempered little troll was sweet.'

'She's not a troll.'

'She is sometimes.'

'Right, you lot, I'm off,' Friday declared.

'Well, be careful,' Sarah said again. 'Hide behind a tree or something.'

Walking away, Friday flapped a dismissive hand. There weren't any trees in Devonshire Street cemetery, well, no big ones, but there were a few just beyond the wall. She'd loiter there.

Tagging along behind the slow-moving funeral procession, she was glad she was wearing her comfortable black boots. It was quite a walk up George Street to the burial ground — past the Haymarket and nearly as far as Ultimo. Also, it was a windy day and going down the long hill on the south side a sharp breeze picking up the brickworks' red dust, constant except during all but the heaviest of rains, seemed to be blowing most of it into her face. She wrapped her shawl around her mouth and nose and yanked the brim of her hat down low. As always, the cattle market gave off an eye-watering stink and dung clogged the road outside its pens and paddocks, but she trudged on, ignoring the temptations of the Old Black Swan, the Dog and Duck and the Wheat Sheaf hotels. The odour changed to the sharper tang of horse and bullock shit mixed with hay as she passed the carter's barracks on the corner and turned onto Devonshire Street, and she ducked through a lychgate and into the cemetery itself, forgetting about hiding beneath the trees.

A long row of carriages sat parked along the cemetery wall, their drivers smoking pipes, chatting to one another or sneaking sips from hip flasks. After Clarence Shand had been buried, they would return to their masters and mistresses and report that etiquette and propriety had been suitably observed. The mutes had disappeared, probably into nearby hotels.

The hearse, Friday noted, was empty. As it started to rain, she crept through a field of headstones and flat ledger stones towards a small knot of people in the distance. Choosing a particularly tall headstone, she ducked down behind it. There was a fresh chip missing from the sandstone — someone had been a bit clumsy with the grass scythe. Peering out, she saw to her surprise that Clarence was about to be lowered into a grave in the Roman Catholic section of the cemetery. Fancy that. Only Bella stood at the graveside, her live-in companions Becky Hoddle and Louisa Coutts hovering some feet away, looking suitably sober and also wearing black.

The priest was speaking, waving his hand theatrically over the coffin as the gravediggers lowered it jerkily into the yawning hole. There was a faint splash as it landed in a puddle left by the previous evening's downpour.

Crouching on the sparse grass as rainwater trickled irritatingly down her neck, Friday wondered why, really, she'd come. She quite often wasn't very good at working out why she did things. She wanted, she supposed, to see Bella show some sort of feeling, and preferably for it to be grief or pain. God knew she inflicted enough pain on other people. Just once, it would be so satisfying to see her keen, or cry, or even just be sorry about something. But her veil was still lowered, and for all Friday knew she could be grinning her head off. She probably was. Her marriage to Clarence Shand had been one of convenience so she'd hardly be heartbroken at his passing. Also, she was fantastically wealthy now and, according to gossip, Clarence had recently 'bought' her a ticket of leave, which meant she could do more or less as she pleased.

It wasn't fair. Bella Shand was a nasty, evil, blackmailing bitch who didn't deserve any of it, and Friday hated her guts.

The wind changed and she caught the priest's final petition: 'May his soul and the souls of all the faithful departed through the mercy of God rest in peace.'

Bella took a shovel and unceremoniously dumped a heap of soil onto the coffin, then turned to Louisa for a handkerchief to wipe her black gloves. The priest crooked his elbow, which Bella ignored, and they headed back to the lychgate, Becky and Louisa trailing behind.

Friday crouched even lower as they passed quite near her hiding place, and almost had a heart attack when the priest said: 'One moment, if you please, Mrs Shand.'

They stopped.

'I realise that Mr Shand's passing was sudden and must be a terrible shock for you, but have you given any thought to some sort of headstone? I can recommend several good stonemasons.'

Bella finally lifted her veil and tucked it into the band of her hat, revealing perfectly dry, kohl-rimmed eyes. 'No. That is not something I've had the time to consider.'

'May I suggest, then, that you choose something behoving of your husband's prowess as a businessman and his standing in the community?' The priest made a sweeping gesture with his arm. 'Why not leave these parsimonious little headstones to the Quakers, the Presbyterians and the Wesleyans? It would be a fine thing, I believe, to memorialise your husband's passing, and at the same time celebrate the glory of the Catholic faith, by commissioning something at least a little grand. Something that will perhaps reflect your status now as Mr Shand's widow, and a very wealthy woman in your own right. After all, we can't let ourselves be outdone by the Anglicans, can we?'

You cunning article, Friday thought, shifting slightly to ease the nipping cramp in her calf.

'Is that so, Father?' Bella said, her voice taking on an irritated edge that the priest possibly didn't know her well enough to recognise. 'And what would you consider appropriate?'

'A sculpted monument, perhaps. Or a finely carved chest tomb?'

'Perhaps. I'll think about it.'

They moved away then, much to Friday's relief — her leg was killing her. She could stretch but didn't dare move until Bella, Louisa and Becky had been driven away in their hired carriages.

A chest tomb? You could pack twenty dead Clarences into one of those. Then she remembered that the corpse usually went in the ground, leaving the tomb above it empty.

And that gave her an idea.

Harrie went straight home after she left Sarah and Friday. She was due at the Barrett household at two o'clock to assist Nora with a gown she was sewing, but she wanted to make sure Charlotte had had her dinner and a proper sleep before they went. Home was now on Bent Street as James had bought a much larger house in April and rented out the cottage. Harrie thought the new place was far too big, but James had insisted.

It had five bedrooms, for a start. The house was lovely, but why on earth did they need five bedrooms? She and James had one, and Daisy Miller, their housegirl who slept with Charlotte, had another, which left three more for Daisy to dust and sweep every day for no reason. And there were also a parlour and a sitting room, a shelf-lined study for James, a dining room, a kitchen directly attached to the rear of the house, a laundry with a huge copper, a storeroom, plenty of cupboards, a cellar, and a small carriage house with adjacent stables. A wide verandah ran along the front of the house, down one side and halfway round the back, from which you could glimpse Sydney Cove. The view was even better from the bedrooms upstairs. The wife of the shipbuilder from whom James had bought the property had clearly put time and effort into the garden, and Harrie was looking forward to spring when the bulbs, shrubs and trees flowered. Angus the cat also appreciated the big garden. Judging by what he was leaving on the verandah, the yield of mice, spiders and lizards was much more bountiful than at the York Street property.

They'd not had enough furniture to fill the place and she and James had gone on a spending spree soon after they'd moved in, buying sofas and chests and carpets and wash stands and clothespresses and all sorts of bits and pieces. Harrie had never seen so much money spent in her life. James had even bought furniture for the spare bedrooms — 'In case we have guests,' he said.

Some days she wandered from room to room, wondering just how she'd arrived in such an elevated position. Her home in London for years had been a tiny, dingy tenement with a single window, shared with her three younger siblings and her ailing mother. No matter how much she'd dared to dream then, she had never, ever imagined she would end up living in a house like this, never mind married to the man who owned it.

She'd paid a price for it, though. She'd lost her sanity. But James — lovely, decent, steadfast James — and Sarah and Friday had saved her, and that was behind her now. The voices in her head and the dreadful, crushing guilt had gone, and her mind was her own again.

Rachel had gone, too, and Harrie missed her, but she understood that it was time now for her to live life with James and Charlotte.

Unfortunately, Bella Shand hadn't gone, and neither, she suspected, had Jonah Leary. But she was so much stronger now than she had been even just a few months ago, and she knew that whatever happened next, she would manage. She wasn't quite the same Harrie Clarke who'd arrived in Sydney in 1829, but, like an animal hide that had been vigorously soaked, scraped, stretched and tanned, she'd become more resilient.

In a funny way, love had cured her. The love of Friday and Sarah, and of Nora, Leo and Charlotte, and most of all, James. Honestly, it all would have been a lot easier if she'd married him years ago.

Having spent four hours in her favourite pub, the Bird-in-Hand, it was almost dark by the time Friday staggered back to the Siren's Arms Hotel. She made her way unsteadily along the alleyway connecting the pub to the brothel on Argyle Street, determined to speak to Elizabeth Hislop.

She knocked on Elizabeth's office door, didn't wait for an invitation, and barged in. 'I've had the cleverest idea,' she blurted.

'Good evening, Friday. Please, do come in,' Elizabeth said tartly.

'Ta.' Friday flopped into a chair.

Elizabeth fanned her face theatrically. 'For God's sake, girl, have you been in the pub all day?'

'No, just the afternoon. I was at the burial ground before that, watching old Clarence Shand get planted.'

'You take some risks, don't you? I can't think of anything more likely to irritate Bella.'

'Don't worry, she didn't see me.' Friday leant urgently forwards, almost fell off her chair and grabbed wildly at the edge of Elizabeth's desk. 'Whoops. Listen to this, though. Clarence might be getting a chest tomb. What do you think of that?'

'Good for Clarence.'

'No, I mean, think what we could put in it. Or should I say, who?'

Elizabeth shook her head, the auburn curls of her wig quivering. 'I'm afraid I have no idea what you're talking about. As usual.'

'Yes, you do. Gil! We could put him in Clarence's tomb!'

Appalled, Elizabeth stared at Friday. 'Are you saying we should put my husband in with Clarence Shand's corpse?'

'Well, Gil's a corpse, too. And not exactly a fresh one either. Anyway, I don't mean right on top of Clarence. He'll be in the ground. I just mean in the tomb bit. It'd be a lot better than keeping him here in your cellar. You'll go to the gallows if the police ever raid this place and find him.'

'Yes, I do know that, thank you very much,' Elizabeth snapped.

'Keep your wig on. I'm only trying to help.'

'Sorry.' Elizabeth rubbed her hands over her face. 'It's just that I'm so used to having him near me. I … well, I draw comfort from him.'

Friday couldn't think of anything more bizarre than keeping the shrivelled remains of the husband you murdered in your own cellar, much less drawing comfort from them, but each to their own, she supposed. She knew Elizabeth had had a long, difficult and complicated relationship with Gil, and it wasn't her place to cast judgment.

'You still could. You'd just have to go to Devonshire Street to do it.'

'You mean stand in the middle of a graveyard and talk to thin air?'

'Isn't that what you do here? And it's what everyone else does in graveyards.'

'But I'd be standing over a grave with someone else's name on it.'

'Stop splitting hairs. You'd just have to make sure no one else is around.'

'But how on earth would I get him there?'

'Let me worry about that.'

'Oh, I don't know, Friday.'

'You do so know. You can't keep him here. It'd be like me keeping Gabriel Keegan's corpse under my bed.'

Elizabeth's worried expression suddenly turned into a scowl. 'Hang on, you said he *might* be getting a chest tomb. I'm not worrying myself sick about moving Gil if you don't know for sure. Anyway, it could be a whole year before that woman puts anything on her husband's grave.'

'It won't be,' Friday said with the supreme confidence of a pissed person.

'How do you know?'

'Bella likes to be … what's the word? … continuous with her dosh.'

'Conspicuous.'

'Yeah, that. If she can throw it around, she will. She won't leave Clarence's grave covered in shitty old weeds if she doesn't have to.'

'Most folk wait twelve months. It's the tasteful thing to do.'

Friday barked out a laugh. 'Well, there you go. There'll probably be a dirty great marble pillar with a ten-foot statue of God on it by dinnertime tomorrow.' Then she frowned. 'Mind you, we put a headstone on Rachel's grave straight away. Well, Harrie did. And she's not tasteless.'

'That was different,' Elizabeth conceded. 'Also, don't you have to wait for the ground to settle, after you've buried someone?'

'Dunno.' Friday shrugged. 'Wouldn't think that'd matter, if you're having a chest tomb. They're pretty solid.'

'But you don't know if she actually is.'

'I can find out. And if she does, will you let me move Gil? Please? It's for your own good.'

'Christ almighty, I never thought I'd see the day when *you'd* be telling me what's good for me.'

'But will you?'

Elizabeth sighed. 'I'll think about it.'